MEET THE MAKERS OF T.N.T.

Enter the glittering, cutthroat, big-money world of daytime television drama, where writers, actors, directors, and ambitious executives jockey for power. The scenario played out *behind* the cameras is rated X. The leading players:

Rita Martin—*Creator, head writer, queen bee. Her thirst for power is unquenchable, her carnal appetites insatiable. Beware her casting couch!*

Nan Booth— *Rising network executive, pretender to the throne. A ruthless, voluptuous redhead with a dark sexual secret.*

Al Peterson—*New dialogue writer, current fair-haired boy, 4-star stud. He's a pawn in the ladies' power game, but there's more up his sleeve than a well-muscled arm.*

Mel Jacobs— *Staff writer on the skids. When the going gets tough, he hits the bottle . . . and his wife.*

William Delligan

TIME NOR TIDE

PINNACLE BOOKS

NEW YORK

Special thanks to Bob Simon for his critical expertise and for his inexhaustible patience.

TIME NOR TIDE

A Pinnacle Books edition, published by special arrangement with E.P. Dutton, Inc.

First printing, February 1984

ISBN: 0-523-42148-6

Can. ISBN: 0-523-43135-X

Cover illustration by ENRIC

Printed in the United States of America

PINNACLE BOOKS, INC.
1430 Broadway
New York, New York 10018

9 8 7 6 5 4 3 2 1

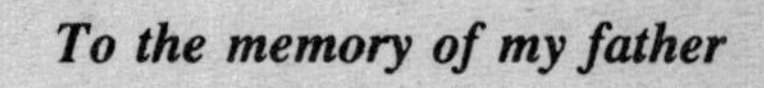

To the memory of my father

Time nor tide tarrieth no man.

Robert Greene,
Disputations, 1592

Time Nor Tide (*TNT*). Created by Rita Martin. Produced for the ITC Network by Alex Thorpe. Directed by Gordon Tate. Written by Rita Martin, Mel Jacobs, Tom Wesley, Patricia Fellows, Loretta Minor, Eleanor Davis. Set in Laurelton, U.S.A., *TNT* centers around the Hewitt and Reynolds families and the sisters, Betty Hewitt and Martha Reynolds. Since its debut, *TNT* has become the crown jewel of daytime television. Its devoted—and often fanatical—followers are women *and* men who represent every social, economic, and age level. Although *Time Nor Tide* is deemed one of the most popular soaps ever created, it has never won official recognition by being presented the coveted Emmy for Outstanding Writing for a Daytime Drama Series.

Marlene Turente,
The Soap Watchers' Guide,
New Outlook Press,
New York, 1979

"I think *Time Nor Tide* has such a loyal following because it reflects the way people think and act. I try to present a realistic picture of the world around us. If I—and the other writers—*didn't* draw on our own experiences, our own triumphs and tragedies, the show just wouldn't be honest."

Rita Martin,
interviewed in *Time*
cover story,
March 18, 1978

Time Nor Tide

PROLOGUE

Frank Cameron slipped quickly from his seat the minute he saw that Rebecca Danforth was alone. While the other orderlies were busy gulping down hot coffee and even hotter hospital gossip, Cameron had more important things to do. He had been waiting for this opportunity since he first entered the hospital coffee shop fifteen minutes earlier.

He looked around to make sure no one nearby was paying attention to them. "I want to talk to you," he commanded.

Rebecca Danforth glanced up from her cash register. "I have nothing to say to you, Mr. Cameron." Then she returned her attention to a roll of pennies she was wrapping.

Cameron's face went red with suppressed anger. "I don't care what you've got to say, Becky baby . . ." She started, surprised by his language and the tone of his voice. "I said I want to talk to you . . . now!" He spat out the last word loud enough to interrupt the conversation of two doctors at a nearby table. Cameron lowered his voice. "Now, unless you want me to raise a real ruckus, Mrs. Highfalutin Danforth, I suggest you join me." He sauntered away from her and found an unoccupied table at the back of the coffee shop.

Hate filled Rebecca's eyes as she watched Cameron sit down. For a moment she hesitated joining him, but after a second's thought she decided she had better. "Sally, watch the register for me, please. I won't be but a minute." She pulled herself to her full height and went to Cameron's table, carefully keeping her distance from him. "What is it, Mr. Cameron?"

"Hey, let's be friendly about this, okay? Have a seat." He smiled and pulled out the chair next to him. When she didn't accept his offer the pleasant facade immediately fell. "Sit down!" She did. "Now, isn't that better? I'd hate to think that one of our first ladies of society had to stand when she could sit." A sudden and totally insincere smile creased his face. "Oh, but I forgot. You're used to standing in your line of work—or should I say your former *line of work."*

Rebecca Danforth's face paled. "How dare you say that to me? You have no right!" she said louder than she had intended. "You're disgusting," she hissed, and she attempted to push away from the table.

Cameron grabbed her by the wrist and twisted. "Not so fast, sister. You're not going anywhere until I say so."

"Stop it! You're hurting me." She tried to wrest herself free from his grip, but it was no use. Cameron clung to her with the tenacity of a moray eel. Only after she relented did he release his grip. "I'll give you five minutes, that's all."

Cameron bowed his head as if honored by this capitulation. "I want . . . no, I need *some money."*

"That seems to be the human condition—but why come to me?" She raised her eyebrows haughtily.

Cameron laughed. "Do we really have to go all through this charade? I've already told you I'm on to you." Her eyebrows rose even higher. "All right, have it your own way." He leaned forward too familiarly, but Rebecca held her ground. "You're a big cheese in this town, lady. Rebecca Danforth, the queen of it all! You've got money, social position, power. You do this volunteer gray-lady bit at the hospital three times a week, and then there's the annual charity ball each Thanksgiving—"

"Get to the point, Cameron; I know my social calendar," she interrupted.

"Sure, sure," Cameron replied. "You've got everything in the world—including a past—and that's where I come in. I'm sure all of your snooty friends would just love to know that the leader of this town's high society was once a . . . how shall I put it? . . . a lady of the evening."

Rebecca's mask of composure now fell away completely. She looked old, scared. The elegance that usually marked her appearance was crushed under the enormous weight of

Cameron's knowledge. "That was all a long time ago . . ." she started to defend herself.

"Who cares? Once a hooker . . ." he let the vicious insinuation drift off into space as she sobbed softly. "Hey, now, I didn't mean to upset you. Look, your secret's safe with me." He passed her his handkerchief, which she took, much to his surprise.

"Mr. Cameron, I have lived here a great many years. I have worked for everything I have; everything you mentioned, my position, my friends, and, most of all, my family. If this were ever to get out . . ." She stared at him thoughtfully, with renewed interest, then dabbed at her eyes, drying away the last of the tears. When she spoke again the fear was gone from her voice. In those few seconds, she had summoned up the immense strength of her will and regained control.

"If I pay you this money today, how do I know that tomorrow or the next day or next week, you won't come to me again for more?"

"Guess you'll just have to trust me, Mrs. Danforth."

"Trust you?" She laughed. "I'd sooner trust a rattlesnake." Her eyes traveled the length of Cameron. "How do you know I won't go to the police with this sordid story?"

"Because I know you've got too much to lose."

She smiled. "You're right, of course."

"Don't take it so hard. You've got the dough. You're used to donating money to charity. Just think of me as one of the needy."

She pushed her chair away from the table. "I know your kind, Mr. Cameron. I grew up with them. You get a little taste of money and you want more, then more. You can't *be satisfied. If I start paying you now, you'll drain me of every penny I have."*

The tables, so unexpectedly turned, caught Cameron off-guard. He now looked upon Rebecca Danforth with something close to awe. "So, what are you going to do? Are you really going to force me to tell everyone what I know?"

Rebecca Danforth looked at Frank Cameron with an icy stare. "There is one thing you have ignored about me, Mr. Cameron. I am a survivor. I did not get where I am by child's play. I have fought against adversity and people like you every day of my life. There is also one other thing you should know before I leave—for your own safety: I will not allow anyone or anything to threaten the way I live. Do you understand me, Mr. Cameron?"

Cameron shrugged his shoulders insolently. "Sorry, sweetheart, I never was much good at riddles. You got something to say to me, don't beat around the bush—just let me have it!"

"Very well," Rebecca said softly. "You're a punk, Cameron. Your kind never learns that the easiest way to the morgue is to start pushing around the wrong people." Her eyes blazed with incandescent hate. "If you persist in this blackmail attempt . . . I am going to kill you!" She stood up, immediately becoming a Laurelton dowager once again, and gave Cameron a smile that was as deadly as it was effusive. "Have I made myself clear now?" Without waiting for an answer she walked quickly back to the cash register to finish her work rolling pennies.

Cameron sat quietly after that. He looked stunned, as if she had slapped him. Rebecca Danforth's threat was the second threat on his life that morning. Suddenly it seemed a lot of people wanted to see Frank Cameron dead.

BOOK ONE

1

Rita Martin had two important things to do before lunch: first, buy a nice little gift for Nan Booth at Tiffany's, and second, kill that bastard Frank Cameron.

Standing in front of the gilt-framed mirror that nearly filled one wall of her bedroom's dressing room, Rita thought about Cameron as she applied a light touch of lipstick. Killing him would be no problem. He was nothing more than a cheap, second-rate punk who sold dope and liked to bully women. The city was full of his kind. Sure, there would be some commotion when he died, but Rita knew from experience his death would soon be forgotten—unless she herself chose to keep the subject alive. But that was another matter entirely.

She stepped back far enough from the mirror so that she saw herself head to toe, then half-turned to the left, then all the way around the other way, extending her left leg out behind her. She smiled. She looked wonderful—relaxed, confident, happy—everything she was feeling, in fact, that unseasonably cool late September morning. Rita had delved into her fall wardrobe selecting a dark gray Chanel suit bought years ago in Paris. Though it was now beginning to show its age, this particular suit remained her favorite; it always reminded Rita of how much she had accomplished since her honeymoon in Europe eighteen years before. She turned again and glanced over her shoulder at her reflection. She loved this suit even if it was a little out of date; it was a classic. Besides, it made her ass look great.

Under the suit Rita wore a taupe silk blouse with a wide, fluffy jabot. A small diamond pin with the initials *TNT* sparkled brilliantly on the left lapel of the suit. She patted the pin affectionately. Those three initials had made Rita Martin famous. By the time *Time* magazine's cover story labeled her "at the top" Rita's celebrity had already far surpassed her own wild dreams of success.

At forty-three Rita was the guiding creative force behind a multimillion-dollar television industry. Six years ago she had convinced Jim Goodspeed, president of ITC Entertainment, that she had the golden touch. Playing a hunch based on thirty years in the business, Goodspeed gave Rita carte blanche—it wasn't a mistake. Within two years Rita had mothered her personal vision to maturity and created an American institution. *Time Nor Tide's* popularity had brought ITC, the nation's newest network, a wave of respectability and escalating fees for its commercial inventory that rivaled all the others. Even the hard-nosed cynics who had predicted a quick death for the "upstart" ITC network were silenced.

Although Rita wasn't the only reason for ITC's meteoric climb to success, in the early years Goodspeed brooked no criticism of his protégée. Her uncanny ability to spot and to capitalize on national trends early on made her something of an icon in the unofficial ITC founders' hall of fame. Goodspeed's six-year-old edict had been "Hands off Rita Martin." Protecting her from criticism was the least Goodspeed could do. With Jim Goodspeed on her side Rita Martin was untouchable. All she had to do was keep him there.

Right now, smiling at herself as she smoothed an errant lock of her lustrous black hair into place, Rita was wishing that Frank Cameron were dead. Killing him off would be a cinch—a few carefully chosen words to the right people were all that were needed. It was buying that goddamned gift for Nan Booth that was going to be a real problem.

As executive vice-president of ITC Entertainment for day-time television and Jim Goodspeed's "right-hand man," Nan Booth was someone to contend with. Rita had given the gift a great deal of thought. It had to be expensive, but not ostentatious; a very small gesture of thanks, but not something so insignificant that Nan might be offended. Rita's relationship with that particular honcho was shaky enough. She liked to keep a delicate balance.

On the surface Rita and Nan were as cordial to each other

as any two women working for the same boss, but Rita pointedly ignored Nan's authority by circumventing her entirely in a flashy show of independence. Rita Martin would deal only with Jim Goodspeed. The regular bureaucratic channels and network red tape were for other people. Or, so it had always been.

Lately there had been subtle signals that Rita's position at ITC was changing. This Cameron fiasco was the perfect example—Nan Booth, not her buddy Jim Goodspeed, had confirmed the rumors of Cameron's indiscreet behavior. Last week Rita couldn't even get goddamned Goodspeed on the phone! Either by accident or, more likely, by design, the specter of Nan Booth's corporate presence seemed to loom larger each day. Rather than give credence to her fears Rita wrote off her growing uneasiness as the usual end-of-the-year paranoia. Just to play it safe, however, a little gift for Nan would do no harm.

She shook her head in frustration. What do you get a woman who fancies herself one of the most powerful people—never mind women—in network television, a woman whose personal priorities in life were ratings and audience shares, viewer demographics, commercial minutes, and wooing the FCC like it was an unwilling lover? If there was anyplace on this earth that held the right gift for such a discerning woman, it had to be Tiffany & Co., that little, extravagant bit of heaven on the corner of Fifth Avenue and Fifty-seventh Street. She would stop in before the day was out.

Rita went automatically to the phone to summon her ITC limo for the short trip to work. She'd already begun to dial when she remembered that in an economy measure last week that particular luxury had been taken from her. Nan Booth, she thought angrily as she put her phone on service instead of calling the garage. "Greater women than I have been forced to taxi to work," she said with forced gaiety, trying to dispel the sense of uneasiness that once again marred an otherwise perfect morning.

She switched off the light in her bedroom, went directly to the hall closet, and, in an effort to rescue her flagging feelings, hauled out her favorite daytime coat—a sporty, full-length silver fox, so luxuriant it made Rita feel coddled, as if a man who knew just exactly how to please her were constantly caressing her, bringing her to life. She pushed up the collar, rubbing the soft fur against her cheeks. Frank Cameron was such a fool; if he only had kept his nose out of her cozy relationship with the network, his continued existence would have been ensured.

She grabbed her keys off the hall table and plunged them deep into her coat pocket.

But Cameron hadn't, and now he was going to die.

Rita strode out of her apartment building onto Fifth Avenue. The day was dazzling bright and more like midwinter than the third week of September. She snuggled deeper into the coat and, much to the consternation of the doorman, hailed her own taxi. "The ITC building—Fifty-fifth and Sixth," she commanded.

With bone-crushing speed the taxi pulled away from the curb and sped downtown toward "Television Row," a canyon of skyscrapers on the Avenue of the Americas just south of Fifty-seventh Street. Here were the East Coast headquarters of the national networks. For years CBS, ABC, and NBC had dominated the profitable world of network television. They were the "Three Rocks" : NBC, "30 Rock," the original, nicknamed for its 30 Rockefeller Plaza address; CBS, Black Rock," a bow to its somber, granite headquarters; and ABC, "Hard Rock," a slightly condescending appraisal of the network's interest in pop music and of its once-traditional place as lowest-rated network.

But now there was a fourth "Rock"—"Punk Rock"—an overtly derisive moniker for ITC, considered by television's old guard as the unholy offspring of the network trinity.

ITC was officially born in the imagination of Randall Cartwright, a shrewd and successful businessman who knew that the United States economy was big enough to handle the competition of a fourth commercial network.

Cartwright personally courted the powerful Federal Communications Commission and got its tacit approval for his proposed network. He dreamed of finding, then buying, an already existing television group like Metromedia, Golden West, or Westinghouse's Group W. Next to the networks, these independents were the most powerful organizations in television.

He realized that dream with Group T, the "brand name" of the Thomson Broadcasting Corporation, a badly managed operation that had never fulfilled its potential. But Group T had Cartwright's two basic requisites: It was not affiliated with any major network, and it was for sale.

With the FCC as guardian Randall Cartwright's International Telecommunications Corporation—ITC—was founded. Beefed up by a phalanx of young, enthusiastic television executives skimmed from the other networks' upper echelons, skilled artists and technicians, plus a battery of advertising men, researchers, lawyers, and accountants, and armed with careful marketing plans and an even more carefully created programming schedule, ITC made its national bow on Christmas Day with the lowest recorded ratings in television history.

But by the end of its first year ITC had penetrated an amazing two thirds of the country and by the end of its second year, when Rita Martin came aboard, ITC was giving third-place ABC stiff competition in the Nielsens, and its pretax profits had more than tripled from its paltry first-year revenue. Now ITC was widely admired for its competitive edge, and all those who worked there held the most sought-after and highly paid jobs.

The taxi stopped abruptly in front of the ITC Building and Rita got out. She felt more at home in the ITC Building, amid cold marble and acres of gray-tinted windows, than anywhere. Nowhere else—not even in the book-filled study of her Connecticut home—did she know the peace and self-confidence she knew here. Moving from the throngs of faceless people in the street into this building, Rita felt her personality unfolding, her power grow.

She smiled as she approached the security guard's front desk. "Good morning," she chirped to a new and unfamiliar young guard.

He stared blankly at Rita, taking her all in with one quick glance. "Where are you going?" he asked coldly.

"To the *TNT* office on thirty-five," she said.

"Who are you going to see?" he insisted.

Obviously he didn't recognize her. "I'm not going to see anyone. I'm Rita Martin and my office is on thirty-five," she said, still maintaining a cordial tone to her voice.

The guard scrutinized her for a moment, then opened a thick loose-leaf binder that contained the current listing of ITC personnel. After a minute he looked up at her, slowly shaking his head. "Sorry, but I don't see any Rita Martin here. I'll have to call upstairs before I can let you through."

"I don't have time for you to call *anywhere*," Rita said

angrily, her patience at an end. "Look under Elliott. It probably says Rita *Elliott* on your damned security list." Time was running out. Had it been another day she might have stopped to chat with the guard. After all, he was actually very handsome. But with Cameron's death pending, Rita had no time to play. To stay on top of the situation meant, among other things, getting into the office before everyone else.

While the guard sought out Rita's married name on his list, she slipped through the security barrier, and by the time he looked up to verify her identity and apologize, she was gone.

Directly opposite the bank of elevators on the thirty-fifth floor, written in glossy white across the dark, chocolate wall, was *Time Nor Tide*. This was Rita's baby—once the most popular daytime drama in the United States. Rita Martin had created *TNT*, was its senior head writer and spiritual overseer, and despite Alex Thorpe's listing as producer in the show's credits, it was Rita who had the last word on every facet of production. Each time she saw those three words, each time she fondled the diamond *TNT* initial pin she was never without, Rita felt a rush of pleasure so intense it was almost sexual.

The receptionist's desk was empty. It was nine-forty, and the office didn't open until ten. Rita walked quickly through the lush darkness of the reception area, into the offices where the real work of *TNT* was done. Back here the office was well-lit and sparsely decorated. A few plants hung from ceiling holders, and prints and posters decorated the walls, but by design, this part of the *TNT* "hive" was devoid of any personality. Rita didn't want any of her drones getting too comfortable, nor did she want any distractions from the production-line intensity of the office. In this sterile space three secretaries worked at breakneck speed, typing, answering phones, taking dictation, and ministering to the needs of Rita and her two associate head writers, Mel Jacobs and Tom Wesley. The other four *TNT* writers were dialogists and therefore held lesser positions in the soap opera hierarchy. They worked at home and, unless there was trouble, rarely were invited to the *Time Nor Tide* inner sanctum.

Rita walked past the secretaries' desks toward her private office whose windows looked north over Central Park and east over the city, the river, and, in the distance, the borough of Queens. Unlike both her New York penthouse and her Connecticut home, Rita's office was coldly utilitarian and Spartan in its appointments. This dichotomy of personal styles was a practical necessity, for Rita felt that to appear anything less than flawlessly efficient at work was to undermine her own authority. The office proclaimed to all visitors that Rita Martin was organized and direct, efficient, able to sweep aside old, unimportant business without mercy in order to make way for the new. As a reflection of the businesswoman, the office spoke volumes, but as a reflection of the woman away from the world of network television, the room said nothing.

She threw her coat on a nearby couch, sat down at her desk, and picked up the mike of her dictating machine. She had to get her strategy right. Tom Wesley was very attached to Frank Cameron and would surely put up a fight to save him. Mel Jacobs just might back up Tom—though that was doubtful. They were supposed to be a "writing triumvirate," but in the end, Rita usually got her own way. Still, it was wise to try to keep everyone happy by allowing at least the pretense that the decision was made by committee, and not by Rita alone. So she needed concrete reasons for removing Frank Cameron—one of *TNT*'s pivotal characters. Because Cameron *was* popular, she would have to prove that his elimination was good for the show.

Rita turned on her dictating machine. "These are the reasons why I believe we must reconsider Frank Cameron's future: When we brought Frank in as a hospital orderly he was relatively unimportant. As you remember, Tom, you suggested we provide a new *minor* character to aggravate Penny Hewitt—who had just been raped—to the point where she was driven into the arms of Ted Reynolds. I agreed because I felt the Penny Hewitt story was beginning to bog down; your suggestion seemed to provide a workable solution. Now, I'm beginning to think we made the wrong choice. I never dreamed Frank Cameron would eclipse several of our major characters—which is just what's happened. In short: He's become too big for his britches!"

Rita stopped the tape, rewound it, then played it back listening not only to what she said, but to how she said it. Dictating these notes was the only dress rehearsal she'd have before a later meeting with Mel and Tom in which she planned to outline Frank Cameron's demise. She wanted to sound strong, yet compassionate, determined, but open enough to compromise, if necessary. It was walking a thin line, and as Rita listened, she realized she'd failed miserably. Her voice sounded strained and unnaturally bright, and there was an unmistakable urgency that once or twice actually sounded like desperation. She ran the tape again, angrily admitting to herself that the whole Cameron mess had gotten out of hand.

Unable to concentrate, Rita pushed away from the desk, retrieved her coat from the couch, and hung it on the back of the door. How annoying that her own voice should betray her! Of course only her secretary, Sandy Lief, would actually *hear* the tape—the others would be given typed transcripts—and Sandy was so much in awe of her boss that she'd never believe Rita was susceptible to feeling anything but the loftiest and most noble emotions. It was hardly a comforting thought, for Rita had heard all the pain she'd fought to suppress. In fact, she'd heard a whole catalog of emotions that, in general, she denied ever affected her business decisions.

This was no way to act; she had work to do. With a sudden burst of energy, she returned to her desk, determined to get on with it. Frank Cameron's death *was* good for the show. It was not being able to make a decision that was bad. The feeling of powerlessness that had haunted her during the night vanished and her old self-confidence returned. She was Rita Martin. She was used to calling the shots and she'd do as she damned well pleased. But as she clicked on the microphone, the torrent of anger that had swept her along since talking with Nan Booth yesterday morning abated and she felt suddenly, inexplicably, afraid. A persistent, internal red light warned her to proceed with extreme caution. Taking overt action against Frank Cameron had far-reaching implications, and unless she were careful, Rita Martin and only Rita Martin would be held responsible should disaster—in the form of further failing ratings—ensue.

In the past, even as recently as four months ago, the execution of someone like Cameron would have been ordered without a second thought. But *Time Nor Tide*'s popularity was waning, and because Rita's position was no longer inviolable, there was no longer safety from retaliation for personal vendettas. In fact, the show's drooping numbers were putting Rita's very existence at the network in jeopardy. Dammit, everything seemed to be going wrong. She was losing control and it infuriated her. She couldn't even bring herself to make the simplest decision without feeling a twinge of fear. Losing Cameron would not weaken the basic fabric of *Time Nor Tide*. He had been born solely to fill the minor role of *agent provocateur*. He was never meant to draw attention, but as happens occasionally with peripheral soap opera characters, because of the actor, Rick Cologna, Frank Cameron took on a dynamic life of his own.

Rick Cologna's face began to assemble itself in Rita's mind. Handsome, photogenic, sexy Rick Cologna. The man who'd beaten Rita Martin at her own game—or so he thought. Well, no one knew soap operas better than she, and the game wasn't over until she called final time. She clicked on the microphone again and began speaking rapidly, not caring who heard the tape or how she sounded on it. "Lately I've begun to notice that the actor playing Frank Cameron is growing weak, particularly when he acts opposite Rebecca Danforth. How can our audience believe he's a threat to 'Our Gal Rebecca' when it sounds as if he's trying to sell her insurance instead of blackmailing her?"

For the next fifteen minutes Rita dictated without stopping, her mind jumping from the image of Frank Cameron the character Tom Wesley had created on paper to Frank Cameron the character Rick Cologna brought to life on the television screen. Each time she pictured Cologna's face her temper flared with renewed fury. She wanted Cologna out of her life, off her show. She wanted him banished to the wasteland of toothpaste commercials and underarm deodorants. And most of all, Rita wanted him to know that she'd put him there.

Rita had pegged Cologna as a slickly packaged smooth talker from the moment his image flickered into focus on the audition videotape he'd done for Judy Brown, ITC's casting director. A *TNT* casting call was a major event among unemployed actors, and even though Judy pared the applications down to exactly the right age, type—even height—there were still six tapes for Rita, Mel, and Tom to see. Some were bad. A few were good. But only Cologna's was special. After consulting with both men—and overriding Mel's objections—Rita instructed Alex Thorpe to hire Cologna on the spot.

Meeting the actor in person several days later convinced Rita she'd been right in her assessment of his character. But Cologna was good at being charming and attentive, and because at the time Rita was just beginning to feel the network squeeze and she needed some distraction, she allowed herself to be wooed and finally to be won.

The affair with Cologna lasted nearly seven months and in that time Rita elevated the hospital orderly, Frank Cameron, from minor to major importance by giving Rick Cologna more to do. When Mel Jacobs—who liked neither the character nor the actor—questioned the wisdom of this decision, Rita rationalized her favoritism by reminding him that Cologna got paid his minimum salary whether he said nothing at all, never stopped talking, or wasn't even used—"pay or play" as it was known. It was her *responsibility* as head writer, she pointed out, to see that the scripts used Cologna twice a week—his minimum guarantee—so why not give him something important to say?

The Cameron character caught on, Cologna began working extra days, and his popularity skyrocketed. Rick Cologna's career in daytime might have been established for life, except for one thing: He forgot that, despite studio gossip, the power behind *Time Nor Tide* was still Rita Martin.

Rita heard all the rumors that circulated at the network, including the recent rumblings that Rick Cologna occasionally used her name to gain favors. Rita hardly believed that anyone—particularly someone as ambitious as Rick—would so blatantly play both ends against the middle. It was career suicide! Just to be sure, however, she warned him in no uncertain terms that if he interfered with her professional life he was through. And, just to stop wagging tongues, they'd better not see each other for a while. Rick reluctantly agreed and left her apartment like a little boy who'd been scolded.

That was all two weeks ago and during his absence Rita realized that she missed him, that she'd actually grown quite fond of the scoundrel. It wasn't like her at all. After all, she'd only been looking for a diversion. Still, fun was fun and business was business. An emotional attachment with a younger man was merely a novelty to be discarded when necessary. She could do it as quickly and easily as she could . . . as easily as she could eliminate a character from *Time Nor Tide*. Or so she thought.

Just how wrong she was about herself was proved yesterday when Nan Booth dropped by the *TNT* office and slyly suggested that a few well-chosen words from Rita might curb Cologna's indiscreet name-dropping and growing demands for special attention. Rita feigned ignorance of the situation, but she felt like a fool in the face of Nan's barely disguised mockery. As a parting shot, Nan also suggested that Rick be informed that his newly budding affair with Betty Taylor, *TNT*'s resident ingenue—and a married woman—was attracting too much attention. Several of the soap opera fan magazines were already nosing around and Jim Goodspeed didn't like it. This time Rita's ignorance was real and it was only after Nan was long gone that Rita realized just how much this betrayal hurt.

Rita looked at the clock on her desk: just ten. Outside, the office was coming alive. Mel and Tom would soon drift into the adjacent conference room for the meeting about Cameron, and another work day would begin. Rita felt better now that she'd taken the action to erase Cologna from her life. In fact, she congratulated herself at having concocted a foolproof plan to get rid of the actor and protect herself at the same time; the sheer power of her own inventiveness exhilarated her. Frank Cameron would live—maybe. It was the actor, Rick Cologna, who had to go. If Tom argued vehemently enough for keeping Cameron alive (now that Cameron was so well established, Mel, too, might want to save him), she would give in—on the condition that Cologna be terminated at the end of his next thirteen-week option and a replacement be found. Rita did have a soft spot in her heart for the underhanded yet oddly lovable hospital orderly. If the other two writers didn't fight to keep the character alive, she would order him killed and, in doing so, create a new and exciting story line. Murders and trials always helped the ratings, something *TNT* could use.

The appearance at the door of Sandy Lief interrupted her thoughts. "Morning Rita." Sandy boisterously invaded the office with a handful of mail. "Thought you'd want to see this."

Sandy's intrusion pulled her back to reality. "Have Mel and Tom come in yet?"

Sandy nodded.

"Good. Type this up right away, then bring it back." She handed over the tape, pleased that things would be going her way.

An hour later Rita concluded a fifteen-minute tirade that had Mel and Tom squirming in their chairs.

"The actor has to go; plain and simple. And to accomplish that with the least amount of pain for everyone concerned, I suggest we kill his character." Her eyes scanned the faces of both men. Neither moved nor so much as blinked. "Any questions or comments?" She looked first at Mel, then at Tom. Neither man would speak until asked. "How do you feel about it, Tom? After all, you did bring Frank into this world, as it were."

Tom Wesley let out a sigh and shrugged his shoulders. "You could kill him off, just like that?" he cocked his head in Rita's direction.

She remained impassive. "We've been building to it one way or another for weeks now . . . months."

"What about the story projection?" Tom asked.

"Nothing we do here is engraved in stone," she argued. "This is a dynamic business; things change all the time. And let's face it, this would be a mercy killing!" Both men smiled. Rita became serious again. "I expect you to disagree with me, but you'll have to convince me that Frank Cameron is more valuable to us alive than dead." She folded her hands in front of her. "Well, Tom, convince me!"

Tom shifted uneasily in his chair. It was impossible to get comfortable under Rita's scrutiny. And if that wasn't enough, her office was boiling hot. The windows were sealed and the temperature was controlled automatically all year round. Outside it was a brisk fifty-five. Inside Rita's office the sun gushed in through tall windows and drove the temperature to nearly eighty. He momentarily speculated that the saunalike atmosphere was a part of Rita's scheme to break down opposition to this latest ego trip. Naw, even Rita Martin wasn't *that* calculating. It was only hangover-induced paranoia. The glaring light and the heat had magnified Tom's marginal headache into a demanding, throbbing presence. "There's really no reason to kill Frank. We've got a good story line going with him; he's blackmailing one of our major characters and he's stealing drugs from the hospital and selling them . . ."

"I *know* the story, Tom," Rita said impatiently. At times like this she almost regretted a long-standing promise made to herself to keep Tom on staff, even though it had meant taking over some of his responsibilities. It was the least she could do for an old friend. After all, anyone could see that the job with *Time Nor Tide* was the only thing standing between Tom Wesley and total dissolution.

At fifty-six, Tom was the oldest member of the writing staff. The years—in combination with his drinking—hadn't been good to him. What had once been a craggy face, full of character, was now bloated and his pasty-looking skin seemed always to need a good scrubbing. His once glacial blue eyes were now blurry, the pupils murky, as if they had just been smudged a little. More often than not Tom's curly brown hair needed trimming and his manner of dress bordered on the slovenly. And he was gay, besides.

In short, Tom Wesley was a disaster. But Rita liked to remember him in the days when *TNT* was only half an hour long. The show was spanking new then and going through growing pains none of them had foreseen. *Time Nor Tide*'s success was gratifying and often the small office they occupied rang with heartfelt laughter. They were a team—Rita, Mel, and Tom. Tom was a hard worker then. He was clever and diligent, and as the associate writer whose main job became editing scripts, he was peerless. But, as the work load increased and the pressure to stay successful became an obsession for Rita and Mel, Tom began to crumble. He fell behind while they moved ahead, he failed where they succeeded. And no amount of loving concern was able to alter Tom's course of self-destruction.

"We *could* simply replace the actor instead of the character," Tom was going on, dissolving slowly under Rita's thoughtful stare.

Mel was no help. He looked out the window, watched an airplane descend in the distance, coming in to land at LaGuardia Airport. Mel would let Tom hang himself before he said anything.

"Replacing people isn't as easy as killing them, Tom. You know that." Rita noticed Tom had begun to sweat profusely. He kept wiping his hand across his forehead then over his face. "Are you okay?" she asked.

Tom laughed a little too loudly. "It's just the sun . . . hot in here. Besides I feel I'm about to sign a friend's death certificate . . . I mean, Frank Cameron's."

At last Mel looked at Tom, his brows furrowed, his eyes half-closed in a quizzical stare. Mel knew precisely how Tom felt about the character. It *was* easy to become attached to the *TNT* characters. But now, Mel's silence was for Rita, and for his own benefit.

"You know I sometimes get too involved with these characters," Tom pushed on. "But isn't that exactly what makes people like Frank Cameron valuable? Viewers care about him, even though he isn't exactly a saint."

Rita nodded her head. "If you didn't love our characters, Tom, you wouldn't be able to write them believably or to deal with them and their problems year after year. You have literally to become a character in order to write him realistically, but killing him will be good for *TNT*. And, I'm afraid, the show always comes first."

He had heard this maxim a hundred, a thousand times before, and there was nothing more to say.

"And, this particular Frank Cameron is just too sleazy for my taste. I mean, look at this." She slid an eight-by-ten glossy across the conference table toward Tom.

He picked it up and stared at the familiar face. Rick Cologna was twenty-seven, nice-looking in a rough sort of way, vaguely Italian, and definitely seductive. His smile was wide and perfect, exuding easy charm and prepackaged likability. The tilt of his head was cocky but meant to be endearing. His inky black hair was perfectly in place. Tom liked Cologna's looks, always had. "He looks good to me," he shrugged.

"I guess our taste in men must differ," Rita said as she signaled Tom to pass the headshot to Mel. "How about it, Mel? Am I right?."

Mel barely glanced at the photo. He knew what Cologna looked like as well as the others did. Cologna was no more—or less—sleazy than he had been eight months earlier when Rita had ITC sign the young actor over his objections.

The dumb bastard must have really pulled something to get Rita this mad at him. Or maybe he had just gotten tired of being known around town as Rita Martin's protégé. Well, what did it matter? Her private life had nothing to do with Mel and today he just wasn't in the mood to play her favorite game—improving the past by rewriting it in the present. "He was your choice, Rita, not mine." He scaled the photograph back at her.

Rita's face darkened. "I remember that very well, thank you." The headshot disappeared into her briefcase. "Then it's agreed?"

There was dead silence.

Mel drummed his fingers on the arm of the chair, then finally answered. "Why *not* kill him? It'll add some excitement to the winter doldrums. Replacing Cologna would mean more goddamn auditions, thinking of somewhere to send Frank Cameron during the change, those lousy announcements when the new actor begins . . ." Besides, we'll never find another actor as good as Rick Cologna, was his unspoken thought.

"It'll be best for the show," Tom seconded weakly, now feeling obliged to concur.

"I'll see to it, then." Rita was relieved, buoyant. Each time she thought of Rick Cologna, each time she remembered his voice she wanted to pretend he didn't exist. Now, he didn't exist—not even incarnated by some other actor in the Frank Cameron role. Life is so simple when you're running the show. "I'll personally call 'upstairs' and let them know we're not going to renew Cologna's option. How long does it have to run?" she asked.

"Eight weeks," Mel replied.

"That's not enough time. We'll have to renew his option." Rita hated the thought of Rick Cologna squeezing all that salary from her, but she rallied quickly. "The extra time will allow us to rethink his story line and to finish him off with a bang, just about"—she consulted her desk calendar and grinned—"Valentine's Day."

Cologna had been awarded Rita's standard "gift"—a two show per week minimum guarantee at four hundred dollars per appearance—AFTRA's (American Federation of Television and Radio Artists') lowest salary for a continuing character in a sixty minute soap opera. Rita was not so enamored of Cologna that her business sense was impaired; she had instructed Alex Thorpe not to budge when it came to salary. The two-year contract Alex negotiated was his own idea. Like any good producer he got Cologna cheap for as long as he could. Some soap opera "stars" made well over one thousand dollars a show, were guaranteed multiple appearances a week, and refused to sign for longer than a year, but Rick Cologna didn't have their clout.

"We'll arrange to have Cameron killed on the last day of that week."

Mel merely nodded. In this job he and Tom were little more than kid gloves on Rita Martin's iron fists. But Mel liked to think he had more autonomy than Tom, not only because he was a better writer but also because he'd been with Rita a little longer, and that certainly counted for something considering the way people came and went according to her whims. Besides, he was more "together" than Tom. On any given day Tom usually looked as if he'd selected his wardrobe from the laundry hamper. Not Mel. Mel had learned at prep school that dressing properly, not cleanliness, was next to godliness. And as his decidedly preppy collection of tweed jackets, button-down shirts, penny loafers, and Shetland sweaters attested, it was a lesson well learned.

"Tom, tell Sandy to get me some coffee. Mel, want anything?" Rita asked.

Mel declined. His stomach had been bothering him lately and he didn't want to aggravate it.

"I guess that's all then. Get yourself something, too, Tom," Rita added, unaware of just how sick Wesley was feeling.

Mel studied Rita impassively, noting again what a handsome woman she was. She was blessed with the skin of a baby, soft and supple, glowing with natural radiance that even the most sophisticated makeup artistry couldn't fake. She was tall, just over five feet seven, and slender in a healthy, athletic way, and today she was wearing her silken black hair in a tight chignon that added a touch of bold severity to her striking demeanor.

Rita's features were tantalizingly feminine: full, sensual lips, aquiline nose, cheeks still with a fullness of youth, a graceful neck, and then there were her eyes. Her blue eyes. The blue of the waters of the Aegean down deep where the sunlight barely penetrates. Rita's eyes spoke the myriad of words she could never utter; they expressed the ineffable, they could show love with a desire beyond words and hate with a passion that was boundless.

There had been a time, years before, when Mel had thought he was in love with her. At least he had been deeply attracted. There was a subtle sexual flavor in dealing with Rita Martin—the way she always crossed and uncrossed her legs while talking or casually placed a hand on his wrist to emphasize a point; even the way she unconsciously preened during serious conversations was alluring. Mel had reached the point of making a pass at Rita when he met Wendy, now his wife. Watching over Wendy had taken up too much of his time, so Mel had never got around to asking Rita for even a simple dinner date. And, luckily, Rita had never held it against him. Actually, Mel was glad he had avoided Rita's charms, which could be the kiss of death to a man's career.

Within an hour, Rita, Mel, and Tom knew just how Frank Cameron was to meet his untimely end. His death had to touch not only the lives of everyone involved with the deceased, but also the lives of the millions of viewers who had come either to love or to hate the character. In the world of daytime drama, suicide was generally taboo. A random killing or an accident would stretch the credibility too far. A terminal illness was nice. But murder was nicer.

Frank Cameron was going to be murdered because Frank Cameron deserved it. He was evil. He was unscrupulous. He was a bastard. And although viewers were clearly fascinated by so immoral a creature, fan mail was five to one in favor of punishing him eventually. Tom had once suggested that Cameron be softened a little to give him more heart, but Rita vehemently opposed it. By then she knew Rick Cologna well enough to know that playing the cad was his forte. Written any other way, Cologna's characterization would falter and the valuable hospital orderly would become just another good-natured, soap-opera-style husband/father/brother/fiancé. So instead, Frank Cameron had grown even more surly, avaricious, and rotten with every episode.

Cameron's death was inevitable. Someone so despicable, someone so low and conniving deserved to suffer the justice meted out by the deity of daytime television. The fate that befell characters like Frank Cameron in mythical towns like *TNT*'s Laurelton was nothing short of biblical: swift and merciless, an atonement for past sins. Cameron's murder would provide enough plot material for several months. After all, a killer would be loosed amid a traumatized Laurelton citizenry.

"So, that's it. There's the murderer." Rita pointed out the killer's name on one of the three-by-five cards she used to store information. Mel and Tom nodded. It was right. It was good. In the end, it was just. She sat back in her chair. "Let's see, it's September. The murder—and trial—should take us up through Easter, at least. Now that we've got a real murder on our hands, we can milk it for all it's worth." She smiled at Tom. "How do you feel about Frank Cameron now? I'd hate to think we were being unfair to one of your children."

"I don't like to see Cameron go, but like you said, Rita, it's the best thing for the show." Tom smiled, but he hated Rita for cracks like that. Goddammit, they *were* like his children, the only children *he'd* ever have. Besides, who was Rita to joke about being unfair to children? For Christ's sake, just look at the mess she'd made of her own life. Jeannie, that poor daughter of hers, would be better off in a foster home. And Ben Elliott, how had he managed to put up with an absent wife for so long? Being unfair? Rita wrote the book on that subject.

"Glad you finally agreed," she said, unconsciously patronizing him.

The meeting at an end, Mel and Tom rose simultaneously from their chairs and headed for the door. But Rita stopped them. "Oh, there is one more little thing," she began. Then she changed her mind. "No. It can wait until after lunch."

Both men nodded and left.

As soon as they were gone Rita buzzed Sandy. "Any messages?."

"Alex Thorpe called and said it was urgent. I gathered it has something to do with Nan Booth." She hesitated a second. "And your husband called."

Rita immediately dismissed the idea of returning Ben's call; Nan Booth was far more important now. If she was pestering Alex it probably meant she'd seen the latest Nielsen pocketpiece. "Get me Jim Goodspeed," Rita commanded impetuously. She wasn't sure what she would say, but if it meant undercutting Nan's complaints about the flagging *TNT* ratings, she'd just have to wing it.

The biweekly pocketpiece contained the make-it-or-break-it numbers that showed how a television show stacked up against the competition. Rita had reviewed her numbers before going to sleep the night before. *Time Nor Tide*'s rating was anemic and its audience share was low and even lower after the mid-show commercial break. That meant viewers were changing channels halfway through the show. The demographics showed a marked decrease in the eighteen- to thirty-nine-year-old, middle-income, female audience *TNT*'s advertisers paid to reach. The situation wasn't good, but it wasn't fatal, either. This was just a slump. She'd survived bad ratings before. True, this time *TNT*'s numbers were frighteningly low but it would turn around. Rita always saved the show, always had the last laugh at critics who proclaimed she'd finally lost touch with her audience's needs.

The intercom buzzed and Rita snatched the phone from its cradle without bothering to clear the call with Sandy. "Jim, it's been a long time," she gushed, anticipating Goodspeed's hushed, masculine voice.

"It's Sally Grahame, Mrs. Elliott," Goodspeed's secretary corrected without embarrassment. "I *told* Sandy that Jim is in conference. Let me give him a message for you," she urged.

"Just tell him I called." Despite her coolness, Rita felt a new tightness in her throat. She hung up. Perhaps the mounting list of personal slights and lapses of business protocol were unrelated, accidental, and had nothing to do with her own performance. Perhaps they were not signs of ITC's disenchantment. Perhaps.

To dispel her mood Rita decided to make an impromptu visit to ITC Studio One. Being on the *TNT* set always cheered her. And she could talk to Alex face-to-face. Once the Nan Booth matter was settled and Jim Goodspeed returned her call, the pressure would ease.

Rita donned her fox coat, informed Sandy she'd be gone for at least an hour, and reminded her to have the standard lunch of Diet Pepsi and lowfat cottage cheese waiting at her desk no later than one-fifteen. Eating lunch alone while watching *TNT* was a tradition Rita established the day the first episode aired. It was a good luck charm, just as ITC had been a good luck charm when they had taken a chance on her. Today it looked like she could use all the luck she could get.

Giving Sandy a smile and a conspiratorial wink, Rita sailed out of the office to the elevators wondering just how—unless she ran into him accidentally—she was going to break through Jim Goodspeed's stony wall of silence.

Jim Goodspeed was hired away from CBS to head ITC Entertainment, taking the job on two conditions: that he would have a free hand in devising a nighttime programming format, and that any pet project of his would be given a guaranteed two-season minimum to succeed. No show of his was going to be killed off after a week because it didn't perform in the Nielsens. ITC quickly agreed to his demands threw in an extra twenty-five thousand dollars a year to sweeten the pot, and welcomed him aboard with open arms.

From the start Goodspeed eschewed the usual slapdash situation comedies and insidious, exploitative "docudramas" that bogged down the other networks. Because he had faith in the basic intelligence of the average television viewer, he commissioned hard-hitting dramas, intelligent comedies, and had the classics adapted for the special medium of TV. In its fourth season ITC's innovative programming caught on.

But Goodspeed wasn't content to rest on his laurels. He knew TV audiences didn't live by brains alone so he reinstituted Friday-night boxing as ITC's foray into the lucrative sports market. Eventually the expanded version of his sports programming was the envy of the other networks. ITC entertained with sports and enlightened with culture, and by its sixth season was known in the business as the B&B—"balls and brains"—network.

Goodspeed grabbed his coat and hat and headed out of his office. He was already late for his daily game of racquet ball, which meant he'd also be late for lunch with Muriel, his wife. Jesus, there just aren't enough hours in the day, he thought. For a man chosen last year by *Fortune* as one of this country's top ten executives, I'm a rank amateur at mixing business and pleasure. One of these days I've *got* to slow down.

Goodspeed was tall, lean, and in peak physical form. At sixty his dedication to his health came second only to his allegiance to ITC. Were it not for his silver-gray hair and the web of fine lines that radiated from the corners of his intense, hazel eyes and his full mouth, he might have been mistaken for a man of forty-five.

Sally Grahame didn't care if her boss were one hundred sixty; she was hopelessly infatuated with him. She'd do anything for him. "Have a nice lunch, Jim," she beamed as he appeared at her desk.

"I'll be gone a couple of hours. Anything I should know before I leave?" He smiled, breaking Sally's heart as he did twenty times a day.

"Rita Martin called a few minutes ago. I told her you were in conference."

Goodspeed stopped buttoning his topcoat and stared past the smiling girl, feeling a twinge of guilt for having instructed her to keep Rita at bay. "If she calls back"—he resumed buttoning his coat—"tell her I'll be unavailable all day." He pulled on his gloves.

Five minutes later, having escaped ITC without running into the ubiquitous Mrs. Elliott, Goodspeed happily lost himself in the crowds along Sixth Avenue.

2

In New York City autumn, not spring, is the time of rebirth. In these few weeks all the elements conspire to make New York the most beautiful city in the world. The soaring summer temperatures level off, the humidity releases its suffocating grip, and the air crackles with excitement as things come back to life. People move more quickly, smiles reappear on their faces, the theater rejuvenates, the opera and ballet seasons begin, gallery openings flourish, and everyone resumes the party circuit.

Rita particularly liked the cool weather because she could dress with some style once again. During the summer she forgot fashion existed. But with the first frost that all changed. For her, at least. It was ironic that at the very time in her life when she could afford anything she wanted, at the time when she sported her full-length sable out to the corner deli for cigarettes, working class and jock chic were suddenly *de rigueur*. Army-navy stores and sporting goods manufacturers called the shots along Seventh Avenue. The fashion world had gone mad!

At Fifty-seventh Street a young couple, rosy-cheeked, wearing matching designer sweat shirts, warm-up pants, and running shoes jogged happily by Rita on their way to Central Park. She pulled herself deeper into her coat and thought if she saw the word *Adidas* one more time she would vomit. On the other hand, work clothes were even worse than sports clothes. Rita had spent too many years a prisoner with her own working-class parents to consider this familiar manner of dress as anything more than a compromise between necessity and an empty pocketbook.

She hailed a cab and ten minutes later stood in front of ITC's Studio One, a hulking, gray, former warehouse, as far west as one can go on Fifty-seventh Street without getting wet. A cold wind raced up the deserted street and wrapped itself around Rita who shivered, despite her heavy coat. Here in this no-man's-land the characters she had created eight years before were brought to life five days a week, fifty-two weeks a year. Every set in the studio, every klieg light, every camera, actor, designer, assistant, and technician, every stagehand, floorman, and secretary was there because of Rita Martin—a power, rich and sublime.

She nestled her head against the silky fur of the collar, fully prepared to experience the usual deep satisfaction, but instead felt a twinge of anger as the movements of several workmen unloading furniture off a truck into the dark, gaping interior of the building distracted her. Rita instantly recognized the Victorian love seat two men struggled with—a prop for the Raffles restaurant set ordered weeks before. Getting what she wanted usually thrilled Rita, but Raffles wasn't what she had asked for—it was yet another compromise and that rankled her.

In past years ITC's budget for new sets designed and specifically built for *Time Nor Tide* always allowed Rita five or six really extravagant new sets each year. Rebecca Danforth's familiar and classically elegant music conservatory was an early example. These top-of-the-line sets brought elegance, grandeur, and sharp realism to *TNT* and the time, money, and skill that went into creating them showed on camera. Because of the vast expense Rita did not capriciously write these sets into the scripts. They sprang from the nature of the character—Rebecca's conservatory—or from the story line—the proposed prison sets for Frank Cameron's accused murderer. When Rita did ask for the best, she was never turned down. Until Raffles.

Rita really wanted a health club to supplant the oft-used restaurant and hospital as a logical meeting place for a variety of characters. The network, through Nan Booth, turned thumbs down on the idea. Nan was diplomatic, polite, and very sympathetic while delivering the bad news to Rita: The end of the fiscal year *was* drawing to a close, and ITC's high muckamucks *were* insisting everyone tighten his—and her—belt, Rita Martin included. So, instead of an innovative set, replete with exercise machines, carpeted work-out areas, and a health-food snack bar, Laurelton opened another restaurant, Raffles. It was better than the usual set and it was overseen by a very proper Englishman, but it was still a restaurant, and that left Rita open to the standard criticism that soap operas were afraid to try anything new. Worst of all, the criticism was right.

Directly opposite Rita, painted on the studio door, was the ITC logo: a semicircular rainbow with the letters *ITC* in black nestled underneath. Beneath that, in larger lettering, it said *Studio One*. Rita allowed herself a little smile. It really should have said *Time Nor Tide Studio One*. This *was* the end of her rainbow and *TNT* was still her pot of gold. She smiled at the thought, then opened the door and walked into the small lobby.

The "Soap Factory"—the studio's irreverent nickname—was a honeycomb of hallways and offices circumventing the main studio in the center of the building. From five in the morning when the technical crew began lighting the sets for the day's taping, until midnight—sometimes later—after exhausting hours of dismantling those sets and replacing them with sets for the next day, ITC Studio One pulsed with energy and activity. To enter the studio precincts was to be drawn into a vortex of controlled pandemonium that subsided only when, after twenty hours' work, one episode of *Time Nor Tide* was accurately stored on videotape.

Rita made her way automatically to the studio door, nodding benevolently at everyone she saw. She was a familiar face here even though her presence was entirely superfluous. Rita defended her "visitations" by explaining that the *TNT* cast and crew was her family and, "One can't stay too far away from family." Of course, there was also the matter of keeping tabs on everyone and everything that might possibly affect the success of *TNT*. She wasn't about to let anyone fuck up *her* show.

She plunged into the studio, ignoring the brightly lit, red *Rehearsal* sign, knowing that rehearsals were over for now. It was nearly twelve and everyone should be off the floor—the crew to have lunch, the cast to prepare for a one o'clock camera call and, if they were lucky, to grab a bite to eat. For some reason Rita's presence made the actors edgy, and the director, Gordy Tate, had politely requested she not visit from ten-fifteen until eleven-forty-five, when he blocked out scenes with the actors on the set, and from one until five when the final dress rehearsal and the actual taping took place.

Rita stepped around the edge of a flat and hesitated, unconsciously holding her breath. The studio still thrilled her after all these years. There was magic here . . . her magic. She surveyed its expanse.

Except for a technician readjusting light levels over a set and two cameramen working out a tricky series of camera maneuvers under the guidance of the technical director—unseen in the control room—no one was around. But Studio One was crammed with props and scenery. Laurelton stood proud and tall. At the far wall, heading an open corridor between sets, stood Rebecca Danforth's conservatory—so expensive to build and so often used that it was *Time Nor Tide*'s only permanent set. Opening into the corridor were today's sets—three on the left, two on the right. Rita scrutinized each, ticking off the characters who used them: a corner of the hospital coffee shop where Frank Cameron first confronted Rebecca Danforth; next to it, the Reynoldses' living room; and beyond that, the office of "Hap" Reynolds's auto shop. Opposite stood the beauty salon where Bev Collins, Laurelton's cheerful hairdresser *cum* hooker, plied her trade, next to that . . . Rita drew a blank for a moment then recognized a recent addition—Carl and Dulcie Montgomery's living room.

The Montgomerys were a black couple she had decided to give more play on *TNT*. It might be a risky move, but Rita felt it would be good for the show. After all, the dramatic possibilities of a black couple in an upwardly mobile white community were endless. At the very worst this ploy could be criticized as exploitative, and *TNT* might become controversial. Either way, Rita figured she couldn't lose.

All of today's sets were full three-sided constructions with the camera shooting through an imaginary fourth wall. With their interiors open to the studio's center aisle, it seemed as if a cyclone had descended on Laurelton, wrenching facades away to expose the daily drama acted out in each location—which, Rita mused, was supposed to be the exact nature of the soap opera: to reveal life as the audience knows it.

"Hello, Miss Martin," the lighting technician called down from his perch inches below the hot lights.

Rita merely nodded. She walked past him, nimbly avoiding

a tangle of camera cables and stopped directly in front of one of the "hot" cameras, waiting to be acknowledged.

Within seconds a man's voice boomed over the SA—studio announcement—system: "Good afternoon, *Mrs. Elliott.*" This was a gently ironic joke of someone who knew Rita Martin very well.

"And good afternoon to you, *Mr. Tate,*" Rita replied. "How's everything going?" She smiled sweetly, knowing her image was being monitored by everyone in the control room.

"It's going without a hitch, thanks . . . But I am a little pressed for time . . ."

"I want to see Alex. Is he there with you?"

"He's on his way out."

She started away, then stole a quick look at the Hap Reynolds's office set and turned back to the camera. "Bob," she addressed Bob Lantrey, the lighting man in the control room, "do you think you could take the lighting down a notch or two on the Hap Reynolds set? It looks like you're lighting a meat counter at the A&P." She grinned into the camera then ducked out of range to wait for Alex.

Alex Thorpe was one of Rita's old guard, a friend from way back. Ten years earlier, they had worked together on *Days of Our Lives.* Rita was just a dialogue writer then, Alex an assistant director, a career he later gave up. Alex was talented, cooperative, and Rita knew he liked her even more than she liked him. When ITC agreed to sponsor *TNT* as executive producer for its trial run Rita quickly called Alex and asked him to be her producer. He turned out to be a wise choice.

Because ITC handled all money matters, *TNT*'s producer was mainly a stylistic director. From day one Alex imposed his superb personal taste on everything, and it showed in little ways—the beds in the women's bedroom sets were made up with dainty, feminine, designer sheets; flowers were real *and* fresh; the color green was verboten because Alex said it made actors look bilious. He kept in close touch with wardrobe, makeup, and the hair stylists, suggesting ways for the actors to be dressed and made up to look more "in character." Alex Thorpe brought to *Time Nor Tide* a touch of class sorely lacking in other soaps, and for that he had been awarded an Emmy.

Alex knew he owed that Emmy to Rita, just as he owed her

his "dream" job, his impressive stock portfolio, his New York coop, and the winter house in Mount Snow, Vermont, among other things. And, in return, he was willing to do the little "extras" that weren't in his official job description—fronting for Rita when she wanted something from the network, being PR man to the wags at the studio and over on Sixth Avenue who considered Rita Martin a royal pain in the ass, even putting up with her overbearing pomposity concerning *Time Nor Tide,* which he felt was a childish, almost embarrassing way to make a great deal of money. And being a gentleman, Alex Thorpe was also the perfect go-between for Rita and the actors, Rita and the press, Rita and God.

"Rita!" Alex called out as he entered dramatically through the Montgomerys' front door and walked briskly to her side. "Well, if it isn't the hunter disguised as the fox!" He pulled her close to him, kissing her on the cheek. "You didn't have to come all the way over here; a phone call would have been enough." He slipped his arm around her waist and started edging her toward the studio door.

Rita resisted and escaped his hold. "What's all this about Nan?" She tried to stall her anxiety, which was building again.

"Why don't we talk about it outside," Alex urged.

Rita's answer was to walk onto the Montgomery set and sit down on the couch. "Why don't we talk about it *here,*" she snapped.

Alex acquiesced. "Nan spent the entire day here yesterday," he confessed, sitting down beside her.

"Here?" Rita's voice was brittle. It was unheard of. Nan Booth had no good reason to be at the studio.

"She nosed around here like a horny kid at a peep show," Alex went on. "Of course she came straight to me the minute she arrived and"—he winked—"asked 'permission' to watch, to get the real feel of the show but . . ." he shrugged his broad shoulders and left the sentence unfinished.

"So, how'd it go? Did Nan have any parting words?"

Alex could hear the worry in Rita's voice and tried to soothe her. "It was all very casual. She looked around, talked to some of the crew, took some notes."

"I don't like it. Sending Nan down here to keep an eye on us rubs me the wrong way."

"Maybe she came down all on her own. After all, we've

never had any trouble with Goodspeed so I doubt he sent her."

"Maybe Jim's getting pressure from above," Rita mused, hoping she was wrong. Goodspeed's boss, Jason Weatherhead, president of the ITC Broadcast Group, was a penny pincher and a classic misogynist. As far as he was concerned a married woman's place was in the home, not in the office. He didn't get along with Rita Martin, though he never complained about the profits she brought in. Of course not.

Alex walked Rita back to the elevators. "The ratings haven't been so great lately," he reminded her apologetically.

"I know all about the ratings," she growled. "I know everything about this goddamned show." She softened seeing the flash of astonishment in Alex's eyes. "But what the hell does Nan want down here? Did she talk to any of the actors?"

"Joe Ericson."

"Figures she'd go after him"

Ericson played Ted Reynolds, a medical student who was as virtuous as he was lackluster. Ericson, however, was an egomaniac who constantly complained about everything. With a salary of seventy-five thousand dollars a year, he still wanted more money and more air time. Ericson's goal was to be a star in a medium that discouraged star trips. He had caused trouble in the past, and until his contract came up for renewal in May, Alex suspected he would continue to do so.

"Let's not worry about Ericson . . . or Nan, for that matter," Rita said lightly. "We're tougher than they are. That's what counts." If there was going to be trouble with the network Rita wanted Alex to keep a low profile. As a suave errand boy, he was peerless, but when it came to a crisis Rita only trusted herself. There was too much at stake to let anyone—particularly an old friend—blow it.

She kissed him on the cheek and stepped into the elevator while he held the door. "What you can do is let me know if Nan—or anyone else—comes snooping around again. But don't lose any sleep over it, Alex." She blew him a kiss, and the elevator doors closed.

Nan Booth's gift was beginning to seem more a necessity than a gratuity.

Rita swept through the ground floor of Tiffany & Co., ignoring the fine jewelry and watches, and made her way to the elevators in the rear. The crowded main floor always annoyed her. Tourists wandered about here like lost sheep as they drank in the atmosphere of one of the most famous and expensive stores in all the world. Upstairs, the third floor, was Rita's secret retreat. This floor was definitely not meant for the casual browser, yet she loved browsing up here.

Moments after Rita stepped out of the elevator, Danielle Martel was at her side. Mrs. Martel was a cheerful, middle-aged woman who, rumor had it, was once married to a Grosse Pointe Martel. Whatever the truth of her background, Danielle was a superb saleswoman. She was always Rita's personal guide through the treasures of the third floor. In her presence Rita felt like she was shopping with a friend and indulged her every whim.

"Mrs. Elliott, how very good to see you," Danielle momentarily clasped Rita's hands between her own. "How are you today?"

"In a hurry, I'm afraid, Danielle. I need to buy a little gift for someone who's difficult to please."

"A man or a woman?" Danielle's voice made it clear the question was strictly business.

"A woman. A network executive, in fact."

Danielle nodded sagely. "That will be no problem. We shall find the perfect petit cadeau for your executive. Come." She touched Rita lightly on the arm, then walked off toward the fine china.

For the next half hour Rita shopped. She loved walking up and down the aisles admiring the beauty of the fine china, silver, and gold. A place setting of expensive bone china conjured up romantic images of a warm, cozy dining room, flowers on the table, candlelight. A set of heavy English coffee mugs delicately illustrated with hand-painted fox-hunting scenes reminded Rita of her father, Gus Martin, the big, burly merchant marine who was always traveling about and returning with stories. Once, when he had returned from England, he had filled her imagination with descriptions of rich manor houses and of riding to hounds. Rita had sat on his knee, spellbound at the wonder of the world he created. As she grew older she realized his stories weren't exactly true, but it didn't matter. He made them up especially for her and they enriched her life. She loved him all the more for it. How ironic that anything at Tiffany should remind Rita of him.

Rita chose an expensive set of four French ashtrays for Nan. They were feminine but not at all fragile. In Nan's hands they would have to withstand a lot of heavy use, so they had to be functional as well as attractive. Nan Booth was a heavy smoker and often italicized her sentences by firmly crushing out her latest butt. She hadn't made it to an ITC vice-presidency by playing the sweet young thing.

Rita left the store with two packages in a small, blue Tiffany shopping bag; she had bought the set of coffee mugs for herself. There was just time to get back to the office for lunch and today's episode. And then she would preside over the execution of another *Time Nor Tide* family member: Ellie Davis.

Before being hired as a dialogue writer for *TNT*, Eleanor Davis had been Alex Thorpe's assistant at ITC Studio One. While working for Alex, Ellie got to know Rita Martin. Ellie liked Rita in the same way she liked her aunt Sarah. Aunt Sarah always made Ellie feel she was the most important person in the world, as if no one else mattered. She knew this was Sarah's manner, that she was this way with everyone, but for the little time they were together Ellie felt special. She also felt special with Rita Martin because Rita treated her like family. The sound of Rita's voice made her feel needed. Rita looked after her and cared about her. She was never too busy to take an interest in Ellie's personal life, and as a token of Ellie's first year with the show, Rita had presented her with a small gold *TNT* pin that duplicated her own. Ellie was so touched she had cried.

When one of the dialogue writers left for a position on another soap, Rita offered Ellie the job. Rita had often talked to Ellie about her ambitions. The world of television infused Ellie's life with excitement, and she never wanted to leave it. But she was the first to admit she wasn't a real writer—she'd written some for her college literary magazine, but not much else. Ellie told Rita all this during that first year, and Rita hadn't forgotten.

"Don't worry about being perfect," Rita said as she handed Ellie her first scripting job. "It takes a long time to learn how to write dialogue correctly. I'm a good teacher . . . you'll learn."

The first thing Ellie learned was that her fantasy of a happy team of writers getting together with plenty of hot coffee to create a soap opera was childishly naïve. At *Time Nor Tide,* as at other soaps, the lines of responsibility and authority were as strictly drawn as in the armed forces. The creator and head writer, Rita, assisted by Mel and Tom, plotted the progress of *TNT*'s characters six to eight months in advance. Then Rita and Mel, using their keen sense of dramatic structure, revealed this larger drama day by day through detailed breakdowns that the dialogue writers then turned into words.

Ellie learned that the dialogue writer is at the low end of the totem pole and that the job is a lonely, isolated occupation, bounded on one side by the restrictions of current soap opera conventions and on the other by the demands of the head writer. Nevertheless, doing the script thrilled her. It wasn't perfect, but most of the dialogue sounded realistic. With some trepidation, and a great deal of hope, Ellie typed a final copy and sent it to Rita.

"The script's good, Ellie. Very good," was Rita's verdict a week later. "But there are a few things I'd like to go over." For the next hour they skimmed each page, stopping only for Rita's occasional editorial comments. "Want to do another?" Rita asked at the end of the meeting.

Ellie was paid for her fourth script, which was aired seven weeks later, and thus she became one of them. She joined the Writers' Guild and was given a contract as staff writer. She went to story conferences, had lunches with Rita and the other dialogue writers, and was made to feel a real part of the creative process that got *TNT* on the air each day. Ellie never felt closer to Rita. Rita was the shining light in her life. If it hadn't been for Rita, Ellie would still be a secretary.

It was a good feeling, a secure feeling, like being a daughter.

"We're going to have to let Ellie Davis go," Rita said tentatively to Mel. She'd called him into her office minutes before, while the *Time Nor Tide* credits were still rolling. Because Rita didn't even pretend to include Tom in policy-making decisions, she and Mel were alone.

"What's the problem with Ellie?" Mel asked warily. He liked Ellie and he'd enjoyed watching her talent grow over the past year.

"Her scripts are becoming mundane. I'm tired of them." Rita frowned to make the point. "With all the pressure from upstairs we can't afford any dead weight. Ellie's last script was amateurish. And that reflects badly on me . . . us," she amended.

Rita averted her eyes, a sure sign to Mel that she sensed his disapproval of this move. He should have seen it coming, though. Sacking Cologna this morning was just the beginning. After Ellie Davis, who knew what would come next? The storm warnings had been posted for weeks—the constant headaches over the ratings. Nan Booth's growing interference, Rita's own mounting irritability and touchiness.

"Mel, you're a bigger sentimentalist than Tom," Rita said softly, hoping to dispel his black mood. "You'd have us keep Ellie because you *like* her, and we'll have to waste our valuable time working over her scripts. Two scripts ago I practically had to rewrite the last act, and I just don't have time for that." Rita lit a cigarette, inhaled loudly, and continued. "After a full year I expect any writer to make it on his—or her—own. I thought Ellie had that potential. I don't think so anymore."

Mel picked up a pencil and rolled it between his thumb and middle finger. No matter what trumped-up excuses Rita made, Ellie's scripts were good. They were clever, funny, and, most of all, dramatic. Ellie's innate understanding of soap opera structure couldn't be bought at any price. The contested script Rita had rewritten had been almost perfect. It could have been aired as delivered, but she'd seen fit to go after it. In fact, as soon as Mel had seen the worked-over copy, he should have guessed Ellie was in trouble.

Well, don't just sit there like a statue. Say something!" Rita was irritated that, after all these years, Mel's silences still made her so uneasy.

"I suppose the script could have been better," he said, momentarily feeling as he always did when confronted by Rita's wanton exercise of power: Had he cared more for her, he might have stood up to her. But then, just as quickly, he admitted to himself that letting Rita ride roughshod over him—and everyone else—had more to do with fear than it did with caring.

Once, when he was a new head writer, he had fought for someone who was being ousted in exactly this manner. Rita had listened politely, had even kept the writer on staff. But, eventually, she started finding fault with the outlines Mel was writing. He got the message fast and within a week admitted he'd been wrong in his assessment of the other writer's work. That writer was fired, and Mel kept his job.

Mel and Tom had often discussed the bind they were in; the duplicity, the sham was almost crippling. But they liked the money—it was as simple as that. What other reason could there be? Mel was selling out and so was Tom. Only Rita, with her power and her charm, her devastating manipulations and her wild generosity, wasn't selling out—because her angry talent ran the show. She had created it. She believed in it. And *TNT* was the only thing that made her life worthwhile. Sometimes Mel got so angry he took it out on others. An image of his wife, Wendy, crossed his mind.

"Mel, *please*," Rita harped.

"Oh," he said, startled back to reality, "You could be right. I suppose."

Now Rita began ordering Mel around in a petulant voice. "Tell Tom I want him to start going over Ellie's scripts with a fine-tooth comb. Come down hard on her, as hard as he ever has. Any questions?" Mel said nothing. "Well, that's it then," Rita concluded. "Now, I've got work to do." Mel got up and left without another word.

Alone at the end of the day, Rita paced to the window and stared out over the New York skyscape. Unconsciously, she rolled her head back and around, gently massaging the back of her neck with her hand. There was a lot of new work produced by eliminating Frank Cameron from *TNT*, and now, too, she had to look for a new writer. Then there was the problem of Nan Booth. Never before today had it been so clear that she was looking for new territory to conquer. Well, whatever Nan might have in mind, Rita had no intention of allowing that territory to include *Time Nor Tide*.

She walked back to her desk and caught sight of the message slip sticking up from under the dial of her phone. Ben again. She tossed it into the wastebasket. What the hell, she would have to speak to him sometime.

She buzzed the intercom. "Sandy, get my husband on the phone, will you?"

It was always hard to guess what Ben wanted when he called at the office. Usually it was to ask her to come home to Connecticut for the night. On rare occasions he drove in to meet her for dinner and the theater, but it was too late for that now. During the early years of their marriage, Rita's dream of success had been built around Ben and the house they'd bought together in West Willow. She saw herself as the nucleus of her family—wife, lover, homemaker, and finally, mother. "A career as a writer and a career as a wife just won't mix,'' her mother had insisted. It used to comfort Rita to think she had succeeded where her mother predicted she would fail. Then her daughter, Jeannie, was born, and indeed, the dream had turned into a nightmare.

When Sandy buzzed back Rita took a deep breath. ''Ben?'' she began in her most professional voice.

''Hello, Rita. How's it going down there in the Big Apple?''

''Nothing changes here. How's everything there?''

''Jeannie's been asking for you. She wants you home.''

Rita's temper flared immediately. ''Don't you mean *you* want me home? God, Ben, I hate it when you use her to get to me.''

''Rita, she misses you,'' he persisted.

''Maybe so, but . . .'' she let the sentence dangle. What was the use of arguing with him? It was the truth. Although Jeannie was retarded—at twelve she had the mental ability of an eight-year-old—her need for her mother was very real. Rita had tried to share the responsibility of loving Jeannie with Ben, but it had all gone wrong, and gradually Jeannie was left in Ben's care as Rita solved the family problem in Connecticut by escaping it in New York. ''Ben, it's late and I'm tired. What can I do for you?''

''First you can stop talking to me like I'm one of your lackeys. This is a social call . . . I'm your husband. Now, what time can I expect you home tonight?''

''Oh, not tonight. I've got too much work to do. One of my writers is botching it, and I'm trying to replace her before we find ourselves in a bind.'' Lying with alacrity to Ben had become second nature.

''Rita, *Time Nor Tide* won't go under if you forget about it for just one evening. What do you say? I'd like to see you.''

''Can't it wait?''

''It's six days since you were here. I've already bought steaks for us. We'll cook outside,'' he added hopefully.

Involuntarily Rita laughed. ''You'll freeze your ass off. It's cold out there.''

''Let me worry about that. You just get home . . . about six-thirty, seven?''

She sighed wearily. ''All right. I'll see you then.'' She hung up and hid her face in her hands.

Ben Elliott and Rita Martin met in a writing workshop at New York University after she moved to Manhattan from Baltimore via college and grad school in Pittsburgh. The years at Carnegie-Mellon had somewhat weaned her from the provincial attitudes of Maryland, but they had in no way prepared Rita for the helter-skelter life-style in New York. She knew she wanted to write, she knew she had talent, but she didn't have a clue about where to start her career. As much to anchor herself in the city as to learn her craft, Rita took a job as secretary to a producer at NBC. She also enrolled in that writing workshop because her ambition was to write like the greats she had read in her literature classes.

Ben's aspirations to be a writer were fulfilled two years earlier with the publication of his first novel, *The Magic Tower,* a muckraking family saga that graphically depicted the horror of black lung disease in Appalachia. Although the novel was a general critical success, it failed miserably in the bookstores. But encouraged by the reviews, Ben began a second novel, *Shared Secrets,* which chronicled the domestic hell of a struggling young writer saddled with a wife he was forced to marry and a child he'd never wanted to father. Because this was Ben's own story, he was never able to attain the objective distance needed to complete it. The exercise did, however, serve its purpose, and shortly after putting the manuscript aside Ben divorced his wife, moved to New York, and, on the strength of a review of *The Magic Tower* in the *New York Times,* was hired to preside over the workshop where he met Rita.

Rita Martin was the kind of woman Ben had always wanted to write about. Her personality, which appeared to run a straight and true course, was actually full of unexpected twists and dangerous turns. He fantasized spending paragraphs—pages—accurately describing the way Rita turned arguments against her to her own advantage, or the way her carefully projected sangfroid often covered deep hurts. Shortly after meeting her, Ben began a third novel, this time with a heroine named Rita. He so often found himself daydreaming about the real Rita, however, that he was forced to change her name—first in the book and, eventually, in real life when he asked her to marry him and she accepted.

Ben learned in the workshop that Rita was a talented though limited writer and that at home—particularly in bed where she loved to confide secrets—she was voraciously ambitious. He found this trait disquieting, but forgave her because he suspected that her ambition was rooted in a long-forgotten but deep-seated need to prove her worth to her family, friends, indeed to the world at large. Ben could understand that thinking, though he didn't subscribe to it. External validation had its merits, but they all too quickly passed. But that was a lesson Rita would have to learn for herself. And in the meantime it was just one of the things that made Rita Martin Elliott so fascinating. And Ben loved her for her quirks and her selfishness as well as for her generosity.

Shortly after their marriage Rita quit her job and announced that the time had come for her to prove herself as a writer. Ben saw the determination in her eyes, and when he was offered a lucrative job writing advertising copy, he quit his teaching position. Although Madison Avenue had never held any special appeal for him, Ben's love for Rita (and his belief that she'd settle down once instant fame eluded her) propelled him through his days at Doyle Dane Bernbach. In the end, Ben was wrong about Rita.

Within a year Rita had landed a series of free-lance jobs as dialogist on several soaps (largely due to Ben's business contacts at Procter & Gamble Productions, the largest independent producer of daytime serials), and she immediately knew she was at home with this work. Ben squirreled away money all during this time, and five years after they were married, he quit advertising to return to writing full time, pooled his money with Rita, and bought the house in Connecticut. Not long thereafter Rita discovered she was pregnant.

Rita lit a cigarette, wishing she'd thought up an excuse to stay away from Connecticut, but immediately realized there was no excuse good enough. Going home wasn't a choice, really—her guilt demanded it. After everything that had happened between her and Ben, after the years of her neglect, the pain she'd caused by her attenuated withdrawal from her family duties in the wake of Jeannie's birth, Ben Elliott still wanted her home. Nothing Rita ever did seemed to deter him from wanting her by his side. Ben acted as if the terrible past—the ugly scenes and fights, the accusations and bitter words, always about Jeannie—existed only in Rita's mind.

A rush of conflicting emotions, familiar and unpleasant, swept over Rita. She tried to push her feelings about Ben and Jeannie aside, but it was useless, as always. No matter what Ben said, no matter how he acted, Rita knew the past wasn't dead for either of them. It was very painfully alive in the person of Jeannie Elliott. And if the tragedy of Jeannie's birth still haunted Rita, who rarely saw the child, how had it twisted Ben who lived with Jeannie day after day? Rita could only hazard a guess based on her own feelings, but that was enough to ensure that she'd always find Ben's motives suspect, no matter how loudly he protested he loved her.

The old doubts rose in her throat like bile and she tried to choke them back. How often must I remember this? When will I have some peace? she thought as she began the agonizing, penitential litany of Jeannie Elliott's birth. Since that rainy, August afternoon Rita had dissected the events leading up to the "accident" again and again. There was always some new way of looking at that tragic day, some new nuance of intent to explore. Sometimes Rita blamed herself—she waited too long to call for help. Often she blamed Ben—he'd left her alone when he should have seen her fear. Rita knew the answer that would end her self-torture was there, if only she persisted. In the meantime she'd deal with the guilt one more day. As she had for the past twelve years.

When Ben left that day he hadn't known Rita was frightened because she hadn't known it herself. She was feeling so self-confident about her work that nothing seemed impossible, least of all giving birth. Her dialoging had already earned her a small reputation and there was even talk of giving Rita Martin a shot at the brass ring—head writing! It was the chance of a lifetime. If she hadn't been pregnant she would have thrown herself into her career with a vengeance. But she was pregnant and Ben should have known enough not to leave her that morning, despite her assurances that she'd be okay. He should have known, but he didn't. And he'd left.

Rita ground out her cigarette and immediately lit another one, feeling the real horror beginning. The grotesque memories flooded her mind now, bringing images of being gripped by such fear that it hindered her movements as she tried to reach the telephone to call for help. She had fallen and bruised her cheek. On the floor, terrified she'd injured her unborn child, Rita cried out to Ben. But he was gone and she was alone.

Later in the ambulance en route to the hospital there was only pain—white-hot, blinding pain centered in her belly and between her legs that scraped at every nerve. And there was blood everywhere. Something was terribly, dreadfully wrong. It was taking so long. Too long. The faces of the paramedics who were helping to deliver her were pale with fear. One of them looked at his watch, silently ticking off the seconds . . .

five, ten, forty, one minute . . . two minutes. And then it was too late.

"I won't give in to these useless memories!" Rita vowed out loud as she summoned her considerable powers of self-control. The tidal wave of tears that threatened to engulf her momentarily receded. She reached for the telephone and dialed. Seconds later the attendant in the ITC garage picked up. "This is Rita Martin. Please have my car around front in ten minutes. I'll be going to Connecticut."

There was a short, embarrassed pause. "I'm sorry, Miss Martin, but I don't see your name on my VIP list anymore."

Rita took a deep breath, suddenly realizing that she was exhausted. But not too exhausted to cut through the bureaucratic red tape Nan Booth was trying to wrap around her throat. When she finally spoke, Rita's voice was almost a whisper: "I don't care about your damned list, mister. I expect a car out front, pronto! If not, it means your job!" She slammed the phone down, knowing the car would be there. But there was no satisfaction in her victory. In fact, Rita felt badly that she'd taken out her anger on the attendant. She'd never before indulged herself in that kind of pettiness. But she was beginning to see that she was on the verge of doing a lot of things she'd never done before—both at work and at home.

She crammed enough work in her briefcase to keep her occupied during the drive home, then fled her office, anxious to get away.

3

West Willow was once a quiet little country town. Nestled in the gently rolling landscape of southern Connecticut, it had its share of minor historic sights and enough of a tradition to make local families feel part of that history. With its pristine beaches on Long Island Sound and the rich soil of its farmland, West Willow was an ideal place to raise a family in simple comfort. For two hundred years the town had gone untouched by the hectic, modern world; then New York commuters fled the city and brought progress with them.

Authentic colonial was drowned by mock federal; general stores that had survived wars, floods, and time fell before the legions of sophisticates who needed gourmet food. Antique stores sprouted like crabgrass, crime rose, drug abuse became a serious problem at West Willow High, and the two weekly meetings of Alcoholics Anonymous were filled to overflowing. That little corner of paradise once known simply as West Willow, Connecticut, became another outpost of Manhattan hysteria.

Rita's limousine edged out of traffic on the Merritt Parkway and descended into the narrow West Willow streets. Rita sat quietly, the reading lights dimmed, her eyes closed. A half-finished glass of Scotch from the limo's bar, now in its holder, rattled with the motion of the car. Ordinarily she limited herself to one light drink on the way home, but tonight she'd broken her own rule and had a second, hoping it would help to loosen the knot of anxiety that had centered itself between her shoulders.

Going to Connecticut often reminded Rita of just how helpless and alone she'd felt during the awful days in her senior year at college when her father was dying. Each time she sat beside Gus Martin's hospital bed silently holding his hand, an uneasy balance of love and duty—plus a heavy dose of guilt—was struck. The love and duty sprang naturally from Rita's deep feelings for her father; the guilt was her mother's legacy. If Rita had had her own way she would have sat across the hospital room writing or studying while Gus slept, but Elizabeth Martin's constant vigil over her daughter made anything less than doting seem disrespectful. And after a lifetime of such disapproval, Rita was powerless in the highly charged emotional atmosphere of the sickroom to take a stand against family tradition, no matter how repressive.

Elizabeth Martin firmly believed that living was a deadly serious business. She subscribed to a parlor-sampler morality that the only joy one could rightfully expect from life was attained solely through hard work and from self-sacrifice for one's family. It had worked for Elizabeth Martin and she saw no reason why it shouldn't work for Rita.

Rita was her antithesis and Elizabeth's greatest disappointment. The child's bubbly optimism was truly the gift of her father, and from the start she meant to subdue it. Gus's long absences afforded Elizabeth the perfect opportunity to undermine Rita's aspirations to leave home, to go to college, and to make a life for herself that was not bounded on all sides by kitchen walls. She truly believed she was doing her daughter a favor, and each time her harsh words shattered Rita's self-confidence she repeated to herself: "I'm doing this to save her from grief and anguish in the future. It's for her own good."

Elizabeth never consciously made the connection between her treatment of Rita and her own disappointment in herself and in her marriage to a man who was rarely there. Indeed, self-deception became a household chore to be carried out along with the laundry, cooking, and general cleaning up. And out of its constant practice grew Elizabeth's one, undisputed talent: her unflagging ability to make Rita believe that to achieve more in this world than her mother had achieved was to court disaster.

"In my time, no woman would *think* of working, or want

to for that matter. I know it can be done, Rita. I've seen career women. Oh, yes, I've seen them," she would say in her stern voice. "But I'll tell you something. There's an emptiness that shines through their eyes. I wouldn't give up your father or *you* for the ritziest job in the world." Then she'd cluck her tongue, a cue that the final, icy pronouncement was at hand. "All I know, Rita, is that you can't do both and *I* couldn't live without love."

Nevertheless, Rita was determined: She wanted a husband, a family, but she could not give up accomplishments for herself.

It was only in times of stress or crisis that Rita's faith in herself, in the rightness of the road she had taken, wavered. Then her mother's words came back to her. Going to Connecticut was always something of a crisis; she couldn't help thinking that if she hadn't pursued a career with such single-mindedness, perhaps her personal life wouldn't be in such a shambles . . . perhaps. It seemed an unsolvable problem; for it was *Time Nor Tide* that had rescued her after Jeannie's birth.

Rita opened her eyes as the limo slowed in front of 44 Noah Webster Lane. The house, an oversize, slate-roofed saltbox built circa 1789, sat squarely on the front lip of two beautifully landscaped acres. Its deep red facade was fully visible behind a cluster of denuded birch trees whose leaves, in warmer months, guarded Rita's cherished privacy. She collected her things and sent the driver on his way.

Once inside, Rita stood quietly, savoring these last moments of solitude. Being with her husband and daughter could be explosive, though she hoped not tonight. The days of intimate dinners and quiet conversations by the fire were over. Their marriage was now usually exaggerated politeness or sometimes new bitter arguments about her familial responsibility. The loving middle ground had almost totally eroded. No, she was wrong. Ben was willing, had *always* been willing, to meet her halfway. It was she who couldn't reach out to him.

"I thought I heard you!" Ben beamed, as he entered the foyer from the living room. He went to Rita, kissed her lightly on the cheek, and, when she didn't resist, took her in his arms and gave her a real kiss. "Ummm, you smell great . . . and taste of Scotch."

"I had a drink in the car," Rita equivocated.

"And I had one in the den," Ben winked. "Let me take that stuff." Without waiting for a reply, he relieved Rita of her briefcase, then helped her off with her coat. "You seem tense. Tough day?"

"They're all tough."

Ben rolled his eyes and shook his head. "Mrs. Elliott, did anyone ever tell you that you sometimes talk just like one of your soap opera characters?"

"Only you would dare," she said dryly.

"And that's what makes you mine." He took her by the hand and pulled her into his arms, encouraged by her earlier submission. "It's good to see you. I've missed you." He maneuvered her closer still, but when he kissed her again Rita turned a moment of possible intimacy into farce by returning his affection with an exaggerated, resounding, slapstick kiss.

Ben relented immediately. The night was still young and he knew that Rita's affection was as quixotic as her reserve. So, undaunted, he spun her around and playfully pushed her toward the back staircase. "Come on, I've got a surprise for you."

A minute later they were in Ben's basement workroom standing in front of the fire he'd started in the fireplace minutes before Rita's arrival.

"I decided you were right earlier: It is too cold to cook outside. So, with the help of our handy hardware store, we're improvising." Ben screwed up his face as he examined the flames beginning to lap at the indoor cooking grill he'd purchased that afternoon. "The man in the village promised that this contraption would work just as well as the real thing. We'll see."

Ben was stationed a few feet in front of Rita. His feet were squarely, widely placed, his hands, rolled into fists, rested on his hips as he stared at his newest toy. Rita smiled at Ben's cheerfully flickering silhouette. In so many ways her husband seemed no more than an overgrown kid. His imagination and inquisitiveness were as gloriously unbridled as an adolescent's; Rita's was directed, reconstituted and rechanneled into her show. His creative energy took him into the realms of a youngster's heightened emotional awareness that Rita had all but forgotten existed. She had grounded herself in the reality of *Time Nor Tide* while Ben, in his novels, did cartwheels across the sky. He was willing to risk everything for what he believed in, and she was willing to risk nothing. But no matter how Rita's feeling toward Ben changed from moment to moment, no matter how often it suited her to think of him as a boy, there was no doubt in her heart that Ben Elliott was a man—exactly the kind of man her father would have liked. And that said it all.

In the early days in Connecticut, when Ben's second novel met with some measure of success, Ben Elliott was a darkly handsome, physically imposing man. Though Rita considered herself tall, Ben was taller, and in his arms she felt familiarly enveloped, comfortably possessed. Then, everything about Ben Elliott made Rita ache for him. When he took her face between his hands and tilted her head up to his for a kiss, the heat of his palms made her tremble. As he kissed Rita, as his lips brushed over every part of her body in the darkness of their bedroom, she grew unbearably aroused with passion.

But that was all so long ago, before Jeannie's birth. And that happiness, that handsome man, all seemed lost forever.

Ben would be fifty on his next birthday and his age was beginning to show. His once glossy black hair seemed dulled by the smudges of gray that covered his temples. The light laugh lines around his eyes and mouth had deepened, and although they strengthened the character of his face, they also proclaimed him at the threshold of late middle age.

And where did that leave her? She was still running while Ben had settled down. With the advent of *Time Nor Tide*'s success, the only constant in Rita's life was change. But even the excitement of the unknown, the indescribable thrill of pushing higher, was beginning to pall with time. And despite all the validations of the past—from viewers, sponsors, the network, from Ben himself—there was no security in Rita's life, not like there was in Ben's. Once he'd quit advertising and returned to his own writing he'd taken root. The vast unhappiness on Madison Avenue that capped each working day like a crown of thorns was erased and was supplanted by the joy of his work, his home. And his daughter.

"I'm going upstairs to get the steaks and fix a drink. Want one?" Ben interrupted Rita's meditation.

"No, thanks," she said, feeling a sudden rush of tenderness. Ben nodded and started toward the stairs. "Ben . . ." she stopped him. She was going to run to him, and be taken into his arms, kissed. But when he turned and looked at her expectantly, the feeling passed. "On second thought, I'll have a white wine." It was the story of the last years of their married life.

While Ben was upstairs Rita surveyed what was now his room. Before Jeannie was born, this pine-paneled refuge from the world was theirs. They'd decorated it with soft, overstuffed furniture just made for snuggling into, some good antique pieces from local shops, and a series of nineteenth-century hunting scenes that Ben loved so much. Before Jeannie was born, a day rarely went by when Rita and Ben didn't escape downstairs together.

Now, Rita hadn't been down here in over a year. Ben had expanded his work space to include a wall of bookcases, a grandfather clock, and an enormous double-sided English partners' desk that was the focal point of the room. Other than those changes, everything looked pretty much the same. What was different was the *feel* of the room. Rita walked around touching familiar objects, wondering why she felt so alienated. Every object held some memory for her. No, it held a memory for *them*, that was the difference. In the rest of the house, leading a life separate from Ben seemed perfectly natural; down here it was foreign. And that recognition at first made Rita feel uncomfortable and then, finally, sad.

Rita sat down in an easy chair and closed her eyes. The coziness of this room always made her sleepy. She was just giving in to her exhaustion when a loud *thud* on the stairs startled her awake. She turned, expecting Ben, but instead saw what had to be Jeannie.

At the top of the stairs two legs protruded from just out of sight. The feet were encased in shiny, red lace-up roller skates, the legs in scarlet tights topped by an abbreviated skirt. Rita watched, amused, as the skates moved cautiously down to the next step and a child's behind thumped into view. This preview of coming attractions was quickly followed by a torso and arms, neck, and, finally, all of Jeannie Elliott. She was so intent on the mechanics of her descent that she didn't notice Rita until she'd come to rest on the bottom step. But when she did see her mother, the smile on Jeannie's face said more than her delighted words could ever express.

"Mommy, you're home!" Jeannie giggled, immediately pulling herself up to her full but shaky height of four feet.

"Careful, dear," Rita admonished, half-rising from her chair.

"I'm okay. Daddy and me have been practicing," she said

in the slow, deliberate way that marked all her speech. Although her confusion with words was occasionally charming (she'd once asked about Rita's "hen house," and it had taken Rita and Ben several minutes before deciphering the real word—*penthouse*), more often than not, the fumbling over the easiest of sentences grieved Rita in a way she could never have conveyed verbally to anyone—including Ben.

"If you've been practicing, then go ahead and show me what you can do, honey," Rita said. "But please be careful."

"Oh, I will," she said as she pushed away from the safety of the newel out onto the polished wooden floor of her imaginary skating rink. Jeannie was less than an accomplished skater, but there was a simple beauty to her movements. She held her slender arms out from her sides, palms down, as if to dare the floor to interfere with her, while she kept her head proudly upright. As she moved, her long black hair, caught up in a red ribbon to match the color of her outfit, danced at the back of her neck. She was smiling proudly. For the moment, Jeannie Elliott looked like any other beautiful child performing for the mother she adored.

At first, Rita held her breath, every second fearful that Jeannie's feet would fly out from under her and the tears would begin. More than anything, Jeannie's tears tore at Rita's heart. The child was so at the mercy of her volatile emotions. But as Jeannie successfully circumnavigated the room a second time, Rita relaxed and began to enjoy the spectacle before her.

Though Jeannie's coordination was not as good as an average twelve-year-old's, there was a definite grace to her movements that came as a surprise to her mother. And for a moment, Rita allowed herself to think that even after all this time, the doctors' diagnosis of permanent brain damage might be wrong. They had condemned Jeannie to a life lived as an eternal child in a maturing body, a life that rarely went beyond the mid-twenties. But who was to say for certain that one day Jeannie wouldn't fully recover? Where was it written that she might not shoot up mentally as pubescent boys suddenly gained inches in height almost overnight? It was a hope Rita rarely allowed herself because for the first four years of her daughter's life, her grim determination to love away Jeannie's condition had been the only thing that stood between her and a terrifying abyss of guilt. And she had failed.

"Jeannie, are you down there?" Ben called, his voice carrying above the whir of the skates.

"Yes, Dad," she answered, looking up and back toward the stairs.

By the time Rita saw Jeannie's collision course with the couch, it was too late to act. Jeannie slammed into the arm of the couch, lost her balance, and fell to the floor in a tangle of arms, legs, and roller skates. For a moment she just looked stunned, then she began to cry. Her sobs filled the recreation room with pain.

Rita sat motionless in her chair overwhelmed by her own helplessness in the face of her daughter's infirmity. Maybe she couldn't make it all better for Jeannie forever, but she could help her right now. She was about to rise and scoop the child into her arms to tell her it would be all right, that her mother was there, when Ben's strident voice intruded.

"For God's sake, Rita, help her," he commanded impatiently as he surveyed the disaster scene from halfway down the stairs.

Rita turned on him, her eyes blazing with rage. "Don't make this my fault, Ben. I won't stand for it!" She turned her back on him and gently pulled Jeannie to her feet. "Looks like that nasty couch got in your way, honey." She steadied Jeannie then stepped back.

"Nasty couch," Jeannie repeated, aiming a kick at it, lost her balance again, but this time tumbled into Rita's arms.

"You never learn, do you?" Rita laughed, despite herself.

"I never learn," Jeannie gleefully agreed. She smiled up at Rita, then snuggled her head against her mother's breasts. "I love you, Mommy," she cooed. "I love Dad, too. But I love you best of all."

Rita pulled Jeannie a little closer, but said nothing. She was watching Ben who hadn't moved from his position on the stairs. There was now a smug look on his face, as if this loving scene with the roller skates had been a setup, as if he'd finally trapped the elusive Rita Martin into caring openly for her retarded daughter again. For a moment Rita actually hated Ben. He had no idea how she felt about Jeannie. All he had were his own ideas, how he wanted things to be. And Rita bitterly resented him for the unspoken demands he placed on her.

And so, she thought, sides have been taken in the Elliott family again, and I wish I'd never left New York.

"Come on, Jeannie," Ben called out from the stairs, "let's get you to bed. Mrs. Flannagan has cookies for you."

Jeannie instantly unclasped her mother. "Chocolate chip cookies?"

"Uh huh," he smiled at Rita, but her icy stare was a distinct warning to lay off.

Rita carefully assisted Jeannie to the foot of the stairs and passed her on to her father. "Good-night, pumpkin," she leaned forward to give her a kiss, but a trickle of spittle on Jeannie's chin put her off. Instead, she smoothed her daughter's hair.

Ben quickly cleaned off Jeannie's mouth, gave her an extravagant kiss, then hoisted her into his arms for the trip up two floors to Mrs. Flannagan, the housekeeper and Jeannie's nanny, and then to bed.

They ate dinner in the dining room, and afterward Ben tried to entice Rita back downstairs for a cognac but she politely refused. She was still angry that he'd shouted at her earlier. Giving in to his sexual advances in the glow of the fire's dying embers was hardly appealing. So instead of the sybaritic delights of Ben's workroom, Rita sat stiffly on the couch in the living room, watching Ben pour Rémy Martins into snifters he then warmed between his palms.

"Tell me, really. How are you?" He handed her a drink then joined her on the couch, slipping his arm around her."

Rita shrugged. "I'm getting some heavy flak from ITC about the show. You remember Nan Booth? Well, it looks like she's at the bottom of——"

"I asked how *you* are," Ben interrupted. "*TNT* will live forever—it's you I worry about."

"I don't mean to be evasive, but the show is all I have to think about anymore. After all these years I *am* under a lot of pressure and it makes me angry." Telling Ben seemed suddenly to make it less important, somehow. And that felt good. She rested her head on his shoulder.

"That's better," he said, stroking her cheek. "The world's a nicer place when there are people in it you can turn to . . . me, for example. You once used to trust me like this. Is there a chance you might learn to again?"

Rita tensed, but remained silent. How could she trust him

when at the least provocation—earlier with Jeannie was a good example—he seized on her failings without giving thought to how she might feel? Even this gentle coaxing seemed tinged with the sadistic pleasure of seeing her squirm.

"That wasn't an accusation, Rita. It was a simple question and I need an answer."

"I don't know, Ben. I'm tired. Can we talk about it some other time?"

"Sorry," he said quickly, "we have to talk now . . . it's about Jeannie."

"What about her?" Rita sat up.

"She's getting older. She'll be thirteen next August. And I'm not going to live forever, Rita. What if she outlives me . . . or us?"

Rita's anger returned. "Dammit, Ben, how can you be so cruel?"

Ben put down his glass and took Rita's hand, holding it against her will. "There's no running away from this one, Rita. We have to talk. We have to . . . to make some provisions . . . just in case."

Rita stared into Ben's eyes trying to guess what his next move was. It had occurred to her that one day Ben might grow tired of his role as both mother and father, and it further occurred to Rita that to pressure her into moving back home he might try anything—including threatening to wash his hands of Jeannie Elliott entirely. Where would such an ultimatum leave her? What choice would she make if Ben ever forced her hand?

"Are you talking about sending Jeannie away? Is that it? You're talking about putting her into an institution?" Rita's voice trembled as she spoke.

Ben looked at her blankly. Even for Rita Martin, she was outdoing herself. Ben's proposal was simple enough and had nothing to do with sending Jeannie away. But as always, Rita had jumped the gun and gone off on this wild tangent. Obviously the idea of losing Jeannie terrified Rita. Inwardly, Ben sighed. He'd always known that Rita had deep feelings for their daughter—for him, too. It was getting by her iron-clad defense that was the problem. It was also getting her to see that Jeannie's impairment affected them both, as parents, not just her as mother. But Rita had taken the sad circumstances surrounding the birth of their daughter and whipped them up into an epic tragedy. And that, coupled with a fanatical need to point the finger of blame somewhere, was slowly destroying what little was left of their life together.

"I couldn't live without Jeannie any more than I could live without you," Ben finally admitted, quietly, honestly.

"Then this taunting has all been some kind of a game?" Rita's eyes opened wide with fury. "I don't need this kind of treatment, Ben. I don't have to travel all the way from New York to be——"

"Shut up a minute, will you, please?" Ben's patience was at an end. "A very simple evening at home has become another episode of high drama. And it's thanks to you, Rita. You seem to have lost your perspective on things. Daily life is *not* high drama, it's living and loving and compromise." She began to speak, but he raised his hand to silence her. "Yes, I know you'll say you compromise by coming home to be with your poor little daughter and your long-suffering husband. Well, I say it's my compromise that I let you come home at all." He got up from the couch and poured himself another drink.

"I don't know how long this can go on, Rita. All we needed to talk about tonight was setting aside enough money, in a trust fund perhaps, for Jeannie just in case, God forbid, she found herself alone in the world." He sipped the drink and looked thoughtfully at his wife. "You, of course, have turned it into *Medea*. I'm getting tired of it, Rita. And I'm getting too old to coddle two children." He started to walk away.

"Where are you going?" Rita asked. There was truth in what Ben had just said and she didn't want him to stomp away. She wanted to acquiesce, but she needed time. He had to give her another chance.

"I'm going to say good-night to our daughter. Want to come along?" He raised his eyebrows hopefully.

"Sure," Rita said, "I'll be right up." When he'd gone she lit a cigarette. All that crazy talk about Jeannie being left alone was just that—crazy talk. And as for Ben compromising by having her here, it didn't mean he could live without her. At least he hadn't been able to before. The thought of not having Ben and Jeannie and this home was equally as painful as imagining life without her work.

Rita laughed to herself. Life without Ben and Jeannie or

life without *TNT*. Which would she choose if she had to? She laughed again and ground out her cigarette before going upstairs. There was no answer to such an absurd question because life would go on just as it was. She'd never have to make the choice.

4

Nan Booth ground out her cigarette. She still hadn't thanked Rita Martin for the goddamned ashtrays, she suddenly remembered. More than a week had passed since Sandy Lief had hand-delivered them from thirty-five. She'd have to call Rita this very morning. The little bone-china saucers daintily festooned with spring *fleurs* were exactly the kind of gift Rita would expect Nan to gush over. They were *so* feminine, *so* charming, *so* nauseatingly domestic. Nan shook her head in disgust. Getting caught up in petty politicking with the likes of Rita was one of the drawbacks of her job. Accepting second best was another. Not so long ago she would never have even thought of anything but a prime-time television career, but with the state of the economy and the shaky state of the television business, in particular, she had little choice. She was actually one of the lucky ones. And she was glad to be at the top of ITC's daytime heap. Still, she had her dreams.

Nan lit another cigarette and inhaled deeply. The inevitable hacking cough followed. Smoking was beginning to take its toll, but every good actress needs her prop and smoking was as much a part of Nan Booth as her signature. The large gestures and violent, punctuating jabs of the cigarette during conversations were an essential element of her personality. She pulled an ashtray closer, tapped off the cigarette ash.

To have to spend her time with Rita Martin . . . the only thing worse would be to learn to like Rita, to empathize. If she didn't one day get the hell out of New York and the penny-ante world of soap operas, game shows, and easy-to-digest talk shows, this might happen. Nan sprang from her desk and stalked to the window. Her corner office, four floors above the *Time Nor Tide* offices and on the opposite side of the building, faced west. On such a clear day, she could see out over the jumble of Manhattan buildings, past the Hudson River, and far beyond the Palisades to the low, flat reaches of New Jersey. Out there in the hinterlands, in thousands of houses and high-rise apartments that litter the landscape are the women who keep daytime television alive, she mused morosely. Nan knew more about these women than she ever wanted to know, and they were still foreign to her. They still aroused disdain in her.

There were many compensations, of course: this executive office, an impressive title—executive vice-president, ITC Entertainment—a salary of two hundred thousand dollars a year, which was just the tip of the iceberg, and more perks than she could remember. Nan ran interference for Jim Goodspeed at all press conferences and spoke to the media as the "network source" on any matter pertaining to daytime television, and, in fact, she had become the "golden girl" of the ITC Network. She was a celebrity. Her face had appeared on the cover of *TV Guide*. Every leading woman's magazine in the country had done an article praising her for her staunch support of women's causes during every phase of her six-year rise to fame from troubleshooter for Procter & Gamble Productions to her present position at ITC. Barbara Walters had interviewed her and genuinely seemed to like her (they had lunched privately several times since). When she walked into a restaurant she was recognized. People stopped her on the street. Even her mother, calling from "back home" in Wisconsin, would exclaim over and over: "I can't believe how famous you are! Everyone knows you." And everyone did. Just one problem: Nan didn't want to be here; she didn't want to be famous in these particular circles.

For Nan, L.A. was the land of milk and honey. Southern California. She wanted a house in Malibu Colony, on the beach. She wanted Hollywood. Nan wanted the West Coast now in the same driving way she had once wanted the East Coast, New York. How and when, she wondered, could she get it?

Nan Booth was a beautiful woman. Nature had artfully

combined fiery red hair, high, prominent cheekbones, eyes the deep brown color of caramelized sugar, and full pouting lips to produce a classic countenance that had favorably impressed more than one man—and more than one woman. She had made it to the top by a careful blend of cunning, flattery, sexual promises—made and kept—and plain, old-fashioned good luck.

ITC had hired her away from P&G to assist Dave Connolly, a former CBS whiz-kid who had defected with Jim Goodspeed. Her job was one part bullshit and two parts covering up for Connolly whose highest priority in life turned out to be a dry martini with a twist. Nan recognized the situation as her golden opportunity, and using her boss's authority and her own initiative, she began to make a name for herself. From the start Nan sidestepped criticism by placing herself squarely between the mere mortals of the network and the ITC gods, ruling from their fortieth-floor Parnassus, whose favor she curried at every chance.

Taking her cue from the legendary Lin Bolen, who upped NBC's daytime ratings by adding glamour and more money to game shows and who pushed soap operas from thirty minutes to an hour with *Another World* and *Days of Our Lives*, Nan revamped the ITC daytime schedule. She threw out the reruns, bought a controversial talk show for early morning and, after expanding it to a full hour, moved *Time Nor Tide* from late morning to early afternoon, thus making it ITC's daytime centerpiece. In exchange for her services as handmaiden—and in gratitude for the millions she brought in, in daytime ad revenue—the network titans gave Nan more power, more authority . . . and Connolly's title and office.

Nan was "one of the boys"; she still reported to Goodspeed according to the organization chart, but more and more his supervision was becoming just a formality. It was rumored that when J.G. retired Nan was the logical choice to succeed him as president of daytime programming. But as far as Nan could see, Goodspeed would live to be one hundred, and the only way they'd get him out of his office was feet first. Besides, she wanted L.A., and to get L.A., she had to do something so big, so eye-catching that ITC's super honcho Jason Weatherhead saw she was wasting her time with the Mickey-Mouse daytime crap. Not true, she suddenly realized. That ploy would have worked a couple of months ago. Now there was another problem. And, Jesus, it was Rita Martin again!

Nan went back to her desk and retrieved Weatherhead's memo from under her blotter. It was dated the day before and had arrived in an interoffice envelope marked *Confidential*. It read:

> *Nan:*
> *According to latest daytime numbers, you have a problem with* TNT. *It's beginning to look like a loser and I'm beginning to wonder if the operation is too big for you to deal with. Keep me posted on your follow-up.*
> J.W.

She crumpled the memo and heaved it into the wastebasket. Weatherhead was a sexist pig and a mean-minded prick. He disliked women almost as much as she disliked men. The trouble was, he was in a position to do something about it. Nan was caught between the proverbial rock and a hard place. On the one hand she had Weatherhead threatening her if she personally didn't do something to improve *Time Nor Tide*, and on the other hand she had Rita Martin, daytime's gracious grande dame—who turned into the Dragon Lady if anyone dared tamper with her show.

Still, Weatherhead's message was clear: Clean house at *TNT* or else! But how? To launch a full broadside at *Time Nor Tide* without full management support was suicidal, and Jim Goodspeed couldn't yet be counted on if it came to a showdown. Although lately he'd begun dealing with Rita Martin in realistic terms of what she was doing for ITC today, not what she'd done in the past, Nan wasn't foolish enough to make J.G. choose between her and Rita. Jesus, what was she going to do?

Her private line began to flash. "What is it?" she answered.

"And good morning to you, too," Rita said cheerfully.

"Rita," Nan's voice cooled off immediately. "I've been meaning to call you. The ashtrays were a stroke of genius!" She hoped she sounded convincing.

"I was afraid you hadn't liked them," Rita remarked pointedly. "But I guess I can still trust my instincts about what people like, after all."

"They're just . . . adorable," Nan searched for the appropriate superlatives. "I would have gotten to you sooner, but I've been swamped."

"Just as long as you're pleased," Rita sailed along. "There are a couple of things I want to discuss." She paused for just a second. "We're writing Frank Cameron out of the show. We feel we've taken him about as far as he can go."

"Dropping Rick Cologna is a big step, Rita. What's the problem?"

"This has nothing to do with Cologna. We're in a blind alley with *Frank Cameron.*" She emphasized his character name. "He's really too involved in drugs and blackmail to make his rehabilitation believable. Making him a nice guy seems too farfetched. So we decided a juicy murder would spice things up for ITC's February sweeps."

Three times a year, during "sweeps weeks," when Nielsens were measured at the local station level to test network popularity, all the networks "hyped" their schedules with the best programming, sexy specials, and first-run movies. Helping ITC claim the number-one daytime spot in the national rating—and the advertising dollars that go with it—gave Rita a rationale above and beyond her personal reasons for firing Rick Cologna.

"Anything to help is okay by me," Nan agreed. Once again Rita had covered her ass. The problem with Cameron was bullshit, of course. "How do Mel and Tom feel about losing Frank Cameron?"

"They agreed down the line. In fact, Mel was the first to suggest we dump him."

"Well, as long as they agree . . . Personally, I'll be sorry to see him go. Rick Cologna is such a lovable bastard."

"He *is* a charmer. In his own way. But he's only an actor, and soon he won't have a part to play," Rita said. "So, that's it, then."

"Not so fast. I want to clear this with Jim."

"No problem there, Nan. Jim gave me the go-ahead not more than ten minutes ago," Rita purred triumphantly.

Nan's anger flared. Attempting to stop Cameron's murder would have been the perfect opportunity to show Rita that the network intended to have a larger say in the running of *Time Nor Tide*. Chances were that Rita would have gotten her way this time anyway, but Nan would also have gotten her message across loud and clear. Damn Jim Goodspeed! He'd probably caved in just to get Rita off his back. And in doing so, he'd blown it.

Or had he? If Cameron's death weakened *TNT*'s ratings further, it might be the perfect excuse for Nan to declare martial law on the thirty-fifth floor . . . and single-handedly save *Time Nor Tide*. If that didn't impress Weatherhead, nothing would. What a coup to scuttle the unsinkable Rita Martin and salvage *TNT* in the bargain. The idea was practically sacrilegious. The ITC hierarchy were used to thinking of Rita as a network goddess, but Nan knew she was all too human. And there was a five-year contract due to expire mid-June to prove it. June. Only eight months away. It wasn't much time.

As the temerity of her budding scheme sent shivers up her spine, Nan began to plan. "I'll get in touch with Cologna's agent to smooth over any hard feelings, Rita. You just go ahead and kill him off," she said breezily. "It might actually help the ratings—and no one would object to that."

"We've been through slumps before and it hasn't killed us yet," Rita shot back. Then her voice relaxed. "Nan, don't worry. Trust me . . . please."

"Whatever you say." This petty conversation was beginning to annoy her. She needed time to think, now. "Look, Rita, I've got another call, so——"

"This can't wait," Rita interrupted. "I'm not through yet." When there was no resistance, she continued. "Ellie Davis isn't working out. I've given her plenty of rope and I'm afraid she's hung herself."

"There's never been a problem with Ellie's scripts. I've read them myself," Nan countered.

"Well, *I'm* not satisfied, and I'm the one whose reputation is on the line. Look, I feel as bad about this as you do, Nan, but the show always comes first, you know that."

"So, what are you going to do?"

"Look for someone to take her place."

Nan didn't bother to offer ITC's help. It was another familiar Rita Martin scenario; she kept one dialogue writing position in a permanent state of flux, filling it for a while with a newcomer. A long series of women and men had passed in and out of this slot, usually so fast they didn't know they were finished until they were back out on the street.

"When you find someone, let me know," Nan said, hoping that would conclude the conversation.

"You'll be the *first* to know . . . as always. One more thing before I let you go. Has there been any particular trouble down on the set lately?"

Actually, Weatherhead's memo had scared Nan into the visit to Studio One, but she said, "There were a few complaints about Joe Ericson. I wanted to take care of them myself."

Nan was lying again, Rita knew. No ITC executive of her stature would venture to the studio just to talk to a headstrong actor. "Can *I* be of any help?" she asked, innocently.

"If so, I'll let you know."

"Do that," Rita ended abruptly. This time she'd let it go, but next time Jim was going to hear about Nan's highly irregular behavior.

When Rita hung up, Nan walked to the couch opposite her desk and lay down without bothering to kick off her shoes; this was where she did her real thinking.

Within an hour Nan knew exactly what she safely could and could not do to dethrone Rita Martin. She could not directly affect the ratings and viewer response to *Time Nor Tide*, but she could, by demanding script approval, scuttle any new story line that might prove popular. She could not woo Jim Goodspeed over to her side by denigrating Rita Martin, but she could begin a campaign to convince him, by careful documentation (Jim never argued with facts and figures), that Rita was no longer working in ITC's best interests and that his continued support of her was ill-advised. She could not wantonly disrupt the assembly-line flow of work on the *TNT* set herself, but she could manipulate a certain hotheaded actor into doing it for her. She could not levy a cash embargo on the show without drawing attention to herself, but she could slowly strangle *TNT* economically with her right hand while proudly displaying the list of savings with her left. And finally, she could not directly be privy to the schemes hatched by Rita on the thirty-fifth floor, but she could enlist the aid of someone who was. Or better still, she could find someone to fill Ellie Davis's spot, someone with a better-than-average chance of rapid advancement.

And that meant finding a writer who was as handsome as he was talented. Who? she wondered. She closed her eyes, the better to think.

* * *

Al Peterson had been head writer on a soap in Canada. He had been in New York for six months and he was still looking for a job.

Now he lit the burner under the coffeepot and fiddled with the pack of matches he'd pilfered last night from the Rainbow Room. Job-hunting was far from his mind. Last night's date, Angela Brite, had come to agree with him that the Rainbow Room was indeed a very romantic spot for a rendezvous. The dapper, sublimely voguish, art deco atmosphere had won her over during the second dance. After two weeks of dating, she had finally let Peterson hold her too close, and she had even rested her head on his shoulder while her long, carefully manicured fingers inscribed tiny circles on his back. The city beyond the tall windows was flecked with dreams, stars, and twinkling lights, and when they returned to his apartment at five in the morning after croissants and espresso at the Brasserie, they made love until the rising sun dazzled their eyes. And now, eight hours later, Al was preparing their second continental breakfast of the day—this time to be eaten while they bathed.

Angela lay in the bathtub with her head back, her eyes closed as the suds ebbed and flowed against her natural "beachfront." Al's entrance disturbed her thoughts and brought her back to reality. "This is service. Good food, a hot tub, and a naked waiter."

Al pulled a small stool over to the edge of the tub, put the tray down, then joined Angela, sighing as the water eased over his body. Taking baths was one of the great pleasures of his life; taking baths with women was *the* greatest pleasure of his life.

"You are the silliest man I know, Al," Angela said, "and, you are one of the nicest, if you don't mind me saying so."

He smiled. "At the risk of sounding like a macho pig, you are one of the most beautiful . . . and desirable . . . women I have ever met. But, I don't have to tell you that, do I?"

Angela blushed. "Enough of this serious talk, let's eat."

Angela watched him while he devoured the food. There was much more to Al Peterson than his longish blond hair, his chocolaty brown eyes, his sensuous mouth; he was a caring human being, someone who liked himself and felt confident enough to like others equally. Every time she waited for him to be bullish or crass, he was gentle and well-mannered. Now that they had had sex, she was pleased to discover that he did not leave her with a terrible letdown, but that he put his arms around her and made her feel more desirable than ever. He was a good lover, and she had found herself agreeing to whatever he suggested and enjoying it. No, adoring it.

"That was marvelous . . . wonderful. It was the best breakfast I've ever had," she said, sliding down in the tub moving her legs around his body until the water lapped around her neck.

He answered by taking her hands in his.

"Al . . ." she began in mock protest, as he pulled her toward him, sending a tidal wave of water over the edge of the tub.

"It's only water." He clasped her in his arms, burying his face in her warm sweetness. "Strawberry jam never tasted so good," he mumbled as his tongue darted around the inside of her mouth. "*This* is what breakfast should be!" His hands slid down the length of her back, gently massaging her until he reached the crest of her buttocks. "You've got a beautiful ass, Angela. Just beautiful." He took the firm cheeks in his hands and kneaded them gently, forcing his tongue deeply into her mouth.

In the middle of the embrace Al's foot slipped at the end of the tub and they slid gracelessly underwater. Gasping and laughing, Angela pushed herself away. "Are you trying to drown us? If you want to play, let's do it right." She stepped from the tub, extended her hand, and helped Al out.

"Playtime's over," he said huskily. "We've got serious work to do." He led her to the bedroom and they finished what the bath together had begun.

Later, as they lay next to each other, Al kissed Angela's eyes and mouth, her cheeks and forehead, the tip of her nose. He tried to speak a couple of times, but there was nothing to say. Contented, he fell asleep.

Distant bells chimed as Al dreamed of Angela's exquisite soft skin and how she tasted when he explored her with his tongue. The bells sounded again, and he turned over, brushing against the real Angela who had been transformed into a Russian princess in the dream. They sat in an open sleigh wrapped in robes of ermine and sable, gliding through a silent world gone white in a Christmascard snowstorm. Beneath the robes they were naked, and he caressed her, bringing her closer and closer to a climax. Angela, her golden hair shimmering around her face, leaned close to him and whispered: "Goddammit, Peterson, answer the phone."

His eyes opened with a start and the snowscape and sleigh disappeared as the familiar shapes of his apartment came into focus. Angela, smoking a cigarette, sat propped up against the headboard next to him. The phone jangled again. He yawned widely, stretched, and reached for the bedside table. "Al Peterson," he croaked.

"One moment for Nan Booth," a male voice chirped.

Before Al had a chance to respond, he was put through to Nan. "It's been a long time, Al," she said in a voice that fell just short of being seductive.

"Last summer, wasn't it?" he stalled, needing a few seconds to wake up fully. Not only did he remember exactly when and where he'd met ITC's executive iceberg, but he also remembered that, in late August, he'd called her office twice to make an appointment and she hadn't bothered to return either call.

"It was the Fourth of July, to be exact," Nan went on confidently, "at the Writers' Guild cocktail party."

"Of course." He pulled himself up in bed and signaled Angela to light him a cigarette. "It *has* been a long time, Nan. How are you?"

"Al, I called for a reason," Nan cut him off. After a week wasted on searching for Peterson's business card then doing a background check on his credentials, she was in no mood for social chitchat. "We're looking for new writing talent for our daytime serials. Think you might be interested?" Last summer Peterson had that wild-eyed look writers get when their bank accounts begin to sicken.

"Can you be more specific?" An unqualified yes smacked of amateurism—or, worse yet, desperation.

"Not really. We're looking for dialogists. I know you've had experience as a head writer, but . . . ." Nan didn't want to sound too negative. Peterson was perfect: He was overqualified, sexy, and broke. ". . . For now that's all I can offer."

"Getting a foot in the door is the most important thing, isn't it?" Al mused rhetorically. "Still I'd like to talk to you personally. Let's meet."

"Absolutely not," Nan responded quickly. "It won't be necessary. *If* you're interested, I'll send you scripts and breakdowns.'' Any connection between them—no matter how tenuous—might sabotage Nan's plan before it got started. ''Are you interested or not?''

''You've got yourself a writer.''

''I'll messenger the material to you this afternoon. Write a sample script and return it to me. I'll——''

''Not so fast,'' Al interrupted. ''What soap are we talking about?''

Nan hesitated. ''It's not definite . . . I'll be sending you material from *Time Nor Tide*.''

''I'm a fan,'' he lied gleefully. For a one-thousand-dollar-plus-a-week job, he'd be a Captain Kangaroo fan. ''You'll have the script within a week.''

''Take your time. You've got to do a bang-up job,'' she coaxed. ''One more thing: Rita Martin is super touchy about outsiders seeing *TNT* breakdowns and scripts. So, keep this under your hat.''

''My lips are sealed,'' he said with polished innuendo. Iceberg or no iceberg, Nan Booth was still a woman, and women were Al Peterson's specialty.

''I'll be in touch,'' Nan promised, then hung up satisfied that the first, and easiest, phase of her plan had gone so well. Now for the tough part—getting Rita to read Peterson's script. Nan knew that Mrs. Elliott never deigned to read anything she hadn't personally commissioned, but she had a way of changing that, at least once. An innocent call requesting that all unsolicited scripts from the *Time Nor Time* slush pile be sent to her office should do the trick—particularly when Nan intimated that the next Rita Martin might be sitting right under their very noses! Nan would set the trap and Rita's vanity would spring it.

If that didn't send Rita scurrying to Peterson's script, then Nan had misjudged her nemesis. But just in case something did go awry, she had an alternate plan involving Alex Thorpe's delivery of the script as a personal favor to ''a close friend.'' Nan liked Thorpe. He was a good boy. And he was also smart enough to see that one day Nan could give him things that made Rita Martin's patronage seem stingy.

Of course there was the chance Rita wouldn't like Peterson's script. In that case Nan was stuck—for the time being. But she was confident that should Peterson make it as far as a personal interview, he was as good as gold—Rita Martin was a known connoisseur of good-looking younger men, and in that Al Peterson was in a class all by himself.

"Jesus, did you hear that? A job with *Rita Martin!*" Peterson pulled Angela into his arms and covered her with kisses.

He crushed out his cigarette and excitedly lit another. Nan obviously thought she was pulling a fast one with her "looking for new writing talent for our daytime serials" vagueness; it was the oldest trick in the book. Something was cooking at *Time Nor Tide;* someone was probably being canned. Hell, it was the nature of the beast. Al Peterson, like many others, could attest to that personally. But this time he was the new kid in town. He didn't care what poor sucker was about to get the gate at *TNT*. More power to Rita Martin! He was about to be rolling in dough again.

"Well, what do you think of that?" He squeezed Angela, not aware of the angry scowl on her face. "Rita Martin, of all people."

"Am I supposed to know who she is?"

"She's the creator of *Time Nor Tide* . . . the soap opera." He got out of bed and began to pace the length of the room like a nervous cat. "I'd better catch today's show for good measure."

"And what about *our* day together?" Angela asked, petulantly, arms folded across her chest.

"We'll watch *TNT*! Bet you haven't done that in a long time."

Now Angela's displeasure was impossible to ignore. "I never watch soap operas!" she snorted and fled to the bathroom.

Peterson shrugged his shoulders. He'd blown it with Angela, but there was no need to compound the error by losing out on *Time Nor Tide*. He flipped on the television just in time to catch the entire last act.

Penny Hewitt, still in her student nurse's uniform, sat alone at a table in the hospital cafeteria, demurely sipping a cup of tea. She brushed aside a wisp of her shoulder-length black hair and smiled to herself. Her green eyes twinkled happily as she remembered an earlier meeting with Ted Reynolds, the young doctor who was ardently pursuing her.

"I'm not going to take no for an answer, Penny," Ted had chided her lightly. "I have something of a reputation at the hospital as a very persistent man."

"That's not the reputation I *was thinking of," Penny had quipped, her voice only barely betraying an underlying anxiety.*

But Ted's throaty laughter had immediately put her at ease. "Touché, Miss Hewitt. Now, seriously, how about having dinner with me tonight? There's a new restaurant I've been wanting to try; it's called Raffles and I've heard it's veddy, veddy English!"

"Well, I don't know," Penny had hesitated.

"I promise I'll have you home by ten. Okay?"

"Okay."

Penny now sighed contentedly at the memory of the smile growing on her face. She was about to take another sip of tea when a shadow fell over her. She looked up, startled by an uninvited guest.

"You're Penny Hewitt, aren't you?" a strange male voice inquired.

Penny's smile vanished. "Yes. What can I do for you?"

The answer was a short, ugly laugh. "You can't do nothing for me, but you can do something for your great-aunt, Mrs. Danforth. Mind if I sit down? The name's Cameron. Frank Cameron."

Penny shook her head in bewildered acquiescence as Cameron pulled a chair from the table, turned it around, and, straddling it, sat down.

"What's this about my great-aunt?" Her voice was tinged with fear, and her eyes danced from one corner of the cafeteria to the other as if she were looking for a way of escape.

"Your aunt and me have a little business deal going, but I think maybe she's thinking of welching on me." Cameron leaned forward, his slicked-back hair glistening in the bright lights. "I want you *to put in a good word for me. Will you do that, honey?" His eyes darted up and down Penny with a frankly animal lust.*

Penny recoiled at his familiarity. "I don't know what you mean."

"You don't have to understand, just pass along the message." With the speed of a rattlesnake hitting its prey, Cameron's hand darted out and ensnared Penny's. "Tell Mrs. D. if she don't get a move on there's going to be plenty of trouble for her . . . and for those she loves." his smile turned into a sneer.

Penny tried desperately to withdraw her hand, but Cameron held tight. "Please let go," she whimpered. "Please . . ."

"Any trouble here?" a voice called out.

Both Penny and Cameron turned at once and saw Ted Reynolds standing behind them.

Cameron immediately released Penny's hand. "No trouble at all, Doc. I was just leaving." He leaped from the chair, took one last look at Penny, then fed.

"What was all that about?" Ted asked as he took Cameron's vacant chair.

Penny lowered her head and shook it slowly back and forth without answering.

"Penny, what is it?" Ted's hand glided out to comfort, but the minute he touched her she pulled away. "What did that creep say to you?"

"I don't want to talk about it," Penny said quietly. "It was nothing."

"Penny . . ." Ted started to coax, but he never finished. With lightning speed Penny pushed her chair back and got up.

"Ted, I'm sorry, but I won't be able to have dinner with you after all. Something's come up. Please don't be offended. I just can't do it now . . . or ever." Without another word she fled, leaving Ted Reynolds utterly confused.

The Time Nor Tide theme rose in the background and the picture faded to black.

Rita leaned far back in her office chair. Today's episode of *Time Nor Tide* sparkled. There were no production problems; it was well-directed, and Nancy Carson had shaded Penny Hewitt with real emotion. Rita saw Penny as not much more than a child in a woman's body, a naïf whose habit of trusting the wrong people would always lead to great disappointment. But Penny was a survivor. The fact that she had been raped by Bob Garrick, a respected lawyer, had then lied about the identity of her molester to protect Jane Garrick—Bob's wife and Penny's best friend—had then suffered an almost fatal miscarriage in an automobile wreck, proved that nothing could kill Penny Hewitt. And that's the way it would always be, because Rita had modeled the character after herself.

She signaled Sandy she was ready for the two-thirty story conference about Penny Hewitt, and minutes later, Mel and Tom joined her. "Nancy Carson did a good job today, don't you think?" she asked them simultaneously.

"If she keeps up like this, we may have a real actress on our hands," Mel answered immediately.

"Be fair. She's really growing into the role; I think we should give her more to do." It was a statement, not a question.

Mel made a note in his pad. "I agree; the time's right. Ever since the rape, she's been hiding in the shadows."

"The story projection has Penny marrying Ted Reynolds," Tom threw in for good measure.

Rita scowled and started chewing on the nail of her thumb, a habit she evoked when she was deep in thought. "Penny Hewitt and sex . . . again?" Her nail snapped under the pressure from her teeth, and she looked at it with annoyance. "But it can't be blind sex . . . lust. We have to ease poor Penny into this—maybe the Ted Reynolds idea will work. After all, he is a psychiatric resident at Laurelton General." She perked up. "They can work through this trauma together with tender loving care . . . then be married."

And live happily ever after in a vine-covered cottage, Mel finished the thought in his mind. The story was shit, plain and simple. It was the same crap Rita Martin had been churning out for the past six years and everyone knew it was beginning to tire the viewers. He'd seen the Nielsens. The soap opera magazines had all run articles saying the same thing: Make *TNT* more modern, infuse it with young blood—and young love—get away from the unrealistic, claustrophobic world of living rooms full of sweet talk and kitchens full of hot apple pies and freshly brewed coffee; adultery was no longer the end of the world, abortion and miscarriages happened to nice people as regularly as the mail delivery; impotent men and frustrated women went to clinics for their sexual problems. Life was moving faster, but *TNT* was standing still.

On top of that Mel had heard reports through the grapevine that *TNT*'s actors were rebelling against weak scripts, and that Nan Booth had been snooping around the set asking a lot of questions. Inwardly Mel sighed. There might be no diplomatic way to approach the subject, no way not to offend Rita, but for his own peace of mind, he decided to risk it. "Rita, it's possible that old chestnut won't work . . ."

She turned toward him slowly, the words *old chestnut* still ringing in her ears. "Oh?" she said softly. "Then please tell me what *will* work."

There was silence in the room. Only the muffled sound of

distant traffic intruded. Suddenly an entirely new Penny Hewitt story surged into his brain. "Penny arranges to marry Ted in a small ceremony. She's affectionate with him but only to a point. Ted, being the understanding soul he is, puts up with her remoteness. Penny confides in her mother that she's afraid of sex and Betty offers some reassuring words of wisdom. So it's done. They get married and take a honeymoon to"—he was stuck for just a second—"I don't know, one of those Caribbean islands. That's it. They go to the tropics where there's political unrest and they—she—gets captured by rebels," Mel said, totally swept away by his own words.

"Mel, that's ridiculous. It's utterly preposterous and . . . I *love* it!" Rita exclaimed, leaping from her chair. "What do you think, Tom?"

"It's got possibilities," he said, wishing he'd thought of it.

Now Rita's mind took over, immediately filling in all the blank spots of Mel's story. She sailed around her desk and gave him a wet kiss on the cheek. "It's perfect! I feel like the show's just been given an Emmy," she gushed. "I don't know how people can do anything that's less satisfying than this job. Mel, you're a genius!"

"I had a good teacher." He held her hand for one second too long. No matter what his opinion of Rita Martin, no matter how often her pushy brand of business irked him, she was still one damned fine-looking woman.

"Now, you two scat," Rita commanded in a cheerful voice that was almost girlish. "I've got a lot of thinking to do."

When she was alone again Rita burst out laughing. Let the Cassandras of ITC beware! Rita Martin hadn't lost her touch after all. She and her team were about to put *Time Nor Tide* back on the map again! It was a simple strategy: Take one neurotic student nurse, one horny medical student, throw in a Caribbean uprising for spice, and mix carefully. There'd be plenty of sex, violence, location shots, and best of all, Penny and Ted were *young*, and everyone in the business knew from witnessing the resurrection and ascension into rating heaven of ABC's *General Hospital* that if you had the young adults with you, you were almost assured of success. So, *TNT* would have a new Romeo and Juliet, and Rita would take the credit.

She laughed again. It was going to be a good day. Charting the fate of Penny Hewitt assured many months of good scripts; some *had* to be Emmy quality. Rita felt good about being alive, about being Rita Martin, and unless her intuition failed her, Jim Goodspeed was going to start feeling good about her once again, too. She'd been too easy on him lately.

She reached for the phone to dial his office when the memory of his recent evasions shook her confidence. She hung up, stymied for the moment. Well, what the hell. If Goodspeed wanted to play "hotshot executive," two could play that game as easily as one.

She dictated a brief memo outlining the Hewitt/Reynolds plot, then gave it to Sandy to transcribe. And, breaking a four-year embargo, instructed that one copy be sent directly to Nan Booth.

Two days later, following a daily pattern, Jim Goodspeed finished his morning running with a final sprint down Sixth Avenue from Central Park to the office. He had been a runner long before it became *de rigueur* for social acceptance and the faddists crowding the park impressed him as nothing more than dilettantes. As he ran on this chilly, drizzly, mid-October day, his thoughts were all about Rita Martin.

He took the express elevator to the fortieth floor, quickly showered in the bath/dressing room off his office, dressed, and was at his desk half an hour before anyone else. Like Rita, Goodspeed knew the psychological impact of his arriving at the office early and leaving late. It created a competitive tension among his colleagues and underlings that resulted in better work in the optimum amount of time. But unlike Rita, Jim Goodspeed was devoted to his family, too. He had a wife he loved, children he respected, and grandchildren he adored. And he wanted to spend time with them all. Business was left on his desk each night and resumed again with his first cup of coffee in the morning.

Now he opened an interoffice envelope that had lain on his desk since late yesterday and shook out its contents. A flurry of clippings from soap opera magazines, daytime stars magazines, and every other crackpot television publication sold in supermarkets and drugstores cascaded onto his blotter. Damn Nan! What a cutthroat, pushy bitch!

Sifting through the latest mass of carefully selected clippings it was easy to see Nan was being true to form; each one had something bad to say about *TNT*. Well, he could understand Nan's concern—the show's ratings reflected on her own capabilities as vice-president. And Weatherhead's interference was probably scaring the shit out of her. But her tactics were odious.

He'd followed the ratings, knew the damning figures proclaiming *Time Nor Tide* a failure, but he also knew Rita Martin. There was no way she'd blow it. She never had before. You don't give up everything else in your life for a fucking *television show*, then let it go down the tubes. Nan could piss and moan all she wanted; he was following his instincts and that meant giving Rita this last chance to redeem herself.

He liked and admired Rita. She could be a pain in the ass, but she was right up front about her demands; not like Nan. Nan was the kind of woman who one minute said she was on the pill and the next said you'd knocked her up. Jim would take Rita over Nan any day. But just in case she failed him and didn't pull the *TNT* rabbit out of the hat, he was keeping her at arm's length. If Rita's dismissal of Rick Cologna was done with future ratings in mind—and was not the result of a sexual peccadillo, as rumor suggested—it would certainly show during the February ratings sweeps. If not, Rita might just find herself out of a job come June.

He chucked the sheaf of offending clippings into the wastebasket. Then he buzzed his girl, Sally. "Come in. I have two memos to dictate." A minute later be began. "Use standard memo letterhead on both of these. The first is to Rita Martin: 'Rita, have read your Caribbean brainstorm with interest. But before discussing it or the feasibility of going overbudget with location shooting, I'll need more precise information. Please prepare a detailed story projection from which we can extrapolate extra costs of production. Send a copy to me and one to Nan at your earliest convenience. Jim.'"

He closed his eyes for a moment to collect his thoughts, and when he opened them and smiled at Sally, she blushed furiously. "The second memo is to Nan Booth: 'Nan, included is a new Rita Martin story line that will involve expensive location work if we go with it. Do you think the story merits the expenditure? I've asked Rita to do a polish of the idea, but my personel feeling is that this may be just the shot in the arm TNT needs. When you can, get a breakdown on projected expenses for this and get it to me a.s.a.p. Jim.' "

After Sally had gone, Goodspeed wondered if he'd been too abrupt in his memo to Rita. A little personal aside would have been a nice touch . . . but, no, better to remain aloof. If Rita failed it would be a hell of a lot easier to fire her if they hadn't just had a cozy lunch the day before.

5

Mel Jacobs pushed his way through the front doors of the New York Health & Racquet Club on West Fifty-sixth Street into the warm, plant-filled lobby. Damn, it was cold out! he thought, rubbing his hands together. It wasn't quite Halloween, yet the weather forecast was for light snow flurries. He headed toward the locker room. He hated winter even more than summer. Give me a nice, spring day and I'll be happy, he mused. He'd leave the fascination with extremes to others—like Wendy, his wife.

Today it was Wendy, not his usual antagonist, Rita Martin, who managed to corrode the protective armor of his personality. In fact, Rita had been in a buoyant, good mood for the past two weeks—ever since taking credit for the Penny Hewitt Caribbean story, which she was absolutely convinced would pull *Time Nor Tide* out of rating limbo. Her optimism was unbridled. This afternoon she'd had Sandy collect every unsolicited *TNT* manuscript that had found its way into the office during the past three months. Usually Rita considered reading these scripts a complete waste of time, but today she'd actually said she intended to start her search for Ellie's replacement with these unknowns! She then sailed out of the office early with all seven scripts locked in her attaché case as if one of them were going to change her life. Rita Martin, champion of the aspiring soap opera writer. What bullshit!

But it was Wendy who really irked him. By the time Mel reached his locker he was furious with her all over again.

He'd telephoned her earlier just to say hello, but she was out. Lately, she'd been out a lot. Too much, in fact, for him not to get suspicious. The housekeeper, Lolly Swedeborg, said she didn't know where Wendy was, or when she'd be back, but Lolly would lie through her teeth to protect "poor Mrs. Jacobs." Mel didn't like it at all. Lately Wendy was tense and jittery. She watched him out of the corners of her eyes and jumped at the sound of his voice. They were familiar signs. She was probably falling back into her old ways. No . . . he'd warned her again and again about *that*, and he'd had to *show* her he meant business about her staying on the straight and narrow. Much as Mel disliked violence, it seemed the only thing Wendy understood. Today he decided to give her the benefit of the doubt. If she could explain why she was out all afternoon, she was off the hook. If not . . . well . . . maybe it was time for another "lesson."

He stripped and stood in front of the full-length mirror. He was in pretty good shape—for forty. Mel demanded perfection in everyone, so it was only fair he should start with himself; keeping his body in top form was a way to approach that goal. Mel kept his life full of goals. They took the edge off the general disappointment he felt in himself and in his personal life. In a world full of things to be achieved, any failure or compromise was only a temporary setback easily forgotten by shifting focus onto a new goal. It was an emotional hurdles race to run from the past, and its importance evidenced itself in the aggressive way he shook hands, his bold walking stride, and the loud, raucous laugh that was something of a trademark. Few would have guessed Mel Jacobs felt himself anything but a success. Even Wendy took his frequent moodiness at home personally, believing he was subtly giving her fair warning to toe the mark—or else. Mel's carefully constructed personality accurately reflected the sum total of everything he was—and carefully hid the painful truth of everything he wasn't.

He ran his hand over his chest and shoulders, over the thick mat of black hair. Dark-haired, olive-complexioned, his appearance the indelible stamp of his ancestors, Mel was the antithesis of those he truly admired. Despite all his accomplishments he still envied many of the men at the club—fair-haired, handsome, Yankee features, glistening smooth bodies—and he hated himself for it. For eight years he'd deluded himself into believing he'd broken the traditional barriers of prejudice that had forced many others before him to retreat. When he finally realized that he, too, had failed, he had not only lost all vestiges of his fragile self-esteem, but also forsaken the love and respect of his family.

Mel's father, Sam, was a first-generation American whose background duplicated the backgrounds of countless Russian Jews who fled oppression in search of happiness on the golden shores of America. And like the patriarchs of those other Jewish families. Zev Jacobs—Mel's grandfather—drove himself day and night so that Sam and Sam's son and every other Jacobs to come might live better. Sam's life began on Manhattan's Lower East Side and led to success on Seventh Avenue, a wife and son, and, by the time he was forty-five, a house on Long Island.

The Jacobses' colonial house in the King's Point section of Great Neck was really too big for the family, and Mel was really the only one who used the backyard boatslip on Long Island Sound, but Sam was determined to lavish the best on his little family—which he secretly hoped would increase. His fondest dream on moving to Long Island was that his wife, Minnie, would bear him one more son before it was too late. At forty-one, Minnie considered that it had been too late for at least five years, and when she saw the gleam in Sam's eyes, she politely excused herself "to freshen up" in the bathroom and inserted her diaphragm while saying a short prayer that it not fail her. It didn't and Sam eventually gave up his dream of bringing another scion into the world.

Like many only children, Mel grew up spoiled and very willful. But unlike so many children without siblings, he was not the center of the elder Jacobses' world. Mel was a late child and by the time he was in grade school both his parents were already feeling the pinch of age. Despite an early, loving home life, Sam and Minnie eventually relegated much of Mel's care to household help, and as he approached adolescence, Mel found himself alone more and more. With Sam always working in the city and Minnie busy with her friends, charities, and clubs, Mel learned to fend for himself. But instead of seeking out his peers, he chose to capitalize on his solitude by becoming an expert sailor.

At thirteen, Mel dreamed of a life at sea. Nothing could be more satisfying than stationing himself in the stern of his sixteen-foot sailboat, the tiller in one hand, the main sheet in the other, as he skittered along parallel to the rocky shore of

Long Island. Being in full command of his boat, his course—his very life, it seemed—was a feeling so intensely joyful that it brought tears to his eyes. What could possibly compare to the exhilaration of sailing on a chill, early autumn day, his face roughly caressed by the stiff wind that whipped the waves into an angry froth and drove the boat so far away from home and the loneliness that had been enshrined there? These times alone were the happiest moments of Mel's life, and years later, late at night when he often couldn't sleep, he wished that it were in his power to will himself back to that all-encompassing happiness, if only for one day.

As Mel entered his last year of junior high school, Sam and Minnie made the fateful decision to send him away to prep school the next fall. After all, they rationalized, they had the money, and Mel certainly deserved the best—even though he wanted to stay in school right in Great Neck. Mel's wishes were overridden in favor of enrollment at Saint Paul's New Hampshire, a bastion of upperclass Protestant tradition where, Sam believed, Mel would find the key to true success.

The truth was simpler: Mel's parents felt guilty about neglecting him, and putting him through the ritziest school they could find helped to assuage that guilt. So, the following year they all piled into the family Seville for the long drive to Concord, New Hampshire, never guessing that this day was a turning point for all of them.

At Saint Paul's, Mel Jacobs was a Jew among Gentiles, a well-to-do student among the very wealthy. It took him only a few short days in the dorm and in the classroom to intuit that Saint Paul's was the worst choice his parents could have made for him, and that unless he made every effort to become "one of the guys," the next four years would be unmitigated hell.

But turning WASP overnight seemed an impossible task. And working at accepting and perfecting Mel Jacobs never occurred to him (in the heady atmosphere of Saint Paul's that didn't seem good enough, anyway). It was Chip Farrington, Mel's roommate, who provided the key to Mel's metamorphosis. Mel and Chip were a true odd couple—Mel, dark and swarthy, Chip, with his blond hair and arresting blue eyes, the epitome of the Saint Paul's man—until they discovered they both shared a passion for sailing. From then on they were inseparable. Chip confided in Mel that he'd been taken aside by his father before leaving Oyster Bay and carefully told that even up in New Hampshire, as he put it, marks weren't enough to guarantee success. It was *how* you lived, *who* you knew, not *what* you knew. Mel took Chip's father at his word, and using Chip's friendship as an entrée into Saint Paul's upperest crust, he set out to be popular and, in turn, successful.

The very next month, in a phone call to his parents, Mel regretfully explained that he'd be spending Thanksgiving with a friend and his family in Boston and that he hoped to be invited to Palm Beach for the upcoming Christmas season. To his great surprise, neither Sam nor Minnie was pleased by this announcement. For what they paid in tuition, they expected their son home for the holidays where he belonged. When they pressed him to change his mind, Mel's determination wavered momentarily, but a mental picture of the King's Point home with its miles of flowered chintzes, comfy chairs, and endless bric-a-brac did it. He refused, adding that if they really objected to the Boston trip he'd just stay at school and study. In the end Sam and Minnie gave in on the condition that Mel make every effort to come home to them during the long winter vacation. Mel said he'd see what he could do.

Thus Mel Jacobs entered the closed world whose golden inhabitants all seemed to be beautiful and to whom great wealth was taken for granted. Mel took to this elitist world as if he had been born to it, never suspecting that the camaraderie exhibited by his friends was firmly rooted in their belief that men of their class had a duty to treat everyone politely. Feeling accepted, Mel put his self-doubts aside and believed himself one of the guys.

There were only two problems with this new view of life: the way he treated his parents, and girls.

As each day passed in the rarefied atmosphere of Saint Paul's, Mel found the thought of going home to Long Island more and more distasteful. His new identity demanded he shake off the past to reap the rewards of the future. When Mel was finally enticed home he entered the big house with its unashamed clutter feeling alienated from his mother and father "who worked so hard to give him everything they never had." Though he tried to mask his feelings at home, Mel's sullen manner spoke for itself. Mel began to straddle two worlds—that of his heritage and that of his dream. No amount of mother love, shame, or even strudel from his ancient *bubba* could change Mel's course. During his Saint

Paul's days a family schism formed that was never mended. And when Mel felt guilty about his actions—as he sometimes did—he simply remembered that he had wanted to stay at home for school; it was his parents' idea to send him away. Only after their death did this argument fail to vindicate and soothe him.

Mel's problem with girls was even more troublesome, even humiliating. All the guys had at least one steady girl friend. Usually sweet, always spoiled, and not necessarily bright, these girls, more openly than the boys, looked upon Mel Jacobs as a brooding oddity in their privileged midst. One particularly forthright, if overly romantic, young thing even nicknamed him Heathcliff. It was these *shiksas* who drew the social line over which Mel was not allowed to step. He was introduced to his friends' sisters but never offered a date with any of them. If his sultry, blonde Wendy had been one of the Saint Paul's crowd, Mel never would have been afforded the opportunity to socialize with, let alone marry, her. Invariably when a date *was* arranged, she was either bland as wallpaper paste or a nice Jewish girl from Scarsdale who, like Mel, had broken away from tradition. Subtly, gently, he was ostracized.

At Williams things changed more rapidly. The whirl of his prep school days was replaced by earnest talk of grad schools and careers. Mel's friends grew more distant as they prepared to enter their fathers' businesses or mapped out strategies for enrolling in the best law schools, and then finding positions in the most prestigious firms. Mel's friends began to seem unreliable, and for the first time since the early days at Saint Paul's, he was afraid. He was to receive a bachelor's degree in English Literature, and he'd already set his sights on a life in New York, but what that life would be wasn't clear to him.

As the dean handed him his diploma, a tidal wave of bitterness swept over him. Looking out over row after row of his classmates, Mel realized, without a doubt, that no one out there really gave a damn about him. Sure they'd all promised to keep in touch, but he knew that with the final tolling of the chapel bell at evening, the heady world of old money and social acceptance would be closed to Mel Jacobs as suddenly as it had been opened.

"You okay, Mr. Jacobs?" the locker room attendant asked, startling Mel back to reality.

"Yeah, sure, Joseph," he mumbled, embarrassed to be caught at such a futile pastime as reminiscing.

As Mel pulled on his sweat pants, a sharp pain in his stomach doubled him over. For a minute it twisted inside him like a knife blade, then subsided. Mel eased himself onto a bench, took a couple of deep breaths and wiped the cold sweat from his brow. He was shaking and near panic; for one horrible minute he was afraid he might pass out.

Shit, that was the worst attack he'd had since his ulcer healed a couple of years back. Well, a little pain wasn't going to keep him from working out. He shrugged his shoulders, finished dressing, defiantly slamming the locker door. Then he walked into the gym. Mel Jacobs was a winner. No one and nothing would prove him otherwise.

He finished showering after the workout expecting to feel the familiar glow from muscles worked to their limits, but the earlier pain in his stomach still lingered. I'm working myself too hard, he thought as he dressed. If I don't watch it I'll end up like Tom Wesley, drinking at lunch and taking tranquilizers as if they were candy.

Mel had watched Tom's problem with pills and booze double over the past year. He didn't like it or like how it affected Tom's work, but Mel certainly sympathized with the need to escape. Hell, the pressure to succeed was killing them all. Even his fury at Rita more often than not stemmed from his identification with her frustrations and fear. Success had been touted as a magic elixir, but he, Tom, and Rita had found its taste bitter, its life-giving powers questionable.

Six years before they'd all prayed that *Time Nor Tide* would hit it big when so many others failed. It was their common dream, and like all dreams, the image was nebulous, constantly changing and wavering, its center soft and malleable. In reality success turned out to be sharp and hard-edged, a self-generating monster that demanded to be fed and tended to every minute of the day. If Tom was crumbling under the pressure from Rita, what must Rita be feeling? If her temper tantrums and nervous energy were her safety valves, what terrible personal agonies was she holding back? It was a question Mel didn't want answered. It was a question that, were it not for Nan Booth, might never have been posed.

Nan had galloped into the network like a knight-errant, cutting down everything that stood between her and the Holy Land of the fortieth floor. He sneered inwardly remembering his—and Tom's—first meeting with Nan over a good sherry late one afternoon in her office. She was all smiles and lavish praise until the end of the meeting. Then she got down to business.

"Let's not delude ourselves, boys. Television is not an art form; it's not even an entertainment medium—it's an advertising tool, the most effective and, in the long run, the least expensive. Television exists to sell products. Our product is the viewers who watch our programs. We sell them to the advertisers—in quantity. Got it?"

She finished the meeting with the admonition to write *TNT* with one eye on the competition and the other on the ratings.

"With that attitude we'll be cross-eyed before long," Tom nervously quipped later.

Shortly thereafter *Time Nor Tide* went to an hour and they all began to suffer from the additional work load.

Goddamn *TNT*, and Nan Booth, Mel thought as he pushed his way out of the club.

During the taxi ride to his Central Park West co-op Mel began to feel even worse. Only the thought of a peaceful evening at home with Wendy made the trip bearable. At home Mel was king. He closed his eyes and planned the evening: fireplace blazing, a light drink to soothe his stomach, a quiet dinner, and maybe even a little roll in the hay. Heaven. Mel's preconception calmed his jangled nerves. If only Wendy didn't do anything to upset him . . .

But when he put his briefcase on the hall table and saw a pile of unopened mail, his dreams began to sour. "Wendy, I'm home," he called out. But he knew she wasn't there.

"Mrs. Jacobs still isn't home," a voice from the kitchen answered him.

Mel looked at the stack of mail again and the pain in his stomach returned. "Did she call?" He made no move toward the kitchen.

Lolly Swedeborg, cook and housekeeper, appeared at the kitchen door. She was short, Norwegian, and disliked Mel as much as he did her. "She *said* she'd be back about five," Lolly replied tartly. "Guess she got stuck in traffic." She attempted a smile to no avail. Lolly only stayed on because she felt sorry for Mrs. Jacobs. Her dealings with Mr. Jacobs were always forced and unpleasant. ' 'May I get you anything?"

Mel shook his head.

"I just put up some herring with sour cream and dill. It would be no trouble."

Mel felt a rush of nausea so acute he leaned on the back of a chair for support. "I don't want anything," he snapped. She shrugged and headed back to the kitchen. "On second thought, fix me a sweet martini." He went upstairs to change.

Twenty minutes later as he sipped his drink, Mel's anger over Wendy's absence returned. He had made it clear long ago that he expected her to be home when he got there, unless they made other arrangements. Today she had defied him. The pain in his stomach was now a hot ball of fire even the drink didn't extinguish. One thing was sure: Wendy would pay for this and soon.

"Want another?" Lolly asked a few minutes later.

He shook his head. "If you've finished everything, Mrs. Swedeborg, you can take the night off."

She looked confused. "But, Mrs. Jacobs said . . ."

"I spoke with her this morning. She agreed you deserve extra time off." The maid saw right through his lie, but what Lolly Swedeborg thought of him hardly mattered. Wendy's "friendship" with the woman displeased him almost as much as the woman herself.

"If you're sure . . . ?" This was *his* idea. Poor Mrs. Jacobs. There was going to be trouble tonight.

Mel withdrew a twenty-dollar bill from his wallet. "Have dinner, go to a movie. Don't bother getting back early."

Lolly grudgingly took the money. "Dinner is all prepared; the roast is in the oven and the vegetables are ready to be cooked. She gave Mel one last skeptical look, then departed, banging the back door.

Mel sat quietly at the far end of the living room sipping his drink and watching the sun set with a fireworkslike display of color. The martini fought his anger and gradually won. His stomach relaxed. Half an hour later when the late afternoon shadows gave way to the grainy light of early evening, he fixed himself another.

By now he'd formulated a little plan and a little challenge for Wendy. He sat in the far corner of the living room where the darkness collected like dust on unused furniture. Wendy wouldn't see him until she turned on the light. He would do nothing to give himself away. She'd walk into the darkened apartment assuming Mel was still at work, and that her little scheme had worked. With luck, it might be ten, maybe fifteen minutes before she discovered him waiting in the darkness.

Mel savored the thought of Wendy's reaction. He hadn't always been so cruel. But he'd been naïve then. When they married he never suspected she had a personality problem that would take precedence. He never guessed that life with such a sexy-looking woman would be overshadowed by her bouts of secret, destructive gambling.

Mel had known there were people who said they were unable to control themselves, but he saw their compulsions as sheer willfulness. Certainly no one he knew was that weak. But then, six months after their marriage there'd been that call—from what was his name? Wolfheimer or something—saying Wendy owed two thousand dollars to cover her losses at various tracks across the country. The call had nearly destroyed him. How naïve he'd been to think his own beautiful Wendy might be perfect. And how devastating to discover she wasn't. It was unfair, unjust. He'd already paid his dues at prep school and college. Marrying a beautiful *shiksa* like Wendy was his right. But Wendy was flawed and it now seemed keeping an eye on her day and night was the ultimate price paid for seeking acceptance in a world that clearly cast him as an outsider . . . and it made Mel furious.

The Jacobses had met six years before at the Guggenheim Museum. Mel was full of himself that rainy Tuesday night. He'd just been promoted from dialogist to head writer, an accomplishment few could claim. But Mel had a rare talent. Rita had personally groomed him for his new position and now it looked like life would be rosy: no more worrying about the future, or money, or more insecurities. And as proof, he'd just had drinks at Rita's Fifth Avenue aerie—which was as good as a papal audience in Mel's book.

The storm that drove him into the Guggenheim that night came from nowhere. It swept across the city, clawing at the trees and hurtling sheets of wind-whipped rain down the avenue. Although Mel loathed modern art, the museum was the nearest place to seek refuge. He stood in the vestibule for a few minutes, and when the rain still had not let up, he decided to go inside. Taking heed of the explicit directions in the lobby, he took the elevator to the top of the museum and, a minute later, began his descent down the circular ramp whose walls formed the main gallery.

It's like being inside a goddamned snail, he scoffed as gravity pulled him down the sloping walkway. He was wet and uncomfortable. What he really wanted was a good hot meal and a change of clothes. He paused at the railing, stifling a yawn. Down in the circular distance a lone woman fought her way up the ramp from one painting to another. She wore faded dungarees, tennis shoes soaked from the rain, an oversize bulky sweater, and she carried a sodden trench coat over her arm. Her blonde hair was short, although she unconsciously brushed her hand across it as if pushing aside a great mane. She'd probably just had it cut, Mel figured.

She couldn't have been more than twenty-two or three. Her aura of wholesomeness, even at this distance, immediately attracted him. But what particularly intrigued him was why, when the sign so pointedly said otherwise, she was walking up to the top.

"I've decided you're so taken with the Matisse exhibit that going the wrong way doesn't mean a thing to you," he said, finally having summoned the courage to speak.

She stared at him, quizzically. "Are you talking to me?"

"You're supposed to take the elevator up and walk down." With his index finger he inscribed an imaginary spiral in the air.

The girl shook her head. "It would have been easier on the legs, I suppose. Frank Lloyd Wright must have believed we have to suffer to appreciate art properly."

When she laughed Mel felt a jolt of sexual excitement. For the past few months he'd been so cloistered with Rita that his personal life had all but disappeared.

"Only the artist is supposed to suffer," he laughed along with her. Up close she was more than attractive. In fact, she was breathtaking, and very sexy. She wore no makeup, and unless he'd lost all touch with the mysteries of the female body, under those loose-fitting clothes she was sensational! Mel pictured her naked, the beautiful soft skin of her body under his fingers and between his teeth. "You like Matisse?" He couldn't let the conversation die.

"I get lost in his paintings; they're so beautiful." She turned back to them. "I guess you're an aficionado too." She addressed the canvas, her back still to Mel.

"He's one of my favorites," Mel lied as he examined the voluptuous contours of her ass. "I'm here, aren't I?"

She turned and smiled beguilingly. "I'm here because the museum's free tonight. When it comes right down to a choice between eating or looking at art, my appetite always wins."

She wasn't at all embarrassed by so philistine a statement because it was an outright lie. "I'm a photographer . . . and money's a little tight, that's all." She tossed her head back and laughed.

Mel laughed too. So she's broke, he thought. Well, baby, this is perfect timing. I've got a wallet full of cash. "Food for the soul *isn't* enough?" he asked coyly.

"No. My stomach always seems to get in the way." She gently rubbed her abdomen. Her sweater, pulled tightly against her, outlined her full breasts.

"I'm Mel Jacobs," he announced quickly, his eyes fixed firmly on her.

"And I'm Wendy Moffat." She shook his hand, then waited.

Mel took a chance at a grandstand play. Shit, it was a lousy night, he felt good about himself, and here he was with a beautiful woman. He recaptured her hand and tugged her back up the ramp toward the paintings she hadn't seen. "If you'll permit me to escort you, Miss Moffat, when we've finished we'll take the elevator *down* and have something to eat, my treat. Come on, what have you got to lose?"

What the hell; she was hungry. She'd go. After all, what *did* she have to lose?

By the time Wendy's key clicked in the lock, Mel was primed for the confrontation. As the front door opened, his hand tightened automatically around his empty glass. Wendy paused in the doorway. For a second Mel was captivated by her presence, despite himself. She was as slender as that night in the Guggenheim, but six years had added a gentle maturity to her. There was less angularity to her face; the prominent cheekbones framing her compelling, oversize hazel eyes were less severe. Her shoulder-length blonde hair was pulled away from her face and fastened carefully at the back of her head, adding another sophisticated dash of maturity. To complete the picture of the young matron, Wendy wore the dark Galanos suit she favored for East Side luncheons with friends. Had it been earlier Mel might have believed she was returning from a gossip session with a crony at the Stanhope, her favorite haunt. As it was, he had his own ideas of where she'd spent the day.

Wendy went directly up to the second level of the duplex. A shaft of light spiraled down the staircase and cut through the darkness beyond Mel's lair. Wendy would be so pleased that Lolly had prepared dinner according to plan. She played the role of accomplice with utter conviction. Wendy most certainly now felt secure, undetected—alone. But wait until she came into the living room . . .

The sounds of a shower filled Mel's mind with visions of Wendy's lithe and graceful body. Her slender hips tapered down to long legs, kept nicely muscled by tennis and jogging; her firm, full breasts possessed nipples of deep rose that deepened in color as they grew hard under his touch.

After five years of marriage Wendy had learned never to vary her routine without permission, and as she toweled herself dry, Mel followed each action in his mind. Breaking her spirit had been the first step toward controlling her unseemly behavior. It had been a long, painful procedure of intimidation and abuse, but in the end Wendy agreed that without Mel's guidance her life would probably now be a shambles. Though caretaking for Wendy was often a burden, it was not entirely without its compensations. Whatever ills had plagued Mel during the day at *TNT* were immediately remedied by Wendy's loving attention. The safety of their homelife's regimented stability was in counterpoint to the risky world of daytime television, and Mel considered their marital arrangement a godsend for both of them. He helped Wendy and she, well, she was there when he needed her. Usually. But tonight, regrettably, Mel was going to have to show her that there was still no room in their life together for failure to comply with his rules.

Ten minutes later Wendy entered the living room. As the lights flashed on she realized she wasn't alone. Her first reaction was to scream, but the sound choked in her throat. She wanted to run, but she couldn't move. In the few seconds before she recognized Mel, Wendy felt the bottomless fear so familiar to her since her marriage.

"Hi, honey," Mel intoned softly, almost salivating with pleasure at her obvious terror.

"You're home," she gasped. Her hand flew to her throat as if this might protect her. The frantic beating of her heart thundered in her ears. "Why are you hiding?" She turned on more lights to busy herself.

Mel signaled her to approach. She obeyed. He kissed her, holding her lightly by the wrist, but firmly enough to detain her. "Sit down. Tell me about your day, what you did."

Wendy tried to wrestle free. "Don't run away. You've been complaining that my work eats into our personal time together. Well, here I am . . . we've got the time . . . so, talk!" He yanked her down next to him.

"I had lunch with Madeline. We went to the Stanhope." The words tumbled confusedly from her lips.

"Speak slower, Wendy. You were *where?*"

"The Stanhope. With Madeline," she enunciated. Her voice was shaking.

"So you were with Madeline. Madeline Lamure?"

She nodded.

"What if I told you I ran into Bob Lamure yesterday, and he said Madeline had gone to one of those fat farms out west for a week?" He took his glasses from his pocket and cleaned them meticulously. Wendy waited breathlessly without answering. "Well, what would you say if I told you that?" Wendy's compulsion thrived on irrational and spontaneous outbursts. She never would have had the foresight to draw Madeline into her scheme.

Wendy laughed at the idea of Madeline being out of town, but it came too late. He knew she was lying. Oh God, why hadn't she checked?

Suddenly, Mel's open right hand came out of nowhere and gently grazed her on the cheek. It didn't hurt, but Wendy began to cry. He leaned forward, tucking both hands between his knees. The motion caused Wendy to wince. "Now, tell me, darling," he said evenly, "just where the hell were you all afternoon?"

"I've already told you . . . I was having drinks with Madeline" she replied weakly.

"Drinks? I thought it was lunch."

"It was both . . . oh, Mel, what difference does it make?" She edged herself away from him.

' 'It makes a great deal of difference, my pet, because if you're changing your story now that means you've been lying to me."

"There's nothing to lie about." She kept her eyes fixed on his hands.

' 'Jesus, what kind of fool do you think I am? Admit it, Wendy, you've gone against my orders once again."

"No, no, I haven't," she protested. "I would never do that. Mel . . . never."

"Maybe you really believe what you're saying . . . your

kind is so clever at self-deception.'' He yawned, bringing his right hand slowly up to his mouth, then rested it on his chin.

Wendy stared at the hand, knowing what was sure to follow. Instead of lashing out, Mel shrugged and dropped his hand back to his knee. ''Maybe I am being too hard on you. After all, you did promise to obey me after last time.'' He smiled warmly. ''Will you forgive me for not believing you?''

Wendy breathed a cautious sigh of relief. ''It's my fault, Mel. If I hadn't been bad in the past you'd have no reason to distrust me.'' She touched his knee. ''Forgive me?''

''Of course . . . but not just yet.''

With a sudden backhand slap he split Wendy's lower lip. ''Goddammit, I'll teach you to lie to me!'' He pulled her forward and hit her again and again, feeling the pain of her teeth against his knuckles.

This time she really *had* to learn who was boss.

That same evening when Rita finished reading the sixth unsolicited script, she tossed it onto the floor with the others, slid down in the bed, and closed her eyes. God, what *dreck!* The scripts were all from ardent fans who wanted to show their love for *TNT*. Their loyalty was touching; their ability, appalling. Does writing soap opera dialogue really look *that* easy? Rita wondered. Whatever the answer, these scripts were a testament to her and her writers' ability for making *TNT* characters sound so natural that viewers simply didn't understand that their dialogue was painstakingly crafted, not just accidental.

She picked up the last script and held it at arm's length as if it might soil her if brought too close. ''I might as well get it over with,'' she said aloud as she propped herself back up in the bed, wishing to hell she'd trusted her first instinct and just sent the goddamned scripts to Nan Booth without reading them, as requested.

Twenty minutes later she reread the seventh script, fascinated that she remembered little scenes, words, phrases from her first reading. She'd known just how good it would be after the first page. There was a naturalness to the dialogue, an instinct for setting up characters and situations that was evident from the first speech. No amount of teaching or good intentions could supplant that instinct, she knew. Over the years she had read the work of enough mediocre writers to recognize real talent when she saw it.

The name on the title page meant nothing to her. According to the letter accompanying the script, the writer had experience dialoging for a couple of New York—based soaps, had done a short stint as head writer for a Canadian contender, and was a rabid fan of *Time Nor Tide*. That explained the script's excellence: He was a professional. He apologized if the script was a little shaky, but he hadn't worked from an official outline. It hardly mattered. With a few minor adjustments, the script could have been written by Rita herself. She made a mental note to have Sandy contact him for a meeting. With Ellie Davis nearly out, Rita would have to hire a new writer soon or be caught shorthanded.

Besides, any man—even a stranger—who made her feel as warm as she did right now deserved a place in her life, even if it was only as a staff writer on *Time Nor Tide*. In a burst of impetuous exhilaration, Rita called Mel to tell him the good news.

"That was Rita," Mel told Wendy, as he returned to the dinner table. "She's just found someone to replace Ellie Davis."

"That's how she stays on top," Wendy commented softly.

"I guess now that her boyfriend's out, she's got a lot of free time," Mel said snidely. "Rita's not as lucky as we are. We've got each other." He picked at the overcooked roast beef and watery asparagus under congealed hollandaise. He hated eating slop, but by the time he'd finished with Wendy, the dinner was ruined.

"Wendy, I said we're lucky to have each other. Don't you agree?"

"Yes." Her eyes darted to Mel's for a moment. "We're very lucky, Mel. Just like you said."

They finished the meal in silence and followed it with dessert, a creamy chocolate mousse, and coffee in the living room. "I'm glad you finally decided to tell me the truth, honey. A man and his wife as close as we are should never have secrets from each other." He took a generous spoonful of the mousse and then a sip of coffee. "Considering the high price you pay for your dishonesty, I find it amazing that you still give in to your baser nature. How can it possibly be worth it?"

If there was only some way she could kill him, she fantasized, or better yet, erase him from the face of the earth as if he'd strangled on his umbilical cord at birth. For this, Wendy would gladly have sold her soul. Mel's cruelty was unforgivable. But there was another side, a loving side. And it was this other side that held her loyalty, the Mel who enveloped her in his warmth and protected her from harm . . . and from herself. Mel was right about so many things, maybe he was right to hit her. Maybe she *did* deserve it. When she was good he left her alone and didn't hurt her. He could be so benevolent, so sweet and gentle that she felt like a rare treasure, pampered and shielded from the evils that waited outside in the violent city. When Mel stroked her and told her how much she was loved, nothing else mattered to her. When Mel chose to display his positive side, the pain and terror he inflicted disappeared like an unreasonable nightmare with the coming of the morning light.

"Don't you think you deserved to be punished?" he challenged.

She had asked that question of herself over and over and could never answer it satisfactorily. What she did wasn't a question of right or wrong; it went far beyond that. Mel just didn't—couldn't—understand that there was nothing she could do to stop herself. She hated herself for having gone to the racetrack this afternoon, but the old feelings and the glow of excitement that doubled with the knowledge that this was something forbidden were irresistible. She was so gripped by the track's grubby magic that she had stayed all afternoon, even though she had promised herself it would only be for an hour. Mel didn't care how hard she tried to stay away, how she hated herself for gambling when she promised she'd never do it again. All he cared about was that she had failed him.

"You had a minor relapse, that's all. You won't do it again, will you?" He reached out to her and touched her tenderly.

"I'll try not to, Mel," she whispered.

"Trying isn't good enough, Wendy. Just *do* it." He tightened his grip. "Okay?" When she nodded he released her. "Good. Now finish your dessert and let's get to bed. It's late."

Wendy stalled for time while she cleared away the dishes. Mel would want sex tonight. He always did after he'd beaten her. Maybe it was his way of saying he was sorry, or maybe it was the last vestige of his anger, Wendy didn't know. All she knew was she couldn't bear his touch. Her arms still ached from where he'd twisted them, and an ugly red welt had already formed where he'd slapped her face. Tomorrow she would have a black eye; it wouldn't be the first. Her lips were puffed and split, and there was a small abrasion on her forehead where Mel's nails had scratched her. After such rage the thought of tenderness disgusted her.

She leaned her head against the cool of the kitchen wall and wept. How sad that this misery was so familiar. There was nothing to do but pick up the pieces and get through the next few days without breaking. Mrs. Swedeborg would know, of course. Her tearful sympathy would only call attention to the trap Wendy was in. In fact, everything would remind her: the thickly layered makeup to hide the hideous bruises, the sidelong glances of strangers, and the knowing looks of the doormen who had long ago divined the Jacobses' "secret." And as if it were a diabolical plot, the very compulsion that had precipitated this beating would steal back to cajole her out to the track again. And thus the cycle began again . . .

Wendy wiped her tears on the sleeve of her torn blouse. Was there no way off this stampeding merry-go-round?

Later, after it was over, after Mel was asleep, Wendy crept back into the living room and sat for a long time by the window. The city was peaceful now. Cars hummed in the background along Central Park West like mosquitoes on a summer night. The distant lights of Fifth Avenue twinkled dimly beyond the park. Wendy's tears were gone. She had cried until she could cry no longer.

She sat in Mel's chair, her knees tucked up against her chest, wishing she could extricate herself from the hell of her homelife. But what would she do alone after so many years? She'd already tried being independent by supporting herself with her photography and she'd failed. No, that wasn't the truth. Her talent had failed her expectations and she'd been unable to settle for anything less than her fourteen-carat dream. And the very night she decided to chuck her career altogether and begin looking for someone to get involved with she'd met Mel Jacobs.

Wendy had immediately sensed that she and Mel were bad for each other. They treated each other like longtime lovers almost from the first date, something Wendy had experienced often enough with other men to know that under the placid surface of their growing infatuation there lay far more volatile and dangerous emotions. If her career had been more satisfying she would never have dated Mel more than once, maybe twice. But it hadn't been and her attraction to him was irresistible. And later, because there seemed nothing to replace the dependence, it took over and grew out of all proportion. Now, even though the pain of her commitment to a life with Mel was almost unbearable, Wendy was still unable to pull away.

She looked around the darkened living room feeling more alienated than ever before. If only she hadn't met Russell Bates maybe her life wouldn't have gone so far off course. She shook her head in disbelief at the ease with which she blamed others for her own mistakes. Russ hadn't forced her to quit photography and marry Mel—he'd been against both, in fact. All Russell had done was to tell the truth about herself. Not being able to accept it was her responsibility, not his.

Russell Bates was one of the best-known photographer's representatives in New York. He had built a solid career on flashy arrogance, personal disdain for anything second-rate, and an unflagging ability to spot a trend, particularly in fashion. When Wendy met him he was forty-eight and moderately overweight. He dressed sloppily in ultraexpensive clothes and had moved into a loft in the SoHo section of Manhattan long before anyone imagined it would become the city's hottest neighborhood.

Bates discovered Wendy Moffat's work at a West Broadway gallery in a group show that closed after only a week. While the general quality of the show was insipid and attracted no critical attention, Bates, who made a habit of seeing everything new in town, was intrigued by Wendy's contribution, "Sun Cities," a depressing collection of black-and-white portraits of the ancient denizens of several Florida retirement communities. Despite the maudlin subject matter and the artist's obvious debt to Diane Arbus, the photographs displayed a simple, straightforward narrative technique and an eye for composition that Bates recognized as being perfectly suited to commercial—and therefore, lucrative—work. Whoever Wendy Moffat was, Bates suspected she might rail at the idea of using her talent to make money (selling out was usually the way it was put), but he was willing to try to convince her. A mention of his name to the gallery owner produced Wendy's Chelsea address and her phone number, and a call later that afternoon to Wendy herself produced her portfolio the next morning.

"I can't quite put my finger on it, Wendy," he said cozily on the phone a couple of days later, "but I think your talent lies elsewhere. Now, don't get me wrong, 'Sun Cities' is a competent piece of work, but it lacks that special something that separates the wheat from the chaff. Am I making myself clear?"

"As crystal," Wendy acknowledged so softly that he had to ask her to repeat it.

Wendy had shot "Sun Cities" during her last Easter vacation. She had been a student in the University of Rochester's demanding photography program. Her initial reaction to the grim portraits was bitter disappointment—she'd tried to capture the old people's courage—but her friends back in Rochester were so ecstatic about her "genius" that, during the next few months, Wendy began to believe their hype. And by the time she arrived in Manhattan that fall, Wendy was so convinced of its place in history that she took "Sun Cities" first to the prestigious Light Gallery expecting to be offered a one-woman show.

Light turned her down. As did every other major dealer in the city. Only the small, upstart SoHo gallery was willing to take her on, as part of a group show, with an exorbitant commission—should she sell anything. After her final uptown refusal Wendy reluctantly agreed, and as she watched "Sun Cities" being mounted, the dour faces seemed to be reproaching her for her self-deception. And now it seemed Russell Bates was on to her, too.

"Put more simply, my dear," Bates barreled ahead, "I frankly don't believe your talent is as revoltingly maudlin as those photographs imply. Surely you don't intend to make a career of such stuff?"

"I don't know what you mean," Wendy stuttered, knowing exactly what he meant. He *had* seen through her. He knew he was talking to a fake and it hurt. She had pinned all her hopes on the success of "Sun Cities." If it failed, she failed.

"What I mean is that your portfolio is quite accomplished technically, but much of your work is derivative and, to be brutal, forced. Forgive me for saying this, but I feel you have stretched your talents beyond the breaking point,'' Bates explained later over lunch at La Toque Blanche. ''Gritty realism, 1940s men and women with sharecropper eyes has been done to death, my dear. Now don't get me wrong, I thank God for the Walker Evanses and Dorothea Langes of this world, but times have changed.''

''If you find my style so archaic and inept,'' Wendy said evenly to hide the fear, ''then exactly why am I here?''

''Because I have a proposition for you. Have you ever given any thought to fashion photography?''

''You must be joking,'' Wendy snorted, realizing only after seeing the anger on Bates's face that she'd actually laughed at him. Well, why not? She'd suffered through this miserable lunch while he attacked her work and now the reason behind it was clear: He really liked her photographs, but they wouldn't sell. And fashion did. If he could destroy her confidence in herself she'd gladly jump at a chance for him to rep her. And she'd almost fallen for it.

''I will excuse your rudeness as lack of sophistication, Miss Moffat,'' Bates said dryly, resisting the exquisite temptation to tell her outright that the *only* thing in her portfolio worth salvaging from the dustbin was the lone fashion spread. Everything else was crap. ''I know exactly how you must feel about fashion,'' he went on solicitously, ''it's so ephemeral, it's crass, it's nothing but vanity, and, God forbid, it pays—exorbitantly well, I might add.''

''Making money has never been my object,'' Wendy replied grandly.

''Of course not,'' he replied deferentially. ''Okay, forget the bucks then. You want to do serious stuff. Then do it. Good. Great. I wish you all the best. But how do you plan to live until MOMA calls to enshrine you forever on East Fifty-third Street? 'Sun Cities' is cute, all right, but so are Kewpie dolls.''

''You know what I think, Mr. Bates?'' Wendy asked angrily, ''I think you're pissed off because I'm not willing to sell out. After all, fancy lunches and glitzy friends aside, you are just a rep, and reps make money from working photographers not from artists.''

Bates lay his knife and fork aside and stared Wendy straight in the eyes. ''Why is it that I don't ever learn about the sophomoric artistic temperament? Why is it that every time I'm confronted with such high-blown bullshit I still gag?''

Wendy threw her napkin on the table and pushed her chair back. "I think it's time I left. Thanks for the lunch and the lecture."

"Sit down!" Bates commanded. "I'm not finished yet." When Wendy complied he continued, muffling his anger at her impudence. "You're taking my offer of help as an insult. Why?" He waited for an answer, but got none. "Well, you have your reasons and I'm sure they're good ones. Just one last thing: Don't be so quick to close any doors, particularly not at the beginning of your career."

"I'm sorry," Wendy apologized, embarrassed by the way she'd acted, but grateful he hadn't interrogated her any further.

"Fashion photography is coming of age, it's exploding. Get caught up in it now and you can explore the artistic side of your talent to your heart's content—*and* get paid," he said softly, resisting the urge to take her hand in his. After all, she was a fine-looking woman.

"I'll have to think it over," Wendy said, but as far as she was concerned, the door marked *Fashion Photography* was already closed. "In any case, thank you for taking an interest in me. I really appreciate it."

Bates smiled and gave in to temptation by taking Wendy's hand and giving it a little squeeze before releasing it. "Take your time. But don't wait too long. When you finally make up your mind it might just be too late." He toasted her with his café filtre, wondering if he'd ever hear from the lovely Wendy Moffat again.

Seven months later, on the day before her phone was disconnected for nonpayment of bills, Wendy called Russell Bates.

"Of course I remember you, Wendy," Bates said expansively. "I even saw your 'Mesquite' series of Pueblo dwellings. It was very impressive." He leaned back in his chair and conjured up a picture of Wendy that emphasized her long legs and ample breasts. "Yes, I know 'Mesquite' was never mounted, but I have friends everywhere in town. One of the galleries considering it let me have a peek." And he'd told the owner not to waste his time with such tripe. After all, he owed Wendy one for being such an ungrateful bitch at lunch. And, who knew, if she failed she might even come back looking for help. "So, what can I do for you, babe?"

"I'd like to talk . . . about fashion. Let's have lunch." She felt like such a failure she was barely able to speak. Seven months ago she'd been so confident. But that was before she'd spent the last of the money an aunt had left her to travel to New Mexico for "Mesquite." She'd been so sure it would sell. And yet here she was again, flat broke, knowing that Bates could hear the hunger in her voice as well as she could. The whole thing reminded Wendy of calling her bookie just one more time—after she'd promised herself she'd never, ever place a bet again.

"There's no need for lunch, my dear. You do some testing and if I like it, well, I'll see what I can do." Bates smiled. The prickly independence was gone from her voice and he knew she was as good as his.

"There's only one little problem, I don't have a real space to work in, or models or . . . anything," Wendy's voice dropped audibly.

Bates instantly made a decision. "Not to worry, honey, I'll take care of everything. You still at the same number? Good, I'll get back to you."

An hour later Russell Bates had arranged a test shooting for Wendy. Because testing was a standard procedure that allowed new photographers to work with good models at no fee (other than providing prints of shots for the models' portfolios), it only took a quick call to Eileen Ford to set up an appointment. Bates's second call produced a wardrobe of trendy casual wear from a young designer. And his third call arranged for the services of a makeup artist who'd worked on everyone from Lauren Hutton to Cher.

"Be at my place tomorrow at two," Bates told Wendy later, "the light's great at that time. I'll send my assistant down with the keys."

"Work at your place?" She had no idea where he lived.

"Darling, my loft is ideal for the shooting. I rent it out by the hour on the side and make a fortune. I'll supply the space, you supply the talent," he said impatiently.

"God, I don't know how to thank you." Wendy was breathless. One minute she had nothing, the next she was already booked for her first professional shooting.

"Don't worry about thanking me. Just do a good job for me, will you?"

"I wouldn't dare do anything else," she laughed.

"No, I guess not," Bates mused. This Wendy Moffat was a far cry from the vixen he'd taken to La Toque Blanche. This Wendy Moffat knew she was now in his debt. "And one more thing, honey: When the shoot's over, why don't you hang around? I'll be there by six; make yourself at home. I'd like to see you and catch up on what you've been doing."

There was only the slightest hesitation before Wendy answered. "Of course, Russell. I'd like that, too."

Wendy slept with Bates because she was afraid not to. But it wasn't so bad, really. He wasn't much of a lover, and yet he was gentle and considerate, which was a welcome change from the type of man she usually found herself with. Unfortunately, Russell was so turned on by the sight of her naked body that he climaxed prematurely, then almost instantly fell asleep. Wendy waited half an hour for him to wake up before letting herself out.

The test shots were mediocre. Bates studied the contact sheets two days later while slowly shaking his head. They should have been great. Everything was top drawer—except the photographer. Wendy had blown it. It wasn't an amateur job, by no means—the models could use a shot or two, and there was a couple of close-ups the makeup guy could use if people ever forgot who Cher was—but it was strictly run-of-the-mill, catalog-quality work.

Bates slowly put down the magnifying glass at the thought. Catalog work. It was fast, simple, direct. Jesus, *that's* what he'd seen in Wendy Moffat's portfolio! Christ, I must be getting old, he thought as he dialed an old friend whose small studio got the catalog runoff from the larger houses. Fred Delancy could always be counted on to have something in the works for Sears, J. C. Penney, Montgomery Ward, or any of the other mail-order giants.

"Fred, it's Russ Bates. Look, I've got a new gal here who's perfect for you. Experience? Who cares about her experience? Trust me. Let me send her over. Great, great. Her name's Wendy Moffat. You'll never regret it. And let's have lunch one day soon." He hung up and called Wendy.

Two months later Wendy turned down a contract with Delancy in order to free-lance for the Spiegel catalog. Seven months later she shot the entire Bloomingdale's fall fashion catalog and a month after that spent two weeks in Rio assembling a new brochure for the newest and largest hotel on the

Copacabana. She'd made more money in ten months than she'd ever dreamed possible and had kept herself broke by gambling all of it away.

But Wendy's rising star was matched by her falling spirits. Catalog work came too easily to her. There was no challenge, no risk. She neither got better nor worse. Her attitude was lousy and it showed in a thousand different ways. She grew difficult to work with and often seemed bent on destroying her career by alienating everyone. This behavior would have ruined anyone else's career. But she was Wendy Moffat, and in an incredibly short period of time, that had come to mean something. To everyone but Wendy.

At photographing men in polyester leisure suits, jockey shorts and over-the-calf socks, cruise wear, pajamas and bathrobes, Wendy was faultless. At photographing women in endless ropes of gold-plated jewelry, daytime dresses, garish fashion wigs, peignoirs crafted from synthetic fabrics, she was brilliant. Peerless. Wendy Moffat couldn't fail. She'd found her niche, heard her true calling. And that was not "Sun Cities" or "Mesquite," but mirroring the taste of the middle classes, and it was killing her.

"Let's face it, Russ, I'm the queen of mediocrity," she complained a year later. "My serious stuff just never went anywhere, my high fashion is pure Kansas City, and only the mail-order bra-and-girdle kings think I'm great."

Bates put his arm around her and pulled her head down against his chest. "You make it sound like a curse. We can't all be great talents. You've realized your limits and you work within them. Quite successfully, too."

Wendy pulled away from him and sat up in bed. She'd practically been living in his loft for the past eight months, yet each time he praised her for what she still saw as taking the easy way out her paranoia flared and she began to think he was no better than any man who lived off a woman. Some were called gigolos, some were called whores, and some were called reps. His job was to find her work and to keep her in her place so she kept the bucks rolling in.

"Russell, to hear you talk I should be happy making money hand over fist by doing something I absolutely don't believe in," she taunted.

Bates's sigh was audible and pointed. "My dear, what else is there for you to try? You've gone the whole route from artsy-fartsy Georgia O'Keeffe ripoffs to *Interview* type glitter and you landed right square in the middle. Do you seriously believe there's anywhere else *to* go?" He hopped out of bed and ambled naked to the refrigerator. He returned moments later with a cold chicken leg. "I appreciate your disappointment that you couldn't make it artistically, but face it baby, that's life in the big city."

"That's one kind of life in the big city," she said as she got out of bed and went to the closet. "But there's got to be another kind." She began to dress, keeping her back to him.

"Sure, there's poverty, too. But remember you tried that and didn't like it." He plunked himself down on the bed and watched her while he took a bite of the chicken. "Face it, doll, you've got a problem accepting yourself. You want to be someone else, you want a different talent, a different life—but you're stuck with this one. And, believe me, all the phone calls to all the bookies in the world won't help you feel any better about yourself."

Wendy turned on him, her mouth frozen into a tight smile. "Did I every tell you, Russell, that you remind me of a talking pig?"

Bates shrugged and continued eating. When he finished he carefully laid the greasy bones on the bedside table and lit a cigarette. "Did I ever tell you, Wendy, that you reek of failure? You've got a handle on something good right now. Sure, maybe it is only catalog work, but you could be the best at that, if you wanted to. But you're stubborn and you've decided you don't want to. And why? Because that might mean facing up to a few truths about little Miss Moffat. And that just might be too painful."

Wendy merely shook her head in disgust, finished dressing, then put on her trench coat; it was pouring out.

"And where are you headed on this fine day?" Bates picked a bit of chicken from between his front teeth, examined it on the end of his finger, then licked it back into his mouth.

"I thought I'd go to the Guggenheim. There's an exhibit I've wanted to see, but I've just been too busy with my *art,*" she said sarcastically. "You don't object if I leave, do you?" She opened the door and waited for his answer.

"By all means let Matisse console you. Let his genius inspire your own. Just one thing, Wendy," Bates retrieved the ravaged bones and began to nibble at what he'd missed earlier, "when you're done with the Guggenheim, please don't come back. You can send for your stuff. Will you do that for me, sweety? I've had it up to here with your self-pity."

Wendy took a taxi all the way to the Guggenheim feeling absolutely nothing. Continuing the relationship with Russell seemed no more fruitful than ending it, so she decided to take him at his word; she wouldn't return. Ever. How had she allowed herself to believe that Russell Bates, of all people, could possibly understand her? Men, in general, seemed to have the knack for missing the point when it came to her needs. Her father had been the first. He'd walked out on her when she was only five, and sometimes Wendy still blamed herself for his desertion. Perhaps if she'd been a better daughter he wouldn't have turned his back on her. And as if to validate her feelings that there was something deeply, disturbingly wrong with her, her mother walked out, too, after putting her upbringing into the hands of her sister, a straight-laced woman who, for the next fifteen years, prophesied that Wendy would never amount to anything because she was tainted by the sins of her father and mother.

So Wendy's guilt was firmly set. She felt inadequate, incomplete, and whenever anyone contradicted that self-image she quickly proved how wrong they were, no matter what the cost to her personally. Being Wendy Moffat just wasn't enough. She needed to be something bigger, someone more important. If she couldn't be the best photographer in the world, then she couldn't be a photographer at all. Maybe what she needed was to be something *to* someone. All her life she'd waited for the right opportunity to make amends for her own personal guilt and to prove herself worthwhile.

But where to begin? The easy compliance that masked her true feelings about herself always brought out the worst in the men she dated. Their ill treatment, provoked by her subtle self-deprecation, verified her own worst fears about herself and thus kept the cycle in motion. Gambling helped ease that pain a bit, but not much. And often it put her in the position of being truly needy, not only in spirit but in reality. Sex occasionally worked, but that too had very diminishing returns. Work had provided the best escape, but she could no longer take any pleasure in doing something she despised, so even that seemed to have been taken from her. So what else was left?

Wendy paid the cabdriver and dashed into the museum, wondering as she shook the icy rain from herself if she'd ever find the answer to her happiness.

Ten minutes later she met Mel Jacobs.

6

Tom Wesley could see that Ellie Davis was sick with worry. He'd had her script for five days without word and now, suddenly, he had asked to see her about it. It was the fourth time in the two months since Rita voiced her displeasure with Ellie that he'd hauled her in on the carpet. She had to know—or intuit at least—that she was in trouble.

In mid-September Ellie had been under Rita's protective wing. Now, as Thanksgiving approached, her ties to Rita were cut. Ellie was dealing with Tom only. He knew she didn't trust him for a minute and that only made him feel sadder about what he had to do; he was probably the last friend she had at *Time Nor Tide*. The hatchet job Rita ordered on Ellie's scripts was odious to him. In the days when the show was a half hour, Mel cheerfully weeded out unwanted writers. But when *TNT* expanded Mel became too busy to deal with such unsavory details. Tom, as low man on the totem pole, inherited the unpleasant task.

"What's this all about, Tom?" Ellie asked trying to control the little wobble of fear in her voice.

"We've got a problem. Rita feels your whole second act just isn't right. She wants it rewritten." He felt like shit. He wondered if Ellie could hear that in his voice. Could she hear how weary he was of playing the paid assassin, how disgusted he was with himself?

"I just dropped in on Rita. Why didn't she say something to me herself?"

"Rita's busy with other things. Now let's get started; it's late."

Fifteen minutes later Ellie broke down, the psychic burden of Tom's onslaught finally too much to bear.

"I'm sorry, Tom," she sniffed through her tears. "I've had a rough week." She dabbed her eyes with a tattered Kleenex.

Tom was horrified by this explosion of emotion. It confirmed his worst feelings: that he—not Rita—was directly responsible for destroying a writer's confidence. "Would you rather we did this some other time?"

Ellie shook her head. "The script is late already. I'd rather we didn't do it at all, but I'll need a full day for the rewrites, so go ahead." She bravely tried to stop the tears but without success.

Tom looked away from her, disgusted by his role in this ugly charade. "I'll tell Rita you're not feeling well. You can have a few extra days."

"For the past couple of months everything I've done has been wrong. A few days won't make any difference. Give me a week on this script, and there'll still be problems. What's really wrong?" she asked in earnest.

"Have you been reading all the outlines thoroughly?" he fielded the question.

"I read everything, including the other writers' scripts, *and* I watch the show every day."

"Then I don't know what to say," Tom equivocated.

"Has this ever happened to any of the other writers? I mean, have they gone through periods where their work just hasn't been up to par?" If she could find a common ground, perhaps she wouldn't feel so bad.

"You'd have to ask them, Ellie. Writing a soap opera isn't easy. It takes a lot of time and practice——"

"For over a year I've been passing with flying colors, and suddenly I can't do anything right," she interrupted.

"If there was anything more I could do to help, I would," he snapped. "Now, please, let's just finish, okay?" At that moment he promised himself that Ellie Davis was his last "victim."

"Mrs. Elliott will be right out, Mr. Peterson," Sandy told the handsome stranger whose handshake had made her blush. She was more than willing to forgo a few minutes' work to chat. Peterson's easygoing charm and all-American good looks had immediately won her over.

Sandy Lief was in her early forties. Her bright manner attested to the fact that she was not at all self-conscious about her age. On the contrary, a mischievous spark of life danced in her dark brown eyes and her sensuous mouth looked ready to be kissed. She was immensely attractive, Al Peterson thought.

Sandy blushed furiously when she caught him staring. "Are you familiar with *Time Nor Tide*, Mr. Peterson?" she fumbled for words to hide her embarrassment.

"I've been watching for the past few months. I guess that makes me a new fan." It was an outright lie, but he had done his research to back up the claim. A phone call to thank Nan for her part in getting him the upcoming interview with Rita Martin, albeit clandestine, elicited not only hearty congratulations and a strict warning to keep Nan out of it, but a day later she sent a copy of the original *Time Nor Tide* bible. Al was now a *TNT* expert. But he knew feigning ignorance to inflate a *TNT* insider's ego wouldn't hurt, either. "I've probably missed a lot over the years." He actually sounded wistful.

"You've missed a lot *this* year."

"Hey, we've got a couple of minutes. If you don't mind, why don't you fill me in?" He flashed Sandy his sexiest smile.

Sandy obliged by delineating the original *Time Nor Tide* characters and stories. It was the usual soap opera history—love, lust, infidelity, insanity, alcoholism, divorce, greed. But Sandy's cheerful narrative made *Time Nor Tide* sound fresh and exciting. Obviously, she loved her work. Al wondered if everyone who worked for Rita Martin was so happy.

"So, that's it for the first year," Sandy gasped for air after her nonstop speech. "Now, would you like to hear about the second year?"

Al applauded the recitation. "You're a wonder! I'd never be able to keep so many plots in my mind . . . and I've got a good memory."

"You'll get the hang of it," a soft voice interrupted from behind.

Peterson turned and confronted Rita Martin. There was no mistaking her. She looked exactly as she had on the cover of *Time* magazine a few years ago. He had no idea how long she'd been eavesdropping, but Sandy had never once given her presence away.

"Mr. Peterson," Rita said warmly, stepping forward to shake his hand, "I'm Rita Martin."

He stood up immediately. Her handshake was firm. He liked that in women. "It's a pleasure to meet you . . ." He almost said *Mrs. Martin*. ". . . Rita." Her eye contact was steady and natural. She flashed a smile perfectly balanced somewhere between friendliness and good manners.

"Sandy is a warehouse of facts about *Time Nor Tide*. I don't know what I'd do without her. Come into my office and *we'll* talk."

Al found himself watching the gentle sway of Rita's ass as she walked; she had good hips that tapered into what were probably beautiful legs—not as good as Angela Brite's, but then Angela was only twenty-six. Rita Martin had to be in her forties. Al had spent a lot of time with women of all ages, and he recognized something special when he saw it. Rita Martin was a real traffic-stopper. She carried herself proudly and erect, but there was something sensual, vaguely inviting in the way she moved. It was just enough of a tease to make Al's juices start flowing.

He immediately chastised himself. Sex and business just didn't mix. With women like Rita Martin who had made it to the top by sheer willpower, one wrong move and it was all over.

"Your script was very good, Mr. Peterson." Rita folded her hands on the desk top looking more like a glamorous school teacher than a one-woman industry.

"Al," he interrupted. "I don't like being formal."

She smiled and continued. "I get many requests for jobs and more résumés than you'd believe, but this is the first time I've ever arranged to meet someone who sent in a *Time Nor Tide* script unasked." She unclasped her hands and leaned back in her chair. "I'd begun to think there were no firsts left."

"Surely a woman in your position *creates* firsts." He wasn't sure she was testing him but a little flattery never hurt.

"That's a nice thought, but it doesn't always work out that way." It was time to get down to business. "Writing your own story projection was a risky thing to do."

He nodded.

"Surprisingly enough, you were almost on target," she

continued. "Of course, there are things about *Time Nor Tide* you could never know, but I took that into account." She waited for his reaction.

"It took a lot of work to come up with that script. If I'd been doing any other soap, it would have been a cinch; but *Time Nor Tide* just isn't that easy to pin down. It's got a flow all its own." He flattered her unashamedly, sensing now that she expected it. Rita's half-smile proved him right.

"It's a tough market, Al. Only the best survive." She abruptly changed the subject hoping to shatter his cool, confident—macho—demeanor. "What happened to you in Canada?"

"I could come up with a lot of baloney about why I gave up a head writer's job, but I want to level with you from the start. I missed the good old U.S. of A. Seven months in Toronto and I was ready for some New York—style hustle and bustle."

Rita smiled. She knew what Al meant. She, too, thrived on the raw energy of New York. Al Peterson seemed a kindred spirit. "So you packed up and left without giving a thought to your career?"

He shook his head. "It was one of the hardest decisions I've ever made. But I finally decided my career is only *part* of my life."

"And what are the other parts . . . if you don't mind me asking?"

"The usual; the same things you do when you're not working, I imagine."

Rita liked that answer. In fact she liked Al Peterson. "Judging from this script, I'm glad you made that decision. Pull up your chair and let's go over it."

He moved just close enough to read the script.

"There were a few minor problems." Rita moved slightly closer and her knee just touched his. "For instance, here . . ."

Forty-five minutes later they finished.

"I'd like you to do another sample for me. This time you'll have outlines and *TNT* scripts to work from. Get it back to me within a week." She rose from her chair. "Sandy has the package waiting for you. If you have any questions, please call me." She thought for a second, then amended. "Better yet, give Mel Jacobs a call."

"Mel Jacobs?"

"You haven't met." She picked up the intercom, and a

minute later Jacobs joined them. "This is Al Peterson, Mel. I told you about him."

"Peterson? Oh, sure," he grudgingly shook Al's hand. One look at the handsome writer and Mel knew Rita had filled Ellie's spot. "You did a sample script?"

"I've asked him to do another," Rita jumped in. "Give him your home phone number in case there are any problems." She knew full well that Mel valued his privacy away from the office, but establishing her supremacy was more important.

Mel stiffened for just a second, then relaxed. "I don't think there'll be any problems we can't take care of during office hours."

"Just in case, give him the number."

Mel scribbled down his phone number and handed it to Peterson. "Try to keep it to business hours," he instructed.

"That's it then." Rita extended her hand. "Make an appointment with Sandy to see me next week. And good luck with your script." The interview was over.

Al felt good about the meeting, but he wasn't about to congratulate himself just yet. Although Rita had involved him in a subtle power play over Mel Jacobs's phone number, she was still keeping him at a distance by insisting he do a second sample script. She, more than anyone, knew that writing for *Time Nor Tide* was a plum job and that she could keep any writer in limbo ad infinitum if she so chose. Women like Rita Martin could be treacherously self-indulgent when the mood struck them, and much as he disliked being anyone's patsy, Al decided on his way to the elevators that if Rita Martin said "jump" he'd jump . . . at least for now.

Alone in her office once again, Rita had time to reflect on Peterson. He was good-looking, talented, and to top it off, Peterson was straight. So many writers applying for jobs these days were gay. Rita didn't exactly dislike homosexuals, but they made her edgy. She hadn't figured a way around them, and it irked her. With no sexual subtext to play with, her relationships with gay men were usually strained and invariably came to an unpleasant end. Peterson would be easier to handle.

He wore his masculinity like a well-fitted jacket, and Rita wanted to climb right into his breast pocket. She didn't intend to fool herself, however; Peterson obviously knew how to handle women, particularly those from whom he wanted something. She pegged him as an opportunist, professionally and sexually.

Still, she closed her eyes and smiled serenely as his handsome face moved in and out of her memory. God, there was nothing more exciting than a real challenge. Al Peterson might just be the first man in years to give her a run for her money. But first things first. Before exploring Mr. Peterson's rather obvious charms she'd have to hire him; no use giving the network gossips a loaded gun to aim at her. That meant ending Ellie's torture soon with a merciful death. And that, in turn, meant another phone call to Nan Booth.

Since their last conversation, Nan had kept a very low profile. For just a second Rita tensed at the thought of taking the first step in reopening that particular channel of communication. By rights Nan should be calling her. Hadn't she been sent a copy of the Hewitt/Reynolds story line *after* being let off the hook about her studio visit? But what the hell! Rita could be as magnanimous as anyone—more so. If Nan wanted to pout and not call to say thanks for the story projection because she'd been put in her place, okay. Rita Martin was above such childishness!

She picked up the phone and punched out Nan's private number.

"I was just thinking about you, Rita," Nan said, after a curt hello. "Did you see the show?" Nan knew Rita watched every episode of *TNT* like a hawk circling its prey.

"It was wonderful," Rita replied. "I still marvel at the way we all push ourselves beyond the human limit and come up with a winner. Nancy Carson was the best ever. She lives up to our every expectation of Penny Hewitt."

"Her agent called last week asking why she isn't getting more work," Nan sniped unmercifully. "He hinted there were other offers." Nancy's contract was sewn up for the next eight months, but a little advance agitation never hurt.

"Agents are always hinting something," Rita tossed off the implied crisis without a thought. "Nancy must be bitching about working her minimum again. Don't worry, her agent isn't going to rock the boat when he's getting ten percent of Miss Carson for just sitting on his ass." Still, Rita was slightly annoyed at this hint of disloyalty. After all, she had big plans for Nancy as Penny Hewitt. "Next time you talk to Pete tell him not to sweat his commission—with the new projection, Nancy will be working more than ever." Rita waited for a moment, expecting Nan to acknowledge the Caribbean story line. When she didn't, Rita went on, "It should put *TNT* back on top."

Nan flinched at the thought. "Glad to hear it, Rita," she replied coldly.

"And to ensure the show's success further, I have found us a new writer," Rita pushed on. "Of course we'll all be sorry to see Ellie Davis go, but Nan, this guy's dynamite."

"Anyone I know?" She frantically reached for a cigarette.

"Name's Al Peterson. He's had previous soap experience. He sent in a sample script; it was damned good. I've asked him to do another—under my supervision."

"Yes," Nan mumbled. There were times in her life when she could do no wrong, when every throw of the dice went her way. And now . . . Al Peterson was as good as hired. But she'd have to be careful; to step out of character now might alert Rita that she had been cast as Desdemona to Nan's Iago. "I think maybe I'd better read his script, too."

"There's no need to," Rita snapped. "I'm satisfied, that's enough." Damn Nan Booth! Always trying to undermine any good news that didn't originate from her own office.

Nan heightened the sense of her skepticism by sighing before answering. "If that's how you want it, I'll pass the news on to Jim—if I can ever chase him down."

So, she's having trouble cornering Goodspeed, too, Rita thought. Good. The less she says to him about *Time Nor Tide* the better. "I'm about to send Jim a memo, but talk to him anyway. I don't want to interfere with *your* job.

"Rita" Nan soothed "my main concern—*our* concern—is to make *your* show the best, most popular damned soap on the air. Any way *you* can accomplish that is fine with me. Fire the whole goddamned writing staff if it means more share points. Do whatever it takes, but do it!"

"I'm glad to hear you say that," Rita replied cautiously.

Nan, guessing correctly that her sudden, impassioned support had momentarily caught Rita off-guard, quickly played the trump card necessary to make this particular hand of cutthroat poker hers. "I also wanted you to know—off the record—that I thought the new Penny Hewitt story was beautiful. It's powerful, intelligent, and compassionate. Congratulations!"

"It's sweet of you to mention it." Rita wondered what she meant by "off the record." "Then, it looks like all systems are go! I'd better get right to work on Peterson's indoctrination," Rita laughed to ease a sudden worry that there might be "official" trouble with the Penny Hewitt story. If so, it would be the first time in six years that ITC hadn't readily approved a Rita Martin story line.

"If you need any help, or advice, call anytime," Nan said sweetly and hung up.

Just before going home Nan sat for a minute staring out over the New York skyscape. The city literally and figuratively lay at her feet. She looked up toward Central Park, then down toward the Battery. She knew this city inside out. She knew the good places and the bad. She could recommend a good secondhand bookstore or an antiquarian bookseller who specialized in priceless first editions. She could tell you where to find designer clothes for next to nothing or where to buy a thousand-dollar Hèrmes handbag. She could take you for an extraordinary ten-dollar dinner or for a mediocre hundred-dollar lunch. For Nan, New York was a city of familiar contrasts that once had perfectly suited her ambitions. Now it seemed nothing more than a dead end. With that in mind she placed a call to Jim Goodspeed.

"Don't you ever get tired of hearing my voice?" he asked with the good-natured familiarity he reserved for women and for his peers.

"You must be joking. I can't *stand* the sound of your voice." She laughed a little too loudly. "Look, Jim . . . I don't want to seem like an alarmist, but Rita Martin was just on the phone and it looks like we're on the eve of another bloody purge at *Time Nor Tide*."

There was a long pause before he answered. "You know how Rita is about shuffling writers, Nan." Rita's memo about Ellie Davis lay on the desk in front of him.

"It's not just Ellie; it's Rick Cologna, too." She tried to make this old news sound like new. "With *TNT*'s ratings all up and down the board, there has to be *some* stability interjected."

"What do *you* suggest?"

The question was a challenge. Nan recognized the tone of voice—it was Jim Goodspeed at his coldest. Damn! In trying to lay a trap for Rita she was unwittingly questioning his apparent lack of interest in the happenings of *TNT*. "ITC must exercise some control over *Time Nor Tide*. If only I——"

"Forget it, Nan," Goodspeed cut her off. "The creative side of that show is Rita's province, always has been."

"But, Jim . . ." Nan wanted to thrash him for his pigheadedness.

"I said forget it! Is there anything else?"

"No."

"See you for lunch tomorrow?"

"Our usual . . . one o'clock."

"Sharp," he amended and hung up.

Nan slammed the phone down. Jesus Christ! For all the facts against Rita Martin, for all the complaints about her personal style, her arrogance, her flagrant favoritism and misuse of power, Jim Goodspeed still kept her out of harm's way. Why? Surely his six-year-old "debt" to her and her show had been paid off in full by now. But what else could it be?

In a rare show of frustration she snatched one of Rita's china ashtrays off her desk and hurled it against the far wall. It exploded in a shower of razor-sharp shards.

No one was going to stand in her way, not even Jim Goodspeed. And tonight's dinner date with Al Peterson was the first step in getting what she wanted.

The Café des Artistes on West Sixty-seventh Street was one of New York's most elegant and glamorous restaurants. Al Peterson limited his visits there to special dates a couple of times a year. He was always captivated by the magic of the rooms. Des Artistes was full of illusions. At the front it looked like a peaceful French inn with hanging plants at the small-paned windows. In back with its hidden bar it might have been an elegant twenties speakeasy. Tying the decor together were the glorious, golden murals of once famous Ziegfeld Follies girls encircling the rooms, adding a touch of refined naughtiness. Des Artistes was a sybarite's delight, and tonight Al Peterson was fully prepared to indulge every appetite.

Sitting opposite the luminously chic Nan Booth, not only was Peterson's romantic spirit fired, but also his curiosity. He wondered just what made Nan Booth tick. Until they met in the lobby of her apartment, he had forgotten just how stunning a creature she was. He had managed to re-create a hazy image of the self-assured beauty, but this picture paled in her authoritative presence. Nan wore a forest green suit with a silk blouse the color of lime sherbet, a single pearl at each ear, and a subtly expensive Piaget wristwatch. This low-keyed ensemble showcased her flawless beauty, her aura, and in the flattering light of the restaurant, she seemed actually to glow.

The iciness in that radiance intrigued him more than anything. Like the fiery star in a perfect sapphire, Nan Booth's inner spark was distant, unreachable. She seemed to exist to be admired, never touched. Al knew other women with this same demeanor—all were as successful or more so than Nan—and the aloofness they shared immediately stoked his competitive spirit. Somewhere along the road to success these women had forgotten exactly what it meant to be feminine. Surrounded by tough, male executive types, they were forced to protect their vulnerability by encasing it in an impenetrable exterior. Even though Nan was truly hard-boiled, Al felt it would only be a matter of time before he made her forget she was an executive and reminded her that, first and foremost, she was a woman.

If he had known that each move Nan made, each time she let him light her cigarette and gently touched his hand to steady the flame, each time her throaty voice rumbled with laughter, it did *not* mean "come hither," Al might have reacted differently, but he responded by drawing closer, wanting more. To him Nan Booth was a magnificent puzzle, and before the night was over he intended to put all the pieces in their proper place.

"This is my favorite restaurant, Al. When I first moved to New York, I used to walk here to stare through the windows. It has such a quality of rosiness and warmth."

"Like a kid with her nose pressed against the candy store window, eh?" he prompted.

She shook her head disdainfully. "I've always made it a point to eat *only* in fine restaurants. With des Artistes I liked knowing that something so beautiful was so *close* to where I lived. You have to agree that New York is sometimes short on beauty." She sipped her after-dinner Chartreuse.

"You go a long way in correcting that." He regretted the remark when he saw Nan's frown. "Beauty is more important when it's in short supply," he added slipping deeper. Christ, it was a losing battle. All through dinner he had been complimentary, and Nan had managed to reject every personal allusion.

"Personally, I disagree," she opined, casting aside his

remark. She had to make it clear to Peterson that dinner was business and nothing more. His offhand compliments might have charmed other women, but Nan wasn't in the mood to be manipulated. "I understand Rita's offered you a second script." It was getting late, she might as well get down to brass tacks. She'd already wasted a couple of hours with small talk.

"She'll have it next week. I guess then the ball's back in her court."

Nan toyed with her drink. "I wouldn't worry *too* much about it, Al. Rita's told me about you. As a matter of fact, she called right after you left her."

"Is that good or bad?" he asked, feeling a flutter of excitement in his stomach.

"Definitely good. Rita doesn't let me in on her little schemes until they're a fait accompli. Because I represent management she sees me cast in the role of the Big Bad Wolf." She frowned slightly.

"And how do you see yourself, Nan?"

"As a member of the *TNT* family," she lied. "Sure, I get skittish sometimes about Rita making changes before first consulting me—the network—but only because it divides us unnecessarily. Rita and her crew on one side, me and the network on the other. After all, we all want the same thing—continued success for *Time Nor Tide*—don't we? Over the years we've all managed to work together very successfully with a minimum of ego problems. But the show *is* Rita's baby. I try to be careful, soft-pedal my part in its operation. Like any good mother, Rita is very protective of her child, and if she senses danger she gets . . ."

"Difficult to work with?"

Nan smiled. "You know how it is. You've worked on soap operas before. There is a very definite pecking order that must be maintained. Why, I would no more think of telling Rita how to write *Time Nor Tide* than she would think of telling ITC how to produce it. If there's any crossing over of authority, feelings do get hurt. You should remember that."

"That's why you didn't tell Rita you engineered my introduction." He smiled slyly and shook his head. "I'll admit I felt a little bit like a cheat letting Rita think I can actually predict what's going to happen on the show because I'm such a fan."

"If you know what's good for you, that's exactly what she'll keep on thinking," Nan threatened.

"I don't get it," he said warily. "I thought once I was in, you'd . . ."

"Al, you weren't listening a moment ago. Rita Martin likes things done her way. She's a fanatic about it." Nan softened her voice. "If I was so much as to intimate I knew you, your job wouldn't be worth a dime." *That* should assure his silence. "So for now, play the game her way. You're Rita Martin's discovery, not mine. But remember ITC owns *Time Nor Tide* and Rita Martin . . . and I represent ITC." *That* should assure his loyalty.

Peterson silently digested this information. "From the looks of all this behind-the-scenes drama I'd say the job is mine."

Nan was circumspect. "Rita was very impressed with your script."

"So where do we go from here?"

She looked conspicuously at her watch and signaled for the waiter. "Home. I've still got some work to do."

"Sure," Al agreed immediately.

Fifteen minutes later they were standing outside Nan's apartment. She had wanted to say good-night in the lobby, but Al insisted on escorting her upstairs. Not that he had any intention of making a play for her tonight. No way. But his innate sense of being a gentleman would never allow him to leave a lady in her lobby.

"Thanks for dinner Miss Booth" he said. "And thanks for the help . . . and for the tips."

"It was my pleasure," Nan cooed.

For the first time in years Al Peterson was at a loss for his next move. "So . . . I guess it's good-night then." He wanted to kiss Nan, because it was as much a part of his style with women as shaking hands with a man, but Nan Booth was a breed apart. Deciding to trust his instinct, Al took her quickly in his arms and pressed his mouth against hers. When Nan stiffened, he knew he'd made a mistake. The kiss abruptly became a peck on the lips as he pulled away almost immediately. "I'd like to have dinner again sometime. I could take *you,*" he said, stumbling foolishly over his words.

"I'll have my secretary check my calendar," she said as she unlocked the door. "Good-night, Al." And she was gone.

* * *

In many ways Nan's apartment was a mirror image of her office. Subdued backlighting silhouetted the chic, modern furniture and cast junglelike patterns from many plants onto the ceiling. Nan walked into the bedroom rubbing the back of her hand across her mouth. The impudent boy had actually kissed her! What inexperience.

The bedroom, except for a platform bed, two low end tables with lamps, and a chest of drawers, was empty. She sat down on the edge of the bed faced with the depressing prospect of sleeplessness. She was too keyed up, too much was happening. She grabbed a cigarette from an end table and lit it, hungrily devouring the smoke. Al Peterson was in, but now Jim Goodspeed was fast becoming an obstacle. Just who did he think he was kidding? His tacit approval of the Caribbean story was bullshit. Soap operas made him gag. Chances were he'd only skimmed the fucking piece of drivel.

But Nan had read it word for word. And it was her gut feeling, too, that if the story ever got done *Time Nor Tide*'s ratings would skyrocket.

She ground out her cigarette and stalked into her dressing room to change. In this mood there was no way she was going to stay cooped up at home. She needed something to subdue the anxiety and eradicate the fears that were growing inside her. And there was only one place in New York where Nan knew she could find the release that no cigarette, drink, or pill ever came close to touching. She angrily pulled on a pair of slacks, donned a pinstriped oxford cloth shirt and Gucci loafers.

If any other ITC soap had had the lousy ratings *TNT* was currently exhibiting its head writer would have been sacked weeks ago. It made Nan's blood boil to think that she was being raked over the coals by Weatherhead because Ms. Martin was fucking up. She stopped in front of a mirror to take a look before going out. Even though she looked appropriately dressed as she was, the outfit cried out for an extra touch. A waist-length leather bomber jacket the color of milk chocolate from the men's department at Ted Lapidus on Fifth Avenue completed the ensemble.

On Broadway Nan hailed a taxi and ten minutes later she stepped out into a narrow, winding Greenwich Village street. She stood for a minute looking from side to side, then quickly darted into the doorway and down the steps to the George Sand.

The bar was in a large basement and lighted so discreetly that the patrons were no more than silhouettes. Nan edged her way through the crowd to the bar and signaled the bartender.

"What'll it be, Jan?" the bartender called out over the din.

"The regular, Sally," she shouted back over the blaring jukebox, pulling a five-dollar bill from her pocket.

Big Sally was the toughest woman in the George Sand, although others looked more imposing. Wearing dirty jeans and a too-tight tank top that accentuated her ponderous breasts, Sally might have passed for an overly healthy woman to anyone in the street, but to the regulars here her she was a gay stereotype—the fast-talking, no-nonsense bull dyke.

Nan paid for the drink, leaving a hefty tip, then pushed back into the crowd. There were many familiar faces tonight—people who knew her as Jan—but just as many unfamiliar ones. Standing by the jukebox was a short, petite Oriental girl with whom Nan once had a brief affair. She broke it off when the girl started asking too many questions about her career. Nan was discreet about this side of her life and she had no qualms about dropping any nosy bitch who started pushing too much.

Half an hour later Nan was bored. She was about to order a second drink when a young brunette entered the bar alone. She was Nan's height but thinner, with exquisitely drawn features—pert nose, large eyes, succulent mouth. In a way she reminded Nan of Rita Martin, and because of this, even though she wore a good deal of makeup, Nan was intrigued. She waited until the other woman ordered, then followed her across the room.

"My name's Jan," Nan introduced herself, smiling brightly.

"I'm Emily," the other woman replied shyly. "Do you come here often?"

Nan almost laughed. The "do-you-come-here-often" line was strictly fifties. "I come here as seldom as possible. Pickup bars are definitely not to my taste."

"But you're here," Emily observed without sarcasm.

"So I am. Now that we know all about me, let's talk about you." This flippancy was strictly for cruising. Friendly, but not cloying, cute and slightly bitchy, it was just cocktail party chatter. If she and her target didn't hit it off, no one lost face.

"This is only my second time here. I'm new in New

York." Emily nervously sipped her drink, entranced by the beauty before her. "I'm from Kansas. That's about all." She raised her eyes shyly to Nan's.

"So you fled the wheat fields to have a glittering sex life in New York, is that it?" This kid had a lot to learn.

"Not exactly," Emily replied shyly, avoiding Nan's gaze.

"Well, what is it . . . *exactly?*"

"I was lonely," Emily admitted so softly the words were almost lost to the music.

Nan had expected a brittle, stinging New York-style punch line, but there was none. It was a straight, honest answer, right from the heart. In time the Manhattan glitz, glib fast talk, and the one-night stand would become part of Emily's routine, but right now they were conspicuously absent.

Nan removed the drink from Emily's hand and placed it on the bar. "Let's get out of here." It was more than a suggestion.

They held hands in the taxi all the way to Nan's apartment. In the cold night of a New York autumn, holding hands—even with a stranger—could be more rewarding than all the other treasures this city has to offer, Nan thought to herself.

Emily could have been Nan ten years earlier. For a moment she remembered with bittersweet sadness the naïve youngster she had been on her arrival in New York. How quickly she had changed. Now, Nan Booth needed no one.

Nan surrendered to her sexual urges because she considered them biological demands like eating when she was hungry, sleeping when exhaustion overcame her, smiling when something amused her, and fucking when she was anxious . . . horny. It irked her that she was considered something less than human, less than a *real* woman because she preferred her own sex over men. Rita Martin could make heads roll from now until doomsday, but because of her husband and child—testament to her heterosexuality—she would always be considered better than Nan by those in the know. If the word got out that Nan Booth was a Lesbian, she was doomed to suffer, despite her talents. Nan faced double discrimination: She was a woman, and she was queer!

"Anything wrong?" Emily pulled her hand away from Nan's viselike grip.

"Just thinking too much. We'll be home soon." She leaned back against the seat and closed her eyes. She'd prove she was as good as anyone else—better, even. She'd get what she wanted despite the odds against her, no matter what she had to do. And right now that meant eliminating Rita Martin and everything she stood for.

7

Al Peterson rang the doorbell of Mel Jacobs's apartment and waited expectantly. This was some building! With its long spacious lobby, acres of etched mirrors and vases of calla lilies, it was right out of a Noel Coward comedy. But when Jacobs had called that morning at eight, he was in no mood for laughter. He sounded pissed. It seemed Rita had given him some notes for Peterson's second script to be delivered that weekend—no later.

Al gallantly offered to pick them up that afternoon. What the hell, last night's dumb date with Nan had already gotten his weekend off to a bad start, why not polish it off with a visit to Mel Jacobs? When he hung up he looked at the empty place next to him in bed and cursed. Not that he had really expected to woo Nan Booth from des Artistes to his brownstone walk-up love nest, but shit, just in case the unbelievable did happen, he'd turned down Angela Brite's invitation for a midnight rendezvous. Next time he'd know better.

As he impatiently rang the bell a second time, Wendy Jacobs opened the door. Caught in the midst of cooking, Wendy wore Mrs. Swedeborg's apron over slacks, a rumpled sweat shirt, and a kerchief tied carelessly around her head. She was covered with flour from hands to elbows.

"Mr. Peterson?" she asked, blowing a strand of hair back into place.

"I was looking for Mel Jacobs."

"He's not in right now, but he told me you'd be coming. Won't you come in?" She stepped aside to let him pass.

Al took in the apartment in one startled glance. Because he had already classed Jacobs as both humorless and grimly determined to succeed at all costs—the type of man who never gets a joke because he's too busy analyzing the motives for telling it—Al expected a dark, cluttered apartment where the curtains were always drawn to keep out the sun. But the rooms spread out before him were painted photographer's white and shimmered in the autumn sun. A wall of windows at the far end of the living room brought the park and a slice of the East Side into sharp focus. Everything except a pastel painting over the fireplace and a vase of yellow roses was in muted beiges and creams. If the Mel Jacobs he knew lived here, Peterson had obviously misjudged him—at least in his personal life-style.

"Won't you wait in the living room," Wendy offered, brushing some flour from her forehead. "He won't be long." She was about to introduce herself when Peterson interrupted.

"Is *Mrs*. Jacobs at home?"

Wendy smiled mischievously. So Al Peterson thought she was the maid. Well, she'd just have a little fun with this gorgeous hunk. "Of course, I'll get her. May I fix you something to drink in the meantime?"

"No, thanks." For the next ten minutes Al paced around while waiting for Mrs. Jacobs.

"Mr. Peterson, I'm Wendy Jacobs," a voice from behind finally beckoned.

Al turned and gawked foolishly at her. Wendy had removed the apron, washed her face and let her hair down, and changed into a skirt and blouse. Beautifully collected, a hint of a smile quivering on her lips, Wendy glided into the living room, like a debutante.

"Haven't we met somewhere before, Mr. Peterson?" she asked.

Al just stared.

His expression was so silly she had to laugh. "I should have introduced myself at the door, but it's not every day I get mistaken for my housekeeper. Will you forgive me?"

He shook his head. "It's been a long time since I've been caught so completely off-guard, and by such a beautiful woman."

Wendy's reply was a dazzling laugh. "I didn't intend to

mislead you, but when you asked about Mrs. Jacobs . . ." She laughed again and her face lit up in a way that sent shivers through Peterson.

"It's my fault, too, I guess. I had an entirely different picture of what Mrs. Mel Jacobs would be like." Wendy Jacobs was young, beautiful, and a total surprise.

"And what was that?" she asked coyly.

"Just . . . different." He carefully avoided being trapped into describing the timid *hausfrau* he had expected.

"Well, I hope you're not *too* disappointed." It wasn't the first time a visitor had had this reaction. "I ordered us some coffee," she explained as Lolly clattered into the room with a silver tray and the best china.

Lolly took one look at the handsome stranger and began to blush furiously. "If you need anything else, just call." She nearly fell over an ottoman as she backed away.

Wendy smiled, recalling how startled she, too, had been by Peterson's good looks. "Mel tells me you may be working for Rita."

"I'm still on trial," he quipped.

"Once you get this far with Rita, it's usually a cinch. She puts a lot of emphasis on first impressions," Wendy said, trying to mask her contempt for Mel's boss. She put a great deal of the responsibility for Mel's metamorphosis from husband to wife-beater squarely on Rita Martin and her goddamned soap.

And with that the conversation died. At the point where something *had* to be said, Al noticed a double row of framed photographs on the wall opposite. "Are those friends of yours?" he asked, vaguely aware that the glum faces were all quite elderly.

"We met only long enough for me to take their photographs," Wendy said without bothering to turn around. "It was a school project I once did."

"Looks very professional from here," he said.

"The whole series is called 'Sun Cities.' It was part of a group show down in SoHo a few years back," Wendy elaborated, recognizing as she did a dim pride she hadn't felt in a long time. "I'd hoped to make a name for myself, but it didn't work out that way." Now she looked over her shoulder at the photographs and, before giving it a second thought, got up and walked to the display. She stood staring a moment before speaking again. "It's been so long since I've really looked at them, so long since I've thought of them as anything more than part of the furniture."

Being drawn into her private thoughts seemed a silent invitation to come a step closer, so Peterson joined her a moment later. "They're really very powerful. Reminds me of some of Diane Arbus's best work."

"Others have said that, too," she said evenly, noting that the comparison had lost its poisonous sting. "I was younger then and easily impressed. Arbus was a favorite of mine. She smiled vaguely, then quickly returned to the couch. "I met Mel and dropped out of the mainstream of my work, so I doubt I could imitate anyone these days—even if I tried."

"You don't work anymore at all?" Al asked incredulously.

"Not really."

He shook his head. "That's really too bad. You're very talented." He paused a moment, then nodded his head as if he'd come to a mental conclusion. "Let's make a deal: If you ever work again—which I think you should—I'll be your first paying customer." He stuck out his hand and waited.

Wendy took his hand and shook it, laughing as she did. "You've got yourself a deal, Mr. Peterson."

"And you've got yourself a fan, Mrs. Jacobs."

After a moment Wendy realized she was still holding Al's hand and quickly released it. "It's refreshing to meet someone who doesn't think photography means Polaroid. Has it always interested you?"

"I'm interested in anything people create. I tried painting and sculpture, acting once, and some singing. Finally, I settled on writing."

"You must be good at it. In case you haven't heard, Rita is to *TNT* what a lioness is to her cubs."

"I don't kid myself about this kind of writing. Dialoging for a soap is nothing more than filling in the blanks, like a crossword puzzle. Even plotting is mainly a mechanical job. A good memory is more important than a spark of talent in this business." He hadn't meant to be so open, yet there it was.

"Don't let Mel hear you talk like that. He takes *TNT* very seriously."

"I take it seriously, too . . . for what it is. But it'll always be like painting by numbers for me." Once again he looked at her photographs. "Now, what you did over there, that's real art."

"Mr. Peterson, I am highly flattered," Wendy acknowledged, bowing her head modestly. "May I please call you Al? I feel like we've already known each other too long for all this formality."

"Call me anything—and anytime—you want," he suddenly said. Wendy Jacobs may have given up her work to be Mel's wife, but she obviously wasn't satisfied with the role. There was an edgy, excitable quality in her talk that no amount of poise could disguise. Sitting sedately opposite him, her legs crossed, one arm over the back of the chair, Wendy Jacobs looked the picture of contentment, but her flashing eyes and the flush on her cheeks when she talked of photography told Al there was a hell of a lot more woman to her than she revealed.

"And what have you decided?" she asked him point-blank.

He stared at her dumbly.

"I know that look, Al. I see it on Mel's face all the time. He creates whole histories for strangers. You were just doing the same thing. So, what's the verdict? As your guinea pig you owe me a little explanation."

She was as smart, no, smarter than he had guessed. "You asked for it. I was just thinking that you've got your act down pat. You're cool and beautiful, self-assured in certain situations—you play a very convincing maid and gracious hostess—but playing a role can't be enough. You're an artist, and for whatever reasons, you've turned your back on it. And from where I sit, you haven't found anything to replace it. That must leave one hell of a gaping hole in your life, lady."

Wendy straightened up and drew herself inward until her hands were folded neatly in her lap over her tightly closed knees. "You certainly don't pull your punches."

"You asked."

"Now I wish I hadn't."

"Hey, look, I'm not saying I was right. You asked me to speculate and I invented a story. It was presumptuous of me to get so personal. I sometimes wish I could be more diplomatic."

"Let me make a statement about you to even the score," she countered slyly. "It's only fair. You *can* be diplomatic . . . when it suits you, but right now you think you'll get the upper hand by being rude, or should I say 'honest'?"

"I just open my big mouth and walk right in. Forgive me?"

She nodded.

Christ, he'd only been there fifteen minutes, and he'd insulted Mel Jacobs's wife. There was no telling how much the couple confided in each other, but they had to be pretty thick for Wendy to give up a promising career to play house. One wrong word from her and his job would be worth shit.

"Look, I can pick up that material from Mel on Monday. I've taken too much of your time already," he apologized, preparing to leave.

"Sit down, Mr. Peterson," she commanded. "This is the most stimulating conversation I've had in months, and I'm not about to let you get away that easily."

She rang for Lolly.

"Now, how about a *real* drink?"

When Mel walked into the living room half an hour later, Wendy and Al were sipping white wine and talking just above a whisper, it seemed.

Mel hadn't liked Peterson on sight at the office, and now, seeing him comfortably ensconced in his own living room—with *his* wife—that dislike intensified. Peterson's collegiate type was all too familiar—good-looking, quick witted, attractive to women and easily accepted by men—but this time it was Mel Jacobs who had the upper hand. Even though Peterson had already spent time alone with Wendy, they were on Mel's home turf and he intended to make it very clear to whom Wendy belonged.

"Well, Peterson, I thought you'd call first. Hope it hasn't been too boring for you."

"Your lovely wife has been entertaining me."

Mel kissed Wendy on the cheek. "Always the perfect hostess," he said endearingly.

"Wine, dear?" Wendy was slightly flushed from the two glasses she'd already consumed.

He shook his head.

"Well, I'll have another glass. Al?"

"It'll just hit the spot." He extended his glass.

Mel didn't like the atmosphere. It was too chummy, too clubby. Peterson had obviously been there long enough to be on a first-name basis with his wife. "I'll get Rita's notes," he said brusquely.

He returned minutes later and remained standing, an obvious sign for Peterson to leave. "If you have any questions . . ."

Al gulped the last of his wine. "I'm sure they're very clear. Sorry to have troubled you."

Wendy looked at the two of them. Mel was on the short side, with dark features and jet black hair and moustache; Al was clean-shaven, tall and angular with hair almost as blond as her own. She and her husband were opposites; she and Peterson almost seemed to belong together. Wendy liked this Al Peterson, and now that Mel was back she didn't want Al to leave. It had been so long since they'd had company, particularly someone *she* liked. Spurred on by the wine, Wendy decided to take a chance just this once. "I've invited Al for dinner . . . next Thursday. Right, Al?"

"Next Thursday is Thanksgiving," Mel interrupted rudely. Then he softened his voice and put his arm possessively around Wendy's waist. "I'm *sure* Al has plans, dear."

"Of course he has plans; he's having dinner with us," Wendy insisted as she pulled away from him. Mel was furious, but it was too late to renege on the invitation now. Besides she *really* wanted Peterson there.

"It's very nice of you to ask . . ." Al began to decline. Being the birdie in a game of domestic badminton wasn't usually his idea of a good time. But something about this situation intrigued him. Maybe it was Jacobs's obvious discomfort. Or maybe it was, more simply, the beautiful Mrs. Jacobs. ". . . and I can't think of anywhere I'd rather be," he concluded.

"Wonderful. Thanksgiving it is," Mel acquiesced with little grace. "Now, I think I *will* have that drink." This time he'd let Wendy have her way, but she'd pay for it sooner or later—he'd see to that.

"We'll have a wonderful time, Mel. After all, we *are* members of the same family—the *Time Nor Tide* family, that is," Wendy said breezily, suddenly happy that Peterson had accepted. "So, we'll see you next Thursday, Al? Eight sharp."

Peterson bowed slightly in her direction. His eyes were full of admiration. Wendy Jacobs was turning out to be quite a woman. "Well, I've got work to do. Thanks for the drink, Wendy . . . and for the notes, Mel. Until Thursday."

Al got out of the Jacobses' apartment as fast as he could without running. Jesus, talk about the beauty and the beast! In the elevator, he suddenly realized just how eager he was for another encounter with Wendy Jacobs next Thursday.

* * *

Rita cast aside Al Peterson's newly arrived script and lit a cigarette to calm her anxiety. She had hoped that bringing him into the *TNT* fold would revitalize her, establish new work goals—at the very least reinstate her as resident sage of the daytime serial at ITC. But Peterson's script was watertight. Any reworking would be nit-picking, a waste of time. So, she couldn't even nurture one of her own dialogists. For a fleeting second Rita wished she had Ellie Davis back. Maybe easing her out was a mistake, after all. Rita was plagued with self-doubts.

She swiveled her chair around to face the window. It was the day before Thanksgiving, a gray and rainy Wednesday, the kind of New York day that always made Rita wish she were at home with nothing more important to do than the shopping for that evening's dinner. "Dreamer," she snapped angrily, turning back to her desk. "You tried that route and what did it get you?" Going home never cured the way she felt about herself on days like this; it only seemed to make the problem worse.

With sudden urgency Rita crammed Peterson's script into her briefcase alongside the final draft of next year's Penny Hewitt story projection. Penny Hewitt was to be her savior, not Ben Elliott or Jeannie or Ellie Davis or the very late Frank Cameron or some new, hotshot dialogist.

Savior was the role Rita usually reserved for Rita. She was used to living life on the brink, stepping so close to the abyss that pebbles were set free by her feet to tumble forever down into the dark nothingness. Nothing gave Rita more pleasure than to salvage a situation and save the day. This was Rita Martin triumphant! The Rita Martin who surmounted all obstacles, winging above all others like a great bird in flight, untouched. This was the Rita Martin who for six years had ruled undisputed at *Time Nor Tide*.

She lit another cigarette, only barely aware that she was chain-smoking. An eerie calm had descended over *TNT*. Since Goodspeed's rather impersonal note concerning Penny Hewitt, there had been no word from him *or* from Nan Booth. It should have been a good sign. It should have instilled in Rita the confidence that she was back on the right road. But instead the silence terrified her. Negotiated power plays and backroom intrigues were too subtle and too slow-moving.

Dealing with dragons head on was her style, smiting them down with her terrible, swift sword.

But now, aside from killing Frank Cameron and preparing for the trial, and making the Caribbean story the best piece of writing she'd ever done, there was nothing to do but wait. A feeling of helplessness so acute that it bordered on despair took hold of Rita. She thought of Ben.

The fatalistic tone of his voice that awful night weeks before had touched something in Rita. What he said about not living forever was an obvious and inescapable fact, but preparing for Jeannie's life were she and Ben to die was a new plot twist—and it made Rita feel her own vulnerability. In her mind she wanted desperately to put her husband and daughter in a neat compartment labeled "the past" and move on, unencumbered. But in her heart she couldn't desert them. Like it or not, Rita was as bound to them as she was to the show. She had put *TNT* ahead of her family in order to realize a dream. But now that the show seemed threatened, the image of the unshakable family she had conjured up for the citizens of Laurelton seemed just as comforting for herself. Love, tender caring, devotion had made *TNT* soar to the top. If she now turned these powers on her family in the real world, couldn't she win them back?

With lightning speed she ground out the cigarette, barked some hasty instructions to Sandy on the intercom, and, a minute later when the light on her phone flashed, listened in, careful not to make a sound.

"Ben, it's Sandy Lief. How are you?"

"Couldn't be better Sandy. Anything wrong?"

"Rita wanted to let you know she'd be home *tonight*. She would have phoned herself, but she's in conference."

"What time does she expect to arrive?" Ben carefully hid his surprise. Rita had willingly agreed to spend Thanksgiving at home but had insisted she couldn't make it to Connecticut any sooner than Thursday morning.

"About eight," Sandy turned and looked at Rita through the open office door. When she mimicked someone eating, Sandy quickly added, "And she'd like you to hold dinner for her."

Ben laughed. "You can tell my wife she won't starve. Thanks, Sandy. Nice talking to you."

Sandy turned back to Rita after she'd hung up. "How'd I

do?" she asked mischievously. She took every request from Rita in her stride—no matter how bizarre.

"You were perfect. Maybe we could find a spot for you on the air," she teased.

"Not on your life; I've got enough troubles, thank you very much. Anything else, boss lady?"

Rita shook her head. This wasn't the first time Sandy had covered for her. She was the perfect secretary: competent, intelligent, fiercely loyal . . . and discreet. Sandy never questioned Rita's motives.

After hearing Ben's voice Rita felt a little more confident about her decision to go home that evening. She really *wanted* to go home—but it had to be on her terms. If Ben had sounded at all displeased by her imminent arrival, she simply would have had Sandy call back later and beg off.

But he had sounded pleased—even anxious—to see her, and as she absentmindedly shuffled some papers on her desk, Rita knew that she couldn't explain this trip to Connecticut as a badly needed escape from the pressures of work any more than she could the many trips over the past weeks. She *needed* to go home. She needed to be with Ben . . . and with Jeannie.

Rita called the ITC garage and ordered a limousine to be out front in ten minutes. Getting that luxury back was a small victory, but a victory nonetheless. She lit another cigarette, cursing the habit, but knowing instinctively that to deny herself now, during a time of crisis, was a subtle form of self-sabotage. *During a time of crisis.* She smiled ruefully at the thought. For the first time in six years her future at ITC was not assured. What would life be like without *Time Nor Tide*? she wondered. Or more importantly, what would *TNT* be like without Rita Martin? Well, she'd finally admitted it. Even without her, *TNT* would go on.

So perfectly had she created *Time Nor Tide,* so thorough had she been in dealing with every aspect of the show that it had taken on a life of its own—a life as complete and distinct from her as hers from her family. It wouldn't take much investigation by someone like Nan Booth to see that the show rolled under its own momentum. The characters in Laurelton, U.S.A., were so carefully delineated that plots were a natural extension of their well-established personalities; anyone familiar with the characters could guide them easily into hundreds—thousands—of story lines. Even the mechanics of production—

rehearsals, tapings, money flowing from ITC's coffers—were assembly line. *Time Nor Tide* truly waited for no man. Or woman.

Now the realization that it all could be taken from her at any moment made her angry more than it scared her. She had worked and fought and sacrificed; done everything but bled for *Time Nor Tide*. And for the few years the show was on top nothing in the world was as sweet as the ecstasy of being a winner. But now what Rita had accomplished for ITC, the many millions in ad revenue that had fattened the network's bank accounts, the audience it gave the struggling fledgling network, meant nothing. Old glory was forgotten because *today TNT* was foundering. Rita felt a bitterness so deep she wondered why, in light of the rewards, success had ever been so important. If her accomplishments meant nothing today, then indeed her life had been wasted.

Oddly enough it was Ben who seemed to offer something more valuable than all she had already achieved. Even though it was now second nature for Rita to defend herself against the implication that her career was anything but totally satisfying, Ben's words troubled her. His nature didn't feed off power and position, glamour and highly charged business meetings; it centered around a wife, children, and a home, three aspects of his life that obsessed him as much as *TNT* did Rita.

Maybe Ben's right, she thought, as she put on her mink. Maybe I should give my home life a second chance.

She turned off the lights in her office and headed for the limousine and Connecticut. There certainly was no harm in trying.

Rita arrived half an hour earlier than planned. All the way home she had tried to look upon this evening as a new beginning.

"A latter-day Brillat-Savarin?" she laughed, catching Ben concocting a corn bread stuffing for tomorrow's turkey as she strode into the kitchen. "Don't you ever do anything but cook? I thought you were the 'respectable' writer in this family."

"You're home early," he observed with obvious pleasure. "Don't let this getup fool you. I was writing until half an hour ago . . . and Brillat-Savarin would turn over in his grave from this meal." He looked at her expectantly.

"Ah, but he never tasted your *dinde à l'Elliott,*" she joked.

In the show Rita handled scenes like this easily: The wife approached the injured husband, soothed him, and everything was copacetic within minutes. In fact, Rita believed the world worked that way for everyone else but her. She felt persecuted because something always seemed to go wrong before a true understanding was drawn.

She nestled into Ben's arms and kissed him warmly on the mouth. "How are you?"

"Better, now that you're here," he mumbled between kisses. The usual tension he felt with Rita at home was conspicuously absent. He relaxed. "How about a drink?"

"I'd love one," Rita said. "If you give me a minute, I'll fix them."

As she poured out two martinis a muted sound from upstairs reminded Rita that she hadn't yet seen her daughter. "Is that Jeannie?" she asked expectantly. Since the episode with the roller skates eight weeks before, Rita had been home more often than usual, and while there, she'd genuinely tried to make contact with her family again—particularly with Jeannie. But accepting the child as she was wasn't easy for Rita. It was often exasperating and painful and too frequently her guilt was honed down to a fine-edged anger that lacerated them all. It could have driven her farther away, but each time Rita returned to New York on business she found herself more and more looking forward to her return to Connecticut.

"That noise is Mrs. Flannagan getting ready to go to her sister's for the night. Jeannie is at the Moores'. Helen volunteered to take her until late tomorrow afternoon so we could have some time alone." Ben accepted his drink.

Rita was looking forward to seeing Jeannie, but being alone with Ben was exactly what she needed. "I want to propose a toast," she said, raising her glass to him.

"To what?"

"To you." The sudden tenderness scared her, so she added, "and to your stuffing."

Dinner was an absolute success. Ben was a good cook, but that night he outdid himself. The lamb chops were better than in the best restaurants, and the baked potatoes with sour cream were sinfully fattening but irresistible. Later, in the living room, they indulged themselves further on chocolate eclairs and Irish coffee.

"Remember Vienna? That little café that used Persian rugs for tablecloths. I'd never tasted eclairs so good, until now." Rita sighed happily.

"You thought I wanted to get you fat on pastry so no one would want you but me," he reminded her, thinking of that honeymoon week. "How *did* we end up in Vienna, anyway?"

"You wanted to honeymoon in a city with palaces," she answered.

"Of course. We went to Schönbrunn . . ." The memories drifted lazily back now. It seemed hundreds of years ago.

"Schönbrunn? We went to every goddamned *schloss* in Bavaria. Palaces, indeed. And I thought *I* was the romantic in the family."

"Oh, no, Rita. You're the realist. You're the one who brings a slice of life into everyone's living room each day."

"As if real life weren't enough," she mused. "Well, as long as they'll buy it, I'll keep dishing it out."

Her tone of voice surprised Ben. "Do I detect a note of cynicism?" He leaned forward. "Is it possible Rita Martin is mellowing toward *Time Nor Tide*." It was his great wish.

Rita wasn't sure he was serious, but there was no point taking chances. "It's just the wine talking, Ben. Tomorrow I'll be tough as nails again." Her words sounded pathetic, rather than humorous as she intended.

"You don't have to be tough, Rita. Not with me, anyway," he murmured.

"I'm doing it for me. I can't very well let every ambitious bastard in New York walk all over me." Her voice hardened, but her anger seemed out of place in the quiet living room.

"Do you know what I'd be like if I thought about my work all the time? A basket case, that's what—one of those men who eats too little, drinks too much, and always wonders why his life isn't worth a plug nickel. Writing is my job, not my life, just as soap operas should be——"

"Don't you *ever* worry about the future?" Rita interrupted, amazed that Ben actually advocated living without an eye on tomorrow.

"Only when it concerns you . . . or Jeannie," he answered, perhaps too pointedly. "Most times I'm just too busy with today. Why don't you try it? Relax and enjoy what you've created."

"My work *is* my relaxation."

"I don't believe that, and I think you're beginning to have

your doubts too." He poured himself a second cup of coffee. "A job is a job, no more, no less. It doesn't matter how creative or glamorous it is, there's much more to life than work. Be honest, Rita. You know that. You write about it every day."

Ben seemed to be getting dangerously close to a truth Rita wasn't quite ready to admit. "Please, Ben," she sighed. "I didn't travel all the way to Connecticut to be lectured."

He shrugged. "Admitting to yourself that you've got your priorities all screwed up is only admitting what others have known about you for years. It would be a big step forward, Rita."

She stared thoughtfully at him for a moment, then shook her head wearily and looked away.

"Okay. Have it your own way." He got up. "I've got some dishes to do. I'll be back in a couple of minutes."

Rita wandered around the living room trying to regain the calm she'd felt before Ben's remarks. He just didn't understand. For his own reasons Ben always denied her just praise for her accomplishments. To suggest that people saw her life as unfulfilled and wasted was preposterous, spiteful. No one in his right mind would feel other than envy for *her* life-style. After all, Rita Martin had everything—almost. If she could hold on to control of the show.

Rita lit a cigarette to keep back the feelings. Hell, in one way Ben was right: Thinking about her tomorrows was ruining *this* evening. She was in Connecticut, not New York. At play, not at work. That's why she was here in the first place. She flicked the cigarette into the fireplace and went to the kitchen. Ben had just finished loading the dishwasher.

"Hey, sexy, how's about coming up to my place?" she crooned. "I'll show you my old soap opera scripts."

For a second Ben was swept back years to the Rita Martin he had fallen in love with and married. They'd often joked around like this. "Well, I don't know," he lowered his eyes to the floor and shuffled his feet. "I'm not allowed to talk to strangers."

Rita strolled over to him, leaned close, and whispered in his ear. "You like candy?" He nodded. "Well, I've got plenty." She stuck her tongue in his ear. "Come on, little boy. I'm going to make a man of you."

They had not made love in over two weeks, yet as they lay in bed, the time melted away.

Ben examined Rita's body in the soft candlelight. He brushed her smooth skin with his fingertips like a feather. "You're a beautiful woman," he said, kissing the nape of her neck.

As always Rita responded with total abandon. The physical passion he aroused with his gentleness was something no one else was able to match. Even Rick Cologna's perfectly executed embraces were lame by comparison. Ben's lovemaking flowed from his deepest feelings for Rita, not merely from an urge for sexual release. He cherished her with each touch, took more interest in her pleasure than in his own, and stayed with her until she was satisfied.

This bond of sexuality had never wavered despite the turmoil of their married life. Even during the most difficult times, when all other communications had broken down completely they had enjoyed passionate sexual love.

And now, as Ben's tongue circled the aureole of Rita's nipple, she felt again, through the haze of her ecstasy, what she'd always known: Her responsiveness to Ben was based on love, too; it was a highly intimate experience, not just good sex.

Ben found his way down to the dark cleft between her thighs and Rita opened her legs, allowing him to move in between. His tongue darted over her clitoris, teasing her, sending her skyrocketing toward a sudden, unexpected climax.

When he finally relented Rita was soaking wet. Her mind was riveted on the burning point between her legs and Ben's stiff prick rising toward her. She spread her legs wider still, rubbing the insides of her thighs with her palms. Rita never allowed herself such freedom with the other men. Even in her most reckless moments, she focused on who she was and what she did in order to maintain her distance from them. With Ben there were no limits.

Ben slid himself deep inside her, lifting upward, rubbing hard against her swollen clitoris. Rita gasped and bit her lower lip to stifle a scream. She threw her arms over his back and raised her knees, pulling him still deeper inside. Rita wanted all of Ben inside, deeper, deeper. Ben panted as he began fucking with ever-increasing fury, rocking them both back and forth, sending the bedsprings into an agony of screeching that filled the room like a child's screams.

He watched her face closely, waiting for the exact moment of her orgasm; then he pounded faster into her, coming when she did, kissing her mouth and face, her eyes and neck. He lay on top of her for a minute afterward, gently kissing her before falling beside her, exhausted.

"I love you, Rita," he whispered drowsily, turning onto his side so he could fall asleep holding her.

"I know you do, Ben," she murmured in reply, before falling into a dreamless night's sleep.

Thanksgiving Day the sun shone brilliantly through a cloudless sky. A prolonged autumn made the countryside of West Willow glorious. The forests had exchanged their mantles of green for brazen cloaks of yellow, red, and orange. From the bedroom window Rita thought the landscape looked like a glorious tapestry. It was a beautiful day. She was happy and relaxed. And she was beginning to feel like a woman in love again.

A car horn sounded from the driveway below. Ben waved anxiously up at her from the driver's seat of the family station wagon. Rita smiled and waved back. When they first moved to Connecticut, they had frequently driven far off the main highway to explore the surrounding countryside. Even though times had changed, there were still places within an hour's drive where the antiques and the people who sold them were still the genuine article. Ben sounded the horn once again.

Rita gave her country outfit a last look. Perhaps the opalescent silk blouse and Lauren jacket were a bit much with the tartan plaid wool skirt and brogues, but she didn't give a damn. Today she was spending the day with her husband in a part of the country she loved, and she felt positively girlish about it. Fashion be damned! Tying a Liberty scarf over her hair, Rita fled the bedroom, took the stairs two at a time, and hopped into the car.

"Where to?" she asked breathlessly.

"I'm just going to point the car and let it take over." He blew her a little kiss. "Do you mind?"

"Why on earth should I?"

"Well, it is a holiday," he reminded her with obvious pleasure. "I thought maybe you had something special you wanted to do."

Rita moved slightly closer to him. "Just being here is special enough. So, lead on, Macduff."

Ben kissed her on the cheek. "It could always be like this, Rita," he confided as he started the car.

They drove aimlessly along the narrow country roads, as

wide-eyed as tourists. The foliage, a many-hued umbrella over the road, was occasionally so dense it blocked out the sun, but just when it seemed night had overtaken day, the light broke through and dazzled them once again. They drove through small towns and village greens, around larger towns with traffic jams, and past acres of farmland stacked with dried cornstalks bound in bundles like Indian tepees.

I owe Ben Elliott a great deal, Rita thought as they motored through the Connecticut countryside. Through the torment of the last years' self-doubt, through the fights and bitter recriminations, the accusations and the pain since Jeannie's accident, Ben had never once called Rita on the debt she owed him . . . and it amazed her. It amazed her that he was so selfless in light of her own ambition. During those first anguished years after Jeannie's birth, she had thought him weak. But it wasn't weakness that kept Ben Elliott by her side, it was patience and love of a kind that Rita always denied herself. Rita suspected she didn't deserve her husband, and this suspicion haunted every minute she spent with him.

They stopped for lunch at an old inn complete with a water-mill and ducks swimming serenely in a pond. In the dining room they had a surprisingly good meal and half a bottle of a decent white wine. They lingered over coffee, reminiscing about old times. When they were satisfied, it was back in the car to go home—the long way, meandering slowly, at whim.

By the time they entered the driveway on Noah Webster Lane, the back of the car was full of booty: an old butter churn; a gallon of chilled fresh cider; two bunches of rainbow Indian corn; winter squash; maple sugar candy; and a home-made mince pie to compliment the pumpkin pie Mrs. Flannagan had baked for the holiday. As the car edged up the drive, Rita caught sight of another car parked in front of the garage.

"Who's that?" she asked, not immediately recognizing the two figures standing by the back door.

"It's the Moores." Ben's face clouded. "They weren't supposed to be back until six." It was only four-thirty. Out of the corner of his eyes he saw Rita tense. "Hey, take it easy, honey. Okay?"

"Sure," she murmured bravely, but she already suspected the pleasures of the day were at an end. As they pulled to a stop, she saw her tearful daughter hiding behind Helen Moore's skirts.

Helen and Dave Moore edged to the car in a tight knot with Jeannie. Helen was smiling, but the smile wavered on her lips. Dave shook his head before anyone said a word. Jeannie's face was red from crying. Ben leaped from the car, pulling up the parking brake but forgetting to turn off the motor. "Anything wrong?" he asked, his voice filled with concern.

"She got a little upset, Ben," Dave said, shaking Ben's hand.

"Now don't worry, Ben. Nothing happened. I guess our little girl is just plain homesick." Helen Moore had three normal children of her own, and it hurt her to see the extremes of pain Jeannie Elliott put herself through, particularly when it came to her mother. Helen thought it shocking the way Rita Elliott spent so much time in New York while her family languished in the country.

Rita turned off the car and got out. She looked at the three adults, then at Jeannie.

When Jeannie saw her, the tears stopped and her face lit up. "Mommy?" she squealed in disbelief. "I thought you went away again." She released Helen's skirt and ran full force at Rita. Halfway to her, she tripped and fell.

Rita stared down at her daughter. Was it really possible this poor creature was *her* daughter? She seemed always to be picking the child up after some unnecessary spill. Helen Moore's children exhibited an agility that astounded Rita. Because of Jeannie's retardation Rita often began to think all children were rather slow and thoughtful of speech, tottering in their walk as if they hadn't quite fully grasped the technique of remaining upright. But Tod, John, and Ken Moore were wild ragamuffins whose words were catapulted from their mouths in endless streams and whose skittering, running, climbing, and jumping was only periodically broken by a slow walk. The contrast was startling.

Jeannie's cries jolted Rita back to reality. She ran and scooped the child up into her arms and pressed her tightly against her bosom as tears filled her eyes. How could she make it up to Jeannie? What could she do, say, to make it all better? "Are you all right, sweetheart?" she asked, her voice choked with emotion.

Jeannie sniffled back her tears and smiled sweetly at her mother. "I guess I never learn, do I, Mommy?"

Rita held back a sob and pulled her daughter closer still, turning her head away—and found herself facing Ben and the

Moores who were watching the entire scene with what seemed to be cautious optimism that Rita Martin, mother of stone, had finally begun to crack.

"Let's go; you'll be okay," she said to Jeannie as she checked her own tears and kissed the child on the top of the head. "Let's go see Daddy." She pried Jeannie's hands from her skirt.

"But I want to spend the day with *you*, Mommy," Jeannie said brightly, unaware that, once again, she was the center of attention.

"And I want to spend the whole day with you, too," Rita said with little conviction. "Now, come along." She took Jeannie by the hand and led her up to the others. "Helen, it was very thoughtful of you to take care of Jeannie. She always tells me how much she enjoys being with you and your boys." Rita was so sweet Ben looked away for fear the ax was about to fall.

"Think nothing of it, Rita. We love having Jeannie. In fact we see so much of her I've begun to think of her as a member of *our* family," Helen said sarcastically.

Before Rita could return the insult, Ben intervened.

"How about everyone coming in for a drink? We've got some fresh cider . . . or something stronger, if you'd like."

"Sounds good to me," Dave Moore accepted enthusiastically.

But Helen demurred. "We really must get home, dear. After all it is a holiday and we don't want to forget the kids." She edged him toward their car.

"Are you sure?" Rita coaxed, knowing Helen Moore would rather spend an eternity in hell than another five minutes in the company of a woman she so obviously envied.

"Some other time, Rita. Thanks anyway," Dave said as he and Helen got into the car.

Ben talked with them for a few minutes alone before joining Rita and Jeannie.

As they pulled away, Rita shouted: "Next time you're in New York, Helen, call me at the office. We'll have lunch . . ." When the Moores' car was out of sight, Rita transferred Jeannie to Ben, saying, "You take care of her, will you? Call me when dinner's ready."

"Dinner? Where are you going?"

"I'm . . . I've got work to do and it really can't wait," she mumbled as she raced toward the house. She had to get away from them and be alone, if only for an hour.

Ten minutes later there was a knock on the study door. Rita quickly stationed herself at the desk and spread the Hewitt Caribbean story across its top to hide the fact that she'd just been sitting thinking, not working. "Come in."

Ben walked in and sat down on the edge of her desk, staring down at Rita. "We've got to talk," he announced quietly. "A few minutes ago I was reminded of exactly the kind of loving mother you can be when you want to—we all saw it."

"You and the oh-so-domestic Moores were staring at me like I was a freak, if that's what you mean," Rita replied bitterly. "Tell me, am I the sole topic of surburban conversation or do you and your friends also have other reputations to destroy?"

"Stop being so arch," Ben snapped, "it smacks of playacting, and this is very, very real. What is it about Helen Moore that so angers you? You and she used to be such good friends." He waited for an answer, then continued. "I know you won't believe this, but Helen actually still likes you."

"Hold it right there, Ben!" Rita pushed her chair back and leaped up. "I don't want to know who likes me and who doesn't, because I don't care. Next you'll be telling me who doesn't approve of my life-style, and we both know who heads *that* list."

"You can hardly blame me, can you? I didn't leave New York to set up housekeeping for one. Yet here I am, a single father . . ." Rita began to interrupt but Ben quickly went on, ". . . and my stubbornness in wanting you back is the only thing that's keeping this family together."

Rita looked at him for a moment, then walked away.

"By the way," Ben said to her back, "Helen does disapprove of your way of life. But more than that, she feels sorry that you've given up everything that once gave you so much pleasure."

"She feels sorry for *me?* Who the hell is she to feel sorry for anyone?" Rita stared out the window at the fierce colors of the foliage, but saw only the kaleidoscopic hues of her own confused emotions.

Ben went to her and put his hands on her shoulders. Surprisingly, Rita didn't move away. "Forget Helen. Let's talk about you. I know how difficult it is for you to relax with

Jeannie. In fact, it's difficult for you to relax at all. Ease up, Rita. You drive yourself harder than anyone I know."

"There was a day when ambition wasn't in such disrepute," she said thoughtfully.

"If I believed ambition had driven us apart, I would have divorced you long ago," he said truthfully. "Anyway you don't have to do anything special with Jeannie. Just be here for her. Be patient and love her—in whatever way you're able. It takes time, that's all."

"That's so easy for you to say, isn't it? You've always loved her more than I."

There was a moment's silence, then Ben turned Rita around, still holding her shoulders. "No. You're wrong. There was a time, a long time, when I didn't love Jeannie at all."

Rita stared at him. "I don't believe you," she said softly.

Ben shook his head sadly and walked across the room where he collapsed into a comfortable chair. "You really think I'm superman, don't you? You always have. Well, I guess it's just as much my fault for keeping up my end of the masquerade. After all, who but a 'perfect' husband would let his wife lead a completely separate existence from him and his child without caring? Well, it's all been a lie, Rita. I do care that you're not with me. I care like hell."

Rita stared blankly at her husband, then she said, "Could we just take one thing at a time?" He nodded. "You really expect me to believe that when Jeannie was born you . . ."

"Couldn't bear the sight of her," he finished the sentence. "When Jeannie's brain damage was diagnosed I nearly walked out on *both* of you."

"Why? It wasn't my fault," she said, feeling the old defenses lock into place. It *was* her fault. It had *always* been her fault.

"No, it wasn't your fault," he agreed without hesitation, "but that still didn't make Jeannie like other babies." He lowered his eyes and stared at the floor in front of him. "I'd wanted to have a child with you almost from the day I first saw you in class. I imagined life with you could never be the domestic trap that had already been sprung on me in my first marriage."

"And after Jeannie's birth I guess it looked like you'd made mistake number two."

"Stop putting words in my mouth, Rita," he commanded. "I have my dreams too, you know." He leaned forward and rested his elbows on his knees. "When Jeannie was born retarded the dreams evaporated and I wanted to run, as far and as fast as I could. I suppose I would have had it not been for one thing."

"And what was that?"

"You."

"Me?"

"During those first years you were always with Jeannie, tending to her, loving her. You were always there when she needed you. I've never seen so much love given in all my life." He smiled at the memories. "I remember thinking that it was easy for you, you were Jeannie's mother and that kind of abundant love came naturally. I told myself that a father's love had to be earned, when all along I knew I just didn't want to get involved, and I hated myself for it."

"I was trying to love her sickness away."

Ben shook his head. "You loved Jeannie unconditionally *despite* her affliction. In fact you probably loved her more because she was sick. And I suspect you still do, if you'd let yourself feel it."

She did love Jeannie then, but her love failed them both. So, she had let Ben take over while she embraced a career in daytime television where tangible success was guaranteed.

"I watched you day after day wondering why I hadn't packed my suitcase to leave. Then, one day, I knew why: It was your courage. If *I* were disappointed by our daughter, what must *you* be feeling? You know we never talked about that, Rita. Not once."

"I know" she admitted softly. "There never seemed to be anything to say really. It was done, over. The doctor made his pronouncement and that was that." For her part, Rita had never mentioned it because she was sure Ben would blame her and leave.

Rita went to his chair and sat on the arm, resting her hand on his shoulder. "But we did share everything in those days."

"Everything but that, and that was the most important thing," he amended. "Jeannie's birth could have brought us together, but we let it drive us apart." He reached back and took Rita's hand. "I learned to love Jeannie by watching you. I learned to accept her by following your example."

"And all along I felt that you hated me."

* * *

Ben had wanted Rita to go to the hospital that morning. He'd be in New York all afternoon with a British publisher interested in the rights to his novel, and he didn't want to chance anything happening while he was out of town. But Rita declined. She felt fine, better, in fact, than she had in weeks. The prospect of finally having her baby in her arms was absolutely thrilling. She was up that morning with the sun to see Ben off. Yes, she had the phone number of the local yellow cab. Yes, she had the doctor's phone number. And yes, Helen Moore had offered to drive her just in case, so she would be well looked after.

So Ben left and Rita began polishing a soap opera outline that had to be in the mail that afternoon. The contractions began an hour or so later, but she ignored them in order to finish her work. The rumors about giving her a shot at head writing had proved true and she was busier than she'd ever been in her life. And she was tired. The contractions were growing more insistent, but she couldn't quit just yet, not unless she wanted to blow a chance of a lifetime opportunity in daytime.

Besides, there was plenty of time left. Rita knew about counting contractions. She knew just how long it would take to get to the hospital. But what she didn't know was that she would go into the final stages of labor while still at home. And that by the time she finally called for an ambulance, it would already be too late.

Rita's water broke moments after the ambulance pulled out of the driveway on Noah Webster Lane. The paramedics attending her had seen it all before and their calmness reassured her that everything was in control. But something went wrong. The baby was in the breech position and was not passing easily through the birth canal. A hospital would have been fully equipped to deal with the situation, but this wasn't the hospital. This was a bouncing, screeching ambulance staffed by two paramedics, not doctors.

One of them counted down the seconds that Rita's baby remained trapped without air inside her mother's body, while the other frantically worked against the clock, knowing that irreparable brain damage was only a matter of seconds away. The crucial time was two minutes. And when the second hand moved past the two-minute mark, the tension in the air vanished and neither man looked at his watch again.

The pain grew until Rita feared she might black out, but the soothing arms of unconsciousness never embraced her. She breathed deeply and pushed with each contraction, remembering the doctor's instructions. She pushed and pushed. And suddenly the pain subsided. Between her blood-spattered legs she saw the tiny baby lying in the hands of the paramedic. With dreamlike movements she reached out for her daughter, but one man held her arms down while the other tried to hide the child from view.

But Rita saw anyway. The baby's features were contracted in a grim mask of lingering agony and her skin was deep blue, the color of a recent bruise. Rita stared at her motionless daughter, believing she was dead. All was pain and agony. The dreams and the joys of the last nine months had died with her. Rita was still sobbing hysterically when she was finally wheeled into the emergency room.

There had been permanent damage to the brain's cerebral cortex caused by prolonged oxygen deprivation. Jeannie Elliott would be retarded. Her mental growth would lag far behind her physical growth, and in all probability she would not live much beyond her mid-twenties—if that long.

After that day Rita tried to wish the truth away. She often reconstructed the past in such a way that she got to the hospital in time to be delivered of a healthy baby in the OR under competent medical attention. The words *if only* haunted her every waking minute. Ben was understanding, but Rita sensed something else, too. Almost immediately he asked why she'd waited so long to call for help. She explained that it had all happened so fast there just wasn't enough time. But she didn't mention working because she didn't want him to know she was to blame for Jeannie's "accident." Even though she never revealed her part in the tragedy, Rita was sure Ben knew. Sometimes she caught him staring, just looking at her, as if he could see right into her soul. And it scared her. But when Ben said nothing, she, too, kept silent. She had enough blame and guilt for the two of them.

When wishing the truth away didn't help, Rita tried loving it away. Perhaps love and attention would be enough to prove the doctors wrong. Jeannie Elliott was adorable, the sweetest thing on earth, and love was the great curative. Its restorative powers were legendary. Hadn't her own mother said so? Hadn't she promised that it could remedy anything? But despite everything, Jeannie remained a distant, still-little baby, locked in her own world. The days turned into months, and the months into years, and it became clear that no amount of love would be reparation for Rita Elliott's error.

When loving the truth away didn't work, Rita gave up. By her fourth birthday, Jeannie—who should have been walking and talking and beginning to exhibit a healthy child's curiosity about her world—was still crawling and had only just begun to make sounds that approximated speech. The burden of Rita's guilt began to crush her. She drifted into an incapacitating depression that surrounded her like a shroud. She locked both Ben and Jeannie out of her life, yet she sat for hours on end in the nursery watching her husband care for the child. Ben tried talking to Rita, tried making sense to her, but she blocked out all his words. For two months Rita barely spoke to anyone. Then, suddenly, one day her silence lifted.

And when she did speak, Rita Elliott had become Rita Martin. And that very morning she retired to her study and began composing the *Time Nor Tide* bible. The emotions she no longer could share with her husband—the fear, the anger and disappointment, as well as the love and the joy—were lavished on the characters of Laurelton, U.S.A. Rita Elliott disappeared into a world more in her own control, a world that was far more congenial than the one in which she lived, and a world in which guilt was expunged as easily as coffee stains from a kitchen sink.

"You really wanted to leave Jeannie and me?" Rita asked.

"It was a tough time for me, Rita. My world had fallen down around me. But let's not get bogged down in the past. We have important things to discuss now." He settled himself against the desk and folded his arms across his chest, a pose that always indicated he meant business. "Jeannie is your daughter as well as mine, but for as long as I can remember it's been my job to raise her. That's got to change. It's time you start sharing responsibility for taking care of her."

"I've always been responsible," Rita said automatically.

"I'm not talking about handing out money, I'm talking about love—the very love I saw earlier."

"Oh, for heaven's sake, Ben," Rita said as she deserted the chair to get out from under his stare.

Ben followed her to the window. "We have a real problem here, Rita, and I need your help."

"What can I do?" Rita asked warily. Ben used to ask for her help all the time, but he never did anymore, and that made staying away easier.

"Jeannie's beginning to get used to having you around and I'm afraid your doting on her is just one of your moods, one of your whims. This week you're a model mother and next you're off to New York and the high life."

"That's bullshit," she said angrily.

"That's *you,* Rita. When things get tough in the city you drift back here. And when the crisis passes, off you go again, forgetting all about us. It's not the first time it's happened." Ben paused. Then he went on, "Honey, Jeannie's maturing—slowly, to be sure—but as she does she's becoming more and more aware of your importance in her life. She sees that everyone else has a full-time mother and she's asked me why she doesn't."

"Has she really?" Rita could hardly believe it. She'd long ago stopped looking for any signs of mental growth in her daughter and it excited her to think Jeannie had a world view that went beyond the boundaries of their front lawn.

"For you to dangle your love in front of her one day, then pull it away the next is just plain cruel."

"Is that how it really looks?" Rita had no idea.

"That's really how it *is,* my darling wife. For the past three months you've talked of nothing but the pressure ITC is putting on you. And for the past two months you've been coming home with clockwork regularity. It isn't fair—if you're just going to vanish again." He put his hands on her arms and unconsciously began caressing them. "I won't let you use us like this anymore, Rita. I won't let you love our daughter when you need her, only to reject her when you feel strong again. You've got to decide about your family. Soon. Regardless of what happens to your career back in New York."

"Do I get a time limit for this momentous decision?" Rita asked actually smiling. In a way Ben's ultimatum came as a relief. Now after so many years of vacillating between her homelife and her career, she'd have to make a decision. Or a compromise. After all, she could work on *TNT* from Connecticut. It would mean giving up some authority, but honestly she was beginning to grow a little weary of the never-ending workweek. Maybe Ben's ultimatum was just what the doctor ordered. Maybe she would just give it a try.

"I can't set deadlines for you," Ben said, surprised by

Rita's calm—and hopeful—response. "Hell, from what you've told me, the whole ITC network will collapse if you ever leave. I wouldn't want that responsibility on my shoulders." He winked and gave her a quick kiss before releasing her. "Just don't take too long. Neither of us is getting any younger. And who knows, I might just find some sweet young thing who finds a middle-aged semi-well-known writer irresistible."

"And I could hardly blame her," Rita said, glad that once again the mood had lightened. "Now, let's have something to eat. I'm starving and I don't want to be too late getting back to the city."

"You're going back tonight?" Ben asked incredulously.

"I've got work to do, as usual," she lied. Despite her brave front, Rita was confused. She needed to get away from Ben and Jeannie and the house. She needed to be alone, to examine her life in New York for what it was really worth. Giving it all up would be a big step and she had to be sure that it was the right one to take.

"Then while you're still here, let's talk of nothing but turkey and stuffing and cranberry sauce . . ."

"And pumpkin pie?" Rita asked coquettishly.

Ben's smile vanished and he swept her into his arms. "Jesus, Rita, come back to us," he whispered as he covered her face with kisses. "We can give you everything you want and need."

"Please, Ben," Rita mumbled as she kissed him, then gently pushed him back, "you promised."

"And I'm a man of my word," he said bowing low before her. He righted himself and proffered his arm to her, and when she was safely secured he escorted her out into the hallway toward the kitchen. "Mrs. Flannagan, prepare yourself for Mr. and Mrs. Ben Elliott," he announced, "the hungriest man and wife in the world."

Rita looked at Ben and wondered how she had ever given him up. Yet, as he led her into the kitchen where Jeannie sat playing on the floor with Bert and Ernie Sesame Street dolls, she wondered if this would still seem quite so perfect if she gave up New York and *Time Nor Tide*.

Rita drove her own car back to New York. She drove too fast down the Merritt Parkway hoping that the speed and the danger would stave off her anxiety about Ben a little longer.

It had been a perfect day! Perfect. Thanksgiving dinner was

rich and irresistible and she'd eaten far too much. Jeannie was subdued and spent much of the meal smiling at Rita. Rita and Ben had talked and laughed the way they had during the carefree days of their courtship. The warm feelings should have lasted into the evening. But they didn't.

"By the time Rita eased her car into the apartment building's parking garage, she was again entangled in the net of self-doubt that always seemed cast out for her in Connecticut. Ben wanted her to take her rightful place at home.

Would he insist she sell her penthouse? And what about *Time Nor Tide?* Would her family responsibilities force her to abandon the show? Rita wanted to believe Ben had only her best interests at heart, but for the past eight years she'd left Ben with the burden of raising Jeannie while she struck out on her own. Surely he had to resent her for that, if not for the success she'd achieved, which had to be part of it, too. After all, he'd only published two novels in the same length of time she'd made it all the way to the cover of *Time* magazine and many other popular publications too numerous to mention. Still . . .

Minutes after walking into the empty apartment she was pacing, restless. Where could she go? It was still early. She had to do something, go out, or invite someone over. But who? Mentally she ticked off names on the small list of people she considered good friends and drew a blank. Some were away, some she wasn't talking to, others were sure to be busy on a holiday as important as this one. There had to be *someone* in New York she could talk to.

Reluctantly, Rita went to the phone and dialed Mel Jacobs's number. She didn't make a habit of socializing with her employees, but Mel would do in a pinch.

"It's Rita," she announced when he finally answered the phone. "Am I interrupting?"

"We're just finishing our Thanksgiving dinner."

"You and Wendy?"

"*And* Al Peterson." Mel recognized Rita's tone of voice. She was bored, looking for a playmate, and that immediately gave him an idea. He knew a way out of this interminable dinner. "Al's quite taken with you, Rita," he said. "At least he's talked of nothing but *Time Nor Tide* since he walked in."

"That's very flattering, I'm sure." Unconsciously, she

straightened the collar of her blouse. "It must be *hell* for you," she quipped.

"I can take it." He peered into the dining room where Wendy was gushing over Peterson like a schoolgirl. "Would you like to speak to him?"

"I . . ." Rita's voice caught in her throat.

"Be a sport. Believe it or not, I think he's a little starstruck."

The arrow hit its target dead center. "Put him on . . . and love to Wendy."

Rita handled Peterson's arrival at her door in a most businesslike fashion even though the invitation was purely personal. She had recognized him as a real pro—both in talent and in personality—and that meant treating him with a kind of deference.

"You're a very intelligent man, Mr. Peterson . . . and a very good writer. It's a winning combination," she complimented after they had exhausted every topic from television to the Jacobses' Thanksgiving dinner.

"Does that mean I really have a chance with *Time Nor Tide?*" His tone was cocky, but still charming.

Rita tilted her head in his direction. "The first time we met you promised no baloney between us, so don't start now."

He laughed at her forthrightness. "Okay. So, I've got the feeling I might be around *TNT* for a while. How's that?" He eased back against the couch's soft pillows skillfully maneuvering his arm behind her, yet maintaining a polite distance. "You're right: I am a good writer. But your show isn't the run-of-the-mill soap, either. And, of course, there's the question of us." Rita's eyebrows arched majestically. "I wasn't sure we'd hit it off as well as we have."

"You know as well as I that 'our relationship' could be carried out by mail." Peterson's assertiveness was beginning to excite her.

"Remember, Rita—no baloney." His arm slipped down, just grazing her back. "I don't go for the 'family' bullshit everyone associates with soap operas. Personal antagonism on any level is the quickest way to die in the ratings."

Rita turned and faced him, ready for another verbal joust, but Peterson startled her by gently putting a finger on her lips. "Mrs. Elliott, did anyone ever tell you you talk too much?" he whispered as he ensnared her, his mouth seeking out the warmth of her lips.

Rita resisted for a moment, then sank deeply into Al's embrace, feeling for a moment more like a child in the protective arms of a parent than a woman being seduced. Peterson kissed her tenderly, passionately, and, finally, with great urgency. When he fondled her breasts and began to undo her blouse, Rita stopped him by taking his hand and leading him into the darkened bedroom.

If there had been any doubts in Rita's mind about hiring Al Peterson, they vanished as he undressed her and carried her swiftly to bed, his soft words of love making her forget everything, except that she was a woman.

BOOK TWO

8

The Hewitt living room was peaceful. The late afternoon sun shone through the windows bringing the couch and a large section of the floral carpeting into brilliant relief. Penny Hewitt, basking in the sun on the couch, was just pouring herself a cup of tea. She looked tired and worried. Despite the tranquillity of the scene it was obvious something was bothering her. Penny was remembering an earlier incident:

She and Frank Cameron were sitting at a table in the hospital cafeteria. He was smiling evilly. "Your aunt and me have a little business deal going, but I think maybe she's thinking of welching on me. I want you to put in a good word for me. Will you do that, honey?" his eyes darted up and down Penny with frankly animal lust.

Penny recoiled at his familiarity. "I don't know what you mean."

"You don't have to understand, just pass along the message." With the speed of a rattlesnake hitting its prey, Cameron's hand darted out and ensnared Penny's. "Tell Mrs. D. if she don't get a move on there's going to be plenty of trouble for her . . . and for those she loves."

As she recalled this, Penny looked more worried than ever. "What am I going to do?" she asked out loud, sadly shaking her head at her plight. Cameron had been following her at the hospital and once she'd even seen him outside her home. Penny was terrified.

At that very moment the doorbell rang and Penny, startled, turned toward the door, expecting the worst. She quickly checked her watch, put her teacup down, and cautiously tiptoed to the door. When the bell rang again she answered. "Who is it?"

"It's Ted. Got a minute?"

Penny's shoulders sagged with relief as she opened the door to her unofficial fiancé.

"Hi," he said softly. "Mind if I come in?" Ted Reynolds was tall and handsome, and his hospital whites clearly defined his muscular body. His blue eyes sparkled with delight at seeing the woman he loved. He smiled widely as he walked into the living room. "I had a few minutes off from the hospital and I . . . well . . . I just wanted to see you." He hovered near the couch, waiting to be asked to sit down.

"That was very thoughtful. Sit down, please."

"Thanks."

"Would you like a cup of tea?"

"Tea would really hit the spot. I tell you, Penny, I've been so busy this morning I've barely had time to breathe."

"But you love your work," she said, handing him a teacup.

"You're right, of course. But sometimes it does me good to gripe a little." He sipped the tea. "That's just what I needed." He rested the cup on his knees and smiled at Penny. "I really stopped by to tell you how much I enjoyed the other night."

"Raffles is a beautiful restaurant," Penny quickly sidestepped the compliment.

"I didn't notice," Ted pushed on. "But I did notice how beautiful you were. And I wanted to thank you for allowing me to take you out."

"Why wouldn't I want to go out?" she asked.

"You did turn down my invitation rather forcefully that day in the cafeteria."

"I'm sorry, Ted. It's just that, well, sometimes trying to sort out my real feelings is so confusing." His reference to the cafeteria once again reminded Penny of Frank Cameron; she could still feel the coldness of his hand on hers. It was all so much like the night she had been raped!

"Look, Penny, if it helps, we all feel confused about our emotions at one time or another . . . even me," he smiled warmly.

Penny laughed. "You know, Ted, hearing you say that actually makes me feel better."

"That's because I'm good for you, Penny . . . if only you'd believe that." He moved closer.

For just a second, terror flickered through Penny's eyes. She quickly changed the subject. "Tell me, truthfully, how is work? You do look tired."

Ted pulled back, knowing he had lost this round to Penny's fear. "Lavinia Winthrop was admitted to emergency this morning, and all hell broke loose." He lifted the teacup awkwardly from his knee and the teaspoon rattled around the saucer then dropped to the floor.

For several seconds there was silence, then Penny Hewitt covered the accident with her next line. "Is Lavinia all right?"

Joe Ericson looked at Nancy Carson, and his concentration on the scene vanished. "There was a car accident and it's just too early to say. She's in pretty bad shape." The words almost choked him.

"Sugar?" Nancy asked politely.

"Sugar?" Ericson exploded. "What the hell do you mean sugar?"

Nancy jumped back, startled that he had stepped out of character. "I'm *supposed* to ask you if you want sugar because, according to the script, you're *supposed* to be stirring your tea," she screamed back at him.

"And just how the fuck can I stir my tea when the goddamned spoon is on the floor?"

"Use your finger, meathead," Nancy shouted, getting up from the couch. "You're the big-time actor, Joe, the *star*—improvise! Stick your dick in it for all I care."

"You stupid bitch! You've been in a lousy mood all morning." Ericson carelessly dropped the cup and saucer on the coffee table. They shattered, splattering tea over everything.

"Just what the hell do you two think you're doing?" Gordon Tate's angry voice, doubly amplified by the SA system, pierced the uneasy silence on the set. "In case you've forgotten, I'm on a tight schedule."

"And because of *your* goddamned stinking tight schedule, Gordy, I drop a spoon and you keep the cameras rolling."

"What did you expect, Joey? A retake?" Tate's voice dripped sarcasm.

"You're fucking right that's what I expect. What does it take to make you stop rolling? Maybe the set falls down, or

Nancy here pees in her pants?'' Ericson glowered into the ''hot'' camera, knowing his unseen adversary in the control room was watching every move.

''You're a pig, Ericson, you know that?'' Nancy hissed as she fumbled in her nearby purse for a cigarette.

''No smoking on the set, goddammit!'' Tate momentarily lost control. Then, as quickly as his temper flared, his voice became conciliatory, almost fatherly. ''Now, Joe, tell me what's really bothering you.''

''This whole, lousy shoestring operation bothers me. Christ, Gordy, ever since Christmas everyone has been so concerned with saving time and money that we tape and air any fuckup that doesn't make us look like complete fools.''

''Sorry. That's not my department,'' Tate announced from inside the control room, half-turning his chair to catch Alex Thorpe's eye. ''That's the way things are. Now, if you're ready to continue . . .''

Ericson stood up and moved closer to the camera. ''No, I'm not ready. I'm not going to let this lousy soap ruin my reputation. I've had it up to here''—his hand sliced across the tip of his nose—''with your half-assed production values. How does it look for me—and the others—to be connected with this pushcart operation?''

Alex decided now was the time to step in. He had been watching Ericson's most recent blowup with an anxious mixture of disgust and admiration. The actor was an egomaniac who had convinced himself that *Time Nor Tide*'s audience cared as much about improving the quality of the show as he did. On the other hand, Joe Ericson was a professional who cared deeply about his work. And for that, Alex could not fault him. Besides, he was right. Nan Booth's Christmas present to *TNT* had been a devastating budget cut—effective immediately. It was now only the beginning of the second week of January, yet the tight money had already begun to tarnish *TNT*'s gleaming exterior. Personally, Thorpe identified with Ericson's disgust. But in the end, Alex was a company man. And that meant defending ITC against all detractors.

Alex pushed his chair back. ''I'll handle this,'' he announced taking one last look at Ericson's angry face on the LINE monitor used to show what was being captured on tape. ''Give me ten minutes, Gordy, then call for Nan Booth,'' Thorpe joked ironically.

"In a pig's ass," Tate replied, almost under his breath.

Since her first sojourn to Studio One in late September Nan had become a regular visitor to the set. The October and November ratings had been the lowest ever and Nan's presence was a constant reprimand. She had confided to Alex that her one wish was to boost *TNT*'s status with the "big boys upstairs," yet the budgetary cuts originating from her office were beginning to cripple production. Ericson was right: Quality *was* suffering. And it didn't take long to see the effects of Nan's interference. Craftsmanship began to slip as the care put into production was lost to expedience. Nan may have thought she was whipping the show into shape, but Alex knew she was slowly, inexorably killing it.

He stepped into the brilliant light of the set, and paused, waiting for his eyes to adjust. The control room was a quiet, dark womb where the producer, director, and a select group of highly qualified technicians controlled the chaos of taping the show. Being wrapped in that security, eyes focused on the vast array of television monitors that were the only link to outside reality, accustomed Alex to being in instant electronic control of his world. One command from him and a Joe Ericson vanished from the screen—and from his life—at least momentarily. Dealing with the real man was another story.

As he strode onto the Hewitt living room set, Thorpe felt imminent disaster in the air. Ericson's violent outbursts and temper tantrums were a tangible symptom of the general discontent at *TNT*. Anarchy was becoming the rule rather than the exception.

"Joe, Joe," Alex called out warmly, putting his arm over the actor's shoulder, "calm down. Shouting's not going to get us anywhere."

Ericson pulled away from him. "You tell him, Alex. Tell our esteemed director that he's turning out a piece of crap. Tell him."

"Cool off, Joe. Come on, let me buy you a cup of coffee." As Thorpe followed the actor offstage, he winked into the camera for Tate's benefit.

Over bad coffee from an urn hidden behind the Hap Reynolds's set Thorpe listened with exaggerated interest to Ericson's list of complaints.

"It's not just the hit-and-run way the show is being put together, it's the scripts. Jesus Christ, Alex, right in the middle of talking about Lavinia Winthrop clinging to life, Nancy offers me sugar. That's not the way real people act."

"It's a tease, Joe, a way of breaking the tension," he soothed, wondering what "real people" had to do with *TNT*.

"But the fucking tension hadn't even built yet. No, I don't buy it; it's just bad writing. The script sucks." He drained his coffee. "And this isn't the first one. They all eat shit. Christ, Alex, doesn't Rita see that things have changed since the radio days of *Ma Perkins?* Doesn't she watch ABC's Big Three soaps?" The hot coffee momentarily seemed to take the edge off his temper. "Look, all I'm asking for is a decent script and for Gordy Tate to get his ass out of the rut. You've seen the ratings, Alex, *TNT* is going down the tubes. And if you don't think something as sloppy as a dropped coffee spoon *and* a mediocre script aren't two good reasons why, then you're in the wrong business."

Joe was right about the shoddy production values, but until Nan Booth got off their backs, dropped teaspoons would be aired. Script quality was another story entirely. To Alex the writing was no better or worse than it had always been. But assessing scripts was definitely not his métier. An actor—a Joe Ericson—was more likely to pick up on deteriorating quality . . . and there was talk that Tom Wesley was going off the deep end with his drinking and that Mel Jacobs had some kind of health problem that was beginning to interfere with his work. A stomach problem. Probably an ulcer. No, it was preposterous to imagine Rita Martin letting anyone—even her Praetorian guard—compromise her nearly inhuman standards of excellence; particularly when the ITC rumor mill had her locked in a fight to the death with the network over control of *Time Nor Tide*.

"Have patience, Joe. The new year has barely begun. Things will change."

"Bullshit! The Nielsens agree with me. *TNT* is losing its audience."

"The ratings have climbed steadily since the second week in December. And the audience share has gained a whole point." It sounded great, but compared to the first week in January last year the show was still in deep trouble. Even if Rita pulled off her promised coup with the long-awaited Penny Hewitt Caribbean disappearance, it would be months before the ratings improved. And by then it might be too late for all of them.

"The ratings jumped because of the holidays and this Cameron scam," Joe said distastefully. Rick Cologna was a close friend and his dismissal was infuriating. "Once the holiday viewers go back to work and Rick is killed we'll slide back to *sub*normal. I'm sure Rita is hypoing the murder plot for the February sweeps, but she's still in fourth place behind the other networks." He drained his coffee and tossed the cup aside. "When Rick dies, *TNT* dies, too. Jesus, you'd think a woman with as many smarts as Rita Martin would see that Cameron is the only thing keeping this dog alive."

Ericson's arrogance finally shattered Thorpe's patience. "That's not the point right now. Your actions are. The network—I—won't countenance the kind of behavior you exhibited on the set a few minutes ago. No one in this business is indispensable," he said harshly.

"Do I take that as a threat?"

Alex studied Ericson for a second. "Take it as a statement of fact."

Joe shrugged. "And I'll tell you something. I'm not the only one on the set who's discontented. I'm ready to walk and others are too. Take *that* as another statement of fact."

Before there was a chance to go further, Ericson stormed off. Alex's first impulse was to call Rita for reassurance, but then he reconsidered. With the network breathing down her neck about *TNT*'s failing numbers she already had enough to worry about. Since Christmas she had barricaded herself in her office and disappeared from sight. She wasn't taking any calls. Even if he did escape detection by her secretarial early warning system and broke through to her, what would he say? No one dared to suggest to Rita Martin that the scripts were becoming mediocre. Except for one person, that is.

Alex finished his coffee and hurried back to his office. He wasn't going to work himself into a rage because Rita was giving him the silent treatment. He had her best interests at heart, but he'd seen her paranoia at work before, and frankly, he was sick of it. There was someone else to do the dirty work—neatly, discreetly, without mention of his name at all—someone who would appreciate his concern and who was in a position to reward him a hundredfold if the backstage rumors proved true and Rita was given her walking papers when her contract expired in June.

He closed the door to his office and without hesitation dialed Nan Booth's private number.

* * *

"I wouldn't worry too much about it, Alex. Ericson's contract is up in a few more months. When we start talking money he'll come to his senses," Nan assured her agitated caller.

"Don't count on it. He was pretty steamed up. I know Joe fairly well, and he's a stickler for production details."

"All right, I'll take that into consideration when I talk to him. Anything else?"

"You bet. Ericson's bitching about the scripts, says they're lousy, badly written . . . old-fashioned."

"Since when did Joe Ericson become a Pulitzer Prize—winning author? That is definitely not his domain," she snapped, quickly jotting down a note. "Do you agree?"

"I have to admit the ratings seem to indicate he's right."

Nan wrote Alex's name on her memo pad, then *x*'d it out with bold strokes of her pen. "Look, if there's any more trouble from Ericson, call me immediately. You've done a good job, Alex. Thanks."

She leaned back in her chair and smiled. So, Alex Thorpe had seen the handwriting on the wall. And like a true rat, he wanted Nan to know he would be the first to desert the sinking *TNT* ship. If Alex and the others in Rita's charmed circle were a seismograph of the show's inner stability, there was going to be an 8.3 quake one day very soon!

Nan lit a cigarette and scanned the latest confidential memo from Al Peterson. These biweekly reports, ostensibly "just to keep in touch," were actually payment for services rendered and reminders of promises yet to be kept.

Nan,

Tom Wesley's on the brink of dissolution. Rita now considers him a liability. His work backlog has created a definite bottleneck and Rita is exhausting herself in an effort to keep the situation under control.

Mel Jacobs is curiously lethargic and has become a problem in his own right by his absenteeism. Stomach problems. Rita finally insisted he get a complete medical checkup.

Since giving up on Goodspeed Rita is short-tempered and irritable. She's cheered by the good ratings since the Cameron "murder" story got under way, but knows it will take more than that to reestablish her. She feels the Penny Hewitt Caribbean story is her ace in the hole. I wouldn't be surprised if Rita tried something desperate to save her neck.

A.P.

Nan shook her head in wonder. She had pegged Peterson from the start as ambitious, but the depth of his treachery impressed her. The mundane crap about *TNT* he had learned at the office, but the really important stuff *had* to have been revealed in bed. Nan didn't care how Peterson really felt about Rita, as long as he kept the information coming. Nan filed the memo with the others, thinking as she did that Peterson, for all his cunning, had made one mistake: He should never have put anything in writing.

Now Nan leafed through her morning phone messages. There were two from Rita. In the past, all this attention from Mrs. Elliott would have been flattering; no longer. When Goodspeed made it clear his special guardianship of Rita Martin was terminated, she simply turned her attention to Nan. That Rita was scared was gratifying; that she called once or twice a day was simply annoying. Nan tossed the messages out and turned her thoughts to a new instrument of sabotage: Joe Ericson.

Right now an irate actor could be of more use to her than a lame-duck head writer.

Nan let two days pass before calling Ericson into her office. But in that time, his fury had not abated.

"It's a goddamned cheat, that's what it is. Everything about *Time Nor Tide* is steeped in hypocrisy," Joe Ericson fumed.

"Now let's not go overboard," Nan soothed. "Calm down and tell me exactly what the problem is."

"I don't want to calm down! I want to stay hopping mad, so I don't forget the issue—quality versus quantity. I won't be bought off this time," he said self-righteously. "Why is it that every flunky in television thinks all you have to do is wave a roll of greenbacks, and everyone will compromise his standards? Maybe that's how it is with some assholes, but not with me, not by a long shot."

Sprawled in the chair before her, Ericson reminded Nan of a second-rate James Dean. He exuded the same sullen arrogance, demanded perfection, and displayed vociferous disdain for company politics and bureaucratic rules. The only thing Ericson lacked was Dean's talent. Nan disliked Joe intensely for his vulgar, showy ego, but she found his anger exhilarating and actually admired him for his unwillingness to compromise. And whether he knew it or not, his discontent was going to do her a big favor.

"So you're not going to complain about money? That will be refreshing," she teased.

"If you want to hand me a thousand more a week I won't complain, but that's *not* why I'm here." For the moment his anger dwindled and his handsome face looked deceptively adolescent.

"Then what *is* it?" Nan coaxed carefully. "If you have a legitimate complaint, I'll see what I can do."

He smiled easily now, the actor in him once again taking over. "I took this lousy job with *TNT* because I was promised that the part of Ted Reynolds was about to take off. I deserve a leading role, but took second best because ITC—and Rita Martin—promised Ted would emerge as a pivotal character. And, goddammit, I'm still at my twice-a-week minimum slogging my way through the same old mundane crap every day." He shook his head in disgust and stared beyond Nan, for the moment lost in his thoughts.

But Nan needed him angry. "Everything Rita promised you was true . . . at the time. Things have changed. Sorry." She sounded helpless.

"And just what the hell does that mean?" Ericson pulled himself upright in the chair, coiled as if to strike.

"It simply means that Rita hasn't come up with a good story line for you yet." The Penny Hewitt/Ted Reynolds story projection would make Ericson a star, but there was no need for him to know about that. He was only good if he thought he was getting shafted.

Ericson pounded the arm of the chair with his fist. "I should've known. When it's all said and done everything comes back to Ma Martin. What is her problem . . . other than she's crazy as a loon?"

"Let's not go too far, Joe. Rita may have her idiosyncrasies, but . . ."

"Fuck her idiosyncrasies! I want a new contract in May. I want a larger part in *Time Nor Tide*. I'm sick of playing that pussy-whipped wimp Ted Reynolds," he yelled. "Sorry if I've offended you, Nan, but this is my *career*," he backed off a bit, still close to hysteria. "Do you understand?"

Nan shook her head hopelessly. "Any change in your contract will have to be sanctioned by Rita. And I can't very well step in and demand she give you a three- or four-appearances-a-week minimum, can I? That would be network interference," she intoned sanctimoniously.

"So, until Ma Martin decides it's time to come to her senses, I sit around and rot, is that it?" He shook his head. "Maybe I should talk to her myself."

"Don't." Nan didn't want that. Rita would certainly tell Ericson about the Caribbean story and, at the same time, tumble to Nan's cat-and-mouse game. "Rita's a fair woman, but she has her rules. Rule number one is, all contact between actors and writers be kept at a minimum. If there is contact, it must be done through the network—me." She smiled. "I know how tough it is playing a back-burner story, but in time . . ."

"Back burner? I'm not even near the stove."

Nan laughed involuntarily.

"You may think it's funny, not me! When I leave you and Rita Martin holding the bag, you'll both be laughing out of the other sides of your mouths," Ericson threatened.

Nan let that one pass—for the time being. "What do you think is wrong with *TNT*?"

"Do you watch the show?"

"Every day," she answered warily.

"Well?" He leaned forward and spoke very confidentially. "I sometimes feel I'm playing an extended run of *East Lynne*. I'm surprised our villains don't wear handlebar moustaches and tie people to train tracks." He sneered at the thought.

"Don't you think the average viewer wants to escape the harsh realities that surround her?" she probed, for the moment playing the devil's advocate. "I thought that's what made *TNT* such a success."

"Of course they want to escape reality, but not the way Rita handles it. Shit, look out the window, read any newspaper or watch television newscasts; the world is in a mess. Revolution is just around the corner, but *TNT* still shows Laurelton as though time stood still somewhere in the mid-sixties, even earlier. Today's values are very different."

Nan shook her head. "Sorry, Joe, I don't follow you."

"Viewers still want to escape through love, romance, candlelit dinners . . . sex; but they also want to see a world they can identify as their own. After all, soap opera fans are intelligent; they don't live in a vacuum."

"You might have something there," Nan complied uneasily. Ericson's analysis of *TNT* duplicated her own. Only he wanted to spread the word that love painted with bold, realistic strokes attracted a larger audience than the Norman Rockwell version, and Nan needed to keep it quiet.

"Why don't you—the network—do something about Rita? Or have you started already?" he queried slyly, watching for some giveaway.

Nan remained impassive but she felt a jolt of anxiety. "Started *what* already?"

"Do you really think your expeditions down to the set go unnoticed? The grapevine has it you've been telling old Gordy Tate how to direct." Ericson's eyes twinkled mischievously.

"That's the trouble with rumors, Joe. Once they get started they get blown all out of proportion. I was merely scouting out the situation to see what—if anything—could be done to jazz up production," she explained, only half-lying. "Telling Tate how to do his job was definitely not part of it."

"Then maybe you *should* come down on Tate—and Alex Thorpe. Neither man has had an original idea since crystal radios were in vogue. And talk about pussy-whipped! Ma Martin has them both in her back pocket. They're nothing more than dead weight, Nan."

Ericson was beginning not only to overstep his bounds but to sound like Nan herself. It was time to remind him who was boss. "That's enough. I sympathize with your predicament, but we can't completely redo *TNT* just to get your name up in lights." It was a stinging blow, gently placed. "I promise to take your ideas into consideration. Believe me, no one wants *Time Nor Tide* to succeed more than I do."

"Careers don't thrive on promises . . . from anyone," he countered. "Unless there are some changes in my favor pretty damn soon, ITC—and Ma Martin—are going to dig up a new Ted Reynolds come May."

Nan walked him to the door. "Don't be too hasty about making any career decisions. You've got a solid audience following, and the network has always liked you. Give me some time to work on it," she encouraged, resting her hand on his arm—a ploy that usually inspired confidence.

"If things haven't changed by May, I'm walking," he reiterated. "Thanks for taking the time to see me, Nan."

She returned to her desk exhilarated by the sheer drama of the con game she was playing. By not placating Joe Ericson, Nan had taken another decisive step in placing herself as an obstacle between *Ma* Martin and the network. Everyone assumed Nan automatically channeled information from Rita to Goodspeed and he, in turn, assumed she passed his pronouncements back on down the line. Her careful manipulations since the beginning of December, however, were now producing a bottleneck of communication with Nan at the center. There was always the danger of a screw-up—Ericson could go directly to Rita with his grievances, or Rita herself might storm Jim Goodspeed's office—but Nan was confident that the predictably slow-moving bureaucratic process would provide her with an impenetrable cover.

So her course was set: promote as much confusion and dissension in and around *Time Nor Tide* as possible.

After reviewing her meeting with Ericson, Nan decided it would be politic to use this bitter exchange to plant another seed of doubt in Goodspeed's mind about Rita and the whole *TNT* operation. She picked up the phone and punched out his extension. "It's Nan Booth, Sally. Is he in?"

"I'm sorry, Miss Booth. He can't be disturbed right now." The secretary's voice faltered just long enough for Nan to realize that Goodspeed was probably in the middle of his afternoon meditation.

"Thanks, anyway," she said, hanging up. Now was the perfect time to catch him. She headed for the door.

Nan rushed past Goodspeed's secretary and barged into his office. The curtains were pulled against the afternoon sun. The room was warm and diffusely lit. Goodspeed lay on the couch, his eyes closed. Nan's intrusion shattered his concentration. "Sally, I told you to stay out!" he growled.

It's Nan. I wouldn't have disturbed you, but it's important we talk." She found a chair near him and waited while he regained full consciousness.

"What's up?" He finally pulled himself upright. Nan was so goddamned pushy, he thought.

"We're heading for real trouble with *Time Nor Tide*."

His groan was audible. "What is it *this* time? Christ, doesn't a day go by without you complaining about Rita Martin?"

"It's Joe Ericson. He's threatening to quit." The worry in

her voice had more to do with Goodspeed's reaction to her than to the issue of Ericson.

"He's always threatening to quit. It's in an actor's nature to complain. What is it this time? A burned-out bulb at his makeup table?"

"They do have ego troubles, don't they?" Goodspeed had little patience with actors, so Nan artfully began to direct the conversation away from Ericson, toward Rita. "This time, though, it's more serious, I'm afraid. He's stirring up a hornet's nest of trouble on the set."

"Can't Thorpe handle it?"

"He wants us to step in. Frankly, I wish Alex were less beholden to Rita. I'm up to my neck juggling our new morning schedule; running down to the *TNT* set every other day is starting to cut into my time."

"That's Thorpe's job, not yours. What's the use of having a producer if he can't produce?" There was a silence. "What's Ericson's bitch this time?" Goodspeed grumbled.

"Bad direction, bad writing . . . the usual," she carefully intimated these were actual, ongoing problems, not simply the target of Ericson's wrath and her own cunning.

"Tate again." He focused on the direction, carefully avoiding the writing problem and the sacrosanct Rita Martin. "What do *you* think Nan? What's the problem?"

"Certainly direction is part of it. Tate hasn't done anything new since I've been with ITC . . . and that's four years."

"On a scale of one to ten, how would you rate him?" It was one of his favorite devices.

"Six," Nan answered without hesitation, knowing that to Goodspeed anything under an eight indicated incompetence.

"That bad, huh?" He'd pegged Tate as an eight, exactly. If Nan weren't so hell-bent on making *Time Nor Tide* a showpiece for her own competence he might have been more worried. As it was Jim took her continued agitation as self-serving hype. "Think we should look around for someone else?"

"It'll be tough to justify his removal to Rita," she pointed out, not for a minute questioning the proposal.

"She'll do anything to get back on top. Rita's more sensible than you seem to believe." Nan's badmouthing of Rita to ITC management since Christmas was bordering on indiscretion. Jason Weatherhead may have lapped up the idea of these two women going at each other's throats, but to the others on the fortieth floor, it was just a distasteful display of power plays and ego trips. "In case you hadn't noticed, *TNT*'s ratings are up. It's this Cameron story, I presume."

"Without a doubt." Nan was disheartened by his enthusiasm. "The ratings did pick up the second week of December once it became clear Cameron was to be murdered."

"Let's give the devil her due: The solid numbers for the second week were bettered by the third and fourth weeks. *Time Nor Tide* hasn't been this healthy since the end of last spring. And there's no indication that will change." He'd force the truth out of Nan one way or another.

Nan blushed furiously. "I'd love to believe that, Jim, but those figures are inflated by holiday viewers. I've just checked the local ratings and *TNT* is backsliding again for the first week of January." She hoped next week's national ratings would verify the local slump.

Goodspeed remained silent for a minute. Nan's drive to secure recognition as *TNT*'s possible savior allowed no room for Rita Martin's achievements whatsoever. It was a dangerous situation. Nan, despite all odds, was well liked by Weatherhead and his was the final word about Rita's future. Still, Jim knew Nan would be less ruthless if he let her see he was on to her dirty tricks. "What's happened to the Penny Hewitt story?" he demanded.

"What?" she mumbled, caught totally off-guard.

"You were sent a polish of the *Time Nor Tide* Caribbean story just after Christmas. What's its status? And where the hell is that list of projected location costs I wanted extrapolated?"

"I'm still compiling a breakdown, Jim. It takes time," Nan lied smoothly. The figures were on her desk, but she'd just have to stall Goodspeed until she came up with another way to kill the story. Nan had hoped to sabotage Rita's tropical fantasy financially—by pleading extravagant production costs, tight money, etc.—but, based on previous years' spending, *TNT* had actually come in *under* budget at the end of the fiscal year, thanks to Nan's own corner-cutting. It was disheartening to think she'd actually done something to *help* Rita Martin, but it was a mistake Nan promised herself never to make again.

"Then what about the story projection? What'd you think of that?" Goodspeed grumbled.

"It's a little farfetched, but I passed it on to broadcast standards . . . and to Weatherhead," she admitted slowly.

"And why did you do that? It seemed innocuous enough to me." The standards department—the censors—had an uncanny way of condemning anything that was sent to them for inspection, particularly if an accompanying letter indicated condemnation was called for.

Nan fought to keep control of her voice. Jesus, she knew he'd grill her about that, yet she'd walked into his office without a prepared answer. "I felt the story would play, but that it was politically iffy."

"What the hell are you talking about?"

"Jim, the plot is set in some banana republic. It's about rebels—antigovernment rebels. Either directly or indirectly the story is going to be for or against them . . . and that raises serious political issues about ITC's policies of neutrality."

Nan looked so smug, so self-assured once again that Goodspeed's first impulse was to pull her from the chair and shake her. She was so goddamned perfect. And so unflinchingly lethal. "That's a crock of shit, Nan, and you know it," he fumed.

"Now just a second Jim, I resent that."

"And I resent this campaign of yours to destroy the reputation of a woman who has been so influential in establishing the network!"

" 'Has been' is right." Nan gripped the arms of her chair, surprised that this confrontation had come about so suddenly. In her mental timetable thrashing things out with Goodspeed was still several months down the road. "I have nothing against Rita personally, nor am I out to destroy her reputation. I am, however, out to sweep aside the debris that has collected over the years. Rita Martin has been relegated to a safe corner where she has been invulnerable. People come and go around her, yet she remains untouched. I have no objection to favoritism—the industry thrives on it—but in this case, it's making me look bad and I won't stand for it."

So, it was finally out in the open. And that presented Goodspeed with one hell of a problem: ease Nan's pressure by explaining that if the February sweeps didn't reestablish *Time Nor Tide* as a contender for most popular soap, Rita was out, or let Nan stew in her own juices, creating enemies and hard feelings with each passing day. He opted for the latter. The die was already cast. The February ratings would speak for themselves. No matter how much he pushed to keep Rita or Nan pushed to dump her, the A. C. Nielsen Company was the final arbiter. And Goodspeed disliked Nan just enough to hope that she cut her own throat between now and then.

Nan's features softened. She managed a smile. "I'm sorry, Jim. I've been under a great deal of tension with this whole *Time Nor Tide* mess." The smile deepened. She sat back and languidly crossed her legs. "I have one great fault: I love ITC and would do anything for it."

"That makes two of us," he said perfunctorily. There was no way he was getting into a chummy conversation with Nan at this point. "Look, I understand your position . . . and I sympathize. Do a complete recommendation for me about available directors, producers . . . anything, anyone that might inject some life into *TNT*."

"Does that include writers?"

What she meant was head writer, Rita's job. Goodspeed hesitated for a moment and then conceded, "Everything." After all, there were many options. Firing Rita was just one of them. And if Nan was as company-oriented as she said, keeping Rita on wouldn't bother her in the least. "Get it to me by next week, Nan. Once this damned holiday season is over, we've got to get moving on this."

"Sure thing." She fled the office without looking back. With Goodspeed's blessing, Nan would now reorganize *Time Nor Tide*—on paper—and set into motion the plan that would catapult her to the top . . . and to California.

The following Friday morning as Goodspeed read Nan's recommendation for the restructuring of *Time Nor Tide,* Rita invited Sandy into her office for coffee before officially beginning the day. Rita usually reserved these *kaffeeklatsches* for times when she was feeling expansive, generous. But today she was more unsure of herself than she'd been in years and she needed Sandy by her side, if only for a momentary distraction.

" 'Disco attire,' indeed," Rita sneered, holding her invitation to the *TNT* Valentine's Day party at arm's length as though it might infect her. "In my day, Sandy, it was either 'formal' or 'informal.' " The fact that she and her secretary were almost the same age eluded her. Rita spoke to anyone not her business peer as though they couldn't possibly be a contemporary.

"I don't know what 'disco attire' means to anyone else, but to me it means the slinkiest Von Furstenburg my budget will allow." Sandy loved just chatting with her boss. "I get to dress up once a year, so I'm going all out."

"I'm sure you'll be lovely," said Rita, patronizing her unconsciously. "One of Diane's little dresses: absolutely the right choice."

"And what do you intend to wear?"

"The Halston will have to do." She laughed at her own irony. "You're really looking forward to this, aren't you?"

"Quite frankly . . . yes. It's my only chance to meet our actors."

"Why would you want to meet *any* actor?" Rita sniffed. "They're just like you and me . . . worse," she amended.

"But they're so glamorous . . . and handsome. That Joe Ericson is a hunk; I'd love to get to know *him* better," Sandy replied. "Besides, they're my family. I've been watching them for so long that I feel I know every one of them personally."

"That's a tribute to their talent, not to their personalities. Believe me," Rita said, thinking particularly of Rick Cologna, "they have very little to do with the characters they play—no matter how convincing they are on the air."

"Well, I'll just hold on to my fantasies, thank you very much. The party is a treat for me, Rita. You already lead a glamorous life."

Rita burst out laughing. "You've been fooled by the soap opera magazines. There's not much in my life other than *Time Nor Tide*. And that's the plain boring truth." She shifted around in her chair. "Now, let's get down to business."

Sandy flipped open her note pad. "Tom called in sick this morning. He sounded like death . . . said it was some kind of a flu."

The kind of flu that pours from a bottle, Rita thought. Tom was skating on very thin ice. "And Mel has a doctor's appointment. Anything else?"

When Sandy shook her head, Rita stiffened. In the past—even though it was well before noon—she would have been swamped with calls: Goodspeed, Gordy Tate, and Alex at the studio, actors' agents complaining about money, dialogists needing information. Al Peterson wanting to see her . . . Ben wanting her home. Now there was silence.

"I guess that's it, then. Except that I'm expecting a call

from Nan Booth. Put her through immediately, will you?" Saying it made it seem possible. The simple truth was that Nan had begun to ignore her. Like everyone else.

"Okay, Rita. Will do." Sandy stood up and left.

Alone, Rita lit a cigarette and surveyed the towering stack of scripts on her desk waiting to be edited. Dammit, that was Tom's job! And today he was "sick." Rita was already swamped with plotting the shows that would follow Frank Cameron's murder. And then there was the Penny Hewitt story to be tackled—if Nan ever okayed it. *Time Nor Tide* was no longer the cozy little soap opera she had single-handedly created. It was a monster. And plotting it was a big job . . . too big for one person. Mel, unlike Tom, was really sick. Seeing the doctor should straighten that out, but in the meantime how the hell was she going to cope with running *TNT* all alone?

If only she could put everything else out of her mind and focus on the show, Rita knew she could do it. But she didn't have the strength. For the first time in years *Time Nor Tide* was taking a second place to the personal problems that had begun to obsess her. She'd never be able to settle down to work again until she knew exactly what her role in the Elliott family was to be—if any.

Since Thanksgiving Rita had tried to make a decision that would satisfy both her needs and Ben's wishes, but she'd failed utterly. Each time she made up her mind to embrace Ben and Jeannie, the siren call of her New York autonomy beckoned and grew more difficult to resist. Yet when she did give in to it by planning to forsake her home and family for her career, the truly inconsequential nature of daytime television crystallized in her mind and the choice seemed dangerously fatuous.

Working at home seemed to offer the perfect solution, but Rita feared that eventually her duties as wife and mother would force her to relinquish some of her authority to the network. And right now, in Rita's mind, Nan Booth *was* the network. And giving in to her was unthinkable.

In the end, because Rita didn't know what to do, she did nothing and a decision was made by default, if only temporarily. After Thanksgiving, not only did she stay away from Connecticut for fear Ben would press her for a final answer, but she didn't phone either. When he, too, remained silent, an unspoken understanding seemed to grow between them that Rita interpreted as permission from Ben to continue on as sometime wife and mother, despite his earlier imprecations to the contrary. But as the year's major holidays neared and she still heard nothing, the silence became more ominous. Finally, unable to concentrate on her work, Rita called to say she would come to Connecticut for Christmas and New Year's.

When Rita arrived on Christmas Eve day she immediately saw that things had changed in West Willow—and that she'd misjudged Ben's determination to make her a part of his life, no matter what the cost to him and to Jeannie. Pleading a severe cold, he moved into the guest room leaving Rita alone in their double bed, feeling for the first time in her life that she truly wasn't welcome. On Christmas Day when he barely tried to make her a part of his and Jeannie's festivities, Rita was shattered. Not only because it seemed Ben had given up on her, but also because there was no joy in the triumph of finally being accorded her independence from her family. There was only loneliness. And confusion.

New Year's Eve was no better than Christmas. During the party at Helen and Dave Moore's, Ben deserted Rita for his friends, and she was so miserable she insisted they leave right after their New Year's kiss.

Desperately unhappy, but unable to tell Ben how much his aloofness hurt, Rita remained silent and left for New York the next morning without explanation. They said good-bye as two people who had once cared a great deal about each other, but for whom time had changed—and diminished—all feelings.

As Ben walked back to the house where Jeannie stood waving by Mrs. Flannagan's side, Rita recognized that it was her own inability to trust Ben's love that was destroying their chances for a happy life together. And it also became clear that unless one day soon she made a real decision about what she wanted from her family, what she could do to be a part of it, fate would take over and make it for her. And when that was done, there would be no turning back.

To quell her anxiety during the ride back to New York, Rita concentrated her thoughts on *Time Nor Tide*, but when she derived no satisfaction from her musings, she immediately turned her thoughts to Al Peterson. Their affair, at least, was something over which she had some semblance of control.

But upon arriving back in New York she discovered that her romance had changed, too. Peterson was no longer the "perfect" lover. His interest was obviously flagging and his company—more often than not a result of "royal command"—rarely distracted her from the problems at work, and never kept her from thinking about Ben and Jeannie. Recent cancellations of their standing Friday-night dates had actually hurt Rita's feelings. Was it possible Peterson had noticed her distracted state, or had he simply decided that keeping his distance was the safest way not to get burned?

She shook her head, amazed by her own naïveté. Who was she kidding? Peterson was a user. He might have wanted her to believe he was deeply attracted to her, but she knew better. He was like every other man she had taken to bed. If it wasn't for *Time Nor Tide* he wouldn't have given her a second look. Yet he was a better lover than most. And there *were* times when she almost believed his affection was genuine.

In the beginning Al presented himself as juggler, riverboat cardsharp, Casanova, circus clown, all rolled into one. He amazed Rita with his openness, enthusiasm, and his carefully polished charm. She had expected respect, good times, and enough sex to keep her occupied. She hadn't been prepared for her reaction to him, however. His mere presence cheered her and his sexual athleticism astounded her. She'd always suspected there were men who truly *liked* the company of women, men whose ability to confide in the opposite sex and make them best friends never hampered their sexual cravings. Until Al Peterson stepped into her office—and into her bed—Rita had never met one of these rare animals in the flesh before.

Yet Al was a thorough professional. He treated Rita publicly with the right combination of awe and respect, and though she expected it from others, curiously enough Rita took Peterson's deference as a compliment. The fact that she had "gone public" with him—something she'd never allowed with any of her other men—gave the liaison the validity of a full-fledged affair. There were evenings at the theater, opera, ballet, dinners at "21," movies where they happily ate popcorn like kids. Peterson made her feel young again and helped her fight the battle against her own self-doubt. If only she'd let herself be so free with Ben.

But during the past weeks the anesthetic effect of Peterson's attention had begun to wear off. And Rita saw clearly that the decisions she was hoping to avoid still awaited her. Compounded by others. She would have to decide about her demi-marriage. That in turn would solve the complex equation involving Al Peterson, Nan Booth, and her own position in the ITC hierarchy.

Well, she wasn't one to leave her future entirely in the hands of fate. There were a few things she could do. Dealing with Tom Wesley once and for all was as good a place to start as any.

She went on the attack as soon as he answered the phone. "Tom, what is it this time?"

"The flu. I feel miserable," he groaned. He had a killer of a hangover; not even Rita Martin's wrath could get him out of bed.

"Really, Tom, you spend more time sick in bed than anyone I know. I desperately needed you here today . . . I'm very disappointed you couldn't make it." She could almost feel him squirming on the other end of the phone.

"Believe me, if I weren't so sick I would have been in long ago." Why today, of all days, did she have to bully him? He was so close to the breaking point; had been since Ellie Davis was unceremoniously fired by Rita the week before Christmas.

"I wish I could believe you . . . but I don't. Your personal life is beginning to interfere with my work schedule," she accused, charitably avoiding the word *drinking*.

"I'm sorry you feel that way." Her words were driving him even lower.

"When you come into the office we're going to have a long talk. We can't go on this way. It's too harmful to *Time Nor Tide*. Try to get better soon." She hung up abruptly. That took care of Tom. Now to take care of Nan Booth.

While Nan finished a phone call Rita stole a look around her office. The room was "done" in good art deco furniture. It was comfortable, but sleek, coolly chic in the thirties style Nan seemed to favor. Rita guessed Nan wasn't partial to any hints of softness—femininity?—but was probably reticent to make a commitment to the total depersonalization of high tech. Bauhaus was the magic compromise. Its elegant simplicity was the perfect cover for Nan's true emotional complexity. Nice though it was, the office still reminded Rita of the ladies' room at Radio City Music Hall.

"Game shows will be the death of me," Nan swore as she hung up. "Women who watch them are almost as bad as women who watch . . ." she hesitated long enough to make her insinuation clear ". . . those morning talk shows." She lit a cigarette and made a great show of using one of Rita's ashtrays. "So, what can I do for you?"

"I realized we'd lost touch since Christmas, and rather than call . . ." Her smile proclaimed: Here I am.

"Am I to take it this is a social call?"

"As a matter of fact, I was thinking of dinner."

"What's the occasion?" She and Rita never socialized. And the fabled Mrs. Elliott didn't suddenly decide to expand her guest list without good cause.

"I feel guilty," Rita said, hearing out loud the words she had said to herself all the way up from thirty-five. "I've been so involved with *Time Nor Tide* that I've neglected the human side of this damned business." She nodded toward Nan's cigarettes and, when she got the go-ahead, filched one and lit it. "Maybe it's just the time of the year—I get sentimental during the holidays. Or maybe I just want to stop this tug-of-war you and I seem to be involved in. It's so unnecessary."

Nan's eyes narrowed. Who the hell did she think she was kidding with this humility bullshit? "Quite frankly, Rita, I don't trust you."

Rita had anticipated this response and was ready for it. "That makes us even." She immediately dropped the neighborly tone of voice. "We're two of a kind, Nan. But right now we find ourselves on opposite sides of the fence. Why don't we help one another instead of trying to cut each other's throat?" She leaned back in the chair and inhaled deeply. "Who knows? We might even become friends."

It was a tricky situation. It wasn't unusual at all for high-level cohorts at ITC to fraternize outside office hours. Being a television executive cast one in a special role, gave one membership in an exclusive club. To deny Rita was to antagonize her. But to agree to dinner was to muddy the issues Nan had worked so hard to make clear in her own—and in Goodspeed's—mind. If only Rita weren't so persuasive . . . and good-looking.

"Okay," Nan replied cautiously. "What have you got in mind?"

"Drinks at my place, then dinner out. Next Wednesday."

Nan flipped open her calendar and jotted down R.M., then circled it twice. "You've got it.

"Good. Eight o'clock, Wednesday." She ground out the cigarette. "But we'll talk before then."

Alone in the elevator, Rita leaned against the wall for support. Her heart was beating wildly and a thin layer of sweat had appeared on her brow. Next Wednesday. Five days. Drinks, then dinner. It sounded harmless. But then, most traps did. Her mind jumped ahead to the evening as she envisioned it and her stomach knotted. Until that moment even Rita had never suspected just how far she'd go to ensure a permanent place at *Time Nor Tide*.

9

That same afternoon, Al Peterson lay naked on his bed, half-asleep as the sounds of *Time Nor Tide* washed over him. But his mind was not on *TNT*. It was on Angela Brite. She had been gone for nearly an hour and her perfume still lingered in the room, stirring up fresh memories of lunch. Together. In bed.

That morning, Angela had called to suggest a noon rendezvous. Al quickly agreed despite his later, standing, weekend date with Rita. That Angela would crave sex during her lunch break was not only exciting, but proved to Peterson that in this affair, at least, he was the dominant partner. Like it or not, being in bed with Rita was always, clearly, fucking the boss. The sex was good, not great. With Angela it was always dynamite.

Angela arrived ten minutes early carrying a picnic lunch prepared by Zabar's gourmet delicatessen. Al could hardly keep his hands off her. "You think of everything, don't you?" He relieved her of the bundles, then kissed her savagely on the mouth.

"I *try*," she said coyly. "Now let me see, have I remembered everything?" She sidestepped him and opened the packages: "Cold poached chicken breasts tarragon, ratatouille, french bread, a nice runny Brie, pears . . . and just enough white wine." She cocked her head. "Oh, yes, there is one more thing." Without another word she scooted into the bedroom, took off her clothes, and lay down on the bed. "This should do it."

An hour later, exhausted by sex and stuffed to the gills with the food, they lay in each other's arms. "I miss you, Al Peterson," she whispered softly. "You're the first man I've ever had such a *casual* affair with." She knew there was someone else, but it didn't matter. Peterson still turned her on, and if she could have him only for a quick fuck at lunch, well, that was better than nothing at all.

"I've told you how it is, Angela. Writing *Time Nor Tide* takes up most of my time."

She pressed a finger to his lips. "No explanations, please. We decided a long time ago to lead separate lives . . . no strings attached. I wasn't pumping you for information."

"Then case dismissed," he joked.

When he'd first started "dating" Rita regularly, Al figured he could juggle the two women on alternate nights. After all, he'd carried on multiple relationships in the past; this should be no different. For a few weeks he tried the old routines but they failed miserably. Rita Martin was a new kind of woman for him—strong, demanding, totally self-sufficient, and oblivious to anyone's needs but her own. Rita made great demands on him, and Al acquiesced without question, telling himself it was purely business when, in fact, that was only partially true.

Rita Martin intrigued him. Gradually he had come to realize that she was more bravado than hard-bitten career woman. In fact, in the relatively short time he'd known her, her actions had forced him to cast aside every preconception the media hype had prepared him for. And that mystified him. Dealing with women like Angela was a straightforward proposition: They told him what they liked, what they disliked, where they came from, and where they hoped to go. The Angelas of the world spun endless tales of aspiration, disappointment, and more dreams. They were reaching for a star; Rita had already captured hers and apparently she'd gotten less than she'd bargained for.

Rita seemed to exist solely through her work. She occasionally alluded to her past or made vague references to a personal future, but these recitations sounded rehearsed, or even more like she were speaking about another person, chronicling the history of a *Time Nor Tide* character. These surface details weren't enough for Al—not if he and Rita really intended to get serious—which was the way it had once looked.

Al had forced her to expose herself, to blast away the facade of her celebrity and parade her nakedness for his inspection. It was an arduous process and several times—after severe arguments—it appeared they'd reached the limits of their relationship.

In the end Rita always, unexpectedly, revealed that under the carapace of power she was more human than even he suspected and he was hooked once again.

He discovered that Rita loved the sound of footsteps in autumn leaves and that she hated pistachio ice cream; he discovered she particularly loved licking her salty, buttery fingers after eating popcorn in the movie, and that horses frightened her; he discovered that she had never been to the top of the Empire State Building—and took her there one cold, windy afternoon—and that she had paid for her co-op in cash. And during those first days, he discovered he was truly beginning to care about her.

But Al soon realized that falling for Rita Martin would be like stepping into quicksand. She demanded his total attention and his willing subservience to her own desires. He might have been willing to risk it had he not observed Rita's treacherousness firsthand, over and over again. Her exercise of will ran from getting testy with a waiter to firing Ellie Davis because she had grown tired of her. What was to guarantee Al that Rita wouldn't turn on him like she turned on everyone else? Getting his balls cut off was not his idea of the perfect end to a relationship, so he held back. At least that was Al's conscious reasoning.

The truth was more painful, more complex. Al sensed, as a man who knew women, that he was merely a substitute for someone else. Second best. Rita's every action betrayed her. At first the feeling was hazy, undefinable, yet it permeated their meetings. As it grew familiar it took on a deadening pattern. Rita seemed to act out her part in their relationship for some unseen observer. She had a way of looking at Al, then beyond him, her body tensed as if she half-expected, half-hoped the door would fly open and . . . who? . . . would storm in to rescue her. Rita acted like a woman salvaging her emotional life from a long, disastrous love affair. She never fully gave herself to Al. Her hands touched his body but expected another's. Her words often were tentative, as if she feared she might call him by the wrong name.

In short, Rita was using him. It might not have mattered so much if Angela were still on tap, or if he'd made a move on Wendy Jacobs and she'd acquiesced, but neither was the case (although he wasn't quite ready to rule Mrs. Jacobs out). Rita Martin was his main lady of the moment, and because he found her genuinely appealing under her tough public image and because he instinctively responded to her vulnerability, the ease with which she accepted—demanded—his attention and time while giving so little of herself in return, hurt. He approached Rita as an equal, while she always made it clear that he was little more than a hired hand. And *that* made him furious.

And it made betraying her easy.

The persistent ringing of the phone brought him out of his reverie. "Yeah?" he answered groggily.

"Mr. Peterson, I have Nan Booth for you," her secretary, Don Sheridan, announced.

"Sure, Don, thanks."

"Al, how are you?" Nan came on cheerfully.

"Great." He stretched and yawned.

"I have a couple of things to ask you. First of all, did you get the *Time Nor Tide* Valentine's Day party invitation?"

"It's right here." He rescued the invitation from a mass of mail on the bedside table and reread it:

THE ITC NETWORK
CORDIALLY INVITES YOU AND A GUEST TO THE
ANNUAL *TIME NOR TIDE* PARTY
VALENTINE'S DAY
AT
STUDIO 54
254 WEST 54TH STREET
NEW YORK, NEW YORK
RSVP **DISCO ATTIRE**

"Tell me, Nan, what does 'disco attire' mean?" For a moment he tried unsuccessfully to imagine the network bigwigs boogying through the night.

"I haven't quite figured that out myself. Lots of glitz, I suppose."

"I'm fresh out of glitz," he said warily. Nan was up to something; she always was when she phoned.

"Well, from what I've heard you've certainly got something," she crooned seductively. "You'll be at the party, of course?"

"There's no way I'd pass up the chance to see Mel Jacobs let his hair down in public . . . not on your life." In Al's estimation Jacobs was a tightass *nonpareil*. If it weren't for sexy Wendy Jacobs he would have written Rita's second off as just another noncom in New York's army of angry, dissatisfied businessmen.

"Now, now. Let's not throw stones. Remember, we're just one big, happy family at *TNT*."

Peterson resisted the urge to call her on that one. "What can I do for you, Nan?"

"How about dinner tonight?"

"No good. I've got other plans."

That could only mean Rita Martin. During the maddening holiday season when everything in the world seemed to grind to a halt Nan was forced to all but disappear from Al's life. But now, after winning the battle with Goodspeed, it was time to move further against Rita. And that meant finally assembling the talent that would keep *TNT* running smoothly during the bloodiest hours of the coup, and in the dark days that were sure to follow Rita's banishment. Peterson was to be rewarded for his loyalty to ITC, and in Nan's mind this step was so close to the ultimate victory that she'd already begun to think of her Wednesday dinner date with Rita as the Last Supper. And the thought was delicious!

"I won't take no for an answer, Al. It's business; no one ever made it to the top by working an eight-hour day," she added, trusting he wouldn't force her to make the request a command.

"Okay," he said without hesitation. "How about eight o'clock at des Artistes? My treat."

"Eight o'clock is fine, but let's make it my place."

"Your apartment?"

She'd scored right on target. "And you thought I couldn't cook. See you tonight."

Peterson got up and lit a cigarette to soothe his anger. Damn Nan Booth! She had the uncanny knack of calling at the wrong time. Not that today's date with Rita was anything more than their usual Friday-night roll in the hay, but he liked to believe that his private life wasn't totally controlled by his business aspirations. Between Rita's and Nan's demands that was a tough one to pull off.

So he'd call Rita and lie. It wasn't the first time and probably wouldn't be the last. A little lie between lovers wouldn't hurt. Besides, dishonesty seemed to be the negotiable currency of their affair. He ground out the cigarette, lit another one, and dialed the *TNT* offices.

"It's the best martini in town, Nan," Peterson said with genuine admiration. He swirled the cocktail over his tongue and swallowed. "You surprise me."

"Then you must have me pegged as a teetotaler—or as one of those women who's a dynamo at the office, but all thumbs in a more domestic situation. Either way, you're wrong." She pushed on quickly, not wanting to get snared in the kind of seductive conversation she suspected Peterson was a master at. "I'll let you in on a secret: I use a drop of Scotch instead of vermouth."

"Very outré," he said taking another sip.

"And very lethal," she laughed. "Be careful or you'll never make it to dessert." Nan wanted him a little tanked up, but not so drunk that he wouldn't grasp the magnitude of the offer she was going to make him.

"I'm usually classed as a perfect dinner guest. I never pass out . . . *before* dessert," he informed her with mock indignation.

She passed a tray of hors d'oeuvres. "I'm really grateful for all the help you've given me since Rita hired you." And you crawled into her bed, she added mentally.

His answer was a big smile punctuated by an exaggerated toast with the martini.

"You know, Al," she leaned forward, pressing her arms together just enough to increase the voluptuousness of her breasts, "it's hard for an outsider to know the real workings of *Time Nor Tide*—the way relationships are established, the true pecking order, how efficiently things get done. Getting your information has been a boon to me."

"Sounds like espionage. Am I your spy 'out in the cold'?"

"You writers," she laughed and shook her head, but was immediately serious once again. "I guess you *are* a paid informant—in a way. Do you mind?"

Peterson barely thought of Rita before answering. "No.

Just one thing: The most effective spies usually are paid by *both* sides."

"We'll get to that after dinner. Have another drink. I've got things to do in the kitchen." She left him.

He refilled his glass. Nan was one slippery lady. For the past six weeks—since he filed his first "report"—they had been working as conspirators right under Rita's nose. Yet even alone the elusive daytime vice-president insisted on talking around the central issue of their complicity. What the hell? As long as he got paid off in the end, Nan could insist he wear a mask to all their meetings.

He wandered over to the kitchen doorway and leaned against the frame. From this vantage point he got a clear view of Nan's beautiful ass hugged by the soft material of her dress as she bent over, inspecting a roast in the oven. She was a damned good-looking woman, but there was something about her he didn't quite understand. In business it was all up-front honesty, but on a personal level she still eluded him. Maybe tonight he'd figure her out.

"Do you only think of business?"

She started, then turned on him, her face blazing with anger. "Don't ever . . ." she began, then immediately regained control. "You scared me, Al. Pass me that fork, will you? Now, what were you saying?"

"Your life seems to be totally involved with work. Is that true? Or am I missing the point?"

"I think of business only when I'm awake." She removed the roast from the oven.

"A beautiful woman like you shouldn't always have her mind occupied by Nielsen," he opined, moving closer.

"Open the wine for us, will you?" That got him out of the way for the time being. "I do have a social life, if that's what you want to know. We're having dinner for a second time. I'd call that pretty social."

"Ah, but you said tonight was business, remember?" he countered, struggling with a stubborn cork.

"So I did," she laughed. "So, let's sit down and talk. I want to know something more about the man who is screwing Rita Martin—both literally and figuratively." She sailed past him into the living room.

When they were seated, Al let his anger show. Her last remark had insulted him.

"Has anyone ever called you a first-class bitch?" He caught and held her eyes. They were cold, unfeeling.

"Many times. It's a quality I've nurtured with great success," she replied frankly.

Her honesty diffused his anger somewhat. But he was now as wary as a man who suddenly found himself locked with a sleeping tiger in a room full of alarm clocks. "Why don't you save us a lot of time and tell me exactly what you want."

She had expected, and was prepared for, his hostility. Once Peterson got over his adolescent defensiveness, he'd come around. "You make me sound so calculating."

"Cut the bullshit, Nan. The only reason I accepted this dinner invitation was to find out exactly what your game is."

"Correction: The only reason you accepted is because you have enough sense to see there's no other choice. I've got you by the balls, Peterson." She lit a cigarette, satisfied by his silence that he accepted the truth of her words. "Now, let's be honest with each other—for a change. We're two of a kind: ambitious, aggressive, totally career-oriented. Those shared traits could have made us the bitterest of enemies. Why do you think Rita Martin hates my guts?" She blew a stream of smoke toward the ceiling. "But you've got more sense than Rita. You know I can do things for you that make her favors pale in comparison."

"Let's leave Rita out of this, shall we?" That she was zeroing in on the dark side of his vanity never occurred to him.

"Leave Rita out of this? Impossible. She's at the very heart of what I'm talking about. Tell me you don't aspire to what she has accomplished. She's success incarnate. She's got it all. She's——"

"You're jealous" he proclaimed breaking into her litany. "You're fucking green with envy. Is that what drives you so hard?"

A slight smile curled the corners of Nan's mouth. "Maybe. But that's beside the point. All I want to know is just how committed you are to success."

"Enough to get by."

"In my book getting by isn't enough. Come on, Al, fess up. I know ambition when I see it. I'm just surprised Rita hasn't caught on."

"Rita's too concerned with Rita to notice much of anything else," he answered bitterly.

That was the answer she was hoping for. Whatever he had once been to Mrs. Elliott, Peterson was now just a hired stud. "You must be starving," she said quickly. "Let's eat."

Throughout dinner the subject of Rita Martin was not discussed. Peterson glibly made small talk to fill the void, but at heart he felt he was reading lines from a play whose plot he didn't quite understand. Nan's reticence ordinarily would have pissed him off had he not recognized that she, like Rita, thrived on drama of one sort or another. She demanded the center ring—in this case, achieved by her very silence.

So he carried most of the conversation. He became slightly drunk from the cocktails and wine, and completely intoxicated by the idea of wealth and power to match—no, surpass—Rita's. Everything became rosier and rosier. He found himself telling Nan the mundane details of his background, and to his amazement, she seemed utterly enthralled.

"I was born and raised in Chicago. I even went to college there. After graduation I knocked around for a while, not knowing my ass from my elbow. I finally ended up with Second City—the improvisational group?"

Nan nodded.

"I soon discovered I was better at writing than I was at acting, so I started writing full time. One thing led to another, and I came to New York, made the right contacts, and found myself writing soaps." He finished his postprandial coffee. "And the rest, as they say, is history."

Actually, Nan had barely heard a word. She was thinking about their important, predinner conversation and sizing up Peterson further. She was not so sure she could trust him. He was good-natured and open, actually amusing, much to her surprise. There was something else—a vulnerable, schoolboy quality that was surfacing now while he talked about himself. It was easy to imagine Peterson drifting into an affair with Rita Martin. They were opposites. They were both ambitious to be sure, but the quality of that ambition placed them at opposite poles. If Peterson was handed an opportunity—as Nan was about to do—he would wheel and deal his way to the top. Rita made her opportunities by going in for the kill, then burying the corpse before it was cold.

Nan pitied any man who thought bedding Rita would ensure job security. Rick Cologna, like several others, had learned the hard way that fucking Rita was only part of the

TNT package. Cologna had gotten too big for his britches. But then Cologna was a *schmuck*.

Al Peterson wasn't. His presence here proved it.

Nan had had enough of Peterson's storybook life. She abruptly asked, "How would you feel about a job as head writer for *Time Nor Tide*?"

"So that's it," Al exclaimed, a piece of a Napoleon suspended on the fork in front of his open mouth.

"Slow down! There's no opening now, as you know, but there definitely will be one in the not-so-distant future. I was asking, not offering." She calmly resumed eating her dessert.

"Back up just a bit. I thought hiring writers was Rita's job, not yours . . . or the network's."

"Don't believe everything you hear, Al. ITC is not exactly impotent, you know. In matters that affect *TNT* policy we do make suggestions. True, Rita doesn't always trust our judgment, but then she fancies herself one of the shrewdest businesspeople in the business." She snapped a mouthful of the rich dessert off her fork. "There are ways of making Rita Martin toe the line."

"So you're going to 'suggest' to Rita that she fire Mel or Tom to make way for me? Just like you 'suggested' she hire me in the first place?"

"*I* am not going to suggest anything, and *you* are going to keep your mouth shut," she commanded, annoyed with Peterson's ironic attitude toward her. "All you have to do is be aware that there will be an upper-echelon shuffle at *Time Nor Tide*." She toned her voice down. "So, can you handle it or do I look elsewhere?"

"I can do it with my eyes closed; it's a piece of cake," he rejoined cockily. Shit, head writer at *TNT* was a bigger prize than he'd expected.

"That's all I wanted to hear. Have some more wine." The bait had worked; the rat was in the trap. Now, more than ever. Peterson was hers.

"You're really fascinating, you know that?" He later swung the conversation around 180 degrees. "And I bet you think because of your position and your high style you can keep people at a distance. Maybe that works sometimes, but not now. I'm a very determined man. I won't back off until I know *everything* about you," he promised.

"Let's take our coffee into the living room before you start *that* particular investigation.'' Nan made a tactical move out of his reach.

In the early days, before she confronted her lesbianism—and acted on it—Nan had dated a succession of men. During college and after, she had gravitated toward easygoing, self-assured men who were not afraid to treat her gently and with love, help her to overcome the fear she made apparent but never explained. She detested any self-proclaimed stud out for a quick lay. Even so, sex with men was always rudimentary, often unpleasant, and generally compartmentalized under the heading ''Learning Experience.'' But at least Al Peterson was this former kind of man, and the idea of going to bed with him—if that would further ensure his loyalty—was not *entirely* distasteful . . .

''. . . so what do you think?'' he asked, interrupting her thoughts.

''I'm sorry, what did you say?'' she fumbled.

Al smiled, then winked somewhat drunkenly. ''You weren't listening. A kind of glazed look came over your eyes.'' He moved closer to her. ''. . . and I decided you wanted me to make a pass.''

Nan stiffened. ''As a matter of fact, you're right.''

He pulled her into his arms and nuzzled her hair with his nose before kissing her lightly on the mouth. When she offered no resistance he kissed her again and slid his tongue between her teeth.

A minute later Nan pulled away, her face flushed.

''Anything wrong?'' She looked scared.

''What could be wrong?'' Her hand nervously patted her hair back in place. She was trying to keep her mind focused on how important Peterson was in her plan to topple Rita Martin, but other thoughts—familiar, ugly thoughts—kept intruding.

''You've heard all about me. Now tell me something about yourself.''

''There's really nothing to tell,'' she lied, hoping he would mistake the fear in her voice for excitement. ''Just love me, Al. Love me!'' She pulled him down on top of her.

Peterson's kisses were wet and warm, and as she forced herself to submit to his caresses, he became more aroused. He slipped his hand into her dress, cupped her breast, then rubbed the palms of his hands over her nipples until they stood erect. His kisses faintly stirred Nan's desire, but she always reached a cutoff point with men beyond which her emotions froze and her intellect took over. As Al placed her hand on the hardness in his crotch, that point was reached.

"You'd better go." She wrestled herself free, then snapped the lights back on.

"But I thought . . ." He was angry and bewildered by this sudden turnabout.

"I don't care what you thought," she shouted cruelly to hide her panic.

"Look, Nan, if I'm going too fast . . ." He adjusted the erection in his pants.

"Sorry. It was my mistake. Forget it." She was close to tears and hated him for seeing it.

He was about to protest, but the look in Nan's eyes stopped him. He'd seen that look once or twice before. Jesus, was it possible . . . ? "Guess I'm a little drunk, that's all." He sprang to his feet.

Nan managed a smile. "And I'm keyed up from work." Please, just get out! she thought.

Peterson accepted his coat at the door. "Thanks for a great dinner." He gave her a brotherly kiss on the cheek. "Let's talk."

'Soon."

"Sure. Real soon."

Al walked leisurely home ignoring the icy January wind that assailed him along Central Park West.

I should have seen it from the start, he scolded himself. Christ, imagine me coming on to a *dyke!* Television is a screwy business, but enough is enough. Well, the evening wasn't a total loss. Nan hadn't quite made him an offer, but it was close enough. Head writer. *Time Nor Tide*. And at least a cool hundred thousand a year!

He lit a cigarette and flipped the match into the darkened park. But who the hell was he going to replace?

10

"Dr. Monroe will be right with you, Mr. Jacobs. Have a seat." The cheery receptionist indicated a row of straight-backed chairs against the wall.

Mel forced a smile and sat on a leather couch that looked more inviting. The stomach pains that had begun months ago were now chronic—and worsening. Suspecting his ulcer was flaring up again, and pushed by Rita to get to the root cause of his recent spate of absenteeism, he'd finally broken down and had a battery of tests. Today the results were in. And if the weekend's crippling attack was an indication, the news wasn't going to be good. What a way to start a Monday morning!

Mel leafed impatiently through an ancient *National Geographic*, hoping to ease his nervousness. He hated being sick and he hated doctors even more. They were all so unctuous. And so concerned. Concern! It was nothing more than thinly disguised greed. He'd had his fill of doctors two years before.

That was his fourth year with Rita, the year when it seemed he could do nothing right. *Time Nor Tide* was on the top. It ran without a hitch like the precision mechanism it had become. It should have been a time of celebration, but it was a time of uncertainty. For reasons he never deciphered Rita was restless, discontent. Staff turnovers were a weekly occurrence; secretaries were used up and discarded like paper clips, and dialogue writers barely made their first appearance on the *TNT* crawl when they were fired. No one was safe.

Eventually Rita relented, but too late. Mel had an ulcer that tormented him day and night. Luckily, surgery wasn't required, but he was forced to follow a strict, bland diet and to take daily regimens of medication to counteract the condition. The meals of tasteless food, the oceans of chalky antacids, the scores of annoying tests were the price he'd paid for surviving Rita's reign of terror. It was the worst time of his life, but he'd gotten through it. Just like he'd get through this.

But this time he didn't blame Rita or his job for his condition. He blamed Wendy and her goddamned insolence. And her gambling.

The intercom buzzed and shattered the silence. "Dr. Monroe will see you now," the receptionist chirped.

The inner office was oppressively furnished with heavy leather club chairs, a thick pile rug, and towering bookcases. The decor was meant to inspire confidence. And Dr. Frank Monroe was a caricature of a reliable country doctor: sixty years old, snowy white hair, cheerfully ruddy face, wire-rimmed glasses, a pipe clenched between his teeth. On a corner of his desk was a framed photograph of his family, and on the wall directly behind him various medical degrees were prominently displayed. Monroe looked like he always had good news.

He immediately rose from behind his desk and shook Mel's hand. "How are you feeling today?"

"About the same." Mel sat down and folded his hands in his lap. "Let's not beat around the bush, doc. Is it that damned ulcer again?"

"Not this time, Mel." Monroe was very serious suddenly.

"What is it?"

"Before we get to that, you should know that in the past few years medical science has performed miracles in controlling disease. Things thought incurable only two, three years ago are now responding to treatment."

"Incurable?" Mel's voice diminished for a second, then rose again with his usual acerbity. "Save the lecture. What's wrong?" he demanded. Inside, he felt at the mercy of his fear.

"Your X rays and the tests show a malignancy localized in the stomach."

Mel cringed. "Are you telling me I have cancer?"

"I'm sorry, Mel."

"Are you sure?" Mel's voice was trembling uncontrollably.

Having cancer meant only one thing: death. Slow and painful. Humiliating and degrading.

"There's no doubt."

"How long do I have?"

"That's hard to say. If we operate—successfully—and catch it all, you could lead a normal life." The chances of that were negligible, but there was no point explaining that now—or ever, for that matter.

"And if you don't operate?"

"If it goes untreated . . . then we're talking about a matter of months."

"Months?" The word hung between them like a jarring note in a minor key. This just wasn't happening! Not to him. Not to Mel Jacobs.

"Discuss it with your wife, Mel. There's always a risk with an operation of this kind. If we don't get all the cancer, we may only aggravate the condition . . ." And then it might be a matter of weeks, Monroe thought morosely. At times like this he wished he'd chosen a career in law like his mother had wanted.

"So I'm damned if I do and damned if I don't, is that it?" Mel laughed bitterly.

"As I said before, we're having greater success with operations of this kind. I can't tell you what to do; talk it over with your wife. An illness like this affects everyone, you know."

"Yeah," he said flatly. "I wouldn't want Wendy to suffer too much." All these years he'd busted his ass slaving to give Wendy a nice place to live, enough money so she didn't have to work, and what happened? She played the ponies. And he got cancer.

"Take some time to think about it. If you decide on the operation, I'll reserve a bed at Memorial Sloan-Kettering. In the meantime, I'll write a prescription for the pain."

Mel was shaking. Cancer was something that happened to other people. The thought of his body consuming itself seemed unreal, but the name Memorial Sloan-Kettering made it ring true. The hospital dealt only with cancer. Mel knew it was famous for its research and expertise in dealing with cancer patients.

"Would you like to stay here awhile?" Monroe asked, as he filled out the prescription blank. "You look shaky."

Mel shook his head. "I need to walk, not sit. This isn't

how I expected to start the day." The smile faltered on his lips.

"I've always wished there were an easier way to break the news, but there isn't. I have to be honest from the word *go* for . . . the patient's sake."

"Yeah, there are things I have to start thinking about—wills, bringing insurance premiums up to date, cemeteries—the little things that make life worth living," Mel agreed bitterly. He wanted to be brave but he was nearly choked by fear.

"Try not to lose hope," Monroe said kindly.

"I'll try to look on the bright side of things." He got up from his chair.

"One more thing, Mel, there are psychological ramifications to this disease; anger at the injustice of it all is only normal. Don't be surprised if your temper flares now and then. There are counselors at Sloan-Kettering—experts. You may want to consult one of them." Monroe showed him to the door. "Feel free to call anytime—day *or* night. And, I'll need your decision about the operation soon."

Cancer.

Counselors for the dying.

Hospitals.

Pain medication.

This wasn't happening. It was all a big, horrible joke. Suddenly Mel had entered a gray world where death was the main topic of the living. Entered against his will, kicking all the way.

He walked to a small park he loved, overlooking the East River at Sutton Place. A nursemaid jiggling a baby carriage at arm's length sunned herself in the cold morning light. Across the river the squat buildings of Queens were crowded with people mindlessly going about their everyday lives. To Mel's left, the filigreed Fifty-ninth Street Bridge hummed with commuter traffic—men and women rushing to work. Life, vibrant and exciting, flourished around him on all sides.

Mel huddled on a park bench, forgetting to button his overcoat against the cold. Bitter tears of frustration stung his cheeks. Why me? The question again pierced his mind. Why not someone else. Rita, Tom Wesley, even Wendy crossed his mind fleetingly. Of course he couldn't wish this on anyone. But why did this happen to him?

"It's not fair!" he yelled into the cold, silent air. "It's just not fair."

The nursemaid studied him curiously for a minute, then turned her attention back to the gurgling baby in her charge.

Life will go on so easily without me, Mel thought. Well, I won't give up without a fight! No one is going to take away everything I've worked so hard to achieve. He stood up, pulled his collar up around his neck, buttoned his coat, and began his walk across town to ITC House. The air would do him good. So would the walk.

Only a sick man gave up. Mel smiled. Sickness was for others. Not Mel Jacobs. If he had anything to say about it, he was going to live to be a hundred!

Halfway to the office Mel realized he'd left his briefcase at home. Such petty forgetfulness wasn't his usual style, but today he excused it with a quick "I must be getting old." He chuckled at the thought as he flagged down a cab. Getting to the office from now on would be top priority. No more staying at home and taking it easy. Mel Jacobs was up to any challenge.

He probably would have forgotten about the briefcase were it not for *TNT* writers' conference at the beginning of next week. These quarterly get-togethers were as much social as they were business. Still, Mel had important papers to be copied for distribution. He'd have to go back home.

Wendy was startled by Mel's intrusion. "I thought you'd be hard at work by now."

"I forgot my briefcase," he admitted. "I guess thinking about a mumbo-jumbo session with Doc Monroe must have done a number on me. Shit, I hate sawbones."

Wendy was suddenly very cautious. Mel was too cheerful. But he looked tired and pale, despite his manner. "So, how'd it go?"

"My ulcer's back." He sank heavily into the couch's soft cushions. "Wouldn't you know it?" His mind fastened on the lie and quickly enhanced it.

"Oh, no," Wendy whispered.

"Oh, *yes,*" he mimicked her out of habit. But a wave of anxiety quickly softened him. "Monroe wants to operate."

"Maybe we should get a second opinion." She sank down next to him and took his hand.

"Forget second opinions." He pulled his hand away. "Well, don't look so concerned. It's not like I'm going to *die*."

"Don't even think that. It's just not funny."

"It wasn't meant to be," he answered sullenly. "You might be better off if I did die." Abusing Wendy provided a flicker of relief from the black depression he had fallen into. "Just think of it—going out anytime day or night, doing whatever you please. Why, you could *live* at Aqueduct, lose everything I've spent years building up. Maybe that would finally make you happy."

"Jesus, what's gotten into you?" His viciousness stunned her. "I don't want you to die, Mel. What would I do without you?"

There was enough of an ironic edge to Wendy's voice to silence him. Sometimes he wondered if Wendy, for all her meekness, wasn't playing him for a fool. Right now the question hardly mattered. He pulled her close and rested her head on his chest.

"You go along day after day thinking everything's great, and suddenly—wham! Ten minutes with a doctor and somebody's pulled the rug right out from under your feet." He kissed the top of her head. "It's not fair."

"An ulcer's nothing these days. You'll be in and out of the hospital in no time."

"Maybe you'd like to have the operation for me?" All the way home in the taxi he'd thought about telling her the truth. Then he'd decided against it. He had to maintain an emotional distance from her. How the hell could he discipline Wendy if, ten minutes before, he'd spilled his guts to her?

"Will you have the operation?" she interrupted his thoughts.

"I haven't decided. Monroe says things aren't critical yet."

"Well, don't wait until it's too late."

"It's never going to be *too* late, understand?" he said, eyes blazing.

"Oh, Mel, I feel so sorry for you." She kissed his cheek lovingly.

He pulled her head back by her hair and stared straight into her eyes. "Feel anything you want, Wendy. But don't feel sorry for me. I'll hate you if you do."

"I meant I'm sorry you're sick, that's all." She wrestled free of his grasp and smoothed her hair. "Why is it you always mistake my concern for sarcasm?"

"Maybe because I've learned the hard way that I can't trust anyone." Even you, my pet, he thought. "Well, I've got to get to the office. Life goes on." He stood up slowly. "Right now plenty of hard work is just what the doctor ordered."

"Why not take it easy for a while?" Wendy suggested. "Driving yourself might make things worse."

"Because if I took it easy, I might end up just like you." He immediately wished he hadn't said it. Wendy was such an easy target. She looked hurt now. But there was no time to comfort her with all the work waiting for him on Sixth Avenue. He'd take care of Wendy later. Hell, there was all the time in the world to make her feel better.

An hour later Wendy was absorbed in her needlepoint when the phone rang. "I'll get it, Lolly," she shouted into the kitchen as she leaned back and popped the receiver into her hand. "Hello?"

"Mel Jacobs, please," a strange, female voice said.

"He's not here. This is Mrs. Jacobs. Can I help you?"

"Hi, Mrs. Jacobs. This is Eileen Kennedy, Dr. Monroe's nurse? Your husband left so fast this morning he forgot his prescription. Do you think he'll be able to pick it up sometime today? Or should I phone it into the drugstore?"

Mel was obviously in no mood to go chasing back to the doctor's office. "I think you'd better call it in. If you hold on a minute, I'll get the phone number." She ran upstairs and got her personal phone directory from her desk. While she read the number of the local drugstore to the nurse, Wendy decided this time to interfere in Mel's private business. He had been so down earlier that her heart went out to him. "Is Dr. Monroe available for a moment? I'd like to speak to him."

"I'll see, Mrs. Jacobs. Please hold."

A moment later Frank Monroe's booming voice came on the line. "Wendy, it's been a long time."

"Yes, it has, Frank," Wendy replied. "How've you been?"

"No complaints . . . and you?"

"I'm okay, but Mel . . ." she hesitated momentarily. Now that she was about to pry into Mel's private life she was unsure of the wisdom of the move. But he *had* looked so depressed. "Look, Frank, I hope this won't offend you, but Mel told me about your prognosis. Do you think a second opinion is in order?"

"There's no point. If I thought there was the slightest

chance the tests were wrong, I'd be the first to point you in the right direction." He paused a moment, then asked, "Mel told you *everything?*"

"Well, yes. Of course."

"Actually it'll make it easier on both of you." His voice relaxed and he opened up to Wendy. "There's a school of thought that says keep the family in the dark. I, personally, think the patient will need all the support he can get."

"Keep the family in the dark," Wendy repeated in her mind. You don't talk about ulcers in those terms. Something was very wrong here. Either they were talking at cross-purposes, or Mel had lied to her about his illness.

"Your love will be helpful to Mel as the disease progresses," Monroe went on, blithely unaware that each word he spoke drove Wendy closer and closer to panic. "Sorry I had to be the bearer of the bad news. If you have any questions about your part in all this, call anytime."

"I . . . I do have questions," Wendy forced herself to say. "May I see you this afternoon?"

"I'm free at one."

"I'll be there." Wendy hung up, then went back downstairs and replaced the receiver in the living room. She started her needlepoint again, but when the clock struck twelve and it was time to get ready to go across town to Monroe's office, she looked at her lap and saw, to her great surprise, that she hadn't done more than three stitches.

Tom Wesley closed his eyes and took another sip of the vodka and orange juice that had started his Monday morning. Somehow he just hadn't been able to stop drinking after the holidays. It was ridiculous; it was already four weeks into the new year and he was still celebrating! Drinking constantly now seemed entirely natural. Besides, he needed it to cure his insomnia, which was back for the first time in years. Only a shot or two calmed him and let him sleep. Trouble was, when he finally dragged himself out of bed, he was still drunk.

"At least there's no hangover to deal with," he chuckled, refilling the glass with straight vodka.

He stumbled into the bedroom. Rita was going to fire him soon. She'd as much as said so. The only reason he hadn't gotten the ax already was her work schedule. She'd been too busy to deal with something as insignificant as finishing Tom Wesley's career. What would it mean after all these years?

There'd be no job, no money, nothing. His worst fear was about to come true—and he didn't give a damn, really. Today was his second "sick day" since Rita's last reprimand.

"I guess I deserve to be sacked," he slurred out loud. "How long could I expect to get away with it? I've lasted longer than I ever dreamed." He finished the drink and put the glass aside. "So what now, Tom Wesley? Where does your life take you from here?"

He turned on the television and watched ten minutes of a game show, sadly shaking his head at the contestants who neared apoplexy each time they won.

"They think their lives are perfect now," he mused. "A toaster, a new car, ten thousand dollars, and life's problems fly out the window. Those poor bastards."

He turned off the television, walked unsteadily into the bathroom, and opened the medicine chest to a rainbow of pills collected over the years. He returned to the bedroom with every bottle.

One by one Tom swallowed the pills, washing each down with a sip of vodka. When they were gone he turned on the television again and lay down.

It was two o'clock.

The screen was filled with the image of sparkling water lapping a sandy beach at sundown. The diffused light played gently off its surface, gulls wheeled and screeched overhead, and a young couple—in dazzling silhouette—strolled barefoot past the camera off into the orange sunset. Lushly orchestrated violin music rose to a crescendo in the background and the words *Time Nor Tide* materialized on the screen.

Tom propped himself up against some pillows and forced his eyes to stay open. He was drowsy already, but he fought sleep. How appropriate that these last moments should be filled with *Time Nor Tide*. What a perfect and fitting end to a miserable life!

The *TNT* logo faded and Rebecca Danforth's living room materialized.

Rebecca sat miserably alone on the couch, absentmindedly thumbing through a magazine. The doorbell rang. She started, then stood up, pulling herself to her full height. As she walked to answer the call her face was set, her lips pursed, a tight frown furrowing her brow. She opened the door to Frank Cameron.

"Well, here I am, Mrs. Danforth. Just like I promised," he greeted her with a wink.

"Come in. I don't want anyone to see you," she said tersely.

"Afraid I might ruin your reputation? Or haven't you already done that yourself?" He sauntered into the living room and whistled. "This is some place you've got."

"Never mind the small talk." She crossed to a small table and opened a drawer, removed a thick, white envelope and handed it to him. "This is why you're here. Take it and get out."

Cameron took the envelope and opened it.

"Don't worry, the money's all there."

Cameron smiled unctuously. "Guess I can trust you, can't I?" He pocketed the envelope.

"Now where are my letters?" she asked quickly.

He reached into his jacket pocket and pulled out a handful of crumpled paper. "For services rendered."

She snatched the letters from his hand and counted them. "They aren't all here."

"Ho, ho, I never said you'd get all *of them at once. I need a little insurance."*

"What you mean is you'll be coming back for more money." She threw the letters on the couch and stared at him with absolute disgust. "Your type is all the same."

"Seeing that you're one of us, you should know, Mrs. High-and-Mighty."

"Get out of here, Cameron!" she screamed, watching him as if he were a cornered rat about to strike out.

"Anything you say. But don't worry, I'll be back."

"I won't give you any more money. Not one lousy penny."

"Then I'll just have to show the other letters to the right people. Imagine their surprise when they find out that under Rebecca Danforth's finery and feathers is Roxy DeVoe, Capitol City's foremost hooker."

"That was years ago. Besides, no one will believe you."

"They won't have to believe me. It's all in them letters in your handwriting. It was pretty dumb of you to put it all down for posterity."

"I could claim they were forgeries," she tried weakly.

"Then why did you just pay me five grand? Maybe you collect forgeries for a hobby?"

"I've had enough of this. Get out and leave me alone."

"Sure thing. But don't get too comfortable, Becky baby, because you haven't heard the last of me." He sauntered to the front door and left.

Rebecca went immediately to the phone and dialed. "Cameron just left," she whispered. "No, he has no idea he was being followed. Yes, I still want to go through with it, but hurry. He's got more letters, and I want them back." She slammed down the phone, picked up the letters, and threw them one by one into the fire blazing in the fireplace. The camera pulled in for a close-up of the burning letters, then the screen faded back to the Time Nor Tide *logo.*

The announcer's mellifluous voice filled Tom's bedroom: "Time Nor Tide *will continue after these messages."*

But Tom didn't hear him.

Rockefeller Center was a roiling mass of shoppers and tourists. The esplanade connecting Fifth Avenue to the open-air skating rink was still ablaze with holiday lights and decorations. Wendy stopped at Saks Fifth Avenue and looked at the expensive dresses in the window. It was a habit. She wasn't in the mood for glamour, far from it. She crossed against the light, oblivious to traffic, and was nearly mowed down by a taxi. The driver's harsh obscenities pulled her back to reality.

Dr. Monroe had told her Mel was going to die.

She paused on the stairs above the rink and watched the skaters. Some were alone, others in pairs, arms linked as they circumnavigated the small space—round and round, smiling, laughing, self-consciously aware that their expertise, or lack thereof, was being scrutinized by the crowds both above and in the lower level restaurants. For Wendy, with death on her mind, ice-skating seemed the most insignificant of pastimes. It was so futile. One skated in a complete circle only to return to the starting point. She wanted to move forward in her life, break the circuit and skate to freedom. Yet she always found herself back at the beginning. With Mel there was no finish line.

But now his death would release her. She hated herself for relying on him—even in death—to make her decisions. If only she would regain the courage she once had and stand up for her own interests, despite Mel.

When Wendy arrived at the Promenade Café, Al Peterson was already comfortably ensconced at a good table with a clear view of the rink. Wearing a light camel's hair sweater over a tattersall check shirt, a rust-colored corduroy jacket, and tan slacks, he looked every inch a writer. His handsome features were set in a half-smile as he followed the controlled pandemonium of the skaters.

Wendy moved toward him, reminded again how sexually attracted she was to him. With any other man she would have written off her desire as the simple human need for intimacy, for protection, in the face of the devastating news she had received. But Peterson was something special. Asking to see him at this critical time proved that beyond a doubt.

Wendy had other friends, friends of longer standing. But it seemed they'd known her *too* long and had grown incapable of—or disinterested in—giving her the desperately needed second chance at life she craved. Peterson seemed different. She'd seen it in his eyes at their first meeting. And later, at Thanksgiving, she'd been so caught up in the swift current of his open fascination that Mel had actually been jealous. That night he accused her of flirting with Peterson. But that was preposterous. Al was just a friend. And she was a married woman. Yet when she'd called him from a phone booth outside Dr. Monroe's office to ask him to meet her, her voice had trembled and her legs had grown weak.

Bearing this in mind, Wendy hesitated. Maybe it would be best to leave well enough alone. Maybe it was more than simple bad luck that Rita Martin had barged in just when Al's charm was beginning to captivate her. Maybe it was a clear warning, fate's "Keep Off" sign. After all, other than a polite thank you note for the Thanksgiving dinner and a Christmas card, there had been only a resounding silence from Mr. Al Peterson.

Suddenly feeling extremely foolish, and very vulnerable, Wendy was about to make a fast escape when Peterson caught her eye and beckoned to her. He rose from the table smiling.

"I was just beginning to think you'd stood me up," he said cheerfully as they shook hands.

"You're early," she said taking a seat opposite him.

"You're late," he bantered. "How are you?" Although Al was pleased by Wendy's call he had no idea why she wanted to see him. Nor could he read anything in her face.

"Tired," she replied truthfully. "*You* look disgustingly jovial."

"It's leftover Christmas spirit, I'm afraid. Holidays just

plain excite me." Wendy may have been tired, but she looked radiant. There was an almost unnatural glow to her cheeks, and her lips looked luscious.

"I wish I felt the same way. Right now all I can think about is a drink. What's that?" she asked, indicating the stemmed glass in front of him.

"Irish coffee. Want one?"

She nodded.

"One Irish coffee for the lady," Al ordered the hovering waiter.

They sat in awkward silence, staring at the skaters until Wendy's drink arrived. She smiled and sipped her coffee, beginning to relax a little. But in her mind, she was a thousand light-years away—after Mel's death—walking through the empty rooms of her apartment. How would she ever pick up the pieces of her fragmented life?

"So, what's all this about?" Peterson asked with an easy smile.

Wendy stared at him in silence, then suddenly she began to cry. There was no use in trying to stop. The tears would either happen here, in the taxi going home, or at dinner with Mel—and *that* was the last thing she wanted.

"Jesus, Wendy, what is it?" He slid his chair closer and took her hand.

She dabbed her eyes with the corner of a napkin. "Mel went to the doctor this morning . . . because of his stomach—you know he's been sick lately."

Peterson nodded.

"He came home and told me that his doctor had diagnosed an ulcer, and . . ." She rambled through the events that led her to Monroe's office, aware that she was terribly frightened. And also aware that being with Peterson made her feel almost safe. "I went to his office initially pretending I knew what was really wrong. It was a horrible thing to do, Al, but I couldn't help myself. Mel has shut me out of his life for so long that . . ." The tears started again, but she managed to choke them back.

"Maybe you should wait . . ." he offered solicitously.

"No. That's why I called you. I knew I would need someone strong and, well . . ." She looked at her hand enveloped in his, "and I thought of you. Do you mind?"

"I'm flattered you turned to me." Wendy was trembling

violently. Al felt as if he were holding an injured bird in his hand. "Just tell me straight out."

"Mel has cancer of the stomach. He's going to die," she hurried the words to be rid of them. "Monroe gave me the details. Oh, Al, what am I going to do?" Her eyes begged for understanding.

"First, you're going to have a big swallow of this coffee." He offered her the glass, and while she drank he quickly digested her grim news. Cancer! Shit, that was the bottom line. "Does Mel know you've been told?"

She shook her head. "I insisted Dr. Monroe not mention I'd been there. He was very kind. He promised to keep it all hushed up."

"Then there's nothing to worry about. Your secret's safe from Mel . . . if you think that's the best way to handle it."

"He'd never want me to know," she murmured.

"He's protecting you, that's all."

Wendy laughed bitterly. "He's protecting his own goddamned pride."

"What's pride got to do with it?"

"For Mel, appearance is all—a nice home, a nice wife . . . a model marriage. Al, it's a lie! My whole life is a series of lies." She sighed and drank more coffee. "Dying can't fit into Mel's game plan. And telling me would bring him down to my level. You see, Mel just keeps me around to make himself feel superior. Maybe someday I can explain, but not now."

"This puts you in one hell of a fix. Living with him without telling him you know how sick he is will be difficult. Can you fake it?"

"Why not?" she shrugged. "It won't be the first thing in our marriage I've faked." She started at the savage sound of her voice and immediately relented. "I sound terrible . . . like a bitter old woman."

"No one's judging you. No matter what your life with Mel is like, this has to come as an awful shock."

"I feel lost," she admitted.

"Well, sure. Losing someone you . . . love . . . never is easy," he probed cautiously.

Wendy smiled, thankful she had called him. "May I tell you something honestly? It's taking a chance, but I have to say it just once . . . for me. If you don't ever want to talk to me again, I'll understand."

"I wouldn't worry about it." He squeezed her hand. Despite the somberness of the situation, being with Wendy was invigorating. She was the antithesis of Rita Martin.

"I don't care about Mel. I really don't." Her voice was controlled, unemotional. "All the way over here I tried to feel something, to feel sorry for him—for us—for the agony he's facing. And all I felt was my own emptiness. I'm worried about me . . . not Mel. What am *I* going to do after he's dead?

"You'll keep living, that's what you'll do. You'll start photographing again and——"

"Stop it!" she yelled. "Don't be so goddamned easy on me. Didn't you hear what I just said? *I don't care that Mel's dying!* I'm his wife, and when he's gone I'll be glad!"

An elderly couple at the next table stopped eating to listen. Peterson glared at them, and they began speaking in hushed whispers.

"What do you want me to do? Slap your hand? Say you're despicable? Come on, Wendy, grow up."

"I *am* despicable. What kind of woman lives with a man for five years and then walks off into the sunset with a happy smile on her face the day he dies?"

"Maybe the kind of woman who has never thought her own life was worth saving. For Christ's sake, are you going to start beating up on yourself because you may come out of this the merry widow? You won't be the first woman death has rescued from a bad marriage." Al wondered if he would have been quite so cavalier if Mel Jacobs were a friend.

"But it's wrong to feel like this," she insisted. "This morning my life was so familiar. Now it's all unknown territory. Will you help me, Al?" she pleaded.

"Call anytime, day or night. I'm here for you, Wendy. We'll meet, if that'll help. I'll do *anything*." Much to the shock of the eavesdropping couple next to them, Al leaned over and kissed Wendy on the cheek.

At that moment Wendy knew what she wanted from Al Peterson. She wanted him to take her in his arms, sweep her out of the restaurant and into his bed. She wanted to be held and comforted and loved.

But all she said was, "Thanks for being a good friend, Al. I think you're going to make the next few months a lot easier for me."

"Glad to be of service, madame." His grand gesture lightened the mood. "Now, how about a walk? The fresh air'll do you good."

Wendy stepped back to admire the dozen yellow roses delivered ten minutes before. How Al remembered she loved roses after all this time—particularly yellow roses—was a mystery, but Peterson was the kind of guy who was full of surprises.

She found herself smiling as she arranged the flowers. Was it only a few hours before that they had met at Rockefeller Center, then gone exploring, pretending to be tourists? It seemed more like years. Al had pulled her out of her depression and got her laughing again. Their disguise as out-of-towners was a simple remedy to put reality at bay for a while. In the meantime, Wendy was a stranger in New York again. She took Al's arm and let him guide her as far away from Mel Jacobs as she had been in five years. It had been a little frightening, but also wonderful.

And just before parting Al promised they'd see each other again soon. Meeting him—even simply as a friend—without Mel's knowledge was a deliciously forbidden idea. Wendy wanted to believe Al was sincere, but she suspected he was just being kind, letting her down gently. On the other hand, there *were* the roses, *And* the card signed *A Secret Admirer*. Maybe this time she really was underestimating herself. Maybe this time Wendy Jacobs might just get a little of the happiness that always seemed earmarked for others. Only time would tell.

The door opened behind her and Mel walked in. He looked more serious than usual. Wendy smiled at him and waited to be engulfed by feelings of pity. But there was nothing. Nothing but the memory of Al.

"Darling, how are you?" She went to him cheerfully and kissed his cheek.

"Beat." He threw his coat over a chair. "I'd be better off if Rita were less crazed these days. Jesus, she's acting like the writers' conference is another Yalta."

"Rita again?"

"Yeah, Rita again." Mel wondered what she'd been up to to put her in such a good mood. "Fix me a drink, will you?"

"Do you really think you should, Mel? I mean, with your ulcer?" Wendy had decided to give Mel every opportunity to tell her the truth. If he chose not to, at least her conscience would be clear.

"I'll get it myself."

The phone rang and Wendy quickly answered it. "Wendy, it's Al."

Oh, God, not now, she thought. "Oh, yes, of course." She managed to keep any excitement out of her voice.

"I called to ask about you."

"That's quite all right. Tomorrow morning will be fine." She concocted a telephone scenario to keep Mel from becoming suspicious. Still, he stopped fixing his drink to listen.

"Tomorrow morning? Are you all right?"

She didn't answer.

"Did you like the flowers?" he blundered ahead.

"Yes, thank you." Mel was watching her carefully now.

"Well, if you're sure . . ." Al wanted to keep talking, but something was wrong. "Is Mel there?" Of course. That *had* to be it.

"Yes," she sighed with relief. "Tomorrow will be perfect. Thank you." She hung up, her hands trembling.

"And just who was that?" Mel demanded.

"I took a dress in to be altered. It'll be ready in the morning."

For a second Mel seemed to accept this, then he turned on her. "Why is it I always think you're lying to me? Tell me, Wendy, who was on the phone?"

"I told you it was the dressmaker," she insisted.

"I could check it out, I suppose, but I don't have the time." As he moved toward her, she stepped back out of his way. "Personally I think that was your bookie. You do still keep a bookie, don't you? What self-respecting gambler doesn't?"

"You're being unfair," she mumbled.

"*I'm* being unfair. What do you think it's like for me? Wondering day in and day out where you are when I'm not at home?" His stomach soured, and he winced. "*This* is the result of your self-indulgence." He beat his stomach several times with his fist. "You've done a fine job, Wendy. A fine job."

His demonstration opened the floodgate of her guilt and the beauty of the late afternoon was washed away. "Please," she whispered, "go upstairs and lie down. I'll call Dr. Monroe."

"Don't you ever call him! Do you understand?" His face

went scarlet. "If you want to make calls, find a doctor for yourself. Find out why you're trying to destroy me and our marriage with your lousy gambling." He pushed her aside, driven by the fire burning in his abdomen. A minute later the door slammed, and he was gone.

Wendy collapsed in tears on the couch. Mel was so wrong about the phone call, but it hardly mattered. Talking to a bookie and lying about another man were the same. They were dishonest. Deceitful. Causes for punishment. Mel was dying and she was glad!

Feelings of resentment and self-loathing that triggered the urge to gamble settled over Wendy. Betting on the horses seemed to offer her what Mel and her marriage denied her—freedom, independence. To strike out on her own and risk punishment for the sake of the big win seemed the ultimate independence. The ultimate defiance. In gambling there *was* freedom!

And shame.

"Did I hear Mr. Jacobs?" Lolly came into the living room, drying her hands with a dish towel.

"He just left."

"Mrs. Jacobs, you don't look right. Is everything okay?" She had seen Wendy's tear-stained face a hundred times before, and it still made her heart ache.

"Mr. Jacobs isn't feeling well, that's all." Wendy carefully avoided Lolly's eyes. She was already too mired in deception to fabricate further lies.

"Anything I can do to help? How about a cup of fresh perked coffee for you?"

Wendy shook her head. "I'd just like to be left alone for a few minutes."

Lolly nodded and started away.

"But thanks for your concern," Wendy added apologetically.

"Everything about you concerns me, Mrs. Jacobs. You know that." She left quickly, before she said too much.

Lolly's intrusion had diminished the intensity of Wendy's guilt but not enough. The anxiety lingered on, gnawing at her. If only there were a harmless way to relieve those feelings!

Wendy stared at the telephone, picturing herself there, dialing Manny Wolfsheim to get the odds for the West Coast races. Then making a bet. Betting would soothe her, but that was taboo. Hadn't Mel just said so? Hadn't he just pointed out the toll her actions were taking on him—on them? To sneak behind his back now, and do the one thing he hated most was to deny all feelings for him.

But she had to!

As Wendy remembered the soothing quality of her bookie's voice, the tension eased. Manny and Wendy went back years. He'd seen her through thick and thin, and even gallantly covered a couple of bad checks in the early days. Manny understood her in a way Mel never would. He appreciated the deep satisfaction Wendy experienced by betting. He was her mentor, not Mel, and right now she needed to hear his gruffly tender voice.

She went to the phone and stood, staring at it, as if wishing the receiver would leap into her hand and take the responsibility from her. It was the most dangerous moment—either she walked away or she gave in to the siren call of her addiction.

Wendy reached for the phone.

An ambulance screeched to a halt outside the emergency room of Lenox Hill Hospital. With detached interest Bob Craig, Tom Wesley's lover, watched as an unconscious man was wheeled through the double doors into emergency. A moment later an anguished relative was stopped at the information window to fill out insurance forms and to give a history of the patient. Just as Bob had done earlier, filled out forms and given details of Tom's life.

A young Chinese intern pushed his way through the double doors into the waiting room. "Mr. Craig, we've moved your friend upstairs."

"Then he's going to be all right?" Bob's voice quavered with worry.

The doctor shook his head. "It's too early to say. Personally. I think he'll pull through. He's in ICU for the time being, though."

The dials and machines of the Intensive Care Unit, the silent patients in dire trouble, flashed through Bob's mind. "May I see him?"

"You'll be better off coming tomorrow; he's still unconscious."

"It doesn't matter."

"Have it your own way, but don't be surprised by his condition. With the amount of barbiturates and alcohol he ingested, his body suffered a tremendous shock. He's on intravenous and we have shackled him down—just in case."

"Just in case what?"

"Sometimes there are convulsions," the doctor replied, "or the patient tries to rip out the IV."

Bob nodded numbly, forbidding the gruesome images to swamp his mind again.

"The contraption you'll see in his mouth is to keep the airway open to prevent suffocation."

"Swallowing his tongue, you mean." Bob's voice was as toneless as the doctor's. "Thanks for the warning . . . and thanks for looking after him. You saved his life."

"I'd say you had more to do with that than I did. If you hadn't called an ambulance so quickly—and brought the pill bottles with you—our job would have been much more difficult. Thank *you*." He shook Bob's hand. "Your friend's lucky to have someone who cares so much about him."

Ten minutes later Bob stood silently at the foot of Tom's bed, tears streaming down his face. All his composure, all the strength he had drawn on to get him through the last, horrible hours suddenly dissolved. He bent over the end of the bed and sobbed.

Tom looked so old, so fragile. Yet somehow he looked at peace. "It's not worth it Tom. To see you like this . . ." Bob moved around the bed and took his lover's hand. "When you get out of here we'll go away. If it's the last thing I do, I'll get you away from those bastards at *Time Nor Tide*."

11

Nan settled back on Rita's couch, just beginning to feel really comfortable. All evening she had been on her guard, waiting for Rita to reveal exactly why she had extended the dinner invitation. As far as Nan was concerned, this was a business meeting. Yet Rita had assiduously avoided any shop talk. The subjects of ITC and *TNT* had only entered the conversation peripherally. They could have been any two women spending a Wednesday evening together.

Maybe she was being just a little too harsh in judging Rita. After all, Rita was a woman—a beautiful one at that—her marriage was a nightmare, and maybe she just craved a little female companionship. Nan certainly understood that need. Still . . .

"What'll you have?" Rita stood by the bar, her hand poised over the array of bottles like a magician about to perform her most astounding trick.

"Rita, if I have one more drink I won't be responsible for what I say—or do," Nan warned, happily.

"Nonsense. I happen to know that one of the prerequisites for any executive position at ITC is a hollow leg," Rita quipped easily. "So, name your poison."

Nan requested a light Scotch. While Rita filled the order, Nan surveyed the apartment. The walls were painted a rich eggshell color, while the delicately ornate woodwork was painted a flat white. The furniture was carefully eclectic, a combination of handsome eighteenth-century English and minimalist *moderne*. This precarious combination of styles worked admirably, and most visitors—Nan included—felt immediately at home here. Two "important" Oriental carpets—over the bare, polished parquet—subtly pulled together the living and dining areas. A veritable spring garden of fresh flowers in a variety of vases completed the impression that this room was a special place to be, that its inhabitant was a person of remarkable style and taste.

Nan had expected something colder, more impersonal—like her own place—and the warm, homey elegance of the penthouse confounded her. But then Rita Martin was a woman of many paradoxes and many appetites—so many, in fact, that Nan allowed herself for a moment to fantasize a brief sexual encounter with her. It wasn't the first time she'd been aware of her attraction to Rita—her girl friend Emily's striking resemblance to Rita was no accident—but it *was* the first time Nan had actually thought of bedding her in exchange for easing up on *TNT*.

It was a frivolous thought, and a potentially dangerous trade-off. But tonight Nan had thrown caution to the wind. Tonight the carefully hidden "starstruck-kid" side of her personality broke through, and she was overwhelmed by the glamour of the evening. Drinks at Rita's was followed by dinner at the Palace; too much champagne and too much elegance was a heady combination. Tonight little Nanette Booth from Smalltown, U.S.A., was dead. Tonight she was Nan Booth of New York City and the most formidable woman at ITC, Rita Martin's equal . . . and newest confidante.

"This is absolutely my limit," Nan said as she accepted the drink.

"Suit yourself," Rita said. "Now, where were we?" All evening she had watched impassively as Nan grew happily drunk, the layers of self-protection peeling away like the skin of an onion, while she herself remained assiduously clearheaded. "You were telling me about yourself."

Nan rolled her eyes. "You don't want to hear about me."

"I find you quite fascinating," Rita urged seductively. If her plan was to work, she'd have to lay the groundwork now. "You must be very determined to succeed. You've already come so far and you're still so young."

"When I first started at P & G I *was* a little obsessed. I mean, the more I realized I could actually have what I wanted

. . ." she confided rapturously. "You, of all people, understand what that feels like."

"Success is a very potent drug. In the hands of a beautiful woman like you, it's a most powerful weapon."

"Exactly," Nan agreed. "Men are suckers for a pretty face. And let's be honest, Rita, except for a few lucky women like you and me, men call all the shots." Nan seemed to grow angry. "It's an uphill fight against those chauvinists."

"But I've aleady reached *my* goal. What does the future hold for you?"

"I'm just waiting for Jim Goodspeed to retire," Nan lied.

It was the obvious next step, but Rita knew Nan never favored the obvious. She was looking for bigger fish to fry. Her scrutinization of *Time Nor Tide* proved that. And unless Rita had misread the signs, she herself was about to be scaled and filleted.

"I sometimes wish I had the security of the corporate structure to fall back on. I feel so exposed," Rita said with just the right touch of pathos.

"Security?" Nan snorted. "I could be out of work tomorrow if I step on the wrong toes. You're practically untouchable."

"I still answer to ITC."

"We all answer to someone," Nan replied. For one amazing moment she felt sympathy for Rita. It passed. "You're in fairly solid. Everyone at ITC seems to have nothing but respect and admiration for you."

"You included?"

"In six years you've accomplished more than most people do in a lifetime. I respect that."

"You see, even *you* do it," Rita sighed. "Everyone connects Rita Martin and business. *Time Nor Tide* is only part of the story." She shook her head ruefully. "How many people on the fortieth floor even suspect that first of all I'm a woman with feelings?"

Ordinarily Nan would have sneered at such a bathetic, self-serving statement. But Rita had primed her for it all evening. Under the witty chatter over drinks, at dinner, a carefully directed undercurrent of loneliness and vulnerability had emanated from Rita to erode Nan's cynicism. That Nan's eyes now sparkled with unshed tears of understanding attested to the power of Rita's performance.

"You always make it a point to seem above it all. What

else can anyone think?'' Nan swallowed hard. Something was happening tonight she had never expected. Rita was actually drawing her into her confidence. This was no bullshit. It was the real thing.

''You're right, of course. It is my own fault.'' Rita got up and paced the room. ''For six years I've given my life to *Time Nor Tide*. It's all paid off—more than even I predicted—but now . . .''

''Now?'' Nan urged expectantly.

''I wonder if sacrificing my personal happiness was worth it.''

''You can't mean you're unhappy . . .'' The idea was unthinkable. It didn't jibe. Nan knew the Martin story by heart: the power struggles and network fights, the overwhelming success, the shattered homelife and retarded daughter, the sexual peccadillos with an army of long-forgotten men. But unhappy? It was preposterous! Rita Martin's career was Nan's own ideal!

''Let's just say that at this particular time in my life I'm hoping there are other things besides a career.''

''I don't believe it! You have everything. And now you're saying you've failed?''

''I haven't failed; I'm just dissatisfied with the results. I expected that when I finally made it to the top I would be surrounded by caring people—friends—but now I see that those closest to me bear constant watching. It appears I have what everyone wants.''

''I suppose that blanket condemnation includes me?''

''Let's be honest, Nan. Our relationship has been strictly business and pretty stormy at that. You're ambitious; you said so yourself. Why should I think you're any different from the others?''

''Because we're kindred spirits,'' she replied.

''That only makes us competitors . . .''

''Is competition between friends so unhealthy?''

''There's that word again: *friends*. I sometimes think my only friends are the *TNT* characters. At least I know when they're lying.'' Rita paused. ''If anything were to happen to *TNT*, I actually think I'd be relieved.''

''You can't really mean that. Besides, *Time Nor Tide* will always survive,'' Nan countered.

Goddammit, I know that, Rita screamed inwardly . . . I want to know what's going to happen to *me!* ''I guess I've fallen into the oldest soap opera trap there is—living out my own life through my characters." She returned to the couch and sat down next to Nan. "What am I going to do, Nan?" she asked, sorrowfully. "I'm forty-three, alone . . . and I'm scared."

Nan took Rita's hand and held it. "Maybe I can help," she whispered softly.

"If only my husband—men—were as understanding as women." She lay back against the couch and closed her eyes.

Nan turned slightly to face her. "Men never seemed to trouble you before."

Rita laughed. "The trick is not to let them know you're using them."

"There are *some* things only a woman can make another woman understand," Nan agreed.

"Such as?" Rita asked, trying to keep her voice level.

"Such as feelings, friendship . . . love." Nan hesitated, then began to caress Rita's hair. "You're a very beautiful woman, Rita. Many men must want you."

"They're only good for a quick roll in the hay. Even that gets tedious." Every muscle in her body was tensed for what, inevitably, was to follow.

"Maybe you just haven't found the right man, or maybe you need . . . something different." Nan tried to control her breathing, which was beginning to betray her growing excitement.

"Different?"

Nan leaned over and kissed Rita's cheek. Rita didn't respond . . . but she didn't pull away. Nan moved closer. "Why not give me a chance?"

"I don't know if I can," Rita answered honestly.

"Trust me," Nan whispered. She nimbly unbuttoned Rita's blouse and cupped her breast, feeling Rita's wildly beating heart. "Only a woman knows what another woman wants in bed." Nan kissed Rita's breast gently and then sucked the nipple like a hungry child, gradually increasing the pressure until Rita moaned. "See how easy it is?"

Rita kept both her eyes closed tight. She feared that the sight of Nan Booth at her breast might make her physically sick. Her mind roamed frantically from Nan to Al Peterson. If she could convince herself that it was Al's mouth enveloping her nipple, Al's hands kneading her body, Rita could carry it off. And she could explain why her body responded. She could allow the ecstasy to build. It felt so good!

Nan caressed Rita's breasts, until the nipples grew hard between her fingers. When her trembling hand edged its way under Rita's skirt, Rita was already wet from excitement and expectation. Embarrassed that her body responded to something her mind abhorred, Rita closed her legs. If only it didn't feel so good . . . If only this were a man making love to her . . . But it was a *woman,* and along with Rita's mounting pleasure, she felt a mounting terror.

When Nan finally kissed her on the lips, her thick tongue snaking its way into her mouth, Rita snapped. "Get away from me!" She pushed Nan back with such force that Nan hit her head on the arm of the couch.

Nan was stunned. She swallowed hard. Tears of humiliation sprang into her eyes. "You liked it," she gasped. "You weren't faking! You liked it!"

"But it's not worth it." Rita quickly buttoned her blouse and straightened her skirt.

"Not worth it?" Nan repeated in disbelief, just above a whisper. And then it all made sense. The whole evening was a trap! The words of Al Peterson's last note came rushing back: "I wouldn't be surprised if Rita tried something desperate to save her neck." *Something desperate!*

"You fucking bitch," Nan screamed. Her eyes blazed with fury.

"You've got it all wrong, Nan." Rita attempted to placate her. "I only . . ."

"You only wanted me on your side because of your fucking show." Nan finished the sentence for her.

Rita dropped her head, unable to reply.

"Poor Rita Martin—so unloved, so friendly. Only the characters in *Time Nor Tide* understand her," Nan mocked. She bolted to the closet and snatched up her coat. "You'd do anything to hang on, wouldn't you? Nice try, Rita. You actually had me going—for a minute." She hurriedly pulled on her coat. "God, I should have known better. You're just another cunt!"

"Please, Nan. Don't go," Rita begged from across the living room. "Let me explain."

"Save your explanations for the network," she spat. And she was gone.

* * *

The following Monday morning Rita strolled into the conference room trying to work up some enthusiasm for the writers' conference scheduled to begin in half an hour. The props were all in order. The six places at the table were each equipped with pencils and pads. At the far end of the room, arrayed on a credenza used to store scripts and outlines, was a gleaming urn of coffee, a basket of fresh fruit, and a mountain of pastries, buttered rolls, and bagels. Because these conferences were designed to reinforce the "family" aspect of *Time Nor Tide,* Rita carefully provided breakfast at the office. What could be more homey than discussing rape, murder, and abortion over a cheese danish and a cup of coffee?

Today Rita should have felt good about being creator and head writer of *Time Nor Tide,* but she felt lousy.

At the window she absentmindedly stared down into the blazing canyon of Sixth Avenue. A steely winter sun hung low on the horizon, and she felt its heat through the thick insulated windows. She tensed her muscles, then relaxed. Wednesday night's fiasco with Nan had sickened her. Her own actions had forced Rita since then to reevaluate everything in her life. And she'd found herself wanting in every area.

But her priorities were changing; the terrible guilt over Nan clearly proved that. Fighting without conscience to remain ITC's reigning soap opera queen was no longer desirable. Or even possible. Rita's growing suspicion that her place at *Time Nor Tide* now had more to do with viewer response than it did with personal drive and network allegiance was given credence by Jim Goodspeed's cautiously optimistic memo, found that morning on her desk. How ironic the memo came when it did! Had it been delivered Wednesday she never would have put Nan—and herself—through such degradation. But then she might never have learned so important and difficult a lesson about herself.

Goodspeed's note reminded Rita that nothing in television is static. Fortunes are made and lost daily. Careers skyrocket overnight and fizzle in the morning. People fall out of favor one day and the next are welcomed home like prodigal children. Into what category do I fall? she wondered. Saint or sinner? She mulled Goodspeed's memo over in her mind.

Rita:
Have followed the TNT numbers with interest. If recent ratings are any indication—particularly December's—

the downward trend would appear to be righting itself. Your Frank Cameron murder seems to be a winner. The February sweeps will tell the true tale. I'm rooting for you all the way.

Jim

Time was running out. The February sweeps had already begun.

Back in her office Sandy informed Rita that Tom hadn't arrived or even called. Mel had been there since eight-thirty. Tom should be there, too. Damn him!

Rita angrily punched out Wesley's phone number. "Tom, it's Rita." She began a mechanical assault when the phone was answered. "In case you hadn't heard, there's a writer's conference today. Just where the hell are you?"

"Miss Martin, it's Bob Craig."

Jesus, it was that *roommate*. "Sorry, Bob. Is Tom there?"

"He's not feeling well. And he's asleep." Tom was still in a coma, but he'd be damned before he told Rita Martin that.

"Do I take it he won't be here today?" On this day, of all days, sick or well, Tom's place was in the office.

"You'll have to ask him yourself. Why don't you call later. Say in an hour or two."

"I won't have time later," Rita snapped. The animosity in Craig's voice was unmistakable. Why was it gay men had such trouble dealing with women? "Tell Tom I hope he's feeling better soon. And have him call me when he . . . wakes up." She hung up.

Wesley was through. If she'd entertained any doubts before, today's disgraceful behavior clinched the decision. Still asleep! Rita had carried him about as far as she could. *Time Nor Tide* was making a recovery, but keeping it healthy surely would double, triple, the work at the office. Tom could never stand the pace.

She put in a quick call to Goodspeed before the writers began to arrive. She wanted to thank him—and avoid that silly secretary who protected him like a lioness. "So, you're still the early bird, Jim," she said when he answered. "Jogging, I presume?"

"Just got finished. You got the memo."

"Yes. Thanks, Jim. I really needed that pat on the back." Only with someone as familiar—and as important—as Goodspeed did Rita confide this way. "I don't mind telling you the past few months have been hell. And when I had trouble getting *you* on the phone, well . . ." The rest was best left unsaid.

"It was Christmas, budget time, the usual bitching and moaning that will drive me to an early grave."

Rita laughed. "You'll bury us all."

"So what can I do for you?"

"Shame on you," she said in her best little girl voice. "How do you know this isn't purely a personal call?"

"Is it?"

"No," she laughed again. "Well, no *and* yes. I really do want to thank you for the memo, but mostly I want to get some word on the story projection I sent you at Christmas; it's getting late.

"I turned it over to Nan. Hasn't she gotten back to you?"

"Not yet," Rita said. The sickening feeling of shame that had haunted her all weekend rose in her throat once again. "Surely the decision isn't solely Nan's. I mean the final word comes from you, doesn't it? You're the big network honcho." This time her laugh was to disguise her nervousness.

"Look, Rita, why don't you call Nan and talk to her personally."

"I've got the writers' conference today. You know what a pain in the ass that is. Jim, would you mind . . . ?"

"I'll tell her you were asking. That's about all I can do."

"That's sweet of you. One more thing: lunch? Next week?"

Goodspeed sighed. "Sure. Have Sandy call Sally to arrange something."

He hung up and closed his eyes. How long had it been since he'd talked to Rita? Six weeks? Eight? However long, it was enough to make him forget just how exasperating she could be. When things were going badly she pushed and pushed to get his protection. And when things were going well she pushed and pushed to get his praise. Christ, dealing with Rita Martin was like dealing with an eight-year-old.

But this time it was his own fault. He was the one who decided to ease off and break his professional silence with the memo. Maybe its friendly tone was deceiving—*TNT* was still in trouble—but, shit, why not give Rita's confidence a boost? Her ratings weren't great, but they were improving; even Weatherhead had abandoned his nonstop complaining that what ITC daytime needed was a good housecleaning—which Goodspeed always took as a euphemism for easing Rita out.

Weatherhead's silence should have taken the pressure off Nan where *TNT* was concerned. Yet, apparently, she was still sitting on the Penny Hewitt story. Why? Probably just being overly cautious until this latest storm blows over, Goodspeed concluded. Hell, Nan wanted to save *Time Nor Tide* for her own selfish reasons, not sink it. She'd get off Rita's back soon enough. There was no reason not to.

He picked up Nan's last major report on Rita and *TNT*. He felt a twinge of leftover guilt as he leafed through it. The report was a list, actually. A list of available writers—head writers and dialogists—Nan had compiled after her last volatile encounter with him about Rita. He hoped he wouldn't need it after all. Still, there was no harm familiarizing himself with its contents. If the worst happened and *TNT* changed hands in late spring, he had to be fully prepared to oversee the transition.

Goodspeed put on his glasses and opened the report. The first name his eyes rested on was Al Peterson.

Peterson tugged the collar of his overcoat up around his neck and ducked his head low to minimize the effects of the icy blast of wind on Central Park West. During the night a light snow had fallen, leaving the city dusted with an iridescent layer of white. Despite the Currier & Ives quality of the setting, the bare trees in the park looked pitifully forlorn.

Al had a bitch of a hangover and his decision to walk to ITC to shake it off now seemed the height of folly. Nothing could make him feel human again, he thought. Two cups of coffee in a greasy spoon on Fifty-seventh Street, however, began to clear the cobwebs from his mind. He had a general idea of what a writers' conference was all about, still he didn't want to be caught off-guard. After nearly three months as a *TNT* staff member, Al had never met the other writers. He fully intended to make a good impression—even if it killed him.

Though it wasn't necessary for dialogists to know or even to like one another, Al's decision was more than simple vanity. After his little tête-a-tête with Nan Booth, he was confident he was slated for bigger and better things at *Time Nor Tide*. And when that happened he wanted to be liked by everyone.

He rode up in the elevator to the *TNT* office with a sprightly middle-aged woman dressed for a dinner party. At nine o'clock in the morning her black satin dress, matching pumps, and pearl necklace were conspicuously outré. Al studied her with undisguised curiosity—short brown hair, small, pretty mouth, and a button of a nose—the kind of woman who laughs at her own jokes, he figured.

When they both exited into the dimly lit *TNT* office, she clutched him by the arm. "You're Al Peterson, aren't you?"

He nodded in complete surprise.

"I'm Patty Fellows. It says Patricia on the outlines, but I only use that professionally. It sounds more legit, don't you think?" Before he had a chance to answer, she continued, "This is your first conference, isn't it? Well, don't worry, Rita's bark is worse than her bite. Actually, with you around I expect this conference might be lots of fun." She actually winked.

"I was expecting a lot of things; fun was *not* one of them," he egged her on.

Patty laughed out loud, a raucous, throaty hoot that defied him not to smile. "My dear Al, what could be more fun than writing a soap opera?" She tightened her grip. "Just think of it: Day in and day out we writers get to lead lives we'd never dream of leading. I mean, do you really believe the world out there is quite so sad and so miserable? Oh, no"—she shook her head—"if it were, no one would have to turn on the television; they'd just look around their living rooms." The thought made her giggle.

"I've never looked at it quite that way before. Then we aren't mirroring *real* life?"

She shrugged her shoulders grandly. "Maybe, but I can tell you one thing: It's not my life." She started pulling him down the corridor toward the conference room.

"But then how do you write believable characters?" He was totally captivated by this bundle of irreverent energy who, he'd been told, had been with Rita from the start.

"Imagination, darling, that's the key." She tapped her head. "And a subscription to *People* magazine." She laughed evilly.

When they entered the room, Rita, Mel, and a woman Al had not met were gathered by the food. Rita was gorgeous. Subtly businesslike in a gray herringbone suit and a prim navy-blue blouse, yet looking as regal as any of the world's remaining crowned heads.

The trio turned as Al and Patty entered. Everyone but Rita smiled. Al had canceled their Friday-night date saying he had a cold; actually he just wanted to be alone. That made two weeks in a row he'd called Rita and begged off at the last minute.

"Morning, all," Patty called out, scampering across the room to kiss each of them on the cheek. "Rita you're perfection." She held her like a trophy at arm's length.

Rita accepted the compliment with quiet grace. "And you're the picture of good health, Patty."

"It's just good, clean living," she quipped, and everyone broke up.

Al hung back near the doorway, until Rita signaled to him. "Well don't be afraid, Al. No one's going to bite you." He quickly joined them. "You know Mel and you've obviously met Patty, so let me introduce you to Evelyn Parsons." Rita stepped back graciously.

Al smiled—but not at Evelyn. So, Rita had dressed for a part. She was playing the role of grande dame today. He was amused and intrigued to see this most imperious facet of her personality yet. "I've seen your name in the credits, Evelyn. It's nice to meet you."

"I know your name, too, Al," she chirped in a birdlike falsetto. Evelyn Parsons was as thin as her voice. She had sharp, angular features accentuated by wire-rimmed glasses and a dowdy wardrobe that surely was secondhand. She could have been fifty . . . or a hundred.

"Now we just have to wait for Loretta before starting. Tom won't be joining us today," Rita announced, not betraying her anger. "Al, why don't you hang your coat in here." She led him to her office.

As he entered he threw his coat over the couch. When he looked up, Rita had settled behind her desk. They were alone. "That's how I want to remember you. Seated on the throne of power," he said.

"Cut the bullshit, Peterson. I called you Friday night to see how your 'cold' was. I foolishly thought I might bring you some chicken soup." Her smile was frighteningly insincere. "You weren't home."

"I unplugged the phone and went to sleep." It was the truth. Only the cold was a lie. "Sorry." He was in no mood to be treated like another Rita Martin flunky—either as her latest bedmate or as her employee.

"Better be careful, Al. Colds like yours have been known to kill more than one brilliant career."

"I'll keep that in mind."

She appraised him silently for a minute, then sprang from her chair and stalked out of the room.

When Al reappeared in the conference room, Patty Fellows pounced. "You know, Al, I've admired your scripts from the start. You're a real writer, unlike the rest of us," she gushed between mouthfuls of Danish.

It sounded like a remark made after a few too many drinks. "I'm flattered you think so, but I've read your scripts, too, and they're always right on target."

She shook her head vehemently. "Dialoging for soap operas is hack work—get the information across without seeming forced. Granted, I do *that,* but your writing has a spark, something else, something I just don't have." She took another bite of the pastry. "Maybe with you on the team we'll have a shot at our first Emmy for writing." She giggled for good measure.

"*TNT*'s never won?" His surprise was genuine. He'd always taken it for granted that Rita had several Emmys stashed away somewhere. But come to think of it she had never once alluded to the coveted award.

"Not once in five years. It's gone to everyone but us. Not that I mind; it's Rita I feel sorry for. She wants that little statuette more than life," Patty confided.

To Al, Rita seemed to want a lot of things more than life—his total attention included. "In that case I promise we'll get it this year."

"With you on the team . . . maybe," she agreed, slugging him on the arm.

Loretta Wyle finally arrived and the meeting began. Loretta was another of the almost nondescript personalities Rita seemed to enjoy surrounding herself with. Mousy and awkward, Loretta spilled her coffee, stepped on Rita's foot, and caused general chaos with the ease of a born *klutz*. Evelyn and Loretta seemed archetypal soap opera writers—dour, plain, taciturn to the point of solemnity, these Cassandras might easily revel in the sensitive and doom-ridden lives that kneaded *TNT*'s daily bread. By contrast the other writers, with their exuberant personalities, appeared oddly unfit to perpetuate characters whose lives were measured out in teaspoons and teardrops.

And beyond that, Al was not only the only male dialogist, but the only subordinate who dared show any initiative with Rita. Even Patty Fellows, for all her boisterous good nature, bowed and scraped when addressed by the powerful Mrs. Elliott. For a moment Al envisioned a roomful of performing seals anxiously waiting to be thrown a fish. It wasn't a pretty picture.

"All right, boys and girls. Work time," Rita announced happily. She took her place at the head of the table. "We have a lot of ground to cover before lunch, so let's get going. Patty, you sit here," she pointed to the chair nearest her. "Loretta and Eleanor, you sit there." She indicated seats on opposite sides of the table. "And Mel, of course, sits opposite me."

The others were too busy finding their assigned places to notice Rita's breach of etiquette. Al took the only place left, and when Rita stole a quick, sly look in his direction, he winked insolently.

They broke for lunch at noon. By then Frank Cameron's death and the conviction of his murderer was old news. And Penny Hewitt had disappeared into the dark Caribbean jungle. Had it not been for Al's confidence in Nan Booth's ability to make good on her promises, he would have been worried by Rita's treatment. She was acting like a spoiled child, rejecting his plot ideas by laughing them away. Apparently she felt publicly humiliating him made her look good. If only she knew how tawdry it actually made her look . . .

But as Nan said, this was not the time to rush things. Part of playing the game was rolling with the punches. If Rita wanted to assert her authority, why not let her? Al knew that in bed he had something she needed. And until that part of their relationship ended, he would always have the upper hand.

As the group walked to a nearby restaurant, Al drifted back to join Rita. "Did I mention before that you look absolutely regal today?"

"How nice of you to notice," she answered, without bothering to look at him.

"Give me a break, will you? I'm sorry about Friday——"

"I know; you took the phone off the hook and went to sleep," she interrupted sarcastically.

"Is that such a crime?" He was torn between the desire to placate her and to tell her to go to hell once and for all.

Rita slowed for a moment, now turning to face him. Her smile was warm, but her eyes were cold. "One thing in my life I will absolutely not compromise is honesty and loyalty to me . . . and to *TNT*. If I misjudged you about our date, I apologize. If not . . . you're going to have a serious problem—with your job and with me."

"I've been warned," he said with a tight smile. "Now, let's forget last week and try to act as though we might actually mean something to each other *today*."

In response Rita quickened her pace and caught up with the others.

For the remainder of the afternoon, Al tried keeping his mind on *TNT*'s convoluted story projections, but it constantly drifted. With fascination he watched Rita conduct the meeting like a ringmaster. Today she was not Rita Martin, the tough, demanding television dynamo; she was not Rita Martin, *Time* magazine cover woman; she was not even Rita Martin, the woman, who in Al's arms exhibited the entire spectrum of feminine emotions. Today she was Rita Martin in the spotlight. Rita Martin the nightclub star who played every corner of the room to ensure that each and every patron believed she was addressing herself directly to him. Rita Martin the school kid who had been given a dollar and who bought ice-cream sodas for the gang. Today she was Rita Martin, matriarch, gathering a large and motley family to her copious bosom.

And today Al Peterson knew his affair with her was finished at long last.

Rita was the first to see Mel clutch his stomach. His face became a mask of agony. He sank into a chair and Rita hurried to him, a postconference Scotch still in hand.

"Jesus, what's wrong, Mel? You look like death," she whispered, so as not to alarm the others.

Nonetheless everyone quickly gathered around him.

"Get them away from me, Rita," he groaned, "please."

"There's nothing to worry about," she said, turning to the group. "Everyone have another drink. We'll be leaving for dinner soon."

The others drifted back to the open bar set up where

breakfast had been. But their stares remained fixed on the pale figure of Mel Jacobs as he gasped for breath.

"Help get him into my office," Rita commanded Al.

"I feel like a damned fool," Mel sighed from the couch in Rita's private office.

"What is it?" Al wondered how Jacobs would react to his knowing the truth.

"It's that damned ulcer," Rita snapped. "Mel, how *do* you feel?"

"I'll have to pass on dinner, Rita. Have Wendy pick me up, will you?" He felt like he might vomit any second. Beads of cold sweat speckled his forehead. But he'd never let on just how bad it was.

"I think we should call a doctor," Rita countermanded his request.

"*Just call Wendy.*"

Rita hesitated, then did as she was told. After a minute she returned shaking her head. "There's no answer. Wendy must already be on her way to the restaurant."

"Goddamn her punctuality," Mel snarled with irony as the pain gripped his insides once again. "Then call me a cab.

"Do it, Al," Rita said. "I'll get a cold towel."

Fifteen minutes later Rita and Al loaded Mel, shaking and in dire pain, into a taxi.

"Are you sure you don't want Al to go with you?" Rita asked.

Mel waved his hand. "I'll be fine. It's just exhaustion. Tell Wendy not to worry. And be sure she stays for dinner." Like a wounded animal, Mel wanted to be alone during this crisis. His first impulse had been to telephone Wendy, but he was now glad she'd already left. Having her fluttering around would only make him angry and, in turn, aggravate his condition.

"Call later, Mel, and take tomorrow off," Rita insisted in a motherly way.

"You can't get rid of me that easily."

"It's an order!" Rita slammed the taxi door. She and Peterson stood silently until Mel was out of sight. "He hasn't looked well for weeks," she mused aloud.

"Probably indigestion," Al suggested. Nan had been very coy about whose job he was taking. But after what Wendy told him, and after this display, was there any doubt?

"Let's go back upstairs." Rita took Al's arm for support.

Mel's attack had shaken her. She hated illness, hated being with people who were sick. Ever since Jeannie's accident, she hadn't even been able to visit anyone in a hospital. Walking through the silent, white corridors that reeked with illness, medicine, and disinfectant, Rita had sensed her own vulnerability, her own mortality, and the dangers of just being alive. For a moment now she felt afraid.

In the elevator when she kissed Al gently on the lips, that fear vanished. "Forgive me for barking at you earlier? Conferences always key me up," she murmured.

"Sure thing . . . no problem, Rita," he said flatly. "We all have our days."

She had expected reassurance, but his distance was hardly that. She looked at him curiously. "Are you angry?"

"What's to be angry about?" He stared up at the flashing numbers. "Here we are."

Rita excused Al's coldness as a reaction to Mel's unpleasant attack. He'd warm up later . . . if he knew what was good for him. One warning was all Rita Martin ever gave anyone. And Al Peterson had been warned.

Rita assuaged everyone's worry about Mel's health and they taxied to the Russian Tea Room for dinner. Once inside the opulent restaurant, the team's mood was light and cheerful. Patty Fellows told racy stories that kept everyone laughing, and even Evelyn Parsons and Loretta Wyle—after cocktails—loosened up.

"How lovely of you to have chosen the Russian Tea Room for dinner. It makes me think of Moscow, though I've never been there," Patty said with a tipsy grin. They had just come in and were waiting to be seated.

"Your imagination is too fertile, even for me," Rita said as she signaled the maître d'.

"One day *TNT* will have a Russian émigrée character, and we shall do all our research here," Patty went on exuberantly. "And here *is* our Russian princess!" she exclaimed as Wendy Jacobs swept into their midst through the revolving doors. "Isn't she just divine?"

"Wendy's always . . . divine," Rita observed with a sly smile. "Darling, how are you?" she called out, kissing her resoundingly almost in her ear. Rita knew perfectly well that Mel's wife despised her, but she didn't mind. As long as Mel functioned as Rita's right arm, Wendy Jacobs would be treated with professional courtesy.

Wendy did look like a czarist grand duchess. Wrapped in yellow chiffon, a discreet rope of amethysts at her neck, she blushed prettily at all the attention. Much as she disliked Rita's insincere pushiness, she'd looked forward to this dinner as the perfect excuse to see Al again. Even Mel couldn't be suspicious. She scanned the group looking for her husband. Where *was* Mel?

Rita saw Wendy's concern, took her aside, and whispered, "Now don't worry. Mel felt a little ill and went home. He made me promise you'd stay with us and have a good time."

Wendy's reflex reaction was to flee the restaurant and go home—Mel's wishes notwithstanding. But Mel had said he wanted her to stay, and Al was here. . . . She smiled at Peterson. He hadn't taken his eyes off her from the moment she walked in.

"If you're sure Mel's all right . . ."

"Then it's settled." Rita ushered her back to the others. "It just wouldn't be a party without *you!*"

Al was startled all over again by just how beautiful Wendy was. The glittering pink background of the restaurant bathed her in an ethereal light. He felt the stirrings of desire. Wendy caught him staring and smiled. "Mrs. Jacobs," he bowed in response.

"Good to see you, Al," she said eagerly.

"I'd forgotten you two know each other," Rita said in her best hostess voice, not for a moment forgetting how she'd snatched Peterson away from the Jacobses' Thanksgiving dinner.

"Oh, Al and I are old friends." Correctly reading the warning in Rita's eyes, Wendy quelled her enthusiasm.

"How very sweet." Rita immediately turned her attention to the others. "Unless we move, our table will be given away. You know 'time nor tide waits for no man,' " she quipped. Actually she was angered by Wendy's coyness and by Peterson's barely disguised lust.

"You never mentioned that Wendy Jacobs was quite so taken with you," Rita whispered casually as they were led to a table at the back of the restaurant.

"I hadn't noticed," Peterson said lightly, "but if you say so . . ."

"Come, come, Al. It's the first thing you *would* notice," she said sweetly. "This is *me* you're talking to, not little Wendy Jacobs," she smiled as the maître d' seated her.

When Peterson was seated next to her she leaned close and whispered: "Hands off, Peterson. And that's an order!"

Al pulled back. "Rita, I'm here to have a good time. So just get off my back." He immediately directed his attention to Wendy, who sat at his right.

The idea of Peterson and Wendy was laughable. Nevertheless, even if she was through with Al, Rita didn't intend just to hand him over to the next woman who came along. Particularly when that woman was Mel's wife. After all, she had her pride.

All through dinner Al paid too much attention to Wendy and too little to Rita. Away from her oppressive home environment, Wendy blossomed.

"I still can't get over how beautiful you are," he said to her when Rita slipped away to the powder room. "You never seem to look the same twice."

"I hope not," Wendy exclaimed. "The first time we met you thought I was the maid."

Peterson smiled at the memory of the farce she had drawn him into.

"Maybe I should have worn an apron tonight instead of this," she touched the sleeve of her dress, "and dusted myself with flour instead of powder," she rested her hand on the milky skin of her breasts, revealed by a rather daring décolletage.

An image of Wendy naked after a bath—her skin moist and pink as she smoothed silky powder over her breasts, thighs, and between her legs—glowed in his mind.

"I definitely prefer the powder." He still imagined her body. "It's sexier . . . not that you need it." His eyes flitted from her breasts, rested momentarily on her full lips, then settled on her eyes.

"Mr. Peterson, are you making a pass at me?" She batted her eyes, meaning it as a joke. But the gesture betrayed real excitement, and they both knew it.

"I just can't keep anything from you, can I?" he asked seriously. "Tell me, do *all* men want to take you in their arms and never let go? Or is it just me?"

"I don't know about all men. In fact I don't know much about men at all." Peterson's undisguised desire was flattering and more than a little frightening. Since their afternoon together, Wendy had often fantasized about slipping into an affair with Peterson, but now that it seemed to be happening she wasn't so convinced she could go through with it.

"I find it hard to believe you haven't been inundated by men. You're beautiful, charming, graceful."

"Spoken like a true male chauvinist. What about honest, sincere, trustworthy, intelligent, creative . . . ?" she demanded, hoping now to keep him at arm's length.

"Those too . . ." He shook his head. "Scratch the surface of any beautiful woman today, and you find a militant feminist."

"The real qualities must come first. Anyone can be charming—even Rita Martin," she went on.

"Touché. I throw in the towel." They both laughed.

As she returned to the table Rita saw Al and Wendy still huddled together like conspirators. Maybe Al really hadn't been lying earlier, but if Wendy's little looks and glances weren't just coquetry, she was hovering on the verge of infatuation. Rita sneered to herself. Wendy was probably ripe for an affair. Mel Jacobs could be impossible when it suited him, and their home life together was probably hell most—if not all—of the time. Rita had seen the bruises and black eyes only partially hidden by makeup. She'd heard the phony excuses, outwardly accepting them while guessing the truth all along.

Wendy Jacobs was the perfect battered wife. She'd given up her own life to serve Mel. In return he gave her protection—the kind of protection that came at the end of a fist. Wendy was such a classic case, Rita had modeled the character of *TNT*'s Jane Garrick after her. Nearly eight months of grueling episodes dealt with Jane's problem—alcoholism, in this case—her husband's discovery of the fault, and his subsequent brutal beatings. Rita could hardly blame Wendy for hating her.

She'd been on to Little Miss Perfect Wendy Jacobs for years. If Al Peterson ever wanted a little something extra on the side, Wendy was there for the asking and Rita could think of no one better for him. In fact, it was a match made in heaven.

Inwardly, Rita sighed. Is there a man anywhere in the world whom I can trust and be happy with?

"There she is!" A loud, drunken voice shattered the hushed reserve of the restaurant. "I told you she was here."

Ben Elliott clumsily weaved his way toward his wife followed by the eyes of every patron and the agitated maître d', shaking his white towel. "If you'll only let me tell her you're here, sir," the harassed man said in vain.

"No need, she'll recognize me," Ben said, dismissing him with a wave of the hand. "Rita . . . !" he said with exaggerated enthusiasm.

"What are you doing here?" she hissed her voice barely audible.

"I'm here to be with my wife, what else?"

He was given a chair next to Rita, edging out Al.

"Well, aren't you going to introduce me to your friends? Let's see, I know Evelyn and Loretta . . ."

He stared at Wendy. "You look sorta familiar. Do I know you?"

"Wendy Jacobs—Mel's wife," she answered quickly. Rita was so uncomfortable she was practically squirming in her chair.

"Well, hi, Wendy Jacobs," Ben got up and reached across Al to shake her hand, jostling the table as he did.

"Will you please sit down," Rita growled.

"Anything you want, dear. And who's this?" He fixed Al straight in the eyes.

Rita tensed. "Al Peterson, our new writer. Meet my husband. Ben Elliott," she introduced them through clenched teeth.

"Glad to know you, Al," Ben said jovially, pumping Peterson's hand up and down. "So you're the one who replaced that writer who was giving Rita such a hard time, eh? Well, I wish you the best of luck."

Neither Rita nor the others missed the irony of Ben's tone and sentiment.

"What can I do for you, Ben?" Rita asked softly. There was no need to draw any more attention than necessary to this brazen display of Ben's contempt. "This is business."

"It's always 'business' with you, Rita. You've got to learn to relax. Waiter, bring me a lemon vodka on ice." He teetered back and forth in his chair.

"Really, Ben," her voice withered, "this is inexcusable. How did you know we were here?"

"It's your favorite restaurant—used to be *ours*. We had dinner here the night you sold *Time Nor Tide* to ITC. Surely, you can't have forgotten?"

'I remember very well." She was embarrassed more by this reference than by his intrusion. Rita kept strict control over what vignettes from her life were revealed. But Ben was drunk and in a vindictive mood. There was no telling what he'd say next.

"Why don't you go to my apartment and have that drink? I'll meet you there soon," she urged, hoping to salvage some dignity.

"But I don't have a key, Rita."

She frantically fished in her purse, knowing now that the evening was ruined. "Here, take it. I won't be long."

The waiter brought Ben's drink. "I'd rather stay," he announced, turning to the others. "What do you say, folks? Do I stay or do I go? Let's have a vote!"

"Let him stay, Rita," Patty burst out, caught up in the spirit of the farce.

"This is none of your business!" Rita barked hoarsely. Then suddenly realizing her loss of control was making the situation worse, she relented immediately. "Okay, Ben stay and have your vodka. We'll leave together."

"Sure thing." He winked at Rita, drained half the vodka in one gulp, then looked around. "So this is the heart of *Time Nor Tide*—very impressive. But I'll never understand how such a nice looking group of people can turn out so much crap, so often, without going out of their minds. Particularly you, Al. I can understand a woman getting involved in soap operas, but . . . how do you do it?"

"It's a job, Ben—plain and simple. Do it and forget it." Al couldn't help thinking that this traitorous statement would have cost him his job a few weeks ago.

Rita jumped to her own defense. "Maybe it's just a job to you, Al, but to the rest of us it's a lifetime's dedication," she proselytized. "No one succeeds in soap operas unless there's room for nothing else in his life."

"That's telling 'em, Rita," Ben applauded. "Unfortunately, you're wrong. *Time Nor Tide* is *your* life. For them it's only *part* of their lives. I'm sure they all have other things to keep them occupied—and happy."

"Oh, shut up!" Rita was on the verge of screaming. She had to do something to stop Ben. He was ruining the evening for her—as well as the others.

At that crucial moment Rita spied Nan Booth being seated at a nearby table with a female companion. Rita prayed Nan wouldn't see her. But fate wasn't that kind. Nan caught her eye and a second later she was at the table, kissing Rita on the cheek. Nan's companion remained discreetly at the table.

"If it isn't *Time Nor Tide* in the flesh," Nan bubbled, perfectly aware of the effect her presence was having on Rita.

"You know everyone—including my husband." Rita maintained a professional smile.

"Sure, Ben and I are old friends. It's been a long time." She kissed him, too. "I usually don't see you until the Valentine's Day party. What's the occasion?"

"Just getting away from family responsibilities," he slurred.

"And I bet you deserve it." She rested her hand on Rita's shoulder and gave it a fast, harsh squeeze. "Being a parent can't be an easy job," she sympathized acidly. "But I'm sure you do as good a job as Rita does with *her* family. Ah, what would *TNT* be without Rita Martin?"

Rita gently extricated herself from Nan's hold. "We'll let you know the day *after* I leave," she said lightly. If this deadly banter went on for one second longer everyone at the table would know something was terribly wrong. She couldn't let that happen. "It's been good seeing you, Nan. We must have lunch soon," she said as if Wednesday night had never happened.

"Yes," Nan replied, "of course, Rita. I *love* your invitations . . . Well, I didn't mean to interrupt you now. I'll let you finish your coffee. Nice seeing you."

Back at her own table, Nan leaned against the banquette and observed the *TNT* crew. It was odd. Neither Tom nor Mel was there. Without them Rita looked physically smaller, totally exposed, and open to attack. For a second Nan almost regretted what she was about to do to Rita. But this maneuver was her trump card. It would demoralize Rita, cripple her, Nan hoped. That's the only way to fight Rita Martin, she thought. If she'd learned anything about Rita Wednesday night, it was to kick her while she's down.

"Just who is that woman, anyway?" Emily asked suspiciously.

"That, my dear, is Rita Martin. She used to be head writer of *Time Nor Tide*."

If Ben's arrival hadn't completely ruined the evening for Rita, Nan's presence did. Feeling angry at Ben, betrayed by both Peterson and Wesley, and terrified of Nan's revenge,

Rita was suddenly at the breaking point. How ironic that for months she'd pretended all was well with *Time Nor Tide* while inwardly she was almost certain she'd lose it. And now, as each day gave new credence to that fear, it hardly mattered. *Time Nor Tide* would always go on—with or without Rita Martin. But if she wasn't careful, no matter what the outcome of her battle over the show, Rita Martin, the woman, would be left with nothing. Absolutely nothing.

She demanded the check, overtipped the waiter with a gesture of largess that only drew more attention to her embarrassment, and prepared to flee.

"It's been a lovely evening, Rita," Patty reassured her. "The story projections are dynamite! We'll get that Emmy yet . . ." her voice trailed off.

Patty's inept words only drove the dagger deeper into Rita's heart.

"Thank you, Rita," Evelyn and Loretta intoned almost in unison. They pushed their way out of the restaurant, to their solitary apartments with their menageries of cats.

"Mel will be so disappointed when I tell him what a lovely time I've had," Wendy said, giving voice to her unconscious thoughts. "That is, he'll be disappointed he missed it," she covered herself.

Rita proffered the obligatory kiss on the cheek. "Nice to have seen you. And don't let that husband of yours out of bed tomorrow. And that's an order!"

Wendy lingered for a moment, her eyes on Peterson, then left. As they had agreed, she would wait for him outside.

"So that's a writers' conference. It wasn't so terrifying after all," Al joked cheerfully, carefully avoiding Rita's eyes.

"Glad you could find the time to join us, Al," she sneered. "Working late can cut into one's social life, but it's the price we pay to stay in television."

Had it not been for Ben, Al might have forced a final confrontation then and there. Instead, he let it pass, tipped an imaginary hat, and walked out.

Rita retrieved her coat from the checkroom, complimented the maître d' on the fine dinner, and left.

Once outside the restaurant, shivering in an icy wind that blew across town from the river, Rita confronted her husband. "Now, Ben Elliott, just what the hell do you think you're doing here?"

12

Wendy and Al snuggled comfortably into the back seat of the taxi they had decided to share. The driver had strict instructions to take his time driving through Central Park.

"Did you see the look on Rita's face when Ben showed up?" Wendy smiled. "Who says soap operas don't mirror real life? Rita could have *murdered* him."

"I didn't notice." Al's good humor suddenly drained away. Being the "other" man in Rita's life put him in a peculiarly sensitive position.

"Didn't notice? Even a blind man could have seen her fury. Now *there's* a story someone could make a fortune from." The river of champagne she had drunk at dinner quickly found its way to her tongue. "I can see it all now—Rita Martin's double life. On the one hand she is creator of *Time Nor Tide*, the nation's favorite soap opera, feeding her fans a daily dose of the golden rule and good rich American apple pie. But in real life? She's a cutthroat, a killer, with a husband and retarded daughter carefully stashed away in the country while she plays footsie with every ambitious stud in New York." She giggled uncontrollably, then put her hand apologetically over her mouth. "Oops, sorry, Al, no offense intended." Just let him try to deny it, she thought.

"None taken," he lied. Usually public opinion of his private life was irrelevant, but hearing the truth from Wendy embarrassed him. He felt sleazy.

She turned and faced him, the shadowy lights from the

street hiding her disappointment. "Let me ask you a straight question, Mr. Al Peterson. How did a nice boy like you end up in a shitty business like this?"

She was so sincere he had to laugh. "Luck, I guess. Like I said at dinner, it's a job."

"Oh, no. You don't get away with that crap with me. There are lots of writing jobs out there, lots of jobs that don't demand you to compromise your self-esteem." She thought for a second. "Or maybe I was wrong about you. I should leave the snap decisions to the likes of Rita. They remedy their own mistakes by cutting other people out of their lives. I'm not that ruthless . . . although it sure would be easier if I were."

"I like you just the way you are—intelligent, creative, trustworthy . . ." he rattled off the list of qualities that had infuriated her when he omitted them earlier.

"Now you're making fun of me," she said softly.

"I've never been more serious in my life, Wendy." With the slightest encouragement he'd take her in his arms and prove it. But she kept on talking.

"I don't know how you come across to the others, but you impress me. I've been around television people a long time now, and they're pretty much the same—they'd sell their mothers to make a fast buck. I thought you seemed different."

"And now you've changed your mind?"

She cocked her head. "I don't know. When Mel told me about you and Rita, I was disappointed in you. Maybe I still am. Besides, you can only get hurt. I've seen it happen before."

"What did you really think when Mel told you I was sleeping with Rita? You didn't know me well enough to care," unless you always cared, he added to himself.

"I thought you were a shit, until tonight."

"Tonight?"

"Rita's taking advantage of you just like she does everyone else. Al, you're handsome, charming, graceful"—Wendy smiled involuntarily—"and you deserve better." She tensed, realizing that too soon she'd be back home with Mel. And it had been so long since she'd really been able to talk to someone. Her emotions were rising. Still, Al's nearness, the faint pressure of his leg against hers, encouraged her to go on.

"Rita's an unhappy woman, but I still can't forgive her for

the way she uses people. Stay away from her, Al. I know what I'm talking about. I'm married to her number-one henchman. You don't know what it's done to Mel . . . and to me." Wendy began to sob quietly. She bowed her head to hide the tears.

Al slid over closer to her and lifted her tear-stained face to his. "Hey, are you going to be okay?"

"You must think I'm an idiot. People usually get giddy on champagne. I get depressed." She wiped at her eyes.

"I really don't know what to think," he admitted. Wendy was confused; that much was obvious. In fact, her apparent romantic longings might just have more to do with escaping Mel than with being captivated by his own charm. It was still a tempting situation, though. And a dangerous one. Wendy was no one-night stand. She was a pretty little bird, but anyone could see she had never really learned to fly on her own. And Al wasn't sure he wanted the responsibility a sexual encounter would almost certainly guarantee.

"I usually don't make a fool of myself until I know someone better," she joked bravely.

"Maybe I know more about you than you might think." He ran his fingers through her silky hair. "You're warm, easily hurt, and maybe you need someone to love you." He kissed the top of her head.

"Funny, that's just what I would have said of you." She raised her face to be kissed, trembling from the excitement of the terrible thing she was doing.

"We're two of a kind then," he tilted her head farther and kissed her forehead, then each eye. "You knew it from the start. I'm the idiot, not you." It was too late. He was on familiar ground. The facile words of love had been waiting in the wings ever since his first encounter with Wendy. Al's resolve to be cautious was quickly superseded by an aching desire for sex. The finely tuned machinery that turned compassion into lust slipped into gear. "How do you feel now?" he asked smoothly.

"Want an honest answer?"

He nodded.

"I'm scared . . . scared because I've opened up to you, Al. I'm afraid I'll go too far, and then there'll be no turning back."

He smoothed her hair, picturing her naked beside him.

"I'm the kind who doesn't take my feelings lightly. I've never done this . . ."

He sealed her lips with his fingers. "Trust yourself. Bend a little . . . give in to the feelings. Don't fight them."

Wendy had been ready for this since their afternoon together. "Trusting myself just isn't that easy," she whispered.

"Let me help you." He kissed her mouth and dropped his hands to her breasts. They were firm and full like he'd imagined, and through the dress he felt her nipples erect with anticipation.

Wendy shuddered, then pulled her head back, gently pushing him away. "I can't yet," she pleaded, her voice vibrating with fear. They were already on Central Park West; and too near Mel.

"Relax," he coaxed. "It'll be great, I promise. Remember, we're two of a kind."

"Al, no." She pushed him away more forcefully when he tried to capture her again. "Not now. Some other time, please." She wanted him more than anything in the world, but taking what she wanted was nearly impossible.

Her resistance excited Peterson even more. "I won't take no for an answer, baby," he moaned.

And suddenly it was over.

"I want to get out, Al, *now!*" She was stunned by his words. One of Mel's beatings couldn't have hurt more.

"But I thought——"

"You thought I was just another piece of ass," she cut him off. "Oh, God," she sobbed, lurching forward toward the taxi driver. "Driver, pull over at the next corner, please."

Al yanked her back against the seat. "Keep going, driver." He held her wrist tightly. "Give me a chance to explain; you owe me that much."

"I owe you nothing. Driver, pull over right now or I'll start screaming," she yelled.

The cabbie looked at her in the rearview mirror, shrugged, then edged the car toward the curb.

"I'll walk from here," Wendy dug into her purse and threw several crumpled bills into Al's lap. "That should pay for the kisses and for feeling me up, 'baby.' Check with Rita to see if it's union scale."

"Wendy, I'm sorry," he apologized blankly. "Please let me take you home."

She pulled farther away from him and opened the door. "I

thought you cared a little about me, Al, but all you wanted was someone to screw.'' She shook her head. ''And all this time Mel's been right about me,'' she added cryptically.

''You've got it all wrong,'' he protested, too stunned by the sudden turn of events to get out and insist he walk her home.

''*You've* got it all wrong. Fucking me won't get you anywhere but in trouble. You're better off keeping your prick on twenty-four-hour call for Rita—she's the one who writes the checks.'' Wendy slammed the door and walked off into the night.

''Where to, buddy?'' the driver asked.

Al gave him the address then fell back against the seat in shock. He really *liked* Wendy Jacobs. But Wendy wasn't the kind of woman you screwed when you had a couple of free hours in the afternoon. She was no Angela Brite. He knew that. Why couldn't he have just told her he liked her and been satisfied? But no, his cock had a mind of its own and now she had a good reason never to talk to him again.

''How dare you break up my meeting!'' Rita stalked into the living room, threw her mink carelessly on the couch, then fixed herself a stiff drink. ''Just who do you think you are?'' she fumed.

''Your husband. No more, no less.'' Ben was unperturbed by his wife's anger. He was a man with a mission and nothing would stand in his way.

''You're my husband for the time being,'' she threatened, feeling that after his treatment of her at Christmas he had no claim on her at all.

''Now, let's not get *too* dramatic, darling. Our marriage is very useful to you. You know as well as I do that it covers a lot of sins for you—if I may use the expression.''

''And just what do you mean by that?'' She tossed her coat aside and sat down, caught off-guard for a second. Rita was positive Ben knew nothing of her affairs. Infidelity was the one thing in their shaky marriage he would never have countenanced.

''Divorce is a big step in anyone's life. In yours it might be a fatal one.''

''And what makes me so special?''

''How would it look for you, Rita Martin, to get a divorce after all the years of 'happy homemaker' crap you've handed out to the magazines? What would your fans say about your perfect home falling apart?'' He took a seat opposite her.

''They'd love it. Those vultures out there would eat up every word of the sadness and bitterness.''

Ben smiled. ''Maybe. Maybe not. A divorce would make you human—no better, no worse than your adoring fans, those vultures. You can't risk coming down to earth, can you?''

''Jesus, I hate it when you act superior. *You* don't even have the guts to confront me when you're sober.''

''Getting drunk was an accident. I was at the bar waiting for you to finish dinner . . . and I had a couple of drinks too many, I guess.''

''You were at the bar all night? You actually sat there and watched me?'' Rita swirled her drink with her finger, keeping her eyes on him. Ben was up to something. At Christmas he'd pretended she didn't exist and now he was spying on her.

Ben leaned forward unsteadily. ''I have to know tonight if you're coming home where you belong. After the past holidays I can't take any more.'' He appraised her for a moment, then looked away. ''I thought I could act like you do, but I can't.''

''What are you talking about?'' Rita asked cautiously. She'd seen Ben drunk before, but never so unsure of himself. And there was a desperate edge to his voice that was new and disquieting.

''Oh, for God's sake, Rita . . . I treated you badly on purpose,'' he blurted out. ''I *wanted* to hurt you. But I love you. Mistreating you made me feel like shit.''

''That's why you didn't call me after Thanksgiving?''

''You didn't call me either,'' he said petulantly, ''so why should I call you? Why should I always make the first move? I'd hoped you'd come to your senses and call me for a change, but you didn't. So the whole thing backfired, didn't it?'' He laughed. ''Being such a prick felt good at first. You looked so damned uncomfortable all New Year's Eve . . .'' his voice wavered, and when he looked up, there were tears in his eyes. ''I won't act like this, Rita. No more.''

''I don't know what to do, Ben,'' she admitted. ''I've tried to make up my mind, but——''

''The answer's so clear, Rita. Why can't you see it?'' he interrupted.

"Because I'm afraid I'll make the wrong choice."

Ben shook his head. "What bullshit! Be honest, Rita. You're hanging on to *Time Nor Tide* not because it brings you so much satisfaction but because you're too goddamned proud to admit defeat. ITC is out to get you—and they will, you know."

"Don't be so sure," she immediately defended herself. "Why just this morning I had a very optimistic note from Jim Goodspeed——"

"Stop!" Ben put up his hand. "I don't want to hear it. You're like a seer trying to read her future in the blood and guts that have already been spilled. Well, to carry out the thought, the runes have already been cast, my dear. Don't you have a contract renewal coming up soon?"

"June," Rita said, surprised that Ben even remembered.

He nodded. "That's it, then. Forget Goodspeed's note. He'll sell you out just as fast as Nan Booth if it means covering his own ass. Don't let him tell you how you should feel about your life. Look in here"—he tapped his chest above his heart—"that's where you'll find the right choice."

Rita looked at him thoughtfully, then lit a cigarette. She wanted to argue but there really was nothing to say. He'd thought it all out, and she hated to admit it, but Ben was making real sense, of a kind she hadn't heard in a long time.

When she still said nothing, Ben continued. "I guess I misjudged you, Rita. I guess all you've got left in your heart is self-pity, isn't it? 'Did you hear about poor Rita Martin? She caused her child to be brain damaged because she didn't get to the hospital on time.' " He laughed. "It's the perfect excuse to avoid all responsibility, isn't it? But you've done your guilt trip to death and I'm sick of it." He got up and walked toward the hall closet.

"You just don't understand, Ben. You never have," Rita countered angrily.

"I understand now that you're the most selfish woman I've ever met, that's what I understand," he flung open the closet door and snatched out his coat. "I'm tired of all this drama. I want you back, but I'm not going to sell my soul to get you. Tonight's a turning point for us. I won't go on being trapped between your hatred of yourself and your abuse of me and Jeannie. I remember how happy we once were. I remember the woman I married, and I want it *all* back."

Rita clenched her teeth to maintain her determination.

"There was a time I might have done anything to keep you, but I'm too old now. The people who would gladly let you destroy yourself are afraid of you. They all have something to lose—money, power, position—by telling you to stop. Not me, Rita. If I lose you, all I stand to lose is a bad marriage." Ben's anger rose. His fists clenched. Since Rita wouldn't answer him, relent, come into his arms, he went on.

"Vulnerability, love, tenderness—they're all weaknesses in your book. Because they're signs of being fallible—human. You've been afraid of getting close to me because I'm the first one to admit I'm human . . . and because I, more than anyone, know you are, too. You're afraid of me because I won't blame you for Jeannie's accident. And I don't want to see you punished because you've made a success of your business life. Isn't that what drives you, Rita? Your fear that if you ever stop running you'll be punished."

"I've already been punished." She held Ben's eyes now, speaking deliberately. "I've already sacrificed everything a woman can. And what I didn't willingly give up was taken from me." Ben had to know she meant Jeannie. "Don't you see? For me to give up *Time Nor Tide* now is to make a cruel joke of the last six years."

"So when does it all end? What goal have you set that will absolve you from your sins?" He'd been ready to write Rita off finally, but this conversation was a revelation. She was telling him what was really in her heart—her anguish. "What will signify to you that your precious career hasn't been self-imposed hell?"

"An Emmy for *Time Nor Tide*."

"It's that simple?"

She nodded.

Ben sat down, stunned by finally hearing the truth. So, her desire for the Emmy was not just vanity, but a desire for absolution. Did she really think something so superficial could make such an important difference? He felt the direness of her quest, and he felt a strong sympathy for her. "Why didn't you confide in me before?"

"Because wanting the award so badly could only seem frivolous and self-indulgent. Even *you* have your limits of understanding." She sat down next to him, yielding to a feeling of love, of need. Telling Ben the truth was gradually opening the doors to her heart that had slammed shut at Jeannie's birth. "So now maybe you begin to understand . . .

a little.'' She rested her head against his shoulder. ''I don't want to be selfish, but I was afraid if it was any other way . . .'' After all the years of pretense, her tears began.

''If only you *had* told me. We could have worked it out together instead of . . .'' Instead of what? There was no point going over the same territory yet again. ''Rita, we don't have our whole lives ahead of us anymore. We're getting older. Surely you can see that.''

She raised her head to look at him. ''We're not getting older, we're getting better.'' The joke was meant to dilute Ben's somberness. But it failed.

''*Older*. There's no time to wait until tomorrow, or the next day . . . or the day you get your Emmy.''

''Three months, Ben. That's all I want from you now. Please understand.''

''There's no guarantee this year will be any different from the last five. What if the Television Academy overlooks *Time Nor Tide* again? Do we wait just one more year?''

Rita's face clouded for a moment. ''If *TNT* bombs again—or even if it wins—I'll . . .''

''Quit?''

''If I quit you'd have a *real* monster on your hands. I'll take a back seat, hire a new head writer, become a consultant.''

''And move to Connecticut where you belong?''

''And move to Connecticut.''

Ben took her into his arms and covered her face with kisses. After the long years of fighting and analyzing Rita's motives the answer was so painfully simple: She desperately needed that final praise—and vindication—that only an Emmy could provide. He gave her another kiss. ''I've always wanted you to bring home one of those babies—just because I'm so proud of you. For that I *would* sell my soul.''

''I already tried,'' she laughed. ''Well, my dear, you seem to have won me over, after all. I hope you won't regret it.''

''It's what I've always wanted.'' Rita's demon had almost won the last round, but Ben's love was too strong for it. There was relief in Rita's eyes. Where icy defiance had once blazed, the warm glow of love now shimmered.

''I think we should celebrate.'' She got up, pulling Ben by the hand along with her.

''No more to drink!'' Ben raised his hands defensively, palms out.

''Drinking wasn't exactly what I had in mind.''

Ben ran his hands over her back, over her ass. "Now that's the best idea I've heard all night."

They headed for the bedroom. Rita was trembling with excitement.

She sat on the edge of the bed while Ben undressed. She was cautiously optimistic about coming to terms with Ben. It relieved a pressure in her heart that had existed for years. Their future happiness was a tempting possibility now. She'd made a promise to Ben she had to keep.

"Forget *Time Nor Tide*, Rita," Ben admonished her as he began to unbutton her dress. "This is *our* time. Better take advantage of it while you can." He was kissing the back of her neck.

"Nonsense," she whispered. "We've got a lifetime together. You'll see."

13

The Saturday of the *Time Nor Tide* Valentine's Day party dawned gray and frigid. The temperature hovered just above freezing, and the weather forecast predicted a heavy snow. Throughout the day the sun vainly sought to break through the leaden sky, but the city remained an alien landscape of bleak vistas. By noon the sky darkened, and the first snowflakes were falling. By three o'clock visibility had diminished to a few yards. For all its claims to modernity, New York quickly succumbed to the weather: Traffic, the city's nemesis, slowed to a crawl; buses skidded on the icy streets; and automobiles honked angrily as they found themselves trapped in congested intersections.

"My God! Are you sure we're in the right place, Al? Just look at that crowd." Patty Fellows peered out the taxi window at the mob outside Studio 54. "This affair may prove too chic for a couple of lowly soap opera writers like us." She squirmed with mock humility.

"Chic? You invented the word," Al replied cautiously. Unless fortune changed abruptly, tonight's party would be about as peaceful as the maiden voyage of the *Titanic*.

"Flattery will get you everywhere," Patty joked, looking out at the crowd once again. "Seriously, though, how do you suppose that rabble heard about our party? They certainly aren't the Studio regulars—not at this hour. I can understand excitement about a movie premiere, but this is television—and just a soap opera at that."

"These are the people we write for," Al observed thoughtfully. "I guess even the lousy weather can't keep them away from their idols."

To a casual observer, the *TNT* party was a good chance to let off a little steam after a year of hard work. To the well-initiated, any network party was a garish arena for making connections, soothing old wounds, drawing new alliances, and proving one's sincerity to ITC. Al had been looking forward to the party since dinner with Nan. It was his first opportunity to rub elbows with the network executives who knew him only as a name on a script. Being cloistered at home writing didn't win big points with ITC—despite Nan's grooming him for more responsibility. Being a brash, eager-to-please young man at a Valentine's party did. Al was an expert at socializing. His easy brand of conversation and charming manner usually impressed executives. His cheek-to-cheek dancing always impressed their wives.

A long, sleek limousine edged its way through the traffic and cut in front of Al and Patty's cab.

"Give 'em a big car and they think they own the world," Patty growled under her breath. "It must be some *actor*."

"How can you tell?" Al leaned forward as the limo door opened.

"Big money, big cars . . . big egos. If we got out of a job like that, Jim Goodspeed would complain we were getting paid too much. But he expects his actors to play the part to the hilt." Maggie Taylor—*TNT*'s Rebecca Danforth—descended daintily onto the slushy sidewalk. "She acts like she's stepping out of a horse-drawn carriage, for Christ's sake." A young man, clearly years younger, appeared and followed carefully at her heels. "So *that's* what he looks like," Patty cackled.

"That's what who looks like?" Al studied the handsome young man who sported a highly visible unseasonal tan.

"Maggie's boyfriend! I swear each time they get younger. Next year she'll probably arrive with a baby buggy."

"Did anyone ever tell you you're a vicious woman, Patty Fellows?" Al laughed.

"Only my best friends," she winked. "You've got to do *something* to amuse yourself after spending eight hours a day churning out oatmeal for our fans."

"I don't know how you manage to stay so level-headed."

Patty was a rainbow in the gray landscape of *TNT*. Her wit, her style, her joie de vivre labeled her a rebel, yet somehow she managed to blend in with the others. She wrote good scripts, handled Rita like a pro, played a minimum of office politics . . . and had survived for six years.

"What's your secret?" he whispered in her ear.

"Daily doses of heavy-duty drugs," she whispered back, then slapped Al on the wrist. "The truth is: Don't get involved. Let 'em *think* you're involved, let 'em *think* you'd kiss every ass on Sixth Avenue to keep your job, but each time you say, 'Yes, sir,' and 'Yes, ma'am,' give 'em the finger," she gestured, "mentally, of course. You might try it . . . if it's not already too late. Now here we are, ready or not."

The taxi halted in front of the club. Although this was a private party, ITC had taken out ads in the television sections of all the newspapers touting the fete. They promised lights, fun, and "your favorite soap opera characters." The ploy worked. At least three hundred curious onlookers waited anxiously in the subfreezing weather for a familiar face. Most were women. They smiled expectantly as Al and Patty passed, but then merely shrugged when they didn't recognize either writer.

"I think they're disappointed," Al said out of the corner of his mouth.

"Fuck 'em if they can't take a joke," Patty replied haughtily. "Lavinia Winthrop and Ted Reynolds are right behind us. That ought to satisfy the savages' hunger for glamour. These peons just don't know real talent when they see it." She swept into the entrance in a parody of queenly deportment.

"I just love network parties. ITC invites four or five hundred of its closest friends. It's so homey," Patty said sarcastically as they dropped off their coats, then started up the staircase to avoid the main-floor crush near the bar and dance floor.

Despite Patty's world-weary attitude, Al felt caught up in the drama and excitement. Network parties—by definition—were flamboyant extravaganzas calculated to impress even the most jaded. The *Time Nor Tide* party was no exception. Hiring Studio 54 for the entire night was a stroke of genius. Tucked between Broadway and Eighth Avenue on nondescript West Fifty-fourth Street, the former television studio gone Hollywood was the most famous dance hall in the world. Through its doors sashayed most every famous person—and personality—ever to be gossiped about in *Women's Wear* and over late supper at Café Un Deux Trois. To celebrities, Studio was a place to drop by to say hello to just about everybody you'd had dinner, drinks, or sex with the night before. To the throngs of anxious tourists who waited outside its front door to be beckoned in at the doorman's whim, Studio was the next best thing to an American Express Gold Card. Be it good or bad, Studio 54 was a perfect setting for a party the magnitude of *TNT*'s. The pulsating lights, the distant thunder of overamplified music, the electricity in the air were harbingers of something extravagant and extraordinary.

Al stopped at the head of the stairs to catch his breath. He was not prepared for the the dreamworld ambience of the main lounge. The vista was one of men in tuxedoes and women in designer gowns—"disco attire" notwithstanding. Enormous baskets of every sort of flower, from gladiolus to orchids, filled the air with the smell of an ersatz—public relations—spring. Tables laden with exquisite food were presided over by three chefs in towering *toques blanches*. Again flowers abounded.

"My God, it looks like the main chapel at Frank Campbell's funeral home," Patty quipped.

"I think we're going to have a great time tonight, Patty," Al took her hand and guided her to the coat check near the bar.

"I'm going to have an *okay* time—drink a little too much, talk a great deal too much, and be the perfect guest. I'll leave 'great' times to you." At the bar she ordered champagne. "Well, what do you make of it? Every man and woman here has something to do with *Time Nor Tide* either directly or indirectly. Frightening, isn't it?" She sipped her drink thoughtfully.

"It's a tribute to Rita," Al said. He'd prepared all day for the ordeal of making many such meaningless statements.

"Come now, Al. This is Patty you're talking to . . . not Mel," she sneered. "Don't be coy. I've heard *all* the rumors. What I want to know is, just where do you fit into all this?" With her arm she inscribed a large, irregular arc in the air drawing the whole disco and everyone into it.

"Same place as you. It's a job."

She looked disappointed with the answer. "I don't blame you for keeping your mouth shut about your ambitions—it's the only way to survive. I, for one, have given up on ambition, so I can shoot my mouth off all I choose. No one cares. Just be careful, darling . . . you may be buddies with someone on Monday and learn Tuesday that they've been canned. It's a dangerous game, Al." She smiled demurely. "I like you far too much to see you fall by the wayside."

"Is that a discreet warning?" Patty and Rita had known each other for years, but Al doubted if she was Rita's business confidante.

"Let's say I'm seeing familiar signs, okay?" She threw back her shoulders bravely, a little carried away with emotion. "Now, let's mingle. There are a lot of people I can introduce you to, people who just might come in handy if the going gets rough." She pulled him away from the bar into the crowd.

Nan warily surveyed the crowd as she and Don Sheridan ascended the staircase to the lounge level. For the past week she'd had "urgent" calls from Rita and hadn't answered any of them. Tonight, however, there was no way she could avoid the bitch. After two weeks' silence, they would be face-to-face once again. Since her humiliation at Rita's hands, Nan's anger had refined itself into a fierce determination to undo *TNT*'s creator at any cost. In the past Nan had tried to camouflage her part as instigator of the network's attack on *TNT*, but now it was time to "go public." She wanted Rita to know the battle had become personal. She wanted Rita to know she was fighting Nan Booth for her livelihood, not just the nebulous structure of the ITC hierarchy.

If the ill-fated "seduction" was an indication, Rita was already running scared. What other reason but survival would drive Rita to pull such a shoddy stunt? The irrational, frantic side of Rita Martin was a revelation. Nan now intended to make it the reason for Rita's demise. If she was careless once, she could be careless again—suicidally so.

Don beamed at Nan, proud to be her "date." His boss's personality was so iridescent that he was sure it reflected on him and made him a little more like her. "Uh oh, there's Joe Ericson." He spotted the actor pushing toward them.

Nan glanced casually in his direction. Ericson was all smiles, and when he saw Nan the smile widened. "Prepare yourself, Don." She glided off to the bar, Don trailing behind.

"Should I sidetrack him?"

"Don't be foolish. Ericson doesn't intimidate me."

"You've got it all wrong," Don laughed. "I just figured he'd bore the hell out of you."

"Oh, Don, whatever would I do without you?" She chucked him under the chin. "I'll handle this. You go have a good time . . . but don't leave without me."

Nan felt supremely confident tonight. A rigid pecking order ruled these network bashes, and the daytime VP was right up there at the top. Tonight all she had to do was look good, smile a lot, and mouth the right platitudes. It wasn't much of a job. Years of parties and frequent business lunches had refined her technique; the mistakes, the tiny slips of etiquette that might ruffle executive feathers were a thing of the past. Nan Booth was the queen of diplomacy. She could make anyone believe anything—when it suited her purposes.

Joe Ericson concluded an informal interview with a *TV Guide* reporter and sidled over to Nan. He pecked her on the cheek and slid his arm around her waist. "The most beautiful woman in the room, alone?"

"For a moment. Where's Nancy? I thought *TNT*'s two most famous lovers were never separated," she said snidely. Off-camera Ericson and Nancy Carson—a married woman—had begun a torrid affair that was the talk of the studio—for that week, at least.

Joe's grin wavered momentarily, then he recovered. "Nancy's out drumming up enthusiasm for the new Penny Hewitt." He released Nan with no prompting.

"The *new* Penny Hewitt?" Nan asked in all innocence.

"Don't try to con me, Nan. If someone sneezes at ITC, word reaches your office in minutes."

"Not true. But it sounds good," she said suppressing her anger. What a pushy bastard!

"Have it your own way," he replied. "Nancy's agent got the word that Ma Martin is beefing up her part. Where does that leave me?"

"Rita doesn't really confide in me, Joe. Try Jim Goodspeed."

"Come off it, Nan. Goodspeed only knows what you tell him."

Nan laughed in spite herself. "You give me credit for a great deal more power than I have. That's what I love about television: Everyone thinks the behind-the-scenes drama is more exciting than the on-screen variety. I gave *you* credit for having more sense."

"I only know what I see. It looks to me like nothing in daytime happens without your approval."

She stared at him blankly.

"All right, play dumb, but remember: I'm not joking about quitting. Unless my part is changed to equal Nancy's, I'm through."

Ericson glowered now, but Nan silently stood her ground. She liked getting this ham angry, and it suited her plans. What she didn't tell Joe was that the "new" Penny Hewitt was already officially dead. She'd seen to that personally last week. A little pressure exerted in the right quarters and *voilà*—the Caribbean plot died an ignominious death. It would be resurrected—correctly rewritten to Nan's specifications by Al Peterson—to be used as her own showpiece to save *TNT*. But that was later. Until then, stringing everyone along, Rita included, was the prime order of the day.

"I'm sure Rita will take your displeasure into consideration," Nan said with sweet condescension.

"Bullshit," Ericson snapped. "See you around . . . until next month." He stalked off.

Nan headed downstairs toward the dance floor. This party might be to honor Rita Martin and her gang, but tonight all the valentines were going to Nan Booth.

Mel stumbled on the stairs and almost fell. Wendy grasped his arm to steady him.

"Get your goddamned hands off me," he snarled. Two martinis at home had exaggerated his already foul mood.

"I was only trying to help."

"If you want to help, leave me alone." He pulled away from her, failing in his attempt to walk a straight line. "I hate these parties. Everyone smiling and laughing with people they'd just as soon see dead. It's mass hypocrisy. Half the people here would gladly tell the other half to fuck off given the chance."

"Why don't you relax and *try* to have a good time? This party is to honor you as much as Rita."

"My champion," Mel said savagely. "Whatever would I do without you?" Several people waved and smiled, and Mel smiled and waved back—while muttering obscenities under his breath.

"I need a drink," he finally announced, staggering toward the crowded bar.

Wendy didn't follow. In the past, she would have feared Mel's brutish behavior, but tonight she immediately forgave him. In fact, during the weeks since discovering his illness she'd adopted a new attitude toward Mel. Forgiveness was now a reflex. For two weeks Wendy had been doing her homework. She'd read books and magazine articles on the subject of death and dying. Mel's explosive personality changes began to make sense. It was one doctor's theory that a terminal patient experiences five distinct phases of emotional acceptance of the dying process. Anger was the first stage—the stage that had completely overtaken Mel. Wendy, now armed with this practical knowledge, protected herself from his outbursts by sympathetic understanding.

But her real feeling about Mel was hardly as detached and clinical as a magazine writer's. Mel had been given a death sentence. He and Wendy were different now; his disease freed her from her own self-torture and punishment. She could no longer blame herself for the miserable state of their marriage. Or for Mel's unhappiness, for that matter. His fate was out of her hands. His life was his own. Mel Jacobs's destiny had been cast. But Wendy would go on living. With that realization, Wendy saw that she was suddenly free to start over . . . . now, if she chose. Mel's fits of uncontrollable rage, his threats of bodily harm were useless against her. The old Mel Jacobs now existed only in her mind. Al Peterson, however, existed in reality. Despite their ill-fated taxi ride, she still couldn't get him out of her thoughts. He'd apologized with more roses and a card that said, simply: Sorry. But he hadn't called and, like it or not, Wendy missed hearing his voice.

Wendy anxiously scanned the jumble of faces before her, seeking out Al's, remembering that once she had as nervously looked for Mel. It was thrilling to anticipate being locked in the arms of someone who reciprocated her warm feelings. How long since she'd felt that way about Mel? How long since she'd felt her heart pounding at the thought of him, the palms of her hands sweaty with the memory of his last caress? Months? Years! Now that excitement was all back again, that urgency to be with him, to hear his voice, to feel a part of him . . . only this time it wasn't Mel Jacobs.

"Well, Miss Holier-than-thou," Mel grumbled as Wendy joined him, "how about a drink? You could use one." Her new calm and unflappability bewildered and angered him.

"No thanks. I'm fine." She caught Mel's eyes for one telling second before scanning the crowd once again.

"Looking for anyone in particular? Perhaps a knight in shining armor?" Mel asked sarcastically.

"I've already found one," she turned back to Mel now. "On second thought, I *will* have that drink. Get me a white wine, will you, dear?"

The thirsty crowd surged and flowed around the bar, eventually forcing the Jacobses to seek refuge against a wall that offered a view of the parade up the grand staircase. Although it was after nine, the hordes of new arrivals showed no sign of abating. Indeed, as it grew fashionably later, the downstairs lobby grew more congested. Some of the guests were familiar to Wendy, but many were totally unknown. She spotted *TNT*'s director, producer, and actors climbing the stairs. Wendy was a guest by marriage only. It suddenly occurred to her that next year there would probably be no invitation.

Next year.

She watched Mel staring dourly down the stairwell and found herself fighting a wave of nostalgia. "Do you actually know all these people?" she inquired to ease the feeling.

"I don't think anyone knows everyone . . . not even Rita."

Wendy scanned the crowd. "Where is Rita?"

Mel laughed raucously. "She'll wait till the last minute then make an entrance that would put Cleopatra to shame. It's the high point of the evening. Once she comes barging up these stairs, the party's over." At parties and business functions Mel felt the old insecurities. In the *TNT* office he was somebody. Here he was merely Rita Martin's second.

Wendy nodded and looked back toward the bar. Al Peterson was there, in the midst of a tight group composed of Patty Fellows, Alex Thorpe, Jim Goodspeed, Maggie "Rebecca Danforth" Taylor, and a handsome, suntanned stranger. It was obvious that the aging but still seductive Maggie was holding court. Her largerthan-life voice and sweeping gestures proved her every inch an actress and the uncrowned queen of *Time Nor Tide*. The others seemed fascinated, laughing when appropriate, but their darting eyes told another story. All but Peterson's. He paid strict attention to Maggie, looking as if he were spellbound. For a second Wendy was jealous. She wanted him to listen to her with that intensity, but that was silly. The *TNT* party was as much work as it was play. Peterson's interest in the old actress had to be purely professional.

"Let's mingle," she said. She planned to move toward Al and the others.

"If anyone wants to talk to me, they can damn well come here. I'm in no mood to be social."

"Maybe we should have stayed home. After all, you haven't been feeling well." She'd discovered that Mel's denial of his illness was quick and spontaneous. One mention of it got instant results.

"Stop trying to make an invalid of me," he growled. "If you had your way, I would be home in bed. Come on." He grabbed her by the hand and led her away from Peterson toward Gordon Tate and some of his cronies.

For Wendy the next half hour seemed like an eternity. She feigned interest in Mel's shoptalk while thinking only of Peterson. Tonight was a night for compliments and puffery, but Mel's flättery was almost baroque. Wendy wondered how Gordy managed to keep a straight face. She hated the superficiality of the television world yet understood the necessity of its rules. With so many delicate egos packed into a single space, the potential for hurt feelings and ugly confrontations was staggering. Mel was a pro at being charming. Wendy wished that once or twice in the past he'd used that charm on her instead of wasting it on these toadies of Rita's. Lately, she'd wished so many things in their life together had been different . . . now that it was too late.

"Why, there you are! I've been looking all over for you two," Patty Fellows practically screamed as she broke up the mini-conference. "Why are you hiding over here in a corner?"

"We're not hiding, we just wanted to get away from the crowds," Wendy responded. She embraced Patty, grateful to have been rescued.

"My dear, have you ever seen so many people? Tell me, are you having a good time?" Patty winked surreptitiously at Wendy.

Wendy caught sight of Al approaching them. "Yes, I think I am," she answered softly.

"You show extremely good taste, my dear." Patty had followed Wendy's eyes. "And you look *so* beautiful. Is that your disco outfit?" Patty stepped back to admire the sexy Mary McFadden Wendy wore as casually as a pair of old slacks.

"It's the best I could come up with," she blushed, "Fiorucci was closed."

Patty took her hand, laughing. "Thank God for small favors. Everyone here seems to have ignored the disco trend . . . except for Loretta Minor." She turned and looked back into the crowd. "That's her—the one who looks like a foil-wrapped baked potato."

Wendy stole a quick glance at the actress who played Laurelton's bighearted hooker. She was dressed in a silver lamé halter top, silver stretch shorts, and balanced precariously on roller skates. "How do you suppose she got upstairs?" Wendy wondered.

"More important, how will she get back down?" Patty broke into wild laughter. "Leave it to Loretta to play her role to the hilt. If she's really clever she may even make a couple of bucks while she's here. Although tonight there's some pretty stiff competition," she proclaimed with a tipsy smile. "After all, everyone here is a whore of one kind or another—present company excluded, of course, my dear."

Wendy was about to agree when Peterson emerged through the throng. Wearing a 1920s-style dinner jacket that made him look blonder than ever, Al Peterson was the epitome of elegance. He'd never looked handsomer.

"Jay Gatsby, I believe," Wendy joked, extending her hand to him.

"And Daisy . . ." He kissed her hand regally.

Patty stepped back to admire them. "Ah ha, the perfect match. Two gold people from East Egg . . . or was it West——?"

"Bad egg, if you ask me," Mel interrupted. "How's it going, Peterson?" He moved forward, edging Wendy out.

Al nodded. "Mighty impressive party."

"Oh, it gets better later on. The network holds games. Remember bobbing for apples? Well, tonight we have bobbing for new contracts." It was meant as a joke, but Mel's bitter edge flattened it.

"So that's how it's done. I always wondered," Peterson continued the jest, trying to keep the conversation light. "What happened to our esteemed hostess?"

Mel slid his arm protectively around Wendy's waist. "I thought maybe *you* could tell us where Rita is."

"Sorry, our hotline seems to have broken down."

Anxious to avoid a scene with Mel, Wendy turned to Mr. Peterson "If I'm not being too forward, how about a dance, Mr. Peterson? That is, *if* you can disco."

He shrugged his shoulders. "I'll give it a shot. Patty, why don't you show Mel how to trip the light fantastic."

She shook her head. "I'll leave self-chiropractics up to you kids. Mel and I will just stay here and discuss world politics. Have a good time." She turned immediately to Mel. "I've just finished reading the new Penny Hewitt story projection. Mel, it's dynamite."

The dance floor was packed with couples gyrating wildly to the driving disco beat. Wendy and Al skirted it and found two places on a cluttered banquette. Despite the surging crowd, Al felt as if he and Wendy had fallen into another dimension where only they existed.

"This is *some* place," Al shouted over the music.

Wendy smiled, almost as if she hadn't understood.

"*Would* you like to dance?"

She shook her head.

"How about talking?"

"I don't know what to say," she admitted. All night she had waited for this moment, and now she was speechless.

"Then let's start with the niceties? How have you been since I last saw you?"

"Confused," she replied.

"About Mel?"

Wendy stared into his eyes and shrugged.

"What then?"

"I wanted to thank you again for coming to my rescue that day at Rockefeller Center. And I wanted to thank you for all the flowers you've sent. And most of all I wanted to tell you what a fool I was in the taxi after dinner at the Russian Tea Room." She felt like laughing and crying all at the same time.

"Is that all?" he joked. "All I can say is, you're welcome, you're welcome . . . and I deserved everything you said in the cab."

"Al, no . . ." she began to protest.

He stopped her with a wave of a hand. "I made a clumsy play for you because maybe for the first time in my life I really thought I was beginning to care about someone. And it scared the shit out of me."

She reached out and took his hand. "You're so different from Mel. He doesn't let himself feel anything. Oh sure, he goes through the motions, but it's like he's already dead."

"And me? What's your diagnosis of me?"

"On the outside you're cool and collected, always saying the right thing at the right time—that's *your* defense. Inside you're . . ." Her words faltered.

"Well, don't keep me in suspense. Inside . . . ?" He wanted to hear her say it.

"You're like me." She quickly squeezed her hand then let go.

Al moved closer. "So what are we going to do about it? Two people finding a soul mate just doesn't happen every day in this city."

"We're going to be very careful. My feelings are beginning to show. I don't think Mel has noticed—he's too preoccupied. But I feel myself change as soon as you're around. I relax, get freer, happier. Mel's no fool. Sooner or later he'll notice how much I . . . like you."

"Would that be so bad?"

"I don't want to complicate my life right now, Al. Surely you can understand that."

"Would it make your life more—or less—complicated if I told you I think about you all the time?" He kissed the back of her hand. "Only dreamers believe that life is simple and uncomplicated. For people like us it can be rotten and unfair. But once that's accepted we've got an edge."

"I just want to be happy with what's really mine."

"Does that mean your marriage?"

"I don't love Mel, if that's what you want to know . . . but he's all I have." It was a terrible admission.

"There you're wrong, Mrs. Jacobs. You have *me* . . . if you want me. Look, I know it's a rough time for you with Mel being sick, but you've got to start thinking of yourself. You've already surrendered too much of your life—and he's misused that trust. You don't owe Mel a thing."

Wendy didn't reply at first. Everything Peterson was saying was true, but that truth frightened her. She was used to Mel making the decisions for her. "So what do I do now?" she finally asked. Deserting Mel now seemed impossibly cruel. Yet, she wanted to leave him. If that's what Peterson wanted her to do.

"I can't make your decisions. But remember: If you want me I'm here. That's all I can offer until you make up your mind." It was more than he'd ever offered anyone before.

"But that puts you in limbo. It's so unfair."

"Let me be the judge of what's fair and unfair, okay?" He took out his handkerchief and wiped away a tear from her cheek. "Smile. How will you explain to Mel that disco music makes you cry?"

She choked back a sob and laughed at the same time. "I can't go back to him," she blurted out.

"You have to . . . for tonight anyway. Don't let Mel, or any of them, intimidate you. Hell, look at it as a challenge, play the role. You're in the company of the biggest group of liars, cheats, and cutthroats in town. Try acting like a bitch for a change—they'll respect you for it."

"I wish I had the guts to," she sighed, fixing her makeup.

"You do. Inside we're both the same, remember: two frightened kids looking for a little love and safety. Don't ever forget it . . . but don't let *them* use it against you."

"We should get back now." She got up and he put his hand on the small of her back and guided her up the back stairs.

Something had changed almost imperceptibly. People were slightly less animated, their voices reduced to hushed tones. Many couples now watched the top of the front stairs, their eyes bright with anticipation. A new tension crowded the air. Even business at the bar had waned temporarily.

"What is it?" Al asked Mel, giving up Wendy to him.

"Rita's here," he replied, casually noting that after disco-dancing neither Wendy nor Al had a hair out of place.

Al found an empty niche overlooking the entrance. Rita, smothered in a full-length tan sable, was chatting animatedly with the blond ITC guard at the door. Once she was finished, Alex Thorpe intercepted her, relieved her of the coat, and left her to get on with the business of arriving.

Rita slowly ascended the staircase, fixing her eyes on a point far beyond the crowds. She knew the effect her appearance was making. She walked regally, slowly, with exaggerated dignity. It was a perfect performance, a royal arrival, properly conducted, properly handled. At the top of the stairs she glanced around, smiling. Conversation stopped completely and someone in the crowd applauded. For a moment the sound of the lone ovation jangled the silence. Then another applauded and another and another. Finally the entire party was clapping for Rita Martin. Now Rita broke into a wide smile. She clasped her hands together before her and bowed ever so slightly.

When the applause died down and conversation began to fill the room once again, Rita joined Jim Goodspeed, who stood alone for the moment at the bar.

"You look radiant, Rita," Goodspeed praised as he accepted her kiss on the cheek.

"How could I not with so many friends around? I hardly expected applause."

"But it's so well deserved. After all, none of these people would be here if it weren't for you."

"I see you haven't changed since last time we had lunch, Jim. Still the flatterer." Their lunch date still hadn't happened, despite Goodspeed's recent commitment to a meeting.

"I'm too old to change, Rita," he replied, sidestepping the inference that she was being neglected. "And I only flatter when it's deserved. How have you been?"

"Busy as usual," she remarked benignly.

"Glad to hear it. Keeping one's head above water gets tougher and tougher each year."

"Well, I think you'll agree that the new story projection will be the final thing to pull us out of the slump," she continued, immediately wishing she had chosen a better phrase.

"We'll see," he said abruptly. Apparently Nan still hadn't told Rita there was trouble brewing with the office of broadcast standards. But tonight was the time to praise, not to criticize. "I presume you've seen the first two weeks' sweeps ratings."

"Whatever makes you think *I* follow ratings?" Rita replied with just the right touch of insouciance.

Goodspeed broke up. "Rita," he said, "I sometimes wish life were just as simple as it used to be. Remember?"

"Don't tell me the venerable Jim Goodspeed is having an attack of 'good old days-itis.' "

He shook his head. "The good old days were just as lousy as today. Life wasn't easier, but it was simpler."

"And friendship counted for so much more," she said almost wistfully.

"The important thing is, *Time Nor Tide* seems to be finding its legs again. The past ratings had us worried." Rita nodded her acknowledgment. "But you're regaining stature now. *TNT*'s got a solid number-three slot in the sweeps so far. Who's to say one day it won't be right back at number one—where it belongs?''

''We'll see,'' Rita replied quietly. After all her attempts to reach Goodspeed, his winning smile now should have been pure gold. It wasn't. His enthusiasm was a cover. Third place in the sweeps just wasn't good enough and they both knew it; particularly in light of ITC's overall fourth-place showing. Inwardly she sighed. What did she expect from Jim? Despite their mutual respect, her well-publicized friendship with him was just that—hype. It had to do with money and ratings, not personal caring. And now, it seemed, Rita couldn't even offer him that.

''Isn't Ben with you tonight?'' Jim asked, changing the subject. ''We never see him in New York these days.''

''You will,'' Rita promised. ''He's on his way. The weather's bad. He said something about an ice storm up in Connecticut.'' In fact Ben hadn't wanted to risk the drive to the city, but Rita had insisted. Perhaps she was just shifting her dependence from *Time Nor Tide* to Ben. It had been remarkably easy.

''And how's Jeannie? If you're anything like me, you must get a great deal of pleasure from your child,'' Goodspeed beamed. ''Of course with me it's grandchildren. But all kids are the same.''

''I wouldn't know what to do without her. There's nothing like having a family.'' She wondered if the real details of her past personal life had ever reached his ears.

''My sentiments, exactly. Now, I really should mingle. Need a drink before I go?'' She shook her head. ''Good seeing you again, Rita.'' He kissed her lightly on the cheek, then vanished into the crowd.

Rita got herself a white wine, took a sip, and had just started to prowl when Rick Cologna came out of nowhere, swept her into his arms, and kissed her roughly on the mouth.

''You never did learn to say 'please,' did you, Rick?'' Rita snarled as she pulled back from him.

''Don't be so touchy, Rita. I only want to say good-bye . . . officially.'' He insinuated his arm around her waist in so calculated a fashion that Rita cringed; she immediately pushed it aside.

''As far as I'm concerned, yesterday's show was your official good-bye, Rick. And it's the only one I ever could be interested in.'' At two-twenty Friday afternoon, February 14,

Frank Cameron was murdered. "Now, if you don't mind, I have some *important* business to attend to."

Rita swept off into the crowds, instantly dismissing her encounter with Cologna as tying up one of *Time Nor Tide*'s many loose ends. That made two: Jim Goodspeed was first. So now there was only one prize left to bag before the evening was out, and that was the biggest prize of all: Nan Booth.

By midnight Mel was far drunker than was safe. He sat listlessly by the bar, barely hearing Patty Fellows's harangue about her nonexistent sex life. His mind wasn't focused on Patty or even on Al and Wendy's latest defection to the dance floor. He was cued into poor Mel Jacobs. He looked blearily around the lounge, singling out first one couple, then another, for his silent curses. How dare they have a good time! He'd already insulted several people—intentionally. Those observant enough to see his foul mood carefully avoided him. Even Rita had walked away—but not before suggesting he ease up on the booze.

Mel's self-pity and anger nearly choked him. Every time he heard laughter it was like a personal affront. What gave anyone the right to enjoy life when he was dying? Until Dr. Monroe pronounced the fatal words Mel had never considered his own mortality. Death for him was a little imp who occasionally forced its way into his consciousness. Banishment was immediate. Confident the best years of his life lay ahead, Mel ignored today. He had no reason to consider death and the end to the world he had worked so hard to construct. With the future on his side, Mel skimmed along on the surface of his feelings, digging just deep enough into real emotion to make his writing believable. Now, he was burdened with the certainty that he had mismanaged his life. He craved a retreat—a Laurelton, U.S.A.—where living was uncomplicated and pain and sorrow, even death, touched others but not him.

"I tell you, Mel, I wish I had your outlook. You're always so positive about everything. Nothing seems to faze you ever. How do you do it?" Patty inquired, interrupting his dreams.

"I'm a realist," he mumbled. "No self-delusions. It pays off in the end." He spilled some of his drink down his shirtfront but didn't bother to wipe it off.

"It must work. You've got it all. A nice home, a beautiful

wife, solid career. Maybe I should try reality . . . for a change," Patty giggled drunkenly.

A beautiful wife, Mel thought angrily. A beautiful wife who's spent most of the evening with another man. Imagining Wendy in Al Peterson's arms was a relatively new idea. Adultery was a form of infidelity Wendy seemed incapable of handling. Gambling was her vice, her outside lover. It was predictable, and with his "help," controllable. But an actual lover? A man who swept her away with his love? That was a *real* threat. Well, he'd nip this little liaison in the bud. No one, particularly that stud Peterson, was going to upset his "domestic bliss."

By the time Wendy and Al staggered back from the dance floor, their faces glowing with barely disguised desire, Mel was in a rage. He waited for them to catch their breaths, then attacked. "You know, Peterson, you've spent more time with Wendy tonight than I have."

"Hey, Mel, you could have had her back for the asking," he said evenly. "You just never seemed interested."

"Since when do I have to ask permission to be with my wife? Most people would consider your horning in on my marriage a definite breach of etiquette . . . or don't you need to be polite now that you're Rita's pet?"

Wendy immediately stepped in. "Mel, I think it's time we went home."

"Do you? Well, I think Mr. Peterson here might have other plans for you."

"Don't bet on it," Al interjected, managing to control his anger.

Mel's eyes brightened. Poor, dumb Peterson had just handed him the solution to the problem. "Bet? Did you ever ask Wendy about betting? She's an expert."

Wendy blanched. Her eyes darted from Mel to Al, then back to Mel again. "Let's go! It's late," she begged, stepping back nervously in utter confusion.

Mel watched her carefully. It was easy to decipher the panic on her face. "So you didn't confess to your friend about your 'problem' while you two were dancing? Shame on you, Wendy."

The blood rose to Al's face. He resisted the urge to grab that bastard Jacobs by the throat and beat the living shit out of him. He folded his arms across his chest. "Why don't you take Wendy's advice and leave! You're stinking."

Mel spat on the floor at Peterson's feet. "And what do you call a hot-pantsed opportunist who can't wait to fuck my wife?" He struggled out of the chair and lurched toward Peterson. Wendy rushed between them and pushed Mel away. "There are a few things you should know about our Junior Miss," he continued, "*before* you invite her into your well-worn bed."

Al had had enough. He grabbed Wendy by the arm. "Come on, I'm taking you home," he announced through clenched teeth.

"She gambles, Peterson," Mel shouted loud enough to attract the attention of several bystanders. "She bets on anything. She'll even bet you how long it'll take a drop of rainwater to slide down a windowpane."

"Shut up, Jacobs," Peterson hissed.

"Oh, she'll tell you it's an illness, but I know better. It's pure selfishness. Wendy wants what she wants when she wants it," he taunted, "and she'll do anything to get it. You're not the first bimbo she's slept with," he snarled.

Wendy turned to Peterson, her eyes brimming over with tears of humiliation. "That's a lie," she said, tacitly admitting the truth of the gambling charges.

"It hardly matters. It's the next step," Mel amended. "Gambling our marriage away and fucking it away are the same thing in the end. She's poison, Peterson." He lurched forward with renewed determination, swinging wildly at his adversary.

Al pushed Jacobs back with the palms of both hands, sending him sprawling into the chair. "The end of your marriage would be a small loss, Jacobs. Now, if you know what's good for you, you won't move, because if you do I'm going to beat the shit out of you right here."

"And what would your mentor have to say if she saw you protecting the honor of another woman? I really don't think Rita would like that," he yelled, seeing Rita move into earshot behind them.

"Fuck Rita . . . and fuck you, too." Al put his arm protectively around Wendy's waist. As he turned her around to make an exit, they nearly collided with Rita.

Rita stepped back, her eyes burning with anger. "Leaving so soon, Al?"

He started to reply but never got the words out.

"Don't let *me* stand in your way. And good night to you too, Wendy."

Al hesitated, then led Wendy to the coat check. "You're coming back to my place for the night," he commanded.

"But I can't," she said, nearly in tears. "You've got to stay and apologize to Rita."

"I'll take care of her tomorrow." But Al knew no explanation would satisfy her—tomorrow or ever.

"Then I want you to take me home." It was the last place Wendy wanted to go, but it seemed a less dangerous alternative than being alone with Peterson.

"After what just happened, you want to go home . . . to him?" He slipped her coat over her shoulders. "Look, I'm not coming on to you; this is just an offer of a place to sleep for the night. Mel's drunk . . . there's no telling what he might do. Come on, Wendy, stand up for yourself for a change."

"All right," she acquiesced breathlessly, "but let's get out of here before I change my mind."

Rita stood directly in front of Mel, her shadow blocking out the glittering lights of the disco. "I want you out, Jacobs. Now! And if I ever see you in this condition again, you're through."

"I'm sorry, Rita."

"You certainly are, but I don't care. Just get the hell out of my sight." Mel was only the fall guy for Rita's anger. It was Al Peterson she wanted to crucify, and that simp Wendy Jacobs.

By 1:30 A.M. the stragglers left at the party were in very high spirits. The buffet tables, long since ravaged, were graveyards of dirty dishes, half-filled glasses, and partially eaten food. Rita worked the thinning crowd, seeking a sympathetic soul, but all the interesting—and important—people were gone. Those who remained were either too drunk or too stoned to divert her. The party was truly over, but she wasn't about to face going home alone just yet. And where was Ben? He should have arrived long ago. In fact, Rita had assumed he was here, lost in the crowd. Now it was clear he was not present.

She sat down. It had been a long, mediocre evening after the tumultuous welcoming applause. No one seemed to care she was there. And the delicate matter of her behavior toward

Nan Booth was still unresolved. Somehow, by design or by accident, Nan managed all evening to be on the opposite side of the room whenever Rita was ready to talk. The tension surrounding this impending confrontation was beginning to gnaw at her insides. Rita had been waiting two weeks to corner Nan, who, as usual, had not bothered to answer her frantic phone calls. And, to top it all off, the traitor Al Peterson had taken Wendy Jacobs off into the night. He was unwisely burning the candle at both ends—and in the middle. She got up and headed toward the coat check.

"Nice party, Rita. Thanks for everything," a drunken cameraman said, waving as he staggered past her toward the stairs.

"Glad you could make it, Tim," Rita smiled, pleased by his look of astonishment that she'd remembered his name. I haven't entirely lost my touch, she thought—at least with the technical crew.

She was about to leave when she saw a last chance to corner Nan.

She was just returning from the dance floor on the arm of Don Sheridan. Nan looked radiant. Unobserved, Rita studied her adversary, marveling at the ease with which Nan hid her sexual preferences. She carried herself gracefully, talking to Don in little secretive whispers as if they were conspirators in an amorous plot. Rita wondered exactly how many others knew the real plot was perverse and that Nan and Don acted as camouflage for each other. For one second Rita remembered Nan's kiss, and closed her eyes to dispel the image.

Nan spied Rita, made a final comment to Don, then proceeded alone across the room. "I've been looking for you all night." She kissed Rita lightly on the cheek.

"I've been mobbed! You'd think I only saw these people once a year," Rita babbled nervously.

"People just naturally gravitate toward you. It was a wonderful party, wasn't it?"

"The best ever. Thanks, Nan," she said, hating herself for sounding like a panderer.

"Don't thank me," Nan laughed. "I have nothing to do with publicity. This was entirely the PR department's handiwork." Nan actually had gone over the guest list with a fine-tooth comb, had suggested Studio in the first place, and had suggested the caterer who was a personal friend.

"I'll have to send Rhoda Hutton a little gift. She's done

such a marvelous job.'' Rita and the head of PR at ITC barely knew each other but that hardly mattered.

''Rita, you're too extravagant. You should save your money . . . there's no telling when you might need it,'' she smiled cutely. ''Well, *I've* about had it.'' She yawned daintily, as if to make her point more emphatically. ''Nice seeing you again.''

Rita froze. Was Nan actually going to walk out without alluding to their disastrous dinner? ''Have you got just a minute?'' she asked hastily.

''I am rather tired.''

''Just a minute, please, Nan. I need to explain . . . I mean apologize for that night. I acted terribly. I don't know what came over me,'' Rita said contritely. ''I know what you must think, but I can explain.''

Nan shook her head. ''What's to explain? We had too much to drink, that's all. Besides, some things are best forgotten. Now, I really must go.'' She signaled Don who now approached carrying Nan's coat and a large envelope.

Rita couldn't let her go. Despite Nan's reassurances, nothing had been settled, and her fear had been augmented by Nan's cool treatment of the whole subject. She *had* to be angry. ''Let me take you to lunch next week. I feel I owe you something.''

''You do owe me something.'' Nan smiled and touched Rita lightly on the arm. ''But lunch? You must be joking.'' She allowed Don to help her into her coat, then took the envelope from him and handed it to Rita. ''This is for you. Happy Valentine's Day, Rita.''

Nan linked arms with Don, and as they exited toward the front door, their laughter echoed in Rita's ears.

Al lit a fire in the bedroom fireplace, then turned down the sheets on his bed. ''You sleep here,'' he said, fluffing the pillows. Wendy didn't hear him. She was huddled in a chair by the window like a lost child. Al wanted to scoop her up into his arms, but that would invariably lead to sex, and he wasn't sure that she could handle that in her present fragile state of mind.

Besides, he'd promised himself to be good. No, that wasn't the truth. He'd promised himself to stay away from Wendy Jacobs completely. Write her off as far too risky an involvement. But the more he tried to forget her the more she occupied his mind. And now, against all logic and common sense, he was alone with her in his bedroom. Jesus!

"If I sleep here, where will you sleep?" Wendy asked in that silky voice of hers.

He knelt in front of her and took her hands. "There's a perfectly acceptable couch in the living room. I've spent many a night there. Don't worry."

"Do you make habit of rescuing damsels in distress? Or is the couch just more comfortable than the bed?" For an instant her humor returned. Her eyes twinkled mischievously.

"Now, would I do that to you?" She was getting to him; she really was. "I just have a habit of falling asleep in the living room while I'm reading. Now, do you need anything?"

She shook her head.

"You'll find pajamas in the second drawer of the chest. I'll put out fresh towels in the bathroom."

Wendy got up abruptly from the chair and went to the window. The cold, dark, night sky lay before her like a swatch of black velvet spattered with diamondlike stars. "I'm going to go home, Al," she said softly.

"What are you talking about?" He went to her, aware of a surge in the urgency of his desire. "You *can't* go home. I thought we'd settled that at the party."

"But . . ."

He put his fingers over her lips. "No 'buts.' If you think it's putting me out to wear my pajamas, don't wear them. If you're worried about my sleeping on the couch . . ."

"You'll sleep with me," she finished the sentence, taking a step forward so that her breasts pushed against his chest. "That night in the taxi I wanted you to make love to me, and *that's* why I wanted to leave tonight." She clasped her hand behind his head and kissed his lips. Al put his arms around Wendy, holding her close, and she melted into his embrace.

She nestled her head against his chest. "You're taking a risk being with me, Al."

"I care about you," he said, wondering if in the end that risk would be worth it. But it was far too late to turn back now, as the ache in his groin told him. "You do believe I care about you, don't you?"

She nodded her head against him. "I wish I cared about me."

He lifted her face to his. "There'll be no more talk like that from you . . . understand? It's not true, and it makes you sound pitiful."

"What Mel said tonight about me . . . about my gambling . . . is true." Wendy's voice dared Al to slough that off.

"Do *you* think you have a problem with gambling?" he demanded.

She nodded her head.

"Do you want to do something about it?"

"I don't know if I can."

"But all you need is a desire to stop."

She nodded her head again. "I want to stop."

"Then we'll find someone to help you." He kissed her again, hoping to soothe her self-doubts, trying to calm the excited trembling he wrongly guessed was fear. "Life's not all that complicated, Wendy; it's really rather simple—if you don't let yourself be taken in by the bullshit artists."

"Show me how simple it is," she said huskily, and she took him by the hand to the bed.

They shed their clothes quickly and slid between the warm sheets. In the dancing firelight Wendy's skin glowed seductively. Al kissed her hair, rubbing his face against its silkiness. He nibbled her ear and then kissed her long, lovely neck.

"You're so beautiful," he whispered.

"Did you really think I'd let you sleep alone tonight, Mr. Peterson? It was very gallant of you to imagine my honor needed protecting, but that's one decision I'm not afraid to make for myself." She moved her hand to his hard cock and moaned with anticipation.

Peterson was overcome by desire. He kissed Wendy's breasts, her flat throbbing abdomen, and finally between her legs. She moaned under his touch, pulling at his hair, wondering how she had managed to deny herself the pleasure of his touch even this long.

Wendy and Al seemed designed for each other. From her responses Al knew that in his fantasies of making love to her he'd instinctively mapped out her pleasure points. She twisted under his hands and mouth, her body writhing with unabashed pleasure. And seeing her excitement, her face so absolutely wanton, Al surrendered to his own deepest cravings. He devoured Wendy with the hunger of a man starved for love.

With Mel, Wendy was completely restrained in her lovemaking. Mel worked on her, repeating the familiar pattern of kisses and embraces that guaranteed him a swift climax. Wendy bore his rutting as part of her punishment. Tonight, Wendy felt like all women, drunk on her own sexual power. She matched his lovemaking—from sharp bites on the nipples, to the lavish attention paid to his genitals. There was nothing she couldn't do with Peterson. Nothing she didn't want to do. Nothing she didn't do.

And just when they both were moved to the brink from extreme desire, Al plunged himself into Wendy without warning, thrusting himself deep inside. He flung his arms around her and crushed her to him. He drove himself into her over and over again, responding to her cries by accelerating his pace. Wendy climaxed first. She clutched Al's back and moaned with the unbearably sweet pleasure. And when it was over for her, she kept her eyes fixed on him, now tense with the physical expectation of approaching release. When he did come, she pulled him deeper still, pushing her hips against him.

Mel stumbled into the bedroom and fell heavily into a chair. The room was spinning dizzily before him. He closed both eyes and felt even worse. How would he get to bed without falling? Dr. Monroe warned him about drinking, but Mel knew better than any sawbones what was good or bad for Mel Jacobs. Still, his stomach was burning and the nausea that started in the taxi erupted into his throat. He dashed to the bathroom just in time.

When the attack was over, Mel stripped off his sweaty clothes and took an ice-cold shower. By the time he was in his pajamas the pain was gone, and he was feeling considerably better. Risking the danger of mixing alcohol and drugs, he took a pain pill—just in case. After all, what was the worst that could happen? The combination might be lethal.

"Shit, I'm going to die anyway," he admitted to his image in the mirror. He closed his eyes and gripped the edge of the sink. "No! I won't die. Doctors have been wrong before. What gives *them* the power to say who will live and who won't?" His stomach rumbled and for a minute he feared he might be sick again. "No wonder I don't feel well . . . look at all I drank. I'll lay off the booze for a while, that's what I'll do."

Mel stared at himself in the mirror. He looked like hell. His skin was ashen, and newly formed dark circles under his eyes made him look a weary ten years older than he was. To make matters even worse, he'd lost weight over the past weeks. His clothes no longer really fit properly, and he looked badly dressed. He tried a brave smile but stopped when he saw his gums had gone a deathly gray.

Mel staggered back to the bedroom. He hadn't really expected to find Wendy home, and the sight of the untouched bed was grimly satisfying. Mel liked to think he knew his wife better than she knew herself. At that moment she was shacked up with Peterson, probably telling him what an ogre Mel Jacobs was. Maybe tonight she has a right to bitch, he thought ruefully. I went too far with that gambling stuff. But she deserved to be slapped down. If she thinks I'm going to play the happy cuckold, she has another thing coming. They both do.

As far as he was concerned she could set up housekeeping with Peterson—they deserved each other. Let Peterson try to support Wendy's life-style on his measly writer's salary, which—if Mel had anything to say—would soon be cut off. He'd seen the hate in Rita's eyes. It wouldn't take much prompting to convince her that Peterson was just so much dead weight. Mel would make sure he personally fired that cocky bastard.

Despite the hour and the effects of the booze, Mel was too keyed up to sleep. He rummaged through his briefcase and found the videotape of yesterday's show. He'd been too busy to watch it on the air and it was a red-letter day—Frank Cameron was to be murdered. He turned on the television, slipped the cassette into the player, and climbed into bed with the remote control in his hand. Because Cameron died in the last five minutes, Mel scanned the tape through the last set of commercials. Then he lay back to savor the final minutes on earth of Frank Cameron.

Cameron sat quietly in his furnished room going over his checkbook. He stared at the pages intently as he added up the columns of figures. When they were totaled he smiled. "Frankie, baby, you're about to become a very rich man." He stashed the book in a desk drawer and poured himself a drink. "Yessir, you've really written your own ticket this time."

The phone rang, and he quickly answered it. His voice was low and cautious.

"Yeah? Who is it?" The tension drained from his face, and he grinned. "Oh, sure. How ya doin'?" He nodded his head at the answer. "You want to come here?" He thought for a second, looked around, then nodded to the unseen caller. "Sure, why not? You've got the address."

After hanging up Cameron poured himself another drink, then lay down on the unmade bed. "Will wonders never cease?" He turned up the lamp but the room became too bright, so he turned it back down. He emptied his glass, got up, straightened the bed, combed his hair, and waited.

A minute later there was a light knock on the door.

"Coming." He adjusted his clothes and opened the door. "This is an honor," he bowed slightly. This was Frank Cameron at his cockiest.

The visitor entered the room. Whoever it was wore an overcoat and a slouch hat. It could have been a man or, as easily, a woman. From any angle, it was impossible to tell which.

"Well, now, what can I do for you? Maybe you want to borrow a little money, huh?" He laughed a short, ugly laugh.

The stranger said nothing.

Cameron's smile disappeared. "Well, what do you want?" he demanded, his voice harsh.

The visitor moved farther into the room and reached into the trench coat pocket. Seconds later a gloved hand leveled a small revolver at Cameron's abdomen.

Cameron stumbled back a pace or two, his face contorted with fear. "Hey, what's the idea? What kind of game are you playing?"

The visitor raised the gun and slowly squeezed the trigger once . . . twice . . . three times.

"Oh, my God," Cameron wheezed as he doubled over and fell to the floor.

The murderer quickly moved to Cameron's crumpled form and, with the tip of a boot, pushed him over onto his back. As Cameron's lifeless face filled the screen the Time Nor Tide *theme swelled up in the background and the picture faded to black.*

"Exit Frank Cameron, exit Rick Cologna," Mel mused with a shake of his head. "That's *last* year's dirty laundry all tied up in a neat little package. Let's see what the new year brings. How much more blood will go down the *TNT* sluices before next year's Valentine's party?''

Next year!

He slammed his fist down hard on the bed over and over again. Then he picked up the bottle of pain-killers and threw them against the blank television screen. The bottle shattered, scattering pills all over the carpet.

Rita sat numbly on the couch in her living room, Nan Booth's empty envelope at her feet. In her lap was the proof that her worries had been justified. With a quick, reflex motion Rita pushed the copies of Al Peterson's memos to Nan to the floor. They made her sick.

How had she been so naïve? If Nan had bought off Peterson she must have gotten to others, too. But who? It didn't take long to peg Alex Thorpe's recent emotional distance as guilt. That wasn't so surprising, really. Thorpe's talents were limited and he—more than anyone—knew that if there was a shake-up at *TNT* he'd be one of the first to go.

Mel was in too high a tax bracket to turn traitor. And Tom was through, although Rita hadn't yet made the official announcement. Tom's behavior was a real disappointment. After all their years of close association on the show, the least she'd expected from him was a formal notice of his intention to quit. Nothing had been forthcoming. And except for a few terse reports she'd practically had to pull from that goddamned smug roommate—the latest story had Tom on an ''extended vacation'' to the California desert—Tom Wesley no longer existed. With him now totally out of the picture, that was four down and how many left to go before uncovering more defectors to Nan Booth's side?

Suddenly Rita was exhausted by the prospect of reviewing her ranks to weed out betrayers. The whole business was shabby. From the looks of it, it was too late to mount defenses anyway. And it looked like there was no one to blame but herself. She had become a major—if unwitting—accomplice in her own undoing, not only a key figure who helped construct the bomb that would destroy her, but the very person whose job it was to detonate the explosion. If only she had been less demanding of Al Peterson, she might have kept his loyalty. If only she had not had dinner with Nan, there might have been a good shot at mediation over *TNT*'s problems. Now the case was closed. She was painfully, desperately alone. If only there was someone she could turn to. But there was someone . . .

She reached for a cigarette. The Lucky Strikes on the coffee table were months old, but she hungrily inhaled the acrid smoke. She looked at the clock—three A.M.—and reached for the phone anyway. Obviously Ben had decided not to come to town. Rita smiled as she pictured him asleep. He'd be madder than hell when the phone woke him—until he heard her voice. God, it was good knowing he was there for her. She could hardly wait to hear his voice. But the phone rang endlessly. Rita slammed down the phone.

Had Ben deserted her, too?

Ten minutes later she was agonizingly preparing for bed when the phone shattered the silence. With one swift motion she snatched it from its cradle. "Ben?"

"I'd like to speak to Mrs. Benjamin Elliott," a strange, male voice requested.

"This is she. Who is this?"

"This is Sergeant Cromwell of the Connecticut State Police."

Before he said another word Rita was already scared. She braced for trouble. "What can I do for you, Sergeant Cromwell?"

"Mrs. Elliott, there's been an accident involving your husband and daughter."

"How bad is it?" Rita's voice was barely audible.

The police officer remained silent.

"How bad is it?" she demanded, her voice now tinged with hysteria.

"Your husband was driving on the Merritt Parkway . . . with the ice storm, conditions were treacherous . . . the car skidded out of control," he said flatly.

"And Ben?"

There was a long silence. "Mrs. Elliott . . ."

Rita closed her eyes. "He's dead, isn't he?"

"Your husband died in the Greenwich Hospital about an hour ago. We've been trying to reach you all night," he said apologetically.

"I was at a party," she confided for no particular reason. "A party for me. Ben was supposed to be there." Only when she tasted the saltiness of her tears did Rita know she was crying. "He didn't want to come but I made him change his mind," she sobbed.

"Is there anyone you can call to be with you?"

Rita shook her head in answer. "No. What do I do now?"

"I'm afraid you'll have to come up here tomorrow. Will you be able to do that?"

"Yes, of course." Visions of the long black ITC limousine, now so funereal, came to her mind. How often had she cursed the drive to Connecticut, because it took her away from the things she thought she cared about to a family she wasn't willing to love?

"I'll have someone meet you at eleven, if that's convenient."

No, it's not convenient, she wanted to scream. It's not convenient that Ben is dead, and I'm going to have to identify his body. No, no, no, it's not convenient at all.

"Mrs. Elliott?"

"Eleven will be fine. The Greenwich Hospital. Thank you, sergeant."

"Mrs. Elliott, your daughter was with your husband. Did you know that?"

Rita gagged. How much could she take? Ben dead . . . and Jeannie too? "Is she dead, too?" Her voice was so emotionless it scared her.

"Your daughter suffered some minor contusions, and the doctors had to take a few stitches. The padded hood of the parka she was wearing saved her life. She keeps asking for you."

Rita broke down completely. She rested the telephone in her lap and cradled her head in her hands. Jeannie was asking for her.

Summoning up all her strength Rita spoke to the police officer once again. "Tell my daughter Mommy is on her way. Tell her . . . I'll see her tomorrow," she sobbed.

"She's a beautiful child, Mrs. Elliott. You're very lucky."

"Thank you, sergeant, that's nice of you to say," Rita mouthed the words incoherently. "Thank you for your understanding." She hung up.

Rita needed to talk to someone. She picked up the phone, then hesitated. Who could she call? With whom could she share her pain? After a minute she replaced the receiver. There was no one who cared about Rita Martin. She had isolated herself from friendships as a way of making herself invulnerable. And now there was no one to turn to.

BOOK THREE

14

Rebecca Danforth looked regal. She wore her hair coiffed high on her head and accented by an antique comb. Her eyes sparkled with life as she smiled. Had Rebecca not been dressed in a shapeless gray prison dress, she might have been hostessing a dinner party for Laurelton's finest.

Dark shadows from the prison bars fell across the dingy cinder-block wall behind her, symbolizing her incarceration. Rebecca Danforth was no longer a free woman. She sat quietly at a long oak table opposite Bob Garrick, her lawyer. In a corner of the consultation room, a mannish, uniformed matron observed the proceedings with exemplary caution.

Although Garrick was no longer in the prime of youth, he was still strikingly handsome. Therefore it was odd that today he looked old and tired. "Rebecca, you must tell me the truth."

"I have *told you the truth, Bob. There's nothing more to tell," she replied quite seriously.*

He leaned back in his chair and shook his head. "I've known you for quite a number of years, haven't I?"

"Since you were a baby, though I don't expect you'd remember that."

He smiled tolerantly. "And during those years I suspect I've gotten to know you—and your habits—quite well."

"As well as anyone."

"Then why are you lying to me?" he almost leaped at her.

Rebecca's face froze, and the charity-ball smile vanished.

"I resent that, Bob. Why would I lie to you? You're my lawyer."

"That's exactly what I can't figure out. Rebecca, you're in trouble. The charge is murder one, not a parking violation."

"You sound like one of those dreadful television policemen now," she noted testily.

"This is real, *Mrs. Danforth." His formality was an attempt to convey the gravity of her situation. "You are accused of murdering Frank Cameron. Yet you choose to treat the entire matter as a joke."*

"I'm sorry if it seems I take the charge lightly. I do realize the danger I'm in, but there's really nothing to be done, is there?" She stood her ground firmly.

"Maybe if I take another approach, you'll understand what I'm trying to say. You knew Frank Cameron, didn't you?" She nodded slowly. "And you knew he was—how shall I put it?—not the most savory character ever to live in Laurelton."

"All you had to do was look at him to see that, Bob."

"Then why did you invite such a person into your home?" he snapped back.

For a moment Rebecca was at a loss for words. "Who said I invited him into my house?"

"The prosecution has a witness who will swear that Frank Cameron was seen on more than one occasion being admitted into your house by your maid."

"I needed some landscaping done," Rebecca lied quickly. "Mr. Cameron once mentioned to me—at the hospital—that he was experienced in gardening, and there were some trees that needed pruning——"

"Was your regular gardener ill?" Garrick interrupted. "Or did Cameron work with him? How did they get along? Will your gardener verify your story?"

Rebecca fell back against the chair under the weight of Garrick's staccato onslaught. "Please stop badgering me! You act as if you're cross-examining me," she said haughtily.

"My treatment of you is nothing compared to what the district attorney's will be; I'm your friend, he's not." Garrick paused and lit a cigarette. "Well, how would you answer those questions?"

"I finally decided Mr. Cameron was not suited to the job."

"And it took three visits for you to make that decision? Come on, Rebecca, you're lying to me and you know it."

Without another word she pushed her chair back from the

table and signaled the matron. "I'd like to return to my cell now," she announced softly.

Garrick reached across and took her hand. "Please, for your own sake . . ."

Rebecca pulled her hand away. "I will not sit here and be called a liar by someone who is supposed to be defending me . . . and who is also supposed to be my friend." She stood up. "Perhaps, Mr. Garrick, I made a mistake in hiring you." She turned and strode from the room followed by the matron.

Bob Garrick crushed out his cigarette and stared after her, his face contorted with concern.

Rita turned off the television, aware that she had only half-watched the last three acts of *Time Nor Tide*. Inattention was something new in her life, but since Ben's death so much was new. After the funeral the most devastating revelation was the certainty that her independence had been totally dependent on Ben's being there. There was safety in him standing in the wings while she pirouetted center stage.

Kathleen Flannagan, their fiftyish, staunch Irish-Catholic housekeeper, came to the door. Her immense bulk blocked the light from the hall. "Will you be having dinner with Jeannie again, Mrs. Elliott?"

"Yes, I'll be here, thank you." Rita smiled to break through the housekeeper's stony reserve. Mrs. Flannagan was a charter member of the "I hate Rita Martin" fan club, but since Ben's death she'd actually verged on being friendly several times. That was yet another change in her life. "Please set the table in the dining room, will you?"

"The dining room? What's wrong with the kitchen?" Mrs. Flannagan hated unnecessary work as much as she disliked people who put on airs. "*Mr.* Elliott always had dinner with Jeannie in the kitchen," she said defiantly.

"And I'm sure he had good reason. But now that Mr. Elliott's gone, let's try it my way, shall we?"

"It's *your* house, Mrs. Elliott."

"Mrs. Flannagan . . . you don't like me very much, do you?" Rita said suddenly.

The housekeeper looked surprised. "You sure don't beat around the bush, do you?"

"I find it easier to deal with people by being honest. Now, answer my question . . . please."

"I can't say I don't like you . . . because I don't really

know you. You've never been around long enough for that to happen,'' she said, matching Rita's disarming candor. ''What I don't like is the way you've been with Jeannie in the past. For heaven's sake, Mrs. Elliott, that poor child lives on love. The minute you take it away, well, I just don't know what will happen.'' She shook her head sadly at the thought.

''I wouldn't worry too much about Jeannie. She'll be well provided for.''

Mrs. Flannagan looked fearfully at Rita, trying to read her expression. ''You won't be sending her away, will you?''

''If that should happen, you'll have plenty of notice,'' Rita remarked.

''Never mind me. It's the child I'm worried about. With Mr. Elliott gone, how's she going to survive on her own?''

''She's not 'on her own.' Now please do as I asked.'' Rita watched Mrs. Flannagan retreat to the kitchen. God, I'm losing my touch with people, she thought to herself. What the hell's wrong with me?

She lit a cigarette and settled herself on the old couch in her study. This was her room. Her escape. Much more than the New York penthouse with its lavish appointments. The study was cheerfully furnished with heavy pine chairs and a couch upholstered with garish tartan plaids, miles of bookcases, an ancient rolltop desk, and the first electric typewriter she'd ever owned—a gift from Ben. Once she had escaped here to destroy her pain by creating *Time Nor Tide*, now she was back again to destroy another kind of pain.

Ribbons of sunlight rippled through the windows and danced like an oasis mirage over the radiator. Winter was over. Spring was creeping into the countryside. From the back lawn the first crocuses, their leaves like spiny green fingers, reached for the sun in random patterns. When the flowers blossomed they spotted the grass yellow, white, and purple, like spatterings from a hastily cleaned paintbrush. Everything was coming to life again. Yet Rita could only sense death.

Since Ben's death she'd been unable to concentrate on anything at all. This distraction was such a problem that she'd fallen dangerously behind in the preparation of outlines for her dialogists. It was already mid-April and there was barely enough story line delineated to carry *TNT* through the last week in May. What little work Rita did accomplish was now tackled at her Connecticut home. In her present state of mind New York's Sixth Avenue was too hostile to cope with.

After Ben's memorial service in a picturesque West Willow church, and the interment, Rita had had a small party in the Irish manner, a helpful suggestion of Mrs. Flannagan's. Rita hoped this gathering of the "family"—friends and business associates—might restore her flagging spirits and prepare her to reenter the world of soap operas. It had done just the opposite.

No matter how valiantly she tried to be brave, she failed. No matter how she tried to involve herself in the money talk of the network executives and the plot manipulations of the writers, she was more and more reminded of the ephemeral nature of their power and of their worries. The party had become more somber than the funeral. Even her staunchest supporters fled after an hour. Rita wasn't so surprised, however, when she caught sight of herself in a mirror. Where she usually saw her smiling business face was a drawn, tired mask of grief, eyes red from weeping.

Rita didn't remember actually crying for Ben. There were those tears while talking to the state trooper. But that was all. Or was it? After the guests paid their final condolences and hurried away, she sat down in the living room and surveyed the rubble of half-filled glasses and the remnants of Mrs. Flannagan's buffet. Within minutes she was crying. And as she sobbed she tried to remember a time during the past few days when she had not let her feelings get the better of her. There was none. Ben's death was like a final verdict of guilty. He was taken as reparation for her sins without a warning, without the chance to say good-bye. And when she finally, irrevocably, understood she would never again hear his voice, Rita prepared herself to face the life of loneliness she knew had been her destiny all along.

She walked through the weeks after Valentine's Day like an automaton, but deep inside her there was a core of grief that hurt so much. She wanted to tear at it, to lance it like a festering boil. But she could not. Her fury at Ben's death and her self-hatred seemed complete and all-consuming. She hardly remembered who the old Rita Martin was. How she acted and dressed. What the important things in her life used to be.

And Rita wasn't the only one to see the change. It was reflected in the faces and actions of those nearest her. Sandy became overly solicitous. Mel actually challenged her decisions. And worst of all, Nan Booth had intervened twice. She gave Alex Thorpe the ax the week after Ben's death . . . and she hired that traitor, Al Peterson, as a free lance to cover for Tom Wesley, in addition to his regular work, until someone full-time could be found.

For a time after this overt move against her and *Time Nor Tide,* anger conquered inertia and Rita had tackled the mountain of leftover work with renewed vigor. But all too soon, as the long days and interminable nights went on, her interest in *TNT* began to flag. Rita blamed her antipathy on a variety of causes. Ben's death certainly was important, and Al Peterson's betrayal ranked high on the list, too. Since his despicable behavior had come to light, Rita had tried to cut him out of her life, but his new duties often put him precariously close. Their affair now seemed folly, a way to pass time while fate prepared to deal its inevitable blow upon blow.

Now Rita was determined to work again. She opened the script and tried to concentrate. But fifteen minutes later she threw her pen down and got up. "I can't do it. It's just no good," she said, and fled the study.

Bright shafts of warm sun fell across the wide plank floors of the hallway. Rita passed the kitchen and went downstairs to Ben's study. In a far corner his cherished grandfather clock ticked metallically, jangling her nerves. She ran her hands over the familiar curves of the furniture and fleetingly touched precious, sentimental objects, hoping they might explain what she really felt. But the ominous, painful knot of sorrow that strangled her heart refused to yield. She paced aimlessly about the room, trying to muster up some sense of purpose. It was useless.

Although Rita was more comfortable in Connecticut than at any other time since Jeannie's birth, there was a dramatic change in her feelings toward the house itself. The rooms seemed too large. The house was meant for a family of four or five, at least. Now that her family had been cut to just two, Rita felt trapped in a vast maze of rooms whose inner secrets she could never possibly hope to explore. Maybe one day soon she'd sell the house and return to New York forever. She'd forget Ben and find a good school for Jeannie. Then the past would be buried. And everything would be okay again. Or would it?

Angry that her feelings had once again interfered with her work, Rita broke away and went directly to the kitchen. Mrs. Flannagan stood at the sink peeling potatoes for dinner. She looked up briefly as Rita entered, then silently continued her task. Rita opened the refrigerator and searched for something to eat. She wasn't hungry but she needed something to get her mind off herself.

"Is Jeannie home from school yet?" she asked as she took out a wedge of cheese.

"Here I am, Mommy," Jeannie replied before Mrs. Flannagan could answer. She was sitting on the pantry floor running a large wooden spoon around the inside of an empty bowl.

"What are you doing, honey?" Rita asked.

"Cooking dinner for you and Daddy," Jeannie answered solemnly.

Mrs. Flannagan stopped her work and waited for Rita to reply, for a moment looking sympathetic. "Come here, Jeannie. I want to talk to you," Rita said evenly. She'd promised herself to give up trying to explain Ben's absence to Jeannie, but each time she mentioned him, asked where he was, Rita renewed her efforts to make sense of a death she, herself, didn't understand.

Jeannie carefully rested the spoon in the bowl, then ran wildly across the kitchen to her mother. Ben was right, Rita thought as she extended her hands to her daughter: Jeannie *is* growing up. Hoisting the child onto her lap, Rita grunted, "Oh, you're getting to be a big girl. You're going to be a young lady soon."

"Like you?" Jeannie asked, all smiles.

Rita caught Mrs. Flannagan's eye, and they exchanged smiles. "You've got a few more years to go before you're as young as I am, darling." When the child looked at her uncomprehendingly, Rita simply smiled and brushed a wisp of Jeannie's hair off her forehead. "What were you making for dinner?" she asked, unsure how to approach the subject of Ben.

"Pizza," Jeannie giggled inordinately.

"Pizza?" Rita laughed. It was her daughter's favorite. "You'll get fat if you're not careful." She tickled Jeannie into a fit of laughter. Now for the hard part. "And who are you making pizza for?"

"Me and you and Daddy . . . and Mrs. Fannigan," she mispronounced the housekeeper's name as she had since she'd learned to talk.

Rita looked her daughter straight in the eyes. "Daddy won't be here for pizza, Jeannie."

Jeannie's eyes opened wide with disbelief. "Oh? He's still not coming home?"

Rita cradled her daughter's head against her breast and smoothed her hair again. "Daddy had to go away, dear. He wanted me to tell you how much he loves you and how much he'll miss you," she explained barely above a whisper. Rita had no idea what these words meant to Jeannie. Ben had been so important in her life that his absence could never fully be explained. Rita had tried over and over again, but Jeannie only seemed to understand that he was gone for right now—not forever.

But today Jeannie held tight to Rita as tears filled her eyes. "You won't go away, too, will you, Mommy?" she asked, her voice full of anguish. "Will you leave me all alone?"

The pain, the sharp, new loneliness of life without Ben that was mirrored in Jeannie's question stabbed at Rita and she began to tremble, closer to despair than she'd been since the funeral. "No, honey, I won't go away . . . ever."

Jeannie smiled and wiped away her tears. "I love you, Mommy."

"And I love you, too." Rita smiled through her tears. "Now why don't you go finish making your pizza? And don't forget that I like extra cheese." She kissed her on the cheek and helped her down.

Jeannie darted back into the pantry, taking one last, long look at her mother before resuming her culinary chores.

Mrs. Flannagan put her work aside and turned to Rita, her face shiny with tears. "Would you like a cup of coffee, Mrs. Elliott? And a couple of brown sugar cookies?" She dabbed at her eyes with the corner of her apron.

"That would be very nice, Kathleen." It was the first time Rita had ever called the other woman by her Christian name. "A cup of coffee would just hit the spot." She took one last glance at Jeannie and went back to the study.

Half an hour later Rita determined to fight one last fight for control over *Time Nor Tide*. She had neglected so much of her life in favor of the show that to give up on it now was to admit her sacrifices were nothing more than selfish whimsy. And that wasn't true. No matter how ruthless she'd been, her mistake had been to tip the balance, ignore the personal for the business. Ben might have been taken from her, but she could still do something to make his death less a sacrifice.

She'd get back control of *TNT* and show the bastards down on Television Row that Rita Martin wasn't through quite yet.

But this time she'd do it for Ben.

Four days later Rita was ready for action. She'd moved back to the city to keep a close watch over the workings of *Time Nor Tide*. Two late nights at the office revealed the exact nature and extent of the damage she'd allowed to slow the progress of the *TNT* machinery. In true mass-production style, a mishap at one section of the production line had put the entire plant out of order. Rita pinpointed the weak links between story line inception and the final taped version of that show—and discovered the major fault was hers. She was understaffed and overworked. Her story lines were fragmenting. The daily shows often bogged down in recapping past plot while barely advancing the various stories. Despite Frank Cameron's death, nothing new was happening at *TNT*. The murder investigation was dragging on endlessly. It was the same old crap day after day. And even an amateur knew that boredom was the kiss of death for a soap opera. And yet no one at the network minded that after *TNT*'s weak showing during the February sweeps the show still had not improved.

Or so it seemed.

ITC's latest silence about their former number-one soap's gradual deterioration was curious. So curious, in fact, that Rita gave it a great deal of consideration. Had it not been for Alex Thorpe's dismissal right at the time when her defenses were at their weakest, Rita might have been lulled into believing that Goodspeed, Weatherhead, and the others were overlooking the trouble at *TNT* for the time being in deference to her personal grief. But Thorpe *had* been dumped. And that could only mean that, despite the placid surface of the network waters, Nan Booth was working her black magic in the depths. The silence now resounded with menace.

Repercussions of Nan's choice of producer were just being felt. The new man, though experienced and reputable, had the personality of a rattlesnake and the patience of a man on amphetamines. He'd already so alienated most of the cast and crew that it was showing on the air. This was an insidious form of sabotage, but effective nonetheless. And the voluminous complaints all fell on deaf ears. Nan's ears. And the bitch was still sitting on a completely revised Hewitt/Reynolds Caribbean story Rita had been forced to submit.

The week after Thorpe's dismissal, Nan had made one of her infrequent descents to the *Time Nor Tide* offices. She'd heard Rita was back in town for a couple of days, and armed with a copy of the original Caribbean story, she'd burst into Rita's office unannounced.

"Broadcast standards has a problem with your new story line." She heaved the folder onto the desk. "It has to be straightened out to certain specifications . . . if you ever want it to air."

Rita fought to remain cool, but Nan's intrusion truly rattled her. "What's the problem? I thought you'd *personally* cleared this way back before Christmas."

"I did. The censors didn't. They want changes. I've made notes in the margins." She turned to leave. "Read them over, then get back to me."

"Don't go," Rita commanded. "I'd hate to have you waste a personal trip down here. You tell me about these changes."

"Have it your own way." Nan sat opposite her. "You'll have to tone down the whole Caribbean concept. There's a dangerous political overtone to Penny Hewitt's abduction. By introducing rebels on to the show, you'll eventually have to take a stand on them—either pro or con. ITC can't allow that."

Rita instantly saw red. "Has everyone in the standards department lost their minds? The country we describe is mythical. It doesn't even exist! How the hell can there be political overtones?"

"Be realistic, Rita. You *say* it's a Caribbean island, even though it's nameless—or imaginary. But the fact is there is a lot of political unrest in the islands right now, and ITC doesn't want to get involved." She lit one of Rita's cigarettes and inhaled deeply, savoring the smoke and also Rita's obvious discomfort. "Just about every island paradise is up to its ass in racial troubles, so you see the issue can't be skirted by just 'making up' a country. Viewers will think it's the Dominican Republic, Saint Croix, Jamaica . . . even Bermuda." She blew a stream of smoke in Rita's direction. "It just won't wash."

"This is bullshit, Nan. Pure and simple." Rita was so angry she had to force herself to keep from throwing Nan out of her office bodily.

"Maybe," Nan replied archly, "but that's the network's

position." Her own position was to stall Rita as long as possible.

"I have never once, in six years, had a single story line questioned before. It's unheard of . . . unthinkable. If ITC starts dictating what I can—or cannot—do, we're dealing with outright censorship." She, too, reached for a cigarette and lit it angrily, aware now that her own inertia was a key factor in the crisis. More than ever, *Time Nor Tide* needed the Caribbean story if it was ever to regain its stature. Rita knew it. And so did Nan.

"In the broadest terms it is censorship, of course, but Jim also believes it's the best way to handle the problem right now."

"Jim?" Rita barked through a cloud of smoke. "I can't believe he'd sanction this disgraceful hatchet job."

"Shall we call him?" Nan reached for the phone but Rita stopped her.

"Don't be so goddamned condescending," Rita hissed. "What else does the network object to?"

"It's all there," Nan calmly reiterated. "Read over my notes, and let me know if there's a problem."

"You're damn right there's going to be a problem. If you think I'm going to sit back and let you or any other two-bit executive tell me what to write, you're even crazier than I thought!"

Nan leaned forward, drawing precariously close to Rita. "Handle this any way you want, Rita. But let me forewarn you: There will be major changes made at *Time Nor Tide* and if you don't make them, I will."

Rita would take care of Nan later. Right now there were more direct steps she could take to salvage *Time Nor Tide*. She drew up a list of things to get done. Finding an immediate replacement for Wesley was one. Finding a replacement for Al Peterson was another. But right at the top of the list was Mel Jacobs's name. Without him fully on her side the battle was lost. She'd ask him to lunch tomorrow. Rita no longer deluded herself that she could do the show alone. Like Jeannie it had grown up. And also like Jeannie it had developed a life of its own—one that could be tended to by Rita, or ignored.

"Rita, you look marvelous. What happened?" Mel asked, then immediately realized his gaffe.

Rita snuggled against the banquette of a choice table at the Russian Tea Room and laughed. "I *have* been looking like a wild woman, but now I'm here and ready for action again."

Mel raised his kir in a toast. "To Rita Martin . . . I've missed you."

"How very sweet of you." She sipped her champagne cocktail and smiled. "I'd begun to wonder if anyone even noticed I was gone."

"It's been hell with you away," he confided. "Particularly now that Tom's drying out like a prune in the California sunshine."

"Now, now, Mel. We mustn't make jokes at poor Tom's expense." Rita was barely able to suppress her displeasure. "He was very loyal for many years. Even you'll admit that."

"The last couple of years were a bust."

"There are things in everyone's life that just can't be controlled. Tom's was drinking," she said sympathetically.

"It still irritates me when people give in to their weaknesses," he replied sullenly, thinking of his own daily struggles against the mounting pain of the past six months.

"Not everyone is as strong as you—and me—but it's unfair to hold their shortcomings against them," she mused. "Now, give me all the dirt. I feel like I've been on another planet!"

"Nan Booth has become the resident executive *yenta* down at the studio. She's watched over *TNT* like a mother hen ever since Thorpe was sacked. His replacement is a tyrant. He chews up the cast and crew but fawns all over Nan."

"Uh huh. What about Gordy? He hasn't called in weeks. *He* should have told me this, not you," she said, registering the first ripple of a tidal wave of suppressed anger.

"Tate's wrapped around Nan's little finger. The scuttlebutt has them lunching at least once a week."

"That sniveling bastard," Rita exploded. "What the hell kind of game does he think he's playing?"

"He's playing it safe, Rita. Personally I think Tate is past his prime. He's been too comfortable for too long, and now that ITC is breathing down your neck, he'd decided to choose sides—and you lost."

Mel discussed ITC's presence on the set as if it were already a forgone conclusion that they were edging Rita out. Mentally, Rita pulled herself up straight at the news, renewing her determination to be strong. After all, why bother to return to New York if she was only going to fall victim to a network plot? "And what do *you* think ITC has up its sleeve?" Mel's insight was often right on target.

He sipped his drink thoughtfully. "I don't like it . . . not at all. We're losing our autonomy. ITC is fucking us over."

"They wouldn't dare," Rita said out of habit.

"Let's be honest for a change—it's the only way we're going to get out of this alive." Rita stared at him frigidly, but remained silent. "The days when creativity and talent held sway are over. It's money now—no more, no less. Remember, television is a selling medium; it's what makes the advertising world go round."

"I don't need a lecture on television," she snapped.

"Rita, you asked me a question. Do you want an answer or not?" he silenced her without hesitation. "The whole fucking world is going to hell in a handbag, and TV mirrors the chaos. As reality gets uglier, programming becomes more banal, more a fantasy trip. Christ, just watch any sitcom . . ." His stomach contracted with pain, and he winced.

"Are you all right?" Mel's face had turned ashen.

"We'll get to me later!" A sip of kir dispersed the pain. "Our economy is beginning to act like prewar Germany's. Pretty soon a cup of coffee will cost ten bucks. ITC is no different from any other business. It's fighting for its economic life. Do you know how that makes people act?" he asked rhetorically. "Paranoid—plain and simple. Rita, *TNT* is a victim of forces so large we can't even begin to comprehend them."

"Mel, you sound like a prophet of doom, as if there's nothing we can do."

"I don't know if there *is* anything we can do. It may already be too late," he replied gloomily.

"I refuse to believe I'm powerless. No, Mel, I am not going to let these 'monstrous forces' you talk about interfere with me . . . no way." She signaled the waiter and ordered a second drink. "We'll just work harder than ever before. And the first thing to do is start the new Caribbean story rolling."

Mel sagged visibly. Rita's relocation in Connecticut coupled with his personal problems had almost defeated him. He spent most of his waking hours at the office, fighting a losing battle against a growing backlog of work. The exertion was beginning to take its toll mentally as well as physically. "I don't know if I can make it," he mumbled.

"You don't mean that. Mel, you've never let me down before." She needed Mel loyally at her side and hard at work. "Of course, the increased responsibility will mean more money for you."

"Money?" he pronounced the word as if he'd never heard it before. "Money won't influence my decision."

"Then what will?" she asked hotly. "If it's not bigger bucks what do you want? More prestige? Shared credit?"

Never in their six-year relationship had Rita ever intimated Mel would be anything but a distant second to her. Yet now she was offering him room at the top. Jesus, she's really running scared, he realized. The rumors must all be true. "Rita, I'm sick," he finally admitted.

"You just need a vacation." Her voice was flat and emotionless. "When we get over this hump . . ."

"Listen to me, Rita," he insisted loudly, fighting back the pain that flowered in his abdomen and imprisoned every nerve of his body, "I have to go to the hospital."

"What is it?" Mel was scared and his fear shook Rita's confidence in the possibility of her own success.

"It's an ulcer" he lied automatically, then added, "it's going to lay me up for a while." The denial of his cancer was now so routinized Mel almost believed it himself. Almost.

"An ulcer?" Rita laughed with relief. "*That's* nothing to worry about. You'll be out of the hospital and back to work before you know it."

"Don't be so sure. The doctor tells me there might be a long convalescence."

"Nonsense," she waved the thought away. "You're much too strong. Mel, you're like me. Nothing touches you. It's one thing I've always liked about you."

"No, Rita, I'm not as strong as you are—not this time, anyway." Mel was dying. He'd put off the operation too long, and the cancer was winning a little more each day. It held his body prisoner while it sucked all the life from him. Mel was dying and he finally understood there was nothing he could do about it.

"Don't underestimate yourself," Rita urged, "you'll pull through this with flying colors."

"Whatever you say," he complied listlessly. "Excuse me a minute, will you?" He had to get to the bathroom. Vomiting was so much a part of his daily routine that it was no more than a minor annoyance, like dandruff, to be brushed off and forgotten until it recurred.

He returned looking pale. He'd lost everything—breakfast . . . lunch . . . his taste for living.

"You do look dreadful. Maybe we should go." Rita signaled the waiter for the check. "I was thinking while you were gone . . . remember how it was those first couple of years? We were like a bunch of kids putting on a high school play——"

"Thinking about the good old days is a waste of time," Mel cut her off, embarrassed by her pathetic reminiscing. "We're so far behind with outlines that unless we haul ass, in a couple of months there won't be any *Time Nor Tide* left to worry about."

Rita instantly changed gears. "I want you to start working on Peterson. Get him *out*." It was a goal she'd savored since Valentine's Day, but because of her own difficulty after Ben's death, she had let it slide. Now was the time to act, before Peterson became too firmly entrenched.

"Much as I dislike Al, you *can't* fire him," Mel said. "And even if you could, his absence would leave us up the creek without a paddle."

"Of course I can fire him," Rita snapped. "I still run *TNT*. I can do whatever I want."

Mel looked at her in disbelief, then continued, "Al Peterson is Nan Booth's protégé, in case you'd forgotten." Everyone at ITC had heard the story of how Rita's erstwhile lover was being advocated for promotion.

"Screw Nan Booth," Rita hissed, "I have a way around her. You just do as you're told. I'll take care of the free-lance stuff." Her way around Nan was Jim Goodspeed, but so much had changed so radically Rita doubted he'd side with her. Well, she'd deal with that impasse when—and if—it occurred. In the meantime she'd find her own replacement for Tom Wesley; that would make her case against Peterson more convincing to the management.

"Rita, are you trying to destroy *Time Nor Tide* rather than hand it over to the network?" Mel leaned forward, a sly smile hovering on his lips.

Self-destruction had never occurred to Rita. She now considered it. She could kill *TNT* just as easily as she had created it. What an idea! What a final triumph! Turn her back on the show and walk away. ITC would be left holding the bag. Nan Booth would be disgraced.

"Rita?"

"I was picturing Nan Booth's face if we did dump the whole mess in her lap." She smiled serenely. "What do you say, Mel? Shall we give in to the bastards?"

"I say we stand and fight." If he had to go he'd go like a winner. Mel Jacobs never gave in. Never!

"Good boy! Now, this is what we'll do . . ."

By the time Rita got back to the office she was intoxicated by her own sense of purpose. Sure, there were things about *TNT* that needed attending to, but now she was ready to tackle any challenge. Six years of overseeing the country's most popular soap opera had prepared her to deal with exactly this situation. With a crackling optimism that made her feel ten years younger, she quickly outlined her plan of attack. She made a list of head writers to be interviewed to replace Tom, then got Sandy to start arranging appointments. When she came to Al Peterson's name on her list Rita hesitated for a second, then scratched a thick pencil line through it.

Peterson was through.

Wendy finished a long, luxurious bath, then toweled dry in front of the bedroom's full-length mirror. Lately she'd been paying closer attention to her body by lavishing it with expensive oils and moisturizers; she'd stop the aging process—if it killed her! Even in the silly floral shower cap she looked radiant, beautiful. She smirked at herself, then laughed out loud at such immodesty. God, it felt good to be alive!

She rapidly brushed her hair until it shone with fiery, golden highlights. Finally satisfied, she caught it up in a pink, satin ribbon. Had she not chosen to wear the slinky silk Chinese dressing gown once her mother's, Wendy might have looked like a mischievous little girl. As it was, the pink fabric, dotted with blind-stitch cherry blossoms, magnified the flush of her cheeks and bathed her in a subtle, sexy womanly glow. Convinced she looked something of the seductress—though her peaches-and-cream complexion was decidedly more wholesome than decadent—Wendy darted into the kitchen to silence the food timer's discordant ringing.

The entire apartment smelled of baking. That morning two quiches had come from the oven; in the early afternoon two loaves of french bread, and now, as the afternoon light dwindled in the city, Wendy removed two cake tins of devil's food cake. When did I last bake a cake? she wondered. It seemed like it must have been high school. Or as far back as her *first* wedding anniversary.

To surprise Mel that first year she had fashioned a lopsided three-tiered white cake with gooey, rich buttercream icing that they had practically devoured in one sitting. Since then cooking, like everything else, had become a thankless chore. Oh sure, once in a while she'd shoo Mrs. Swedeborg out of the kitchen to prepare something herself, but that always had more to do with boredom and killing time than it did with a loving, personal touch. How ironic that she'd met Al on one of those rare days when she looked like a happily married woman. And how quickly he'd seen she wasn't.

But now things were falling back into place. Now it was so easy—and natural—to want to do things, to shop and buy fresh vegetables and fruits, to explore recipes for an exotic dish, and, like today to spend the whole day assembling a meal as a token of her love. It was easy because her work was appreciated. And that made her deeply happy. And only occasionally did the thought occur to Wendy that photography, not cooking, was her first love and that, although she'd begun to dabble in it again, her preoccupation with housewifery was based on the plain simple fear that she would again be painfully disappointed by the limits of her talent.

On the other hand, Wendy Jacobs was changing. She wasn't that pitiful creature anymore. The other Wendy was rapidly becoming a memory, part of a Dickensian nightmare about a girl doomed to suffer endlessly. The new Wendy was a woman who stood on her own two feet, took care of herself, and *wanted* to be independent. Still, once in a while, the old vulnerability rose up to overshadow her new persona, and for a moment the world was a hostile place once again. But when that happened Wendy shunted the feelings aside by repeating the phrases that had become her beloved mantra: I *have* changed and I will *continue* to change. And I *will* begin to work seriously.

Once the cake was safely cooling on wire racks, she tested the wine stored in the refrigerator; it was overchilled. She removed the bottles to the kitchen counter, then sailed into the dining alcove with two wine glasses. The table was perfect. Two place settings, her "best" silver, a linen tablecloth and napkins, and a crystal vase overflowing with yellow roses created exactly the right ambience of warm intimacy and love. She readjusted the roses for the hundredth time, carefully arranged the glassware, then stepped back and admired her handiwork. "Not bad for an amateur," she complimented herself. "Not bad at all."

Tonight was their "anniversary," and everything had to be perfect. By six o'clock Wendy had frosted the cake with chocolate frosting, hidden it in a cupboard, and was reading in the living room, frantically feigning nonchalance. Of course the ruse was doomed to fail. Each time there were footsteps in the hallway, she flushed with excitement. And each time they passed the apartment she felt let down. By the time the front door finally did open, Wendy had studiously reread the same page five times—and still had no idea what it said.

"Hey, what's all this?" Al asked, his smile warmed by the romantic lighting of flickering candles.

Wendy leaped up and flew into his arms. So much for playing it cool, she thought. "This is for you—for *us*. Today is our anniversary, don't you remember?"

"Anniversary?" His forehead furrowed in confusion, then he smiled again. "Every day's an anniversary with you, Wendy. Why is today so special?"

"Because it's seven weeks to the day since I moved in, and I've never been happier in my life." She looked deeply into his eyes and lightly kissed his lips. "I love you, Al." She rested her head against his chest and held him tightly.

He kissed the top of her head. "You know, we're very lucky. Just think of all the people in this city—in the world—who live their lives never having any real love and understanding." Shit, he was talking like a *TNT* character again. "Next thing you know I'll be making a speech. Let me grab a quick shower, then we'll talk, okay?"

Ten minutes later he returned in baggy corduroys, an old flannel shirt, and tattered slippers. Wendy shook her head in mock disgust. "Seven weeks and you look like an old married man already."

"And you look like the most beautiful woman on earth," he kissed her. "And taste it, too." How Mel Jacobs had blinded himself to the voluptuous Wendy was a mystery. "Has it really been seven weeks?"

"Since I moved in. Getting to . . . know you started the minute you walked through the door. But I'd say the Valentine's Day party was the clincher."

"It's beginning to look like that party clinched everything." He poured them each a glass of wine. "As they say, the chickens are starting to come home to roost."

"Trouble?"

"It's safe to say that Al Peterson is no longer the fair-haired boy with certain powerful people at *Time Nor Tide*. If Tom Wesley hadn't quit without notice, and if Rita weren't so bent out of shape by her husband's death, I suspect that my job at *TNT* would be the test case to establish exactly who has real power over the show: Rita or the network."

"You're too good a writer to get fired, if that's what you mean," Wendy said dismissing the idea.

"Thanks for the vote of confidence, honey, but you know talent has very little to do with working for Rita Martin. Besides, my career at present is based on promises—first Rita's, and now, more importantly, Nan's." He paused and looked off into the distance as if he could see the true folly of his situation. "But, as they say: Talk is cheap, and I'm not so sure that when the smoke settles and the bodies are counted, good old Al Peterson won't be among the missing in action. Damn."

"But Nan promised you a head writer's job. And you're already taking up some of Tom's slack, so why worry?" This morose analysis of *TNT*'s inner workings was all too familiar to Wendy; Mel had done it almost daily. All she wanted now was to go on with her party and have a good time.

"Nan's promises are as good as a rattlesnake's. But, we'll see; my contract is up soon and that's when alliances will be drawn. Rita hates my guts and I know her too well to think she'll let me stay on the payroll—her payroll—if there's any way she can get me out." He poured himself a second glass of wine then turned back to Wendy and said, almost ruefully, "Since Valentine's Day I have committed two major sins: choosing you over Rita and coming out openly against Ma Martin's *ancien regime*."

"She can't blame you. It's so unfair. I was the one who walked out on Mel. If you remember correctly you didn't want me to leave Mel."

Wendy was only partially right. He didn't mind her leaving Mel. It was moving in with him that was the real problem. Not only was Al not sure he was ready for a live-in relationship, but it was a foregone conclusion that the move would jeopardize his position at *TNT*. Yet, when Wendy had asked to be taken in he had been powerless to refuse.

"None of that matters now. You're living here, and we've got to start from there."

"Maybe you're exaggerating things," Wendy offered. "After all, like you said: Rita's still distraught about Ben's death . . ."

"It's not Rita; it's Mel," he quickly corrected her. "I stopped by the office earlier and he ordered me into his office—then he grilled me about you."

"Oh, Christ, he didn't. He's such a bastard." Her anger flared immediately.

"We *are* living together, Wendy. And you haven't talked to him since you walked out." It sounded like an accusation.

"You're defending Mel now, is that it?" The anger got the best of her. "Well thanks one hell of a lot. Next thing you'll be inviting him over for dinner." She turned away and faced the dining table; it looked suddenly shoddy. "Why are we always dragging those awful people back into our lives?"

Al put his arm around her shoulders. "I know it's tough for you, but we agreed that honesty is the most important gift we could give each other, remember?"

She grudgingly nodded her head.

"I don't want to keep anything from you . . . and that means talking about my work, and unfortunately that includes Mel and some people neither of us likes."

Wendy sat silently for a minute, trying to formulate an answer. If only deep down she didn't feel guilty about deserting Mel, a snappy self-defense would be easy. But she did feel guilty and she kept it from Al because more than anything he wanted her to be strong. Guilt and fear—both connected with Mel—made her feel weak. She was feeling better about herself but she wasn't quite ready to tell the world to go to hell yet.

"Hey, you still there?" Al nudged her.

"I guess part of me still wants to be taken care of."

"Join the club." He pulled her closer. "In the end it's easier to change than not." He laughed. "There I go making speeches again. Writing *TNT* has affected my thinking."

Wendy gladly took the opportunity to change the subject. She lowered her voice dramatically. "Stay tuned for more of *Wendy and Al Face Life*, after these important messages." She then kissed him and pressed her body against his. "I love you, Al Peterson," she whispered.

"You show remarkable taste," he whispered back.

"And you are incorrigible!" She pushed him aside and started toward the kitchen. "Now let's have something to eat before everything is ruined. And for God's sake let's forget the jackals of *Time Nor Tide*."

They dined on quiche and salad, homemade pâté and warm bread. And just when Al thought he'd burst, Wendy returned from the kitchen triumphantly carrying the cake.

"Seven candles for the happiest weeks of my life," she exclaimed. "Now blow them out and make a wish." She hovered over him like an anxious mother at a birthday party.

"There are no more wishes, darling. They've all come true." He blew the candles out wondering if Wendy really believed his corny dialogue. When she applauded wildly, he knew she did. Now if only he could convince himself, too.

"I want to be serious," Wendy said, "just for a moment. Let's not let anyone—or anything—ever come between us. When we shut that door, let's leave the world outside, okay?"

"It's a deal." It was a wonderful dream, but totally unworkable. The long arm of Rita Martin could reach into the most protected corners, even through locked doors.

Al had tried to talk privately with Rita after Ben's death. He'd phoned her several times both in New York and in Connecticut, but she was either not there or was unavailable to him. Because it was before he'd been told Rita had seen copies of the memos to Nan, he interpreted Rita's distance as nothing more than her way of dealing with her grief. When they finally did see each other the week before, he was stunned to see how haggard she looked. He'd expected Ben's death to take its toll, but he hadn't expected Rita to look so . . . defeated.

"I've called you," he reassured her, allowing no trace of apology to enter his voice.

"I know. I've had other things on my mind." Her voice was hollow, echoing unnaturally around the office.

"I'm sorry about Ben. If there's anything I can do . . ."

"It's all been taken care of, thank you. Everyone has been very good to me."

"I think everyone feels your loss as their own."

"Do they?" she asked absentmindedly. "It's just going to take some time for me to adjust, that's all."

Adjust? he thought. Rita almost made it sound like a boarder had moved out unannounced and there might be trouble renting the room. He was inexplicably infuriated by her icy reserve, but he asked her, "Would you have dinner with me one night?"

"Thank you, no." She smiled. "I'm not in New York much anymore . . . there's my daughter to look after."

Al was acutely uncomfortable. Rita left no room for sympathy, and she made him feel irrelevant, not just as a lover—or rather as an ex-lover—but as a human being. She had obviously wrapped herself in a thick, protective cocoon.

"It would do you good to get out. What do you say? Lunch at the Russian Tea Room—for old times' sake?" He suddenly knew he was beginning to sound like an idiot.

"That's very sweet of you, Al, but I think not. It's better if we forget what happened between us." For just a second the familiar edge returned to her voice.

"Have it your way, Rita. You know where to reach me if you change your mind—about lunch." Her impersonal tone made him edgy. He remembered the discussion about the correlation between his job and his loyalty to her and *TNT*. One was contingent on the other. And now, without the romantic backup, Al felt like a trapeze artist working without a net.

"I'd like to discuss work with you from time to time," he threw in as a sop to her ego.

"Mel will handle that. I no longer have the time to be available to everyone." She pushed back her chair to indicate the meeting was over.

He left Rita's office, furious. So, all ties with Rita Martin were finally severed . . . his fate was now in the hands of Mel Jacobs . . . unless Nan Booth came through with her grandiose promises.

"Hey, are *you* still with me?" Wendy's voice shattered his reverie. "Starting right now, no more shop talk . . . unless it's absolutely necessary. This is our night, remember? So, let's celebrate." She took him by the hand and led him to the bedroom.

"There's still more to this party?" Al asked coyly.

Wendy examined the turned-down bed. "Well, *you* must have thought so or you wouldn't have messed up my pretty bed."

"Think that's messy? Wait till you see it an hour from now." He encircled her waist, pulling her against him. "Now for the *real* dessert."

For so long Wendy had lived in fear of Mel's caresses that sex had been an ordeal. Yet as Al slipped the dressing gown from her trembling shoulders, she craved his touch. Peterson was not only one sexy man, but kind and gentle. When he first asked her what she liked in bed, she hadn't been able to answer; it had been so long since anything had pleased her sexually. But in Al's arms they explored the question—and found the answers—together.

Over his meager objections, Wendy undressed him, sliding her free hand under his shirt as she unbuttoned it and entwining her fingers in the silky blond hair that matted his chest. She was the aggressor—forcing him onto the bed, kneeling next to him as she removed his slippers, then his pants. Al responded like a child. He threw his head back, his face radiant with the love being lavished on him. By the time his trousers were off he was already hard.

Wendy ran her hands along the inside of Al's thighs, finally cupping the soft warmth of his testicles. He liked having his balls fondled, so Wendy gave them a little tug and kissed the hard flatness of his stomach. "You're a beautiful man," she whispered as he fondled her breasts. "I've never known a man before with such a beautiful body."

He arched his back slightly as she took him in her warm mouth and he pushed himself deeper into her throat. There were no barriers between them now, no secrets—emotional or physical. Wendy wanted all of Al Peterson, and she wanted him to know it.

He pulled her up next to him. "Oh, baby, it's hard to believe you're mine," he gasped just before covering her mouth with his.

Wendy Jacobs was definitely more than his usual casual affair. Letting her move in proved that. And hadn't he broken off all contact with Angela, too? Starting up with Wendy as he extricated himself from Rita was tricky, but it kept his mind off the way Mrs. Elliott had treated him. When he met Wendy she was in real emotional trouble, anyone could see that, but over the past weeks the angry, lonely woman who'd been so pitiful that day at Rockefeller Center had blossomed with love. Al Peterson had done that! And it made him feel good about himself. The new Wendy actually brought some happiness into his life. The Angela Brites and Rita Martins of the world had been simple diversions. Wendy Jacobs was the real thing.

Al pressed his head between Wendy's legs, savoring the salty sweetness of her cunt. He drank deeply before easing himself up over her body. When he kissed her mouth, Wendy tasted herself on his lips and shuddered with pleasure. She pulled him forward, easing him inside her, hungry for his love.

Driven to the brink of passion, Al came but he continued his long, measured strokes against Wendy's clitoris. Her breathing grew shallow and her eyes fluttered with ecstasy as a shower of orgasms convulsed her body.

They lay in each other's arms like children after their first sexual encounter. Then Al reached for a cigarette.

"Isn't that a bit of a cliché?" Wendy joked.

He inhaled deeply, then blew the smoke in clouds to the ceiling. "Nothing we do is a cliché."

"You've restored life in me, Al." She snuggled closer. "Do you know what that means?"

He tipped her head to him. "Let's give credit where credit is due. You've taken your life back, that's all. I was just lucky enough to be around when you had enough of being Mel's servant."

She shivered, and he put his arm around her. "We're going to make it, Al. Aren't we?"

"Just let someone try to stop us."

"Thanks for believing in me. I love you." Wendy closed her eyes, ready for sleep. If only Mel weren't so sick, she could turn her back on her marriage for good. But the thought of his illness plagued her. Even as she drifted off into an uneasy sleep, Wendy feared that the tiny seed of guilt planted in her heart might one day grow and blossom, releasing a poison that would kill all feelings for Al.

15

Rita walked calmly down the long fortieth-floor corridor toward Jim Goodspeed's office. It was important she look relaxed and self-assured, even though her confidence had been severely shaken. But Rita was a master of illusion, and the various men and women she acknowledged along her route to a guaranteed argument with Goodspeed never suspected just how nervous and insecure she was. Two weeks earlier—the very day she'd promised Mel at lunch they'd fight to the finish—Gordy Tate was fired.

Rita's pilgrimage "upstairs" was mainly a gesture of desperation and she wasn't sure she could successfully hide her fear from anyone—particularly Jim Goodspeed. She was used to giving orders, not taking them, and Tate's dismissal so soon after Alex Thorpe's amounted to nothing less than paving the way for firing Rita Martin when her contract expired the second week of June. Her first reaction to the news was old-fashioned rage—she'd almost stormed Goodspeed's citadel then—but a sixth sense warned her that only a rational approach might avert her own sudden demise. So she received the news with uncommon good grace, then waited until the time felt right to move in and find out just how deeply Nan Booth's ax had cut.

The fortieth floor was as familiar to Rita as her own living room. But today the comfortable, homey feelings she was used to were gone. The high-luster white walls, the gray industrial carpeting with its embossed ITC logos, and the trendy furnishings alienated her. Today the utilitarian decor of the executive suites only underscored ITC's corporate depersonalization, its emphasis on profit at whatever human cost.

The endless corridor was a picture gallery of ITC nighttime celebrities. Inwardly Rita sneered at these high-priced hams—not one of her "stars" had made the grade. The network is nothing more than a tribe of cannibals, she thought. They feed off the carcasses of daytime victims, growing fat and rich, never acknowledging the source of their expensive lifestyles. She turned the corner sharply and headed toward the glass door separating Goodspeed's suite from the rest of the floor.

"Rita, you look wonderful," Sally Grahame flattered her.

"Thanks. Is he in?"

"Jim's expecting you." Sally nodded toward the burnished oak door.

Rita flashed a winning smile then pushed open the heavy door to Goodspeed's inner office. He was seated behind his desk, talking animatedly on the phone. He signaled Rita to sit down and kept talking.

When he finished the conversation, he smiled benevolently. "Good to see you, Rita. It's been a long time."

"I won't bother telling you I feel neglected, Jim," she pouted.

"Now, now, let's not get into that," he warned her gently. "I'm a very busy man."

"In that case maybe I should be thankful you've granted me this audience." The words sounded too harsh, and for a second there was a flicker of anger in Goodspeed's eyes. "But if you're that busy you must be making money for ITC—and for *TNT*." She was trying to rekindle the friendly, jesting spirit of her past conversations with Goodspeed. But he was all business now.

"We'll always find enough dough to subsidize *TNT*, even if we have to make a few changes to insure our investment."

Now they were down to business. "Changes like giving Al Peterson more responsibility than I'd ever trust him with?" She leaned forward. "Changes like firing Gordy Tate? Why wasn't I told about Gordy, Jim?" Her voice unexpectedly was full of hurt.

"What was the point? You'd only have put up a fight and there's no time for that now," he replied curtly.

"So, my opinion doesn't count anymore, is that it?"
"Don't take it so personally . . ."
"How *should* I take it? I was the one who hired Gordy in the first place."
"Correction: *ITC* hired Gordy—at your behest." Goodspeed sighed wearily. "Let's face facts: Alex Thorpe and Gordon Tate were millstones around our necks. They were ineffectual."
"And you're suggesting I'd keep people around who didn't pull their own weight?"
"Your opinion is not the point. Quality is. While *Time Nor Tide* was at the top, ITC was willing to give you limited say in staff organization. That's changed now. Remember, ITC is executive producer of the show—you gave us that power the day you sold us the rights."
Rita swallowed hard. "I have never once forgotten who has the final word, Jim, and I don't think I have ever acted in anything but the network's best interest." This was humiliating. It wasn't self-defense; it was begging for mercy. "Now it seems you don't trust me anymore. Am I right?"
"You're going a little overboard with this, Rita. Tell me, why are you taking these dismissals so personally?"
"Because, goddammit, you are systematically relieving me of my authority at *Time Nor Tide*, that's why!" she barked as her anger took over. "First it was Alex Thorpe and now Gordy Tate. They're all that's left of the old *Time Nor Tide*."
Goodspeed was willing to ignore her rudeness for the moment. "You've always said *TNT* must come before everything else—including your own personal likes and dislikes," he said, as if taking her side. "The network is merely following your own prescription."
"Don't try to pawn this raw deal off on me, Jim. You're doing the firing—or should I say Nan Booth is! After all she's the real hatchet man." Her apt metaphor was not missed by Goodspeed.
"Nan's just doing her job."
"Like an army officer who kills because he's commanded to?" Rita rose and leaned forward across his desk. "I resent this treatment, Jim. I resent the flak I'm getting from your office over the most piddling details concerning *my* show."
"And I'm beginning to resent the fact that I'm wasting half my time these days defending *TNT*'s lousy ratings." When Rita began to protest, he cut her off. "Oh, I know what you'll say: The ratings improved at Christmas and the sweeps

week was even better. True. But that's old news. Once Frank Cameron died mid-February, the story got bogged down and *now*, week by week, you're losing your audience. Goddammit, Rita,'' Goodspeed slammed his fist down on the desk, ''admit it, *TNT* is out of your control. And you don't know what's wrong.'' He sucked in his breath in an effort to control himself, but when he spoke again it was evident he'd barely succeeded. ''If Nan hadn't done some quick thinking and enlisted Al Peterson's help you'd have been so far behind with outlines *and* scripts we'd probably have had to close down production.''

''You know that never would happen,'' Rita quickly defended herself against so unthinkable a situation.

''Maybe not, but someone's got to take control of the show and it's becoming more evident that that person is not you.''

Goodspeed's anger surprised her. He had never yelled at her before, had never been anything but the perfect gentleman with Rita Martin. ''There have been problems,'' she agreed cautiously, ''but there's no need to panic.''

''It looks to me like you're the one who's panicking. You're understaffed, you're behind in your outlines, one of your head writers has quit and still hasn't been replaced, and you tell *me* not to worry?'' He shook his head. ''What else *can* I do when you suddenly seem unable to delegate authority?''

It was all true. Goodspeed knew everything—including the problem with the outlines. Someone must have gotten to Mel, or Sandy or . . . Al Peterson. That traitor again! But now she had to be calm. If she gave into her fear she'd most certainly make a fatal mistake. Reason was essential. Simple, direct, logic . . .

''You are right, Jim.'' She bowed her head. ''Since . . . Ben's death . . . I have been putting off certain actions.''

''Oh?'' he asked skeptically, not surprised that Ben's name had come up. ''Tell me about it.''

''Tom's departure did leave us with more work than I was able to handle, but I couldn't hire just anyone . . . I think I've found someone to replace him now,'' she explained quietly, thanking her lucky stars she'd lined up a few interviews to fill Wesley's slot. ''His name is Dave Hailey.''

'Tell me something I don't know,'' Goodspeed retorted viciously. ''Nan talked to Hailey's agent two days ago.''

Rita stared in stunned silence. The situation was obviously

worse than she'd feared. "The problem at the moment hinges on the writing *quality*. It's plummeted." She scanned his face for some reaction. "I've decided to replace Al Peterson—he's our first weak link."

"Jesus Christ! Fire another dialogist?" Goodspeed exploded, nearly levitating from his chair. "Why don't you just install a turnstile at the *TNT* office?

"I'm only trying to improve the show, Jim. That *is* what you want, isn't it?"

"Yes, that's exactly what I want," he replied. He was tired of Rita's cat-and-mouse game. Just who the hell did she think she was kidding? Nan had carefully explained Rita's special relationship with this guy Peterson. It stank! Sexual favoritism was the bottom line for Goodspeed, and he now wondered if Rita had ever been up front with him about anything in all the years they'd known each other.

"You don't think I'm right?" Rita asked.

"Frankly, no."

Rita got up from the chair and began stalking. She had to play this scene as if she still held the upper hand. "I promise this will be the last shake-up at *TNT*. With Gordy and Alex gone, you've cleaned up your end of the business; now let me clean up mine." It was more a demand than a request. The situation was all too obvious: She'd lost Jim Goodspeed to Nan Booth. Either she took full command of *Time Nor Tide* once again right now or they would take it from her.

"I'll give you one last chance, Rita."

"Is this it? One last chance to make good or Rita Martin is through?"

Before he had time to answer, the office door opened and Nan swooped in. "Jim, I wanted you to see . . ." She saw Rita and smiled. "Rita, I had no idea you were here. Sorry. I'll come back." She took one polite step back.

But Goodspeed signaled her in, saying, "That's okay, Nan. Rita and I are finished."

Nan settled back comfortably in the chair Rita had occupied stiffly five minutes earlier. Sally had warned that Jim was tied up with Mrs. Elliott, but Nan had barged into the office anyway. It looked good to have access to Goodspeed even when he was in conference.

"Trouble with Rita?" she asked innocently. "She looked a little miffed."

"We just had a little heart-to-heart about *TNT*."

"And?"

"And she's willing to do anything to get it back on top."

Nan sighed. "Let me guess what that means: She's finally decided to replace Tom Wesley and hire this guy Hailey . . . after firing Al Peterson." Her tone was vicious, her guess correct.

For a moment Goodspeed rallied to defend Rita against Nan's gleeful sarcasm. "You're really out for her blood, aren't you?"

"I have nothing personal against Rita Martin." Nan carefully framed her answer. "It's what she stands for that rubs me the wrong way."

Goodspeed tented his fingers against each other. "And what might that be?"

"Indiscriminate use of power, for one. Self-serving decisions, for another. A means-justifies-the-ends mentality. To work with such a warped perspective is to set yourself up—and everyone around you—for one helluva fall. Rita Martin is the kind of woman who would rather destroy everything she's created than relinquish control. And if we're not careful, that's exactly what could happen to *TNT*."

Goodspeed wished he could disagree, instead he merely nodded his head. "I told her we'd give her time, but it's already too late. The time has come to face the inevitable—Rita Martin's through at ITC."

Nan gripped the sides of her chair. It had happened! Really happened! "Are you absolutely sure?" she asked cautiously, hiding her satisfaction.

Doubt flickered across Goodspeed's face for a moment, then vanished. "I don't see any other way out."

"Well, if you feel it must be done," she sighed, throwing the full responsibility of the decision onto Goodspeed. "Will there be any trouble from upstairs?"

Goodspeed shook his head. "I've already got Weatherhead's go-ahead. He asked why we hadn't moved on this sooner." In fact it was the president's pressure that had forced Goodspeed's decision. His recent silence had been the calm before the storm.

"Jason understands the stickiness of the situation. Rita Martin is an institution. You don't just pull down the Smithsonian without careful planning."

"And 'careful planning' means plenty of advance notice,

doesn't it?" he said pointedly. "It was very thoughtful of you to keep Weatherhead so closely apprised of Rita's failures."

"Dammit, Jim, the time has come to stop pussyfooting around. You said it yourself—it's either us or Rita."

"Christ, it's unbelievable! Last spring everything was running smoothly and now . . ." He tilted his head back and groaned as a headache began tensing his neck muscles.

"Hey, Jim, relax," Nan cooed. "No one's worth having a heart attack over."

"Sometimes the injustice of this lousy business still burns my ass."

"Look, everyone knows television is one hell of an unfair racket. To survive, the weak naturally must fall victim to the strong."

"Rita Martin is one of the strongest women I've ever met," he snapped. But since Ben's death . . . I don't know. She's changed." And because of the change, defending her was dangerous once again. Since the recent crop of bad ratings, and particularly since Nan's damning memos, Weatherhead had made a point of expressing his disapproval of Rita and her show at every opportunity. That much of his antagonism was personal made defending her doubly difficult. And Goodspeed was tired of trying. He'd been feeling down lately and had even cut his jogging to three times a week. After thirty years in television the pressure was finally getting to him.

"So, tell me again about your boy, Peterson," he commanded to get his mind back to business. "I'm not convinced that an explaymate of Rita's is a suitable choice as *TNT*'s heir apparent, despite your campaign of hyperbole and flattery."

"He's the best. Outshines them all, except for Rita herself."

"She wants to fire him."

"Of course she does. She's through with his . . . services," Nan put it as gently as possible. "But he's the best shot we have."

"What about Mel Jacobs? He's got a good track record with the show."

"He's one of Rita's 'boys.' When she goes, we should sack him, too." Nan shook her head. "Mel's one of those guys whose sense of duty to Rita will always keep him at odds with her replacement." Another thought came to her. "Besides, he's sick. I saw him last week and he looked like death. Rumor has it he's headed for the hospital." She paused. "No, our safest move is Al Peterson."

Goodspeed turned up his nose in disgust at the thought of replacing Rita with some stud, no matter how talented he was. "Maybe it would be better for everyone to let Rita fire him—start over with a new crew."

"No good, Jim. *Time Nor Tide*'s still very much in trouble. You're on the verge of firing its creator, a woman who once had a lot of clout in this town. If Rita goes and the ratings go with her, you're the one who's going to have to answer to Jason. Peterson knows the show inside out. He's been working on story projections for weeks."

"And whose idea was that? He's still officially only a dialogist." This whole business was beginning to sicken him.

"It was his idea. And let me tell you, he's come up with some winners." Al had been modifying Rita's rewritten Caribbean story. Nan would release it the minute Mrs. Elliott was out on her ass.

"Okay, I'll go with your decision for the time being. Until we break the news of Rita's leaving, let her think she's still running the show. Let her fire Peterson. Let her hire someone else." His headache had grown and pounded dully behind his eyes now. "*You* tell Peterson to get ready to take over. I'll stall Rita as long as possible, joke her along." Jesus, was it possible he was talking about an old *friend*?

"Suits me. What's the timetable on this?"

"The Emmy Awards ceremony is in two weeks. The pickup date of Rita's contract is a week later, so let's wait until then, until after the awards before terminating her officially. After all, we don't want the timing of this to seem vindictive, do we?" he asked sourly.

Nan nodded solemnly, but after leaving the office she had to restrain herself from breaking in to a gleeful sprint to the elevators.

Three weeks! She could practically feel the warm California sun already. It was all happening as planned. Rita was out, Peterson was in. Now all she had to do was tell Al the good news and the rest, as they say, would be history.

Al strolled into the bedroom, a towel wrapped around his waist, his hair still glistening from a shower. Wendy, in a halo of afternoon sunlight, was poring over a batch of photographic contact sheets. He watched her for a moment. She was calmer than when they first met, and her self-assurance was beginning to show in the forthright, confident way she dealt with her work . . . and with him. For the first time in his life Al suspected this particular infatuation might last longer than the standard couple of months.

He padded across the room and put his arms around her. "Anyone I know?" The contact sheets were of a shooting she'd done a week before with Al as the model.

Wendy kept working. "Oh, it's just some guy I met a while ago."

He moved into her field of vision and bent down to examine the series of thirty-six miniature portraits of his face. "Nice looking. What's he like?"

Wendy reluctantly put her work aside, knowing Al would pester her until she responded. "Once you get past his good looks, he's not really a bad sort. Sometimes a bit temperamental . . . and he likes getting his own way far too often; but he's a writer, and you know what they can be like."

"Indeed I do. Anything else?"

"He happens to be keeping me from my work."

Al slipped his arms through Wendy's and drew her up tight. "I want to know all about your being in love with him."

She kissed him lightly on both cheeks. "Be a good boy and let me get back to work."

But Al tightened his grip and began edging her toward the bed. "Do you know how beautiful you are?"

"Let's wait, okay? I have to finish." She pulled away.

"Can't you take just half an hour away from your goddamned work?" he complained. "It's starting to interfere with our sex life."

Wendy's reply was to shrug and get back to work.

A few minutes later, after dressing, Al returned to Wendy's side feeling contrite. "The photos are great. And I'm not just saying that because it's me."

"You really like them, don't you?"

"You know, you should get yourself that studio you're always talking about. I just get in your way here."

Wendy didn't argue. Two people living in Peterson's small, one-bedroom apartment was manageable, but two people working there was hell. Between her artistic self-doubt and his constant "supervision" she was getting fed up with their domestic situation. At least Mel left her alone most of the time.

She looked up at him and absentmindedly touched his leg. "I wish you could hear how depressed you sound. What's wrong?"

"It's a bad case of the blahs," he equivocated. There was a reason for the depression, but after all the wheeling and dealing it had taken to become a functioning member of *TNT*, facing up to the truth of his discontent wasn't easy: The excitement of writing *TNT* was gone. And Al missed it. He missed the thrill of opening the endless packages of outlines and scripts that arrived daily from the office. He missed the satisfaction of creating clever dialogue within the standard soap opera format that hardly allowed cleverness. And like it or not, he missed the excitement of working—and being—with Rita.

Jesus, what a chump he'd been! From that first meeting he'd allowed her every word, every action to seduce him despite the signs that this was nothing more than her standard operating procedure. But Al Peterson could tame her. After all, Rita Martin was nothing more than a woman—in a class by herself, to be sure—but he knew women; they were his hobby. He was sure to have the upper hand. So now what? Rita had retreated to her ivory tower but remained tantalizingly close. And, goddammit, each script he wrote was a constant reminder of the raw deal she'd given him. What was the use of lying to himself? He was depressed because he hurt. And even Wendy wasn't able to make him forget that. She was so wrapped up in herself that he might as well have been living alone.

Writing *TNT* had finally become just a job. A long, tedious chore he did with both eyes closed. How many different ways were there to cover the same plots day after day, week after week? He never seemed able to pull himself away from Laurelton, U.S.A. His very life had been devoured as he wrote scripts and read outlines that prepared him to get on the weekly dialogue treadmill once again. Sure, he had other, clandestine duties—doctoring up the Caribbean caper, creating new story lines—but they were the price of admission to *TNT*'s inner circle and, as such, were done on his own time, without pay. So the main thrust of his workday was still doing scripts, and without access to Rita it was a grind. He wondered if she would still keep her distance when—if—he became a full-time head writer. Or would she mellow toward him, forgive and forget? God, he hoped so. Working with Rita was an exhilarating contest of wills.

He began pacing the room, putting off the confrontation with the blank sheet of paper in his typewriter. Wendy ignored his circuit for a couple of minutes then finally lost her temper. "If you're going to pace, do it somewhere else."

"Sorry if I'm bothering you," he replied sarcastically. Then he softened his voice. "What have we got on for tonight?"

"*I'm* going to a meeting." Wendy had joined Gamblers Anonymous and used the meetings as a second home.

"How's it going?" He perched on the edge of the bed, glad to have a distraction.

"I always thought I was the only person in the world who couldn't stop gambling. God, I was so isolated hiding those terrible feelings and cravings." Her voice lowered confidentally. "Now, I don't ever have to feel alone again."

Al went to her and put his arms around her. "Did I ever tell you that I admire you? It took real guts to do something about your problem."

Wendy rested her head against his chest. "Mel used my gambling against me. He said I was sick, bad, something less than human. All those years I let him make me believe I was beneath contempt." GA had taught Wendy that she wasn't responsible for having her illness, but that she *was* responsible for keeping it under control by attending meetings. At those meetings, as she realized only those with an addiction can fully understand what it is to be addicted, she began to forgive Mel's inept handling of her problem. And she began to see the real strain she'd put on their marriage.

"Forget about Mel. He won't bug you anymore." But ever since Rita had come back to work full time Jacobs had started bugging Al about minor flaws in his scripts almost every day. It looked like he'd fallen victim to the Ellie Davis syndrome. And Nan, though they talked regularly, had still not committed herself by offering him the promised job.

"You don't know Mel like I do. Sometimes I imagine him out there thinking about me. How he must hate me for walking out." She shook her head. "It's scary."

Getting over Mel was a healing process that had only begun to take effect. The last time she'd seen him—the day she packed and left—he'd looked pitifully drawn and pale. To leave him Wendy had had to fight every instinct. Yet, when she did close the apartment door behind her there was no real satisfaction. There were too many old scores to settle, too many things left unsaid. One day she would have to come to terms with the ugly fact that she'd deserted him when he was dying.

"Let's have lunch," Al said, swiftly steering the conversation out of dangerous territory.

"I've got work to do. Maybe later."

"You work yourself too hard. Loosen up."

"What about *your* work?"

Al's lip curled at the implied criticism. "Say no more. I get the picture: no work, no play. The great Protestant work ethic in action."

"Al, if you don't let me work I might as well . . ." still be with Mel, she completed the thought. When Al was like this he was so much like a child—so much like Mel. If she didn't give in to him he'd pout. And if she did . . . where did that leave her? "I'll make a deal with you: Let's both work for another half hour, then we'll have lunch. We can watch *Time Nor Tide* while we do."

Al brightened. "You work, I'll run to the deli and get bagels and cold cuts and all the junk food I can carry." He grabbed his coat and headed for the door. "And when we're finished I'll make wild, passionate love to you."

Wendy's smile was a cover. She'd known for some time that she'd traded domination of one kind for domination of another. Since moving in with Al she'd lied to herself by saying she was finally happy. But was this isolated life precariously balanced between her own self-discovery and placating Al's childish demands *real* happiness? Or was it just running away again? Putting off the inevitable confrontation with herself? Leaving Mel *was* a godsend. But maybe leaving Mel for Al wasn't such a smart idea. And no amount of embroidering the truth would disguise it this time.

Lizzy Alexander sat primly on the witness stand. She wore a simple black dress, a modest straw hat, and very white gloves. Her hands were nervously clutching her handbag and she stared at a point on the railing of the stand. Occasionally, whenever Rex Todd, the prosecutor, raised his voice and scared Lizzy, she looked up at him. The rest of the time she looked down at her knees.

Todd paced before the witness stand, paused to look at Lizzy, then began pacing again. "Miss Alexander . . . may I call you Lizzy?"

She raised her head and a smile flickered over her lips. She may have been a spinster, but she was still partial to handsome men. And Rex Todd was certainly that. "Of course you may."

"Lizzy, you are Rebecca Danforth's maid, are you not?"

"Yes, sir."

"And you have worked for Mrs. Danforth for ten years, am I correct?"

Lizzy nodded.

"How would you categorize your employer?"

Lizzy's face clouded with bewilderment. "Sir?"

"Do you enjoy working for her? That is, is she a fair employer?"

"I wouldn't have worked for her for ten years if she weren't. I may be an old maid, but I ain't crazy!" she said in the funny manner calculated to make people laugh.

Todd waited while the courtroom chuckled in appreciation of this joke. "Of course not. So you liked working for Mrs. Danforth. And she always treated you fairly." He got no argument. "Would you consider her an average person? That is, did she have any peculiar habits?"

Bob Garrick was immediately on his feet. "Objection, your honor. That question calls for a conclusion from the witness. What Miss Alexander thinks is of no relevance here."

Judge Walter Hackett appraised Garrick for a moment. "Objection sustained," he said quietly.

Todd smiled indulgently, but it was obvious he was angry at losing the decision. "Let me put it another way: Would you have Mrs. Danforth as a friend?"

"Why, she is my friend," Lizzy said immediately. "She's always treated me with the utmost kindness. She's never raised her voice to me in all those years." Lizzy pulled herself up even straighter in the chair, indicating just how offensive she found the question. "There are some people who just lord it over people who work for them. Not Mrs. Danforth. Not for one second."

"Very well," Todd interrupted. He didn't want the answer to be a defense of the accused. "And would you classify Mr. Frank Cameron as the kind of man you could be friends with?"

Lizzy's face darkened. She raised her eyes and stared at the prosecutor. "What kind of woman do you think I am?" Again she straightened herself. "Frank Cameron was no good. He was the kind of man who'd stab you in the back while picking your pocket."

Todd looked to Garrick for an objection. Of course there was none. "It seems our esteemed defense counsel doesn't object to that particular conclusion from the witness."

"Never mind the sarcasm, Mr. Todd," the judge reprimanded him. "I'm sure you're not about to object, either."

The court got a good laugh out of that.

But Todd pushed on as if nothing had been said. "So, I gather you didn't have any fond feelings for Mr. Cameron. How, then, did you feel about him spending so much time in Mrs. Danforth's home?"

Garrick again leaped to his feet. "I must object, Your honor. It has not been established that Frank Cameron was ever at Mrs. Danforth's home."

Judge Hackett nodded his approval. "Point well taken. Mr. Todd please leave the courtroom trickery to Perry Mason. I'm sure we all want this trial concluded as quickly and as fairly as possible."

Todd bowed slightly in the direction of the bench. "Miss Alexander, did you ever see the deceased, Frank Cameron, in the home of your employer, Mrs. Rebecca Danforth?"

Lizzy hesitated. And when she answered she sounded as if she were hiding something. "I did, sir."

"How many times?"

"Three," she said quickly. "But, he was never asked more than twice. That last time——"

"Thank you, Miss Alexander," Todd interrupted her. "Your witness, Mr. Garrick.

Bob Garrick stood up and buttoned his jacket before approaching the witness box. When he did he smiled warmly and put his hand on the railing inches from Lizzy's. he'd known her for years and had been comfortable in her presence—and she in his—since he was in law school. When he spoke his voice was charming and soft, oozing confidence and pleasure at being with her. "How are you today, Lizzy?"

She blushed from head to foot. "Much better now you're here. Mr. Garrick."

"That's good to hear. Now I don't want to grill you or put you through any more trouble than I have to. But we're here

to get the truth to help Mrs. Danforth." He stepped away from the bench. "Now, please finish what you were saying to Mr. Todd. You said Frank Cameron was only asked to the house twice?"

"Yes sir."

"And how do you know that?"

"I heard Mrs. Danforth call him."

"Did she say why she was calling him?"

Lizzy thought a moment, then shook her head. "I don't remember exactly."

"Did it have anything to do with gardening? Or the yard?"

Todd's face went scarlet. "Objection. Counsel is putting words in the witness's mouth. She just said she didn't remember."

"Objection sustained. Please strike the question from the transcript. And Mr. Garrick, no more leading questions."

"Let me ask you this, Miss Alexander: How did you know Cameron wasn't invited that third time?"

"Cause I was there when Mrs. Danforth answered the door. She looked shocked, then angry. She even sent me away. That's a real sign there's going to be trouble."

"And did you hear what Cameron wanted? Did he say why he was there?"

Lizzy began to wring her hands nervously in her lap. Her lips began to tremble and she sank lower into the seat. "No, sir, he didn't."

"But Cameron's presence angered Mrs. Danforth?"

"Yes, Sir," she whispered.

"How do you know?"

Lizzy looked up, mouth twitching wildly now. She bit her lip, but said nothing.

"Miss Alexander, I asked you a question: How did you know Mrs. Danforth was angry that Frank Cameron had intruded?"

"Because of what she said when he left."

"She said something to you?"

Lizzy shook her head. "I was out in the hall, but I heard her say it.

"And what was that?"

Lizzy looked up and stared across the courtroom to Rebecca Danforth who was obviously sympathetic to her maid's plight. "She said . . . she said . . ."

"Yes, tell us," Garrick pressed unmercifully.

"She said if he ever bothered her again she was going to kill *him!"*

The courtroom erupted into a cacophony of cries at this news. The camera zoomed in on Lizzy Alexander: then quickly switched to Rebecca Danforth. Then the scene faded entirely.

Al leaped from the bed and turned off the television. "Sylvia's great in those scenes. She plays Lizzy Alexander like she's the heroine of *Rebecca*—so sweet, so naïve, so self-sacrificing." He hopped back onto the bed, rattling the lunch plates, which were carelessly spread around. "Actually, Sylvia's one of the toughest broads on the set. And if it weren't for the TelePrompTer, she couldn't remember her own name." At Nan's insistence, Al had spent several days at Studio One being shown the ropes.

"Nevertheless, Lizzy's a very convincing character," Wendy said, giving the maligned actress the benefit of the doubt. "I believed every word of it. So, tell me: Did Rebecca Danforth kill Frank Cameron?" She asked the question slyly, while eating a pickle.

"Uh uh. No fair asking," Peterson scolded. "That's a professional secret."

"Oh, Al, don't be such a prick. I want to know!"

He remained silent.

"Personally, I don't believe Rebecca would commit a murder just to protect her own reputation. She's much too grand to worry about that. *But* if she's protecting someone else . . . say Ted Reynolds or his fiancée, Penny Hewitt . . ." Wendy caught a glimmer in Peterson's eyes. "That's it, isn't it? Good old Becky Danforth is covering up for someone."

Al fell back against the pillows shaking with laughter. "Jesus Christ, Wendy, you're hooked! You really care about that old crow Danforth, don't you?"

"Well, of course I care. If I didn't I wouldn't bother to watch the goddamned show," she answered tartly.

"Will wonders never cease? Under that gorgeous, intelligent façade of yours there lurks a fan! You really eat up this mush, don't you?" He laughed until tears streamed down his face.

"And you write that 'mush,' so don't be so damn pompous."

"Pompous, huh? I'll show you who's pompous!" He pulled her on top of him, then rolled her over and pinned her down.

"Why I think it's downright cute you're so involved with *Time Nor Tide*."

She struggled against him. "Now you're being condescending. I hate it when you talk down to me." She fought valiantly to release her arms from his grip.

"How else can I talk to you when you're underneath me?" He started kissing her, but she kept bobbing her head from side to side, avoiding his mouth. "Stay in one place, will you?

"Not until you apologize." She wrinkled up her nose.

"All right . . . I apologize. It was unfair of me to joke about one of the driving passions of your life." He broke up again.

"You bastard!" Wendy said in mock rage. "Just as soon as I clean up these dishes, I'll fix you!"

Wendy was already in the kitchen when the phone rang. Al hoisted himself back onto the bed and answered it. "Al Peterson," he nearly giggled, relieved that Wendy had snapped out of her mood.

"Well, you sound like the goose that laid the golden egg," Nan purred. "Want to let me in on the good news?"

Peterson straightened up immediately. "Just a private joke."

"Good. I was afraid my news might be anticlimactic."

"What's happening?"

"Rita's out." Nan had practiced this terse comment several times to herself. What promise was held in those two little words!

"Jesus," Al breathed.

"Exactly. And that means Al Peterson is in. I keep my promises, Al. Congratulations."

"Thanks, but . . ."

"But what?" Nan's question was a threat.

He laughed softly. "I guess I'm just a little surprised about replacing *Rita*. I thought it would be Tom, maybe even Mel . . . but Rita Martin!"

There was a long silence and when Nan spoke again her voice chilled him. "I don't care what you thought or what lies you have to tell yourself to soothe your conscience. All I care about is *Time Nor Tide*." She let that settle in, then quickly asked, "Now, are you ready to take over or not?"

"Of course I'm ready. Where do we go from here?" he replied without hesitation.

Nan outlined her meeting with Goodspeed, carefully leaving out his reservations about Peterson. She would need to see a copy the Penny Hewitt story line; she wanted to move on it right away. When Rita was officially retired, Al would move in immediately. There was no time to lose during the transition of power. Nan would congratulate him officially in her office after the Emmy ceremonies.

Al put the phone down so thoughtfully it seemed like slow motion. "Rita's out." Those were Nan's words. Just like that. After all the plotting and working, "Rita's out." It *hadn't* come as a surprise, yet he'd wanted Nan to think it had. But Nan was too crafty to fall for his bullshit. Why should she? He'd played her game all along, taking every scrap she threw him in hopes of getting more. Nan knew what made Al Peterson tick. Maybe everybody did. Maybe the only person he'd been fooling was himself. But, hell, who could blame him for trying to keep up appearances? Even though it wasn't necessary. In this world it was not how you played the game, but whether you won or not. Wasn't that it? Wasn't fucking over your friends one of the slipperiest rungs on the fabled ladder of success? And attaining self-sufficiency, needing no one, another?

He lit a cigarette and rested against the pillows waiting to feel good. Five minutes later he was still waiting. He was glad he'd gotten the promotion and the extra money and responsibility, but he didn't feel good about it. Not in the way he'd expected. The feeling was hollow. It reminded him of how he felt after Nan accidentally revealed she'd shown Rita copies of his memos.

He ground out the cigarette, disgusted by its taste. And by his own actions. That day when he'd offered his sympathy to Rita and invited her out to lunch, she already knew what he'd done to her. But she hadn't said a word. And he'd been so proud of himself! He'd acted so gentlemanly, so graciously to the bereaved Mrs. Elliott! At that moment Al Peterson wouldn't have sold his life for a dime—if he could have found any buyers.

The phone rang again and he snatched it from the cradle. "What is it?"

There was a momentary hesitation. "It's Mel Jacobs."

"What do you want?"

"I want you at my office tomorrow morning at ten," Mel said just as rudely.

"What for?"

"We'll talk about it then,"

"We'll talk about it now," Al insisted.

"There's a problem with your script, Al. It's lousy. Does that satisfy your curiosity?"

"It answers a question," Al conceded. So Rita did want him out. Well, he could hardly blame her. "Okay, see you tomorrow."

"One more thing: I want to speak to Wendy."

That one caught him off-guard. Wendy hadn't talked to Mel since her exit, and Al wasn't so sure she ought to start doing so now. Mel had a mesmerizing effect on her. There was no telling how she might react. "I'm not sure she'll want to talk to you."

"Let's let her decide," Mel replied evenly.

Peterson hesitated, weighing the pros and cons of Wendy making the decision. Finally he cupped his hand over the phone. "Wendy, Mel's on the phone. He wants to talk to you." There was silence, then Wendy appeared in the doorway looking strangely calm. "Want me to tell him to fuck off?"

"No, I don't think so." She thought a second. Her eyes focused somewhere off beyond Al, then she looked directly at him and smiled. "No, I'll take the call . . . in the kitchen."

He waited until Wendy picked up, then, for one tantalizing moment, contemplated eavesdropping. But, hell, if he couldn't trust her common sense by now, he never could. He hung up.

"Mel, how are you?" Wendy asked, unconsciously running her fingers through her hair.

"Okay," he said quietly. "It's good to hear your voice."

"Yours too." Hearing him wasn't the shock she'd fantasized it would be. Relief was mixed with pleasure.

"I wouldn't have called if it weren't important." Mel cleared his throat. "I'm going into the hospital in a couple of weeks . . . and I'd like to see you before then."

"What is it?" She sat down on a kitchen chair wondering if Mel would tell her the truth.

"The ulcer. I've decided to have it operated on."

The lie was almost welcome. "Are you very sick?"

"Sick enough."

"Oh, Mel, I'm so sorry. What can I do?"

"Have dinner with me."

"Why not?" she agreed without deliberation. The invitation was almost a last request. She'd deal later with its consequences—and with Al's inevitable jealousy.

"You sure it'll be okay?"

"Why shouldn't it be? Where'll we meet?"

"Here? For a drink first?"

"Let's meet at the restaurant. It'll be easier for me." Safer was the truth.

"How about the Top of the Park, then? Seven o'clock on Tuesday?"

Today was Wednesday. That would give her six days. Six days to list all the reasons she wanted to stay with Peterson. "Tuesday will be fine."

"It'll be like old times," Mel assured her. "Back to the scene of the crime, as it were."

Too late Wendy remembered that the restaurant, with its sweeping panoramas over the city, was where they'd celebrated their engagement. But now she couldn't back down. Not without looking like the "old" Wendy Jacobs. "I look forward to it, she mumbled.

"See you Tuesday."

She hung up in utter confusion. She rested her head wearily on the palm of her hand wondering if she'd just made the worst mistake of her life. Why had she agreed to see him? Was it compassion? Or something she refused to accept—that after everything, she actually cared for him?

"What did he want?" Al demanded as she entered the bedroom.

"We're having dinner next Tuesday," Wendy replied, ready now not only for an argument but also to defend herself.

"You're joking!"

"Al, he's sick."

"He's been sick for months, and it's never bothered you before. Why now? Why does he call today, and you say yes? It doesn't make sense."

"He's going into the hospital."

"And you fell for that line?"

"Please. Don't make this more difficult for me than it already is," she pleaded. "He's my husband, and he's dying."

"You seem to have forgotten that not so long ago you were wishing he were dead. What's changed your mind?"

"He's at a safe distance now. I don't have to be afraid."

"Mel Jacobs is the kind of man who's never at a safe distance. You think he's going to let me steal his wife without wanting some kind of revenge?" he snorted. "And you, innocent little Wendy, played right into his hands. You really should have discussed it with me first."

"Fuck off, Peterson," she growled. "I've had my share of that kind of 'innocent little Wendy' talk already. And stop treating me like a child who must be led through life by the hand! Both you *and* dear Mel immediately assume that without proper supervision I'm completely helpless."

"I can only judge you by how you act," Al said cruelly.

"Touché," she said. "Thank you for reminding me of my past." It was a cheap shot, a Mel Jacobs trick. And coming from Peterson it seemed doubly insensitive.

"That was a lousy thing to say." He sat next to her on the bed and tried to put his arms around her. "I'm sorry."

Wendy pulled away. "Don't be sorry. It's the truth. But reminding me of it won't change my mind. I'm still having dinner with Mel. This is my fight with the past—not yours."

"I just don't want you to get hurt again." Al lit a cigarette to cover the anger stirred up by her reprimand.

"There's no way to deal with Mel *without* being hurt." She absent-mindedly took Al's hand and stroked it. "But if I don't start facing the fact that I have this crazy need to be punished and start doing something to change it, I might as well give up."

She kissed the back of his hand. "It'll work out for us—one way or the other." She rested her head on his chest, but when he encircled her with his arms there was no comfort.

The following Tuesday Wendy and Mel sat silently over cocktails at a window table in the Top of the Park. It was a perfect spring twilight. The cloudless blue sky was like a canopy over a newly green Central Park. Miles of skyscrapers shimmered in the last golden sunlight of the day. And the frenetic extravagance of New York City traffic pulsated harmlessly, and quietly, far below them. It was the perfect ambience for lovers, the perfect place to start a new life together. Or, in their case, to eulogize an old one.

Wendy had dressed very carefully, draping herself in a clingy beige wool dress that accented every curve. She wore her hair long and free, eschewing her matronly look for one younger and more sublime. A blush of makeup made her lips look delectable, her skin adolescent. She had artfully assembled this outfit, which was better suited for captivating and seducing an exciting new lover than for rehashing the past with an almost-ex-husband, for a very good reason. There must be no doubt in Mel's mind that she was *happy!* Happy with her new life. Happy with Al. Happy with herself. And more than that, he had to know, without a doubt, what a fool he'd been to have driven her out.

"Has it really been five years since we were last here? It seems like yesterday, doesn't it?"

"We never did come back, did we?" Wendy replied.

"We promised ourselves not to spoil a perfect moment by trying to recapture it. God, we must have been very much younger then," he said ironically.

Wendy rolled her eyes heavenward. "Please, Mel. If you really want to talk tonight, let's cut the bullshit, okay?"

"What do we talk about? It's been so long." Though Wendy's brusqueness had caught him by surprise, it was a pleasant change from her usual dreary, self-effacing style.

"You tell me. You're the one who did the inviting."

"You really despise me, don't you?"

"To tell the truth, I haven't given it much thought," she equivocated. "But now that you mention it, no. I don't despise you. I do despise the way you treated me, though. You really can be quite nice—when you're not acting like a maniac. Do you know how often you acted like a maniac?" Pressing her advantage was cathartic, even though Mel's discomfort was obvious.

"I guess I did—do—have trouble controlling my temper occasionally." He smiled. "The funny thing is, most times when we fought I wasn't really mad at you. I——"

Wendy's fury cut him off. "If that confession is supposed to make me feel better about being beaten up it doesn't." She angrily sipped her white wine. "And if this whole evening is to be an apology for mistreating me, I'm not interested." She grabbed at her purse, but Mel stopped her.

"It's too late for apologies, Wendy. The past is really over." And the future's about done, too, he thought. "I've done a lot of thinking since you walked out and I want you to know you did the right thing." He swirled his drink with his finger, and thoughtfully sucked it dry. "I mean it, Wendy—we'd come to the end. We just couldn't go on. If you hadn't left, I would have."

"*You* move out? I don't believe it! You loved our cozy little arrangement," she said bitterly.

"No, Wendy, I didn't." He leaned forward and rested his hand on hers. "The truth is I always blamed myself for not fulfilling you, for not being able to make you happy." He pulled away at the sound of a tremor in his voice. "When I saw the sadness in your eyes I got angry with myself for not being man enough to satisfy you. And then there was your goddamned gambling, and . . ." he sighed and his voice caught in his throat, ". . . you know where it all led." He covered one hand with the other and quickly put them both in his lap. "We lived in a squirrel cage. Wendy. Always running from each other, working at cross-purposes. It was killing us both."

Wendy sat in stunned silence. To her, their roles were so clearly defined. He was the brute. She was the victim. Mel was deluding himself. He'd never once tried to change the status quo of their marriage. But then, neither had she.

"You make our life together sound so . . . futile," she barely whispered the word. "Where did we go wrong?"

"Now that it's over, there's not much point going back. Is there?" He smiled warmly. "It is nice to be with you in this restaurant again, even though we're breaking a five-year-old promise."

"Promises are made to be broken—you know that better than most," she said as cynically as possible.

"I thought I did, but I made one foolish mistake: I believed when we were married that it would stick for good." He sighed. "I really thought Mel and Wendy Jacobs were going to accomplish something more than increasing the divorce statistics."

"No one goes into a marriage expecting it to fail," Wendy defended herself, not sure why. "If they did . . . why bother?"

"That's a very sensible attitude," he agreed, "but then you're a very sensible woman—I see that tonight more than ever." He hoped his flattery sounded guileless. "I lost track of your ability to deal practically with everyday matters. I lost track of so many of your good qualities."

"I wish I could help you with that one, Mel. I was there all the time—good old Wendy."

"Don't denigrate yourself," he turned on her. "Loyalty is an admirable quality."

"In dogs," she viciously qualified the statement. "I was always there, and you never were—except to punish me."

"I lost myself in *Time Nor Tide*," Mel confessed. "I guess it took over."

"You got lost in your work, and I got lost trying to win you back," Wendy mused. "How ironic. There were times I was so desperately lonely, Mel. I would have done anything for you."

"Jesus, Wendy," he closed his eyes and lowered his head.

"Mel, I can't blame you . . . or me, for that matter. But it's too late now. I gave up my self-respect, and along with that, I stopped loving you. It just happened, that's all." She touched the back of his hand.

"May I be honest with you?" Mel asked.

"I'd appreciate it if you were."

"I miss you, Wendy. Each night when I get home . . . I work very late these days so I don't have to"—he hit his fist on the table stared at it then looked up at her—"it's just not right for you to be gone." He turned his head to the window, his voice choked with emotion. "I'm sorry. I wasn't going to say any of those things.

She took both his hands and squeezed them. "It's no good, Mel. I've been hurt too much already. I don't want to be hurt ever again."

"You can't avoid it, not if you're really living. If you're afraid of these"—he made twin fists—"don't be. I'd never lay another finger on you. But if you're afraid of emotional pain, there's no escape. Not if you care about people. I'm just beginning to find that out. These past seven weeks . . ."

"Mel, don't." Wendy had never seen him so vulnerable.

"Wendy, you've got to listen." Mel's eyes were wide with fright. "I'm going into the hospital in two weeks. I'm scared. I don't want to die."

"Please, Mel, I can't stand to see you like this." His words terrified her. "It's only an ulcer. That's not so bad, is it?"

"An ulcer's not so bad," he repeated listlessly. "Will you do me a favor?"

Wendy tensed. "Of course."

"See me again. Next week. Before I go for the operation?"

"Okay, sure." Her voice betrayed the relief she felt that he hadn't further unburdened himself on her. "How about dinner and a play?"

Mel's head dropped to keep her from seeing the tears. "God, how did I ever let you go?" he whispered.

At Wendy's insistence Mel grabbed a cab and left her to walk home. The air was heavy with the smell of budding trees and early flowers. Wendy crossed to the park side of the street and began walking briskly north. Despite the evening's warmth, she was cold. She turned up her collar and plunged her hands deeply into her coat pockets. The men Wendy had become attached to during her life were all the same—arrogant, selfish, domineering. She'd always blamed those men for encouraging her worst qualities by ignoring her good ones. With Mel she'd grown sullen because unwanted sex and abuse was often forced on her. With Al she'd grown resentful after moving into his apartment because he often regarded her as nothing more than a playmate, while she was dead serious about renewing her career.

A traffic light changed, and she waited on the curb, wishing the beautiful evening were of some comfort. But her malaise was too old, too deep to be wished away, even on a spring evening when the air was thick with the perfume of new life. In exchange for her subservience, she had been allowed the illusion of absolute, unshakable belief in the strength of her men. Wendy was infatuated with authority and called it love.

The light changed and Wendy suddenly began to run. No one would stop her. No one would wonder why a beautiful woman was running up the street as if chased by hoodlums. No one would care. After all, this was New York.

Opposite Al's apartment building Wendy stopped for a moment, then hurried on to the next corner. She had to find a public phone. She felt a high, swelling panic inside herself and she knew there was only one way to quell it.

She dropped a dime into the telephone and hastily punched out the number. Immediately she began to feel relief.

"Yeah?" a gruff male voice responded.

"Manny, it's Wendy Jacobs." She was breathless from the run, the fear.

"Long time no hear, Mrs. J," he said smoothly. "It's kind of late in the day to be calling, ain't it?" But Manny knew it was never too late for someone as hooked as this dame.

"There must be something running. What do you say, Manny? Can you help?"

He paused a second, then laughed. "You're in luck, Mrs. J. There's a West Coast race just about to break. How's that sound?"

Wendy caught her breath. She'd run from her photography. She'd run from Mel. One day she'd run from Al. And all along she'd be running from the one person she couldn't escape—herself. Would she ever stop? Would the phone calls to Manny, the gambling, the dishonesty—the grinding unhappiness—ever end?

"Mrs. J? You still there?"

"Sorry, Manny. I guess I made a mistake." Slowly, she hung up the phone.

On the way back to Al's apartment Wendy planned what had to be done. For years she'd played the horses, hoping for the Big Win. Tonight she realized she'd had the winning combination inside herself all along. This time she was putting all her money on a newcomer named Wendy Jacobs. And she was going to stick with her until the rest of the pack had vanished behind her in the dust.

16

Rita sat disconsolately at her desk drumming her fingers on its slick surface. It was Thursday, the day before the Emmy Awards ceremony, but it felt more like the day before her own execution. Why?

She pulled herself from her chair and stationed herself by the window to survey the city she had conquered. It lay before her, a multi-leveled, roughly textured carpet woven of success, ambition, and greed. Just standing here, higher than the skyline, higher than the dazzling mid-morning horizon, was proof Rita had prevailed.

She sighed. She wanted to pull herself away from the postcard view of Manhattan, but her body resisted. During the few weeks since returning to the city from Connecticut the past had become an insistent intruder in her everyday life. Rita had merely to close her eyes to be swept back through the years, vividly recalling one moment, then another. A moment when she was safe and loved, a moment when love turned bitter. Always love. Always the past.

The intercom buzzed and startled her. With a swift stride she was back at her desk. "What is it?"

"I need to see you if you've got the time," Mel's voice crackled over the speaker.

"Just a minute."

Mel arrived. He was pitifully thin, but less grotesque in his new wardrobe than in the old clothes that had made him look more like Emmett Kelly than Rita Martin's new executive head writer—her equal. If she hadn't been forced to say something, he'd probably still dress like a hobo.

"I expected you to be a powerhouse today—running around, organizing tomorrow," he said, surprised Rita was in such a glum mood. Usually she acted as if the Emmy was her personal party, rather than the network's big rating grabber.

"I've decided not to kill myself politicking. It's never gotten us anything in the past."

"We'll win one of these days . . . if only by default," he said helpfully. "It's a real shame——"

"Mel, please," she interrupted. For five years he'd been telling her how sad it was *Time Nor Tide* had never won.

"Have you heard any network gossip? Any leaks?" he persisted.

"Not a peep. The Academy is very tight-lipped about all this." The East Coast National Academy of Television Arts and Sciences awarded the daytime Emmys while the West Coast version presented the more prestigious nighttime awards. "But I wouldn't worry too much about the Emmy," she said calmly. "It's more an ego boost than a rating of quality. Just think of the number of shows that have won after they've been canceled." Mel nodded mutely. "Besides, there are more important things. After you're out of the hospital, I want you to take a vacation. Get away from it all." Rita hated admitting it, but she blamed herself in part for his physical condition.

"You know that's impossible," he shook his head. "We're understaffed as it is."

"We've got Dave Hailey on the line. That should help." By the time Rita interviewed Hailey to fill Tom Wesley's position he'd already been hired by Nan Booth. The experience was humiliating—and another sign of her loss of control. Once again Goodspeed was unavailable. And Nan Booth had still not approved the Penny Hewitt story.

"We need dialogists. Particularly with Peterson about to leave," Mel said with his seemingly inexhaustible spirit of fight.

"I'll get some free-lance people in. Do you know anyone who might . . ."

"Let's talk about it later," he rudely cut her off. "I came in to find out why I can't just dump Al Peterson without all this crap about demoralizing him. He'll see right through it."

"Simple: the Writers Guild. We have an obligation to be

fair with Peterson—like it or not. Besides, I thought you were looking forward to this. What happened?"

"I don't want to waste my time, that's what happened," Mel replied angrily.

"Okay, then let's make it easy for you. I'm *ordering* you to work with Peterson." Rita fumbled for a cigarette on her desk, lit it, and blew a stream of smoke directly into Mel's face. "Hate *me*, if you have to, but get the job done." Mel was growing comfortable in the habit of stepping on her toes, and equal or not equal his insubordination still riled her.

"I don't like it."

"It must be a difficult position for you . . ." she began, intuiting Wendy as the real cause of Mel's hesitation, ". . . but I always thought you were able to separate your personal from your professional life."

"Like you separate the two?"

"Let's not draw me into this, Mel. We're talking about you. If you really feel incapable of dealing with Peterson . . ." she said with enough condescension to satisfy Marie Antoinette, ". . . I'll be glad to take over."

"Over my dead body you will." He leapt up from the chair.

"Then for Christ's sake do the work and stop complaining." Mel glared at this reprimand and Rita decided she'd better stroke him. "I know the pressure you're under, but we'll be back on our feet soon. Be patient, Mel—with yourself and with me. Okay?" She pursed her lips and bowed her head like a child asking forgiveness.

"Why am I such a sucker for your line of bullshit, Rita?" he asked bluntly. "But perhaps even that's ending. These days I'm beginning to wish I'd never heard of you or your goddamned show." He walked out, slamming the door behind him.

Halfway back to his own office Mel was struck by a wave of convulsive pain that sent him racing to the men's room. Standing in front of the mirror, he searched for the man he'd known all his life. A stranger stared back at him, a man who measured out his life in volleys of pain and handfuls of pills to counteract them. A man who was a twin to his sickness. They walked together, ate together, slept together. A man who was dying.

"Goddammit," he choked as the pain returned. "I don't want to die." He gripped the edge of the sink for support. "I don't want to die.'' But the gray, tear-stained face before him offered no comfort. In that moment, once again, he saw that if he did not reach out to Wendy for understanding, his life would have been worthless. That was why he had to get her back.

Peterson was late, and Mel was slightly relieved. Although he had mustered up enough ego to work professionally with the bastard, he was still antsy about one-on-one meetings with the man who was cuckolding him. Even the years of being second best in prep school and college were nothing compared to the insult of Peterson fucking his wife for all the world to see.

Although no one at *TNT* dared allude to the situation, Mel saw the pity in their eyes and hated them for knowing his shame. When even the secretaries lavished him with warm, understanding smiles, as if to say, ''We understand, Mel. You've been fucked over; it must be tough,'' he wanted blood. Peterson's blood. But he'd settle for getting Wendy back.

When Peterson was announced Mel took a deep breath, straightened up, and flipped Al's script open to the title page.

Peterson appeared in the doorway dressed like a rumpled heap of last week's laundry, but looking very handsome. ''So what's the problem this time, Mel?'' he asked without entering.

''*This* is the problem.'' He shoved the script across the desk. ''It's a mess. I want it redone from page one.''

''This is all your idea?''

''It was generally agreed upon, not that it matters.'' Mel clenched his teeth. ''You're here to work, not to ask questions.''

Peterson sashayed into the office and sat down. ''Just curious, that's all.'' He pulled out a pack of cigarettes and tapped one out. He had no intention of letting Jacobs pull any bullshit today. Mel had already overstepped his grounds by conning Wendy into accepting that phony dinner invitation.

''Do us both a favor—don't smoke,'' Mel requested testily.

Al lit the cigarette and flicked the spent match into an ashtray. ''Let's get on with it. I've got other things to do this afternoon.'' If Nan hadn't called Al never would have dared pull this grandstand play. But she had and he relished seeing Jacobs on the spit.

''Take a good look at this. We'll talk when you're done.'' He had planned to dissect the script page by page, but Peterson was such a prick about the cigarette Mel wanted as little contact with him as possible.

For the next ten minutes, Peterson leisurely thumbed through the script, smiling all the while. Mel's changes—emphatically scrawled in the margins of the text—were ludicrous. Nothing he contributed improved the script . . . nothing. To sweet little Ellie Davis this treatment, even from Tom Wesley, must have been devastating, but to Al Peterson, with ITC firmly on his side, the exercise was laughable.

"The only thing you didn't criticize was the color of my typewriter ribbon, Mel," he grinned, flinging the script back across the desk.

"And what the hell is that supposed to mean?"

"Kind of looks like I can't do anything right around here these days. Has Rita seen your work?" He nodded toward the script. "Your *editing*?"

"Rita is no longer interested in you—or your scripts," he gloated. "You answer only to me from now on. And I resent your questioning my motives." He was building up a good head of steam now. "You've done a lousy job in a business that demands perfection, so what the hall difference does it make who wants your work redone, anyway?"

"I just figured you've got more at stake here than Rita does," Peterson replied. "After all, I *am* shacking up with your wife."

"So now we're down to brass tacks." Mel pushed away from the desk, but remained seated. "I have an ax to grind, and I'm taking it out on your work, is that the scenario? Well, even if it were true, I'm still calling the shots, and I want this fucking script rewritten from top to bottom, got that?" His face was scarlet with rage.

Al nodded meekly. "You're the boss, Mr. Jacobs, sir."

"Then take this crap with you and have it back to me first thing Monday morning."

Peterson stood up lazily and stuffed the offending script into his briefcase. His complacence infuriated Jacobs.

"You're taking this mighty lightly, Al. Mind if I ask why—if I'm not getting too *personal*?"

Al snapped the briefcase shut. "Because I know you're full of shit, and you know it too." He started for the door, stopping at the threshold. "We also both know you're an asshole, and this little drama you and Rita have cooked up is as meaningless as your corrections on this script.'' He patted the briefcase.

Mel sprang from his chair and lurched toward Peterson, stopping a few feet short of him.

''I'll make the corrections,'' Peterson agreed, ''but don't expect me to tremble like Ellie Davis each time you call me in on the carpet, because to be frank, there's no way in hell you—or Rita—can get rid of *me*.'' Maybe it was tipping his hand a bit, but the days of kowtowing to this schmuck were over.

After Peterson left, Mel sat with his fists clenched on the desk. That goddamned, arrogant bastard, he thought. He thinks he can play this game better than I can, but he's wrong. I still hold the trump card, and I intend to use it.

He picked up the phone and dialed Peterson's number. It rang five times before Wendy answered.

Rita returned from a solitary lunch to find a message from Nan Booth. All communications between the two women had broken down, and it was with a mixture of curiosity and trepidation that she returned the call.

Don Sheridan answered. ''Nan's at lunch, Mrs. Elliott, but she left word she'd like to see you at two.'' He paused. ''If it's convenient.''

''No problem,'' she replied angrily, then hung up. Two o'clock. Halfway through *Time Nor Tide*! Rita sighed and began editing a set of ''crib'' notes for Dave Hailey. He had a great deal of catching up to do in a very short period of time. Tom Wesley might have been a disaster, but at least he'd known the show inside out.

At two o'clock exactly, Rita took the elevator up to thirty-nine.

''She'll be right with you, Mrs. Elliott. Take a seat.'' Don casually indicated an uncomfortable chair wedged into a corner of the anteroom off Nan's office.

Rita smiled and remained standing. She was a long way from acquiescing to the rudeness of a secretary. Her eyes drifted to the closed office door and she imagined the woman on the other side. Rita had prepared herself for the worst, although she hadn't a clue why Nan had called this impromptu meeting. Rita's feelings about Nan were easily summarized by now: once a bitch, always a bitch.

''Sorry you had to wait,'' Nan said unctuously as she

appeared through the door. "With the Emmys tomorrow you can imagine what hell my life is." She pecked Rita on the cheek.

"I can imagine," Rita agreed with only the faintest lacing of sarcasm. "But it's a big time for the network."

"Yes," Nan agreed as she guided Rita into the office and indicated a chair for her guest. "ITC only gets the 'privilege' of telecasting the ceremonies once every four years. Personally, I think it's a pain in the butt. I'd just as soon see the other networks share the honors amongst themselves."

Rita chuckled and shook her finger at Nan. "Sounds like high treason to me."

"Well I have to let my hair down once in a while. It makes me feel human." She settled back comfortably, lit a cigarette, and blew a thick column of smoke off into the air. "But even you will admit that working in the sequestered world of Laurelton does rather isolate one. Times have changed in the real world."

Rita laughed. "So I've been told."

"However, we now seem to be over the hump. The ratings are beginning to look healthier, and although your audience share has dropped a little, I'm not that worried."

"I misjudged the competition," Rita mused.

Nan nodded. "If the Frank Cameron murder story had begun six or eight weeks earlier and Cameron had died, oh, say about Christmas, my guess is that *TNT* would have grabbed more than a fair share of the audience and held it through the February sweeps right up until today. As it is, Cameron's death came too late and your ratings proved it."

During those six or eight weeks back in the autumn, Rita and Rick Cologna were still very much an item. He hadn't yet wallowed in the popularity of his character and his ego hadn't yet begun begging for instant gratification. During those six or eight weeks Rita still lavished him with expensive gifts while dangling the ultimate prize of a bigger part on *Time Nor Tide* in front of his eyes. To be reminded of those days now, shamed Rita. The whole affair had been so shabby, and look what it had cost.

"And to compound your problems," Nan pushed on fearlessly, "the other networks *had* planned ahead with very strong stories. It was just a case of bad timing," she gently let Rita off the hook.

"But the Penny Hewitt story is perfectly timed," Rita insisted.

"With the murder trial under way *and* an abduction into the jungle, we'll be sitting pretty once again." Rita didn't like the situation. Nan was being much too magnanimous to believe. A well-placed probe might just reveal what was really going on.

"You go ahead with the Hewitt story. The standards department has gotten over the notion that ITC is taking sides in Caribbean politics. Frankly, I, like you, felt they were taking themselves a little too seriously."

"Of course you did. Or at least I'm glad you finally came around to my way of thinking." Rita went right for Nan's heart—her professional vanity.

"I did it as much for myself as for you," she said tartly.

Bingo! A bull's-eye on the first try! Now Rita was curious to see just how deep the resentment went. "And that's why you fired Alex and Gordy, too. For your own good—and for mine."

Nan's smile wavered on her lips. "Be honest, Rita. Gordy Tate was ineffectual, a hack. And Alex? Well, he had an eye for set decoration, but we have scenic people for that." She lit another cigarette without offering Rita one.

"Gordy was one of the best," Rita pushed on, taking note that Nan didn't palm off the firings on Goodspeed.

"If he were that good he'd still be with us." She nervously flicked a match into a Rita Martin ashtray. "You knew his limitations. Isn't that why you wanted him hired in the first place?"

"My need for control doesn't run so deep I'd commit artistic suicide to prove a point," Rita said evenly.

"Then I must have misjudged you. I thought you'd do *anything* to hang on."

"Not any longer." Rita got up and extended her hand. "Thanks for your support, Nan. Getting a release on the new story line is a lifesaver."

"Don't thank me, thank broadcast standards," Nan said curtly.

"Do it for me, will you?" She walked to the door. "See you tomorrow."

Rita returned to thirty-five, convinced that, whatever it was, Nan's final power play was already under way. Rita prayed she'd have the time to stop it.

*   *   *

"Jesus, you make it sound like I just sold state secrets to the Russians!" Wendy screamed at Al after he chastised her for arranging a second date with Mel. And for that very night—when he'd wanted to get out of the house and go to a movie. "Being lovers doesn't mean you own me. I had enough of that with him." Wendy paced from one end of the living room to the other. "Everything you said is true: You did give me a chance for a new start. But how about giving me some credit, too? It wasn't exactly easy to walk out on a five-year marriage, a comfortable home, and a terminally ill husband for this," she gestured at the cramped room with consummate disdain.

"I'd think a prison cell would be more appealing than sharing a bed with Mel Jacobs," he said angrily.

"What's happening to you, Al? You used to say you wanted the best for me."

"What the fuck are you talking about? I'm not the one headed for a cozy dinner with an ex. What kind of dizzy feminine logic makes walking into a trap a learning experience?" Jacobs had been such a prick about the script that morning, and now this. "Don't you see he's trying to get at me through you?"

Wendy stopped short. "Is that what you really think?"

"What else could it be?"

"Maybe he wants me back." She found a chair near the fireplace and sank into it. "Is that such a preposterous idea?"

"That's not the way he operates. He and Rita want me out. He's been handed the dirty work. You're just a grace note in the Al Peterson funeral dirge."

"You're just plain jealous and you don't even have the guts to admit it." She watched Al closely for a telltale sign that might betray his true feelings. "You're afraid Mel might entice me back, aren't you?" Peterson didn't move. She got up and began to pace again. "Mel wants this, you want that. And nobody cares what Wendy wants."

"I just don't want you to get hurt," he finally managed to say.

"You just don't want Mel to win." When Al's jaw stiffened, Wendy knew she'd finally uncovered the truth. "That's it, isn't it? You want me because I'm Mel's."

Peterson was immediately at her side. "You're talking crazy, Wendy. I don't give a damn about him."

"Or me," she whispered. "What were you thinking that

first time we met? That I was a delectable piece of ass trapped in the lair of the Big Bad Wolf? Of course, what *could* you think? That's how I played it.'' She pulled away from him and nervously ran her hands through her hair. ''It's no wonder you resisted when I suggested moving in here. You probably thought of Valentine's Day as the beginning and end of Wendy Jacobs.''

''Shut up, will you?'' He fumbled in a lacquered box on the coffee table for a cigarette. ''I don't give a damn about Mel Jacobs.'' He lit the cigarette and snapped the lighter closed.

''No,'' she corrected, ''you don't give a damn about *me*.'' It was clear now. The past weeks she had been kidding herself. Al's more frequent fits of temper, his impatience with her work, with her demands to have time to herself, all exemplified a man living a life he regretted. He'd been good at covering up his dissatisfaction, but time had eroded the facade. Wendy had bounced from Mel to Al; he'd bounced from Rita to her. Only Wendy believed her commitment had been real.

She waited for Al to come to her, to put his arms around her, to prove finally she was wrong. Instead he looked at her for one long, painful minute, then stared at his hands, then at the floor. She fought back tears of anger. It was over. Suddenly, they were through.

''Maybe we need a cooling off period,'' she offered, still hoping to salvage some vestige of her pride.

''Does that mean you want your own apartment?''

''We spend so much time trapped in these three rooms.'' Suddenly moving did seem a good idea. ''I'll find a loft in SoHo,'' she said, immediately thinking of Russell Bates.

''Does that mean Mel's out of the picture?''

''I'm afraid it means you are, Al.'' She went directly to the closet and removed her coat. She'd dressed to go out earlier. If Al had been fifteen minutes later this whole conversation would never have happened.

''Well, good luck. I hope when you grow up I'm still around.'' He watched her without moving.

''Oh, you'll always be around, Al. Your type always is,'' she said so snidely it scared her. She left without another word, not bothering to look back. He wouldn't be there asking her to stay. And come to think of it, he'd never really been there from the start.

Wendy hailed a taxi on Central Park West and gave her home address. This time she'd agreed to meet Mel at the apartment. To prove to Al she could do it. And all she had proved was that he didn't care. But there was someone who did care. And maybe this time she could be there for him.

Wendy was apprehensive in the apartment for the first few moments. There were so many memories waiting—good and bad—that she felt her resolve waver. No, she'd be strong. Tonight she'd forget the past and view the evening as a first step into a new future. What *she* needed came first. And right now she needed to be with Mel.

"My god, you've had it painted," she exclaimed with surprise when Mel turned on all the lights.

"Like it? It was so sterile before. I wanted a little warmth."

The photographer's white living room was now pale yellow, the pastel painting over the fireplace had given way to an ornate, antique mirror that added a new depth to the space, and even the furniture had been rearranged. There was a new beige carpet. Wendy walked through the apartment discovering little changes everywhere: Mrs. Swedeborg's room had been converted into a cozy study with towering floor-to-ceiling bookcases, the kitchen had a new stone tile floor, and the ancient wooden cabinets had made way for chrome high-tech utility shelves; upstairs, the bedroom was a fresh, warm rose color, and a king-size platform bed had replaced the creaky four-poster Wendy had always considered an eyesore—even though it had been her own purchase long ago.

When she returned to Mel in the living room, she was breathless from the tour. "It's just not the same apartment. I don't believe it."

"Like it?"

"I love it! And I thought *I* was the only one in this family with any taste."

"You've underestimated me." Mel sulked with mock hurt.

"I've underestimated us both," she replied, seriously.

Mel saw her darkening mood and signaled her to join him on the couch. "What is it, honey?"

"You did this for me, didn't you?" Wendy blinked a tear aside.

He put his arms around her to cover his embarrassment—he'd changed the apartment around hoping not that Wendy might come back, but, like an ancient pharaoh, to remove all symbols of a past regime by obliterating any proof that the woman who scorned him had ever existed. He told himself his obsession was fueled by anger, but as the days dragged on without her, he had seen that the loss and a strong need to deny it drove him to the office for grueling, self-punishing hours of work.

Now Mel pulled Wendy close. "I needed to do something to get my mind off you."

"I *had* something to take mine off you," she sighed.

"Want to talk about it?"

Wendy shook her head. "There'll be time for talk later."

Mel nuzzled her hair. "I missed you, Wendy. Very much."

Wendy stared deep into his eyes. "Is there anything I can do to make things up to you?"

His eyes filled with tears. "Don't ever leave me again."

Wendy pulled Mel to her and cradled his head against her breast while his body shook from a lifetime of tears. Whatever demonic power had driven him during the years of their marriage, it seemed to be gone, cast out by the sickness that slowly took its place. Wendy no longer considered whether she did or didn't love Mel. The question was irrelevant. The fact was, he needed her. In all the time they'd spent together he had never once turned to her for anything but his own pleasure. Their real communion had always been only physical. Now as they sat in the muted lamplight of the living room, they transcended that.

After cocktails and dinner and a long, quiet talk, they fell asleep in each other's arms. Later, Mel slipped out of bed and pulled on his robe. Wendy lay sleeping peacefully. He sat at the edge of the bed to study her. All his life Mel thought he knew every little twist and turn of his mind and soul. Life was at his command and the world played by his rules. But during the last two months he saw clearly just how wrong he was. And things began to happen he'd never counted on or expected. Falling back in love with Wendy was at the top of that list.

Tonight he no longer wanted to hurt Wendy, or himself. All he wanted from life was a peaceful death. With Wendy nearby. He was exhausted from swimming against the tides of his life. He'd pushed himself too hard for too long, and like the song said, maybe now was the time to stop and smell the roses—while he still could.

But before he began his last stand, there was one thing he

had to do. It smacked of the old Mel Jacobs, but hell, no one was perfect. He left the bedroom and descended the stairs to the main floor study. After closing the door, he picked up the phone and dialed Al Peterson's number.

"You take cream only, right?" Rita asked Peterson as she poured a cup of coffee. He nodded. "You see, some things I haven't forgotten."

"I never thought you would." He accepted the cup with a tolerant smile.

"My, my, is that ego I hear talking?" She looked at him reflectively for a moment, then poured herself a cup. "You are a very attractive man, Al. But not totally unforgettable."

Peterson frowned. "It's too late in the game for either of us to play cute, Rita. That's not why I'm here."

"Then by all means tell me why you *are* here. I've been wondering how you got the balls even to call me." She plunged a spoon into the dark, amber liquid, and began to stir it erratically.

Peterson never for a moment questioned the rightness of telephoning Rita to invite himself over. Whether she knew it or not he was her replacement at ITC now—and he'd always been an emotional peer. With Wendy so suddenly gone, he could feel himself drifting. True, he could have stopped her tonight, but why bother? Everything she'd accused him of was true. Still, he'd grown used to her company. Maybe that's why he'd called Rita—just for company.

"You really are a bastard," Rita interrupted his thoughts. "All those nights you must have jumped out of my bed and run straight to the typewriter to tell Nan all. You know I just might create a new character for *TNT* based on your treachery." She stirred the coffee thoughtfully. "No, on second thought, who'd believe such snakes exist?"

"You have every right to chew me out, but don't I detect just a touch of admiration in your voice? I mean, you said it yourself over and over—we're two of a kind."

"Did I really say that?" She shook her head slowly from side to side. "The idea seems pitiful now."

Peterson laughed. "Come on, Rita. This is Al you're talking to, not Mel or the late, hardly lamented Tom Wesley . . . or Nan."

He caught her eyes and held them. Rita felt a flash of real disgust. Did Peterson actually know just what she'd tried to do to secure Nan's backing? Not a chance. Nan Booth was far too practical to go around broadcasting her own humiliation.

"Now that you mention it, I am glad you're here." She patted his hand. "Because you remind me just how far I've come since Ben's death."

Peterson's eyebrows furrowed. "What's that supposed to mean?"

Rita rose from the couch, coffee cup in hand, and walked to the french doors that opened onto the terrace. A warm breeze ruffled the hem of her skirt. "I find the idea of identifying myself with you to be nearly impossible and totally repulsive." She turned back to him. He stared at her uncomprehendingly. "You see, before Ben died, I told myself *Time Nor Tide* was the reason I existed. *TNT* equals Rita Martin. The equation was simple and effective. And most people bought it." She sipped the coffee. "Oh, you probed a little deeper than most, but I suspect that's only because you're more ambitious—and far more selfish—than most."

Now Peterson got up. "Go on, Rita, this is fascinating and most informative." He passed her and continued out onto the terrace. Hundreds of city lights speckled the darkness.

Rita joined him outside. "I might have gone on that way forever, but then Ben died. And in a way, Rita Martin died along with him."

Peterson turned to face her. She was beautiful in the diffused light that came from the living room. "Go on."

She smiled. "That's it. There's nothing more to say. After Ben's death came the realization that in the last six years I've wasted more time being self-indulgent than most people do in an entire lifetime." The words cascaded out now. Odd that Peterson should be the one to hear them. "And I now see that everything I once held sacred is really profane—people, places, things. Everything I once would have sold my soul to possess now seems the emptiest of prizes."

"And that includes me."

Rita remained silent in answer. Then she said, "Shall we go in, Al? It's getting chilly out here."

"Not just yet." With two long steps he was at her side, his arms around her waist. He was angry, filled with fury at her coldness. "You always were an iceberg, Rita. Get too close and you'll freeze." He pulled her against him savagely. "But you see we really *are* two of a kind. That was a very pretty speech you just gave, but save the pap for the show." He buried his head in her neck, biting the warm skin, kissing her roughly.

"Get away from me," Rita commanded, managing to keep her voice low.

But Peterson grabbed her by the hair and pulled her head back. She lost her balance and fell into his arms dropping the coffee cup and saucer. They shattered on the tiled floor. Al crushed his lips to hers, forcing her teeth apart with his tongue. Rita fought back, but was powerless in his grasp.

He edged her up against the terrace railing. Twenty-five stories below the night doorman lit a forbidden cigarette in the shadow of a nearby doorway, bored with the routine of his job. Traffic hummed along Fifth Avenue and car lights sliced wedges from the darkness of the adjacent Central Park. The air was heavy with the promise of spring and flowers, summer and heat waves and beaches.

Rita managed to free one hand. Fiercely, she slapped Peterson's face. He released her immediately and stumbled back. His lips were pursed, jaw set. His eyes hated Rita.

"Get out of here!" Rita yelled. "If you don't, I'll call for help." She ran inside to the entrance hall and stopped, her hand poised over the intercom button.

Peterson followed her inside. He was calmer now, but his cheek was red and still stinging. Instead of leaving, he sat down on the couch and closed his eyes.

"I want you out" Rita hissed. "Or I'll call the doorman and have you thrown out."

"I'll go, but first there are a few things I have to say." Jesus, he felt like he was caught up in a nightmare. This wasn't why he'd come over. He'd wanted to patch things up.

"I have no interest in anything you have to say. I can't believe you'd think I'd want anything to do with you. You must be——"

"Shut up!" His eyes flew open and he suddenly stood up, tense with violence.

Rita's hand instantly hit the intercom button. She was leaning against the wall, pushing herself back to get as far away from Peterson as possible. She was scared.

"Tell him it's a mistake," Peterson warned, coming closer.

Rita shook her head.

"I've got a few things to tell you, Mrs. Elliott. And you'd better listen." He had wanted to tell her about ITC's plan for her; he had wanted to help, but somehow it had all gone wrong.

"Can I help you?" The doorman's tinny, disembodied voice shattered the silence.

Rita looked from Peterson to the speaker on the wall. All she had to do was press the button and scream. Peterson was close, but not close enough to stop her. She trembled uncontrollably, every nerve in her body close to the breaking point. It was all like a scene from *Time Nor Tide*. No, no it wasn't. It was her life. It was real.

"Mrs. Elliott, is anything wrong?" The voice grew more insistent.

Rita looked pitiful crushed up against the wall, tears streaming down her face. So, this was what lay beneath the marble and steel of the Rita Martin facade! Just another human being. Just another frightened kid. Peterson shook his head and closed his eyes momentarily, burning the image into his memory. He didn't want to forget this moment. Ever. Not as long as he lived.

"Rita," he whispered, "I want to save your ass. Will you just give me that chance?" His voice was soft now, almost loving.

And it penetrated Rita's terror and instantly calmed her. She studied his face for a moment longer, then pressed the intercom button. "Max, it's Mrs. Elliott. Sorry, I must have brushed against the button by mistake. There's no problem."

"Okay. Good-night, Mrs. Elliott." His voice trailed off.

"Now, maybe we can talk like two human beings." Peterson guided Rita back to the couch.

They drank two more cups of freshly brewed coffee in silence. Their fight had devastated them both. It had torn away the patina of civility and professionalism, even the facade of casual lovers they had earlier erected. Indeed, they were very much alike, but to see it so undeniably, to come face-to-face with their raw emotions so suddenly, had drained them.

Finally Rita said, "I'm afraid I'm going to have to ask you to explain what you meant earlier about 'saving' me." She poured herself another cup of coffee and offered one to Al who shook his head no. "It's late, Al, and . . ."

"Yeah, I know. I'm tired, too." He was exhausted. Wendy was gone. He'd nearly assaulted Rita. Jesus, what the hell was happening to his life? "First, I'd like to talk about Mel and his strategy to, shall we say, ease me out."

"Are you speaking professionally or personally?" Tired or not, Rita still had the sharpest tongue in New York.

"I resent the approach he—and you—are taking with my work."

"Do you?" Rita cocked her head slightly. "And just how would you like him—us—to approach it? On bended knee?"

"You know you really overestimate yourself," he said, managing for the moment to quell the anger that was threatening once again to erupt. "You may really believe that no one at ITC sees you're behind every dirty trick at *Time Nor Tide,* though I doubt it. But there are at least three people who have your number, and have had for quite some time: Jim Goodspeed is one, Nan Booth is another."

Rita tensed. "And who, might I ask, is the third?"

"Me."

Rita chuckled. "It does my heart good to see that my wicked ways haven't been overlooked by the dialogists." She suppressed a smile. "But don't you think that's rather like the scullery maid censuring the peccadilloes of the master of the house?"

"Your schemes affect everyone."

"Please, be more specific," she urged. "Just what 'schemes' are you alluding to?"

"During the first couple of months I worked for you, I had the dubious privilege of observing your tactics with Ellie Davis. It wasn't a pretty sight. She deserved better."

"How very gallant of you to come to Ellie's defense—six months later," Rita sneered. "But of course you *couldn't* have said anything earlier because, after all, you *did* take her place, didn't you?"

"Did I really take *Ellie's* place? And all along I was under the impression I was taking over for Rick Cologna." He poured more coffee. There was no way in hell he'd sleep tonight anyway. "But now that you and I are finished—despite my writing ability and knowledge of *TNT*, and despite its lousy ratings—I'm out. Is that it?"

"Time will tell," she replied archly.

"You're so damned sure of yourself. So sure you'll always have the upper hand. Well, you may have been able to railroad Ellie Davis, but you won't have that easy a time with me."

"If I didn't know better, I'd say you were threatening me."

Al remained silent. How the hell could he tell her the real extent of his complicity with Nan Booth? How could he reveal the cheapest of shots Nan had pulled that very afternoon without admitting—even indirectly—that he condoned it? Last week he'd decided not to tell Rita anything. She deserved to be shot down in flames. Then Nan pulled today's stunt. And like it or not, he had to admit Rita Martin still got to him. *That's* why he was here tonight. It wasn't the job. It wasn't Wendy. It was Rita herself. Al stood on the threshold of his greatest triumph, but he couldn't just let Rita be led to the slaughter without a chance to defend herself.

"Did you know Nan Booth forwarded my first script to you? Did you know she as much as offered me a job at *Time Nor Tide* before I ever met you?" The words spilled out in a flood. "Did you also know she supplied me with *TNT* scripts and outlines, as well as the original bible?"

Rita's face went white. She smiled, but when she spoke her voice was brittle. "Why . . . of course I knew. She told me."

"You're lying, Rita," Al shouted at her. "You *didn't* know. Admit it. Be honest with yourself this once."

"All right; I didn't know. But what of it?"

"You've been set up . . . from the start." He edged closer to her. "Nan Booth has used you—and me—to push you out."

"That goddamned bitch!" Rita hissed. She rose and stalked to the bar to pour herself a stiff drink. "And just why are you baring your soul to me now? Is your little playmate at ITC fed up with you? Is that it?" She took a long pull from the drink. "Christ, Peterson, I gave you credit for more diplomacy."

"Hey, hold on a minute. You're way off the track."

But Rita wasn't about to be stopped now that the picture was becoming clear. "It's too late for an eleventh-hour declaration of loyalty, Al. You're through." She was in control again. "You were right, though. I did sic Mel on you. He probably went a little overboard, but I can hardly blame him . . . since you *are* fucking his wife."

"And when did adultery become so deplorable to you?" he growled, and noted the hurt that registered in her eyes.

Rita sank down on the couch, defeated for the moment. "That's no longer relevant. Ben's dead, and you and I have long since finished *our* little affair. You were nothing more than a petty amusement, Al . . . a diversion.'' She finished the Scotch in one swallow and poured another.

This time Rita's words struck home. ''Well, let's set the record straight; what do you say, Rita? *You* came on to *me*. You are an attractive woman, and I was willing to give you what you wanted, but only because I thought it might give me job security.'' He laughed. ''What a dummy I was. I never guessed the fastest way to the *TNT* exit was through your bed.''

''Look, Al, I'm really getting tired. If you have something to say, say it and leave, please.''

Al took in a deep breath and began. ''Last week Nan Booth hired me as head writer of *Time Nor Tide*.'' Even though he said it as evenly as possible, the words seemed to explode in the room.

Rita stared incredulously at him.

''She began sniffing around months ago, asking if I could handle the job. I said sure. I figured she knew something about Tom leaving . . . or even Mel.'' He bowed his head and looked at his feet, wondering if Rita would buy the lie Nan had so easily seen through. ''I didn't know what she *really* meant.''

Rita slowly put her glass down on the bar and eased herself up onto a barstool. ''And what did she *really* mean?''

''ITC isn't going to renew your contract. Nan's known about it since last week. She's got Jim Goodspeed, Weatherhead, all the network execs so fired up against you they'd just as soon see you dismissed by firing squad.''

''But our ratings have improved,'' Rita defended herself weakly.

''It's too late. At this point even a fifty share couldn't save you. Ratings were once the issue, but now it's more . . . complicated. It looks like Nan has a great personal stake in getting you out.''

''Then she's just been stringing me along?''

Peterson nodded.

''And she has no intention of putting the Penny Hewitt story into production?'' she completed the thought.

''It is going into production . . .'' Peterson slowly admitted.

''*After* I've left.'' Only now did Rita begin to intuit the extent of Nan's loathing. ''And *you're* going to replace *me*. Is that it?" She kept her head held high, but her trembling voice betrayed her confusion.

"It looks that way," he mumbled apologetically. "Tom's gone, Mel's sick—there's no telling how long he'll be out of commission. The network feels this is the perfect time to revamp the whole show. There's even talk of taking it to California."

"California?" Rita mused. "I never liked California." She picked up the drink and sipped. "And so that's the way the story ends? My friends turn their backs on me, and out I go. Good old Ma Martin, the bitch of the airwaves." She began crying softly, cradling her head in her hands. "I always wondered how I'd react when this happened. I thought I'd probably explode, want to tear Nan Booth's hair out or set fire to that goddamned couch that Goodspeed meditates on every afternoon . . . with him on it. But tears? I never would have guessed." She covered her eyes with her hands.

Peterson went to her and put his arms around her. Rita melted against him. "You're not exactly friendless, Rita. No one is supposed to know, but tomorrow—whether *Time Nor Tide* wins for outstanding writing—you're going to be presented with your own personal Emmy for your contributions in the field of daytime drama."

"And will I be fired before or after the presentation?" she asked bitterly.

He kissed her forehead, then wiped her tears away with his thumb. "It's a great tribute. You should be proud."

"I don't know that I have any pride left. I've done everything I can think of—short of begging—to hold on to my show. You still underestimate me, Al." She smiled. "You still believe I've blinded myself to reality. That's my safeguard. When you're in my position, even though they know you're onto them, you can t let them know how scared you are. All you can do is fight them at their own game—and hope to win!"

"You've known about this all along?"

"Let's just say that since February it has become apparent to me that I'm no longer the most popular girl on the block. All the pressure about ratings, the discontent on the set, the firings, the Penny Hewitt fiasco . . . it was all part of the same thing." She sighed. "Nan's been building a case against me for months, but I'd be damned if I'd give in one inch to those bastards until I had no other choice.'' She wiped away the last of her tears.

Al kissed her on the cheek. ''You are a remarkable woman.''

''That and a token will get you on the subway,'' she laughed. ''So, the bad guys have finally won.'' She considered the idea. ''Nan Booth should come out of this smelling like a rose. Next thing she'll have Goodspeed on the carpet.''

Al shook his head. ''She's playing for bigger stakes. Rumor has it she wants to head west for the big time.''

''And I hope they eat her alive.'' She got up and walked into the hall and looked in the mirror near the front door. She began correcting her makeup, her eyes darting now and again to Peterson. ''Tell me, Al, why did you come here tonight? Aren't you taking an awfully big risk telling me all this?''

He shrugged. ''I don't know—loyalty, guilt, admiration? Maybe I just wanted you to hear it from someone who . . . once . . . cared a great deal about you. I also wanted you to be forewarned and forearmed.''

''I appreciate the gesture, but I don't see that there's much I can do.''

But Al looked at her disbelievingly. Soon a smile began to hover on her lips. ''That's the spirit, Mrs. Elliott,'' he winked. ''Could it be that devious mind of yours is already at work?''

''Now, don't try to second-guess me. You run along home and let me get some sleep.''

''See you at the Emmy Awards tomorrow.'' Al started toward the door, but she stopped him.

''One more thing, Al. Thanks for taking the time to be kind. And if there were anyone I'd choose to replace me it would be you.''

So it was over. The worst thing that could happen *had* happened. And Rita felt nothing. No bitterness. No pain. No regrets. How was it possible? *Time Nor Tide* was her life, her baby. Correction: Jeannie was her baby; *Time Nor Tide* was her job. She reached deep inside and tried to cry again, but the tears had dried up. Even her anger at Nan Booth, Goodspeed, Peterson . . . everyone . . . was gone. She was calm and peaceful, feeling something approaching serenity. It was as if the weight of the world had been lifted from her shoulders.

She waited for the elation to pass and when it didn't, Rita began to savor it. God, I feel unshackled, she thought to herself. I don't believe it. I just don't believe it. But now there were other matters to attend to. Peterson was right; she could take advantage of her knowledge of ITC's plans and do something. What? What she needed now was an idea, something suitable for the death of a soap opera queen.

And by the time she crawled exhausted into bed, Rita had indeed concocted a plan.

Peterson stumbled into his living room and flipped on the light. It was extremely late, two o'clock in the morning. A celebratory drink at Maxwell's Plum for his honest but cautious handling of the situation had quickly become two, then three, and now he was pleasantly high. He tiptoed into the darkened bedroom hoping not to awaken Wendy. The bed was still made. Wendy wasn't there. Shit, he'd forgotten their fight. Well, that could easily be remedied. He'd forgive her.

Al went to the telephone and beat out Jacobs's number. It rang ten times before it was answered.

"Who is it?" Mel answered blearily.

"Is Wendy there?"

"Peterson?"

"Who else did you expect? Now tell me, where the fuck is she?"

Mel took a deep breath. "She's here . . . where she belongs . . . in bed with her husband. There's no need to worry," he added with mock sincerity.

"You fucking bastard!"

"Look, Peterson, I understand your confusion, but I didn't twist Wendy's arm to make her stay. You need to talk to her about this, not me. Shall I wake her?"

"Go to hell," Al yelled and slammed down the phone.

17

To an outsider the main lobby of the Waldorf-Astoria looked no different than it ever did at ten o'clock in the morning. Guests hustled in and out, conventioneers caucused to plan afternoon meetings and late-night revels, friends met for a late breakfast, and the shadowy, efficient staff kept everything running in clockwork order. It looked like any ordinary Friday morning.

But to an insider, the daily routine had changed radically. Excitement filled the air. The usually blasé staff was starstruck as a seemingly endless stream of famous faces passed before them. Television had come to the Waldorf!

After weeks of planning and preparation several squads of ITC technical crews invaded the hotel at six that morning. Their object: the final transformation of the opulent ballroom into a television studio equipped to carry a live, nationwide broadcast of the Emmy Awards ceremony that afternoon at two-thirty. Miniaturization made everything possible, but the work of snaking cables into the room, setting up a makeshift control room that could handle the live feed, planning camera shots, blocking, rehearsals, more blocking, camera rehearsals, all took the better part of three days. It wasn't easy, but as the time approached and the entertainers arrived for a final rehearsal, ITC was ready.

"I'm going down to the drugstore for a moment, Mrs. Elliott. Need anything?" Mrs. Flannagan asked from the bedroom doorway. They had all come to New York yesterday from Connecticut.

"No thank you, Kathleen." Rita looked up, distracted from reading the final copy of an "unprepared" speech she planned to give later. "You won't be long? I have the award ceremony to attend."

"I won't be more than ten minutes. Will you and Jeannie be all right?"

"We'll be just fine," Rita laughed at the motherly concern. "Won't we, honey?" Jeannie was sprawled next to the bed, her Bert and Ernie dolls wrapped in her arms.

"Yes, Mommy," Jeannie replied without looking up from her playmates.

Mrs. Flannagan smiled at the tableau of her two charges finally acting like a proper mother and daughter. Then she collected her gloves and purse and left, fully prepared to meet all the devils of hell in the New York street. She didn't like New York. It was too big, too dangerous. And much too controlled by "the heathens." Kathleen Flannagan's bucolic Irish-Catholic upbringing had never prepared her to deal with the likes of humanity she found crowding the New York streets. In fact, if Mrs. Elliott hadn't become so attached to Jeannie over the past couple of months, Mrs. Flannagan never would have stayed on as housekeeper.

She'd spent six years holding her tongue about Rita's galivanting about. But that was while poor Mr. Elliott was alive. Now that he was dead, she no longer felt constrained to maintain that silence. Not only did Kathleen look askance each time Rita approached Jeannie with less than open affection, but she outspokenly reprimanded Rita's callous treatment of "the poor child." In Mrs. Flannagan's book, what Rita Martin Elliott needed was a good spanking. But in lieu of such drastic measures, an old-fashioned tongue-lashing was nearly as effective.

At first Rita listened impatiently to the unsolicited and unwanted advice. But gradually, Rita began to take an active interest in her daughter's welfare. Routine soon became habit, and the habit became love. Mrs. Flannagan once thought it shameful that Rita was unable to intuit how to deal with the child. She suspended her judgments, however, when it became obvious that she had covertly been enlisted by Rita as a tutor in mothercare. Mrs. Flannagan saw Rita's personal—and business—troubles in clearcut black-and-white terms: She was a sinner *nonpareil,* and through Ben Elliott's death she'd been given a last chance at redemption—in the form of Jeannie. And once Mrs. Flannagan was convinced that she'd been chosen to do God's work, it no longer exasperated her that Rita asked for advice in dealing with the simplest facets of childcare.

When Mrs. Flannagan left Rita looked thoughtfully after her. The old woman was a treasure. And to think for years she'd lost out on a perfectly good friendship by categorizing the housekeeper as an adversary. Kathleen may have looked as tough as peat, but under that craggy exterior was a warm, openly loving human being who genuinely cared for her—and, more importantly, for Jeannie.

Rita put the speech aside and clambered off the bed to join Jeannie. Although the child was sometimes unwieldy, she was most often a pleasure. Rita now classed her daughter—and other children like her—as a most precious flower. Tonight this particular flower wore Dr. Denton pajamas, and Rita noted with amusement that the trapdoor had fallen open.

"Hey, come here, pumpkin. You've sprung a leak." She pulled Jeannie to her and deftly made the necessary adjustments. Jeannie smiled happily, still staring at her dolls, now a few feet away. With a pat on the bottom, Rita sent her scrambling back to her "friends." A moment later Jeannie was in the thick of a thoughtful conversation with Ernie.

Rita stood up and stretched, not at all surprised that her muscles ached. Getting back into shape with triweekly visits to a local health club was arduous. It really hurt to start all over again. But pain was growth, and Rita pushed on. Besides, it was far too late to stop now—in so many ways. She was playing her ace at this afternoon's ceremony. She may have come face-to-face with her own human limitations, but she was also going to triumph. There was going to be sweetness where there was also pain.

Emmy day was the peak of the broadcast year for Rita, although she carefully hid her anticipation and excitement from everyone. Only Ben, who knew every mood, had seen the importance of this day. Today there was a strong aura of nostalgia in the apartment: It was Rita's last Emmy show and her first without Ben's loving support. Winning an Emmy for Outstanding Writing for a Daytime Drama Series meant everything to Rita. It would validate her unequivocal success. That her peers had not granted her this seal of approval since

TNT's inception was a constant source of irritation. Other shows—shows mediocre in style and content—had won *more* than one award. It just wasn't fair!

After the third year without recognition Rita promised herself that when she finally won, she would start thinking about retiring from *Time Nor Tide*. It was actually a ploy, a game with the gods to entice them, to give then an incentive to award her the coveted golden statuette representing the winged goddess of television. Yet each year the gods turned a deaf ear to Rita's promises. And just this past year, she'd made that same promise to Ben. And now she was about to make good on her promise.

Rita always went to the ceremony with Ben. This and the Valentine's party were the times when Rita eagerly put aside her resentments and enjoyed his company. Ben was a perfect escort-witty, charming, handsome. He stood perfectly calm at her side as he was reintroduced to the same people who forgot year after year exactly who he was and where he fitted into the Rita Martin empire.

And each year as *Time Nor Tide* lost out to another soap, Ben comforted Rita, made shuddering love to her in the stillness of her penthouse bedroom, and convinced her that next year it would all be different.

Until this year, next year was always the same.

As Rita sat reminiscing, Mrs. Flannagan returned. And right behind her were the cleaners, delivering Rita's Chanel suit. God, what this suit and I have been through! Rita thought. If there was one thing she considered a good luck charm, it was the dark gray Chanel. But now it was getting a little threadbare, and constant mendings no longer restored it to its original beauty. She noted sadly that today was probably the last time she would be able to wear it. So everything was coming to an end. Her life had come full circle.

"I'll take Jeannie to the park now, Mrs. Elliott," Mrs. Flannagan said. "She'll enjoy the spring air, and you'll get some time to yourself, to get ready for this afternoon.

Time to myself, Rita thought. Time to think about what needed to be done before she embarked on her new career: Rita Martin, private citizen. She undressed and stepped into a hot bath, to relax, to ponder.

First there was Jeannie.

What could be done with her? Sending the child to an expensive "special" boarding school filled with rich castaways was out of the question—Jeannie was far too important for that kind of neglect. So, if the Elliott family stayed in New York, Jeannie would be enrolled in a school for . . . retarded children. Rita said the word to herself, noting that it didn't hurt to say it. Or to admit it, really. But if she decided to retire to Connecticut, then Jeannie would continue on at the school Ben had chosen for her. Rita wasn't quite sure which plan was best, but at least she'd begun to put her daughter's needs on a par with her own. And no matter what her final decision, Jeannie would always be taken care of; the trust fund she'd recently set up would provide Jeannie with proper care for as long as she lived. It was Rita's memorial to Ben.

Now what about about me? Rita wondered. With all this free time staring me in the face, there must be a million things I can do. But what?

She closed her eyes and succumbed to the delicious pleasures of the bath. But after a moment, her eyes fluttered open. I could travel! Even start lecturing again! God knows the fans are clamoring to find out all about their favorite soap opera. Even the talk shows might be interested in booking me. It's certainly worth looking into. For heaven's sake, I could even create a new soap opera!

''Haven't you had enough?'' she asked herself aloud, poking a hole through the thick layer of bubbles with her big toe.

And there's always the chance I might marry again. She pictured her sweet Ben and allowed herself, for only a second, to miss him as deeply as she had missed him immediately after his death. He'd known her so well, and had known her moods, her tricks, her self-deception. Tears filled her eyes. Ben had always warned of the day when Rita discovered too late that in him and Jeannie she'd always had the love and respect she so desperately sought through *TNT*. He'd been right. Tragically right.

Rita finished her bath, snuggled into a robe, then began ticking off the long list of items to be dealt with before this afternoon, *Chanel,* she crossed off the first word. *Flowers.* She had ordered her traditional orchid corsage the day before, in memory of Ben who had started the tradition. *Hair appointment.* She had to leave for Cinandre in twenty minutes. The last entry was *Travel Agent*. Rita thought about that for a minute, then went to the phone.

Ten minutes later she was dressed and on her way out when Mrs. Flannagan and Jeannie returned. Jeannie was dressed in a yellow quilted fleece jacket and cranberry ski pants. She looked like a model straight from the L. L. Bean catalog. With her hair flying and her cheeks shiny red, Jeannie Elliott was a picture of health . . . and happiness.

"We had fun in the park," she announced, charging into Rita's arms. "Do you want to come play with me?"

"I've got to go out this afternoon, honey." Rita kissed the top of her head.

"Going to work again?" Jeannie asked with such disgust that both Rita and Mrs. Flannagan laughed.

"Not this time. I'm going to a television show."

"Can I come, too?" Jeannie asked instantly. "Is it *Sesame Street*?"

"If only it were," Rita mused. "No, this is only for grownups . . ." An idea suddenly came to her. "Or is it?" It was crazy even to think of it, but why not? This was to be her day, and as such, she could damn well do as she pleased. "Mrs. Flannagan, while I'm out having my hair done, get Jeannie to take a bath . . . and do her hair up nice and pretty . . . and dress her in that lovely pink dress Mr. Elliott bought—you know, the birthday dress—and her best black patent-leather shoes . . ."

"And the coat she wears to church with me, and the little straw hat with the flowers . . . and her gloves, I presume," Mrs. Flannagan said, caught up in the spirit of Rita's obvious excitement.

"Exactly." Rita turned to Jeannie. "You *are* coming with me today." Jeannie would go in Ben's stead and Mrs. Flannagan would tag along to watch over her while Rita picked up her special award. "Would you like that, Jeannie?"

Jeannie responded by throwing her arms around her mother's neck and giving her a resounding wet kiss on the cheek. "I want to go everywhere with you . . . even to work," she gushed.

Rita cradled Jeannie against her. "We won't have to worry about that anymore after this afternoon . . . Now, scoot!" She sent Jeannie off with Mrs. Flannagan feeling happier than she had in years.

Al frittered away the early morning doing petty errands to keep his mind off Wendy. He shopped for groceries, took a pair of shoes to be resoled, picked up his good suit for this afternoon, and he still felt like shit. Goddamn Wendy Jacobs! Sweet, simple, "take-care-of-me" Wendy.

At eleven o'clock he sat at the kitchen table nervously drumming his fingers. When he caught himself staring again at the silent telephone, he turned away in disgust. He'd be damned before he'd call her! She knew they had a date for the Emmys. Cocktails were scheduled to begin in an hour at the Waldorf. And here he was in a pair of jeans and an old sweater. And all because of her.

He got up and began pacing, then made a cup of bitter instant coffee, which, after tasting it, he immediately threw down the sink. What excuses would Wendy offer when she finally called? What lies? He picked a half-smoked cigarette from an ashtray and lit it. She'd gone too far this time. There were a lot of things Al had put up with because he was fair-minded. But being fucked over by some dizzy dame wasn't one of them. Sleeping with Jacobs was unforgivable. After all, he had his pride!

Christ, how had he let someone like Wendy Jacobs con him? Well, she was different, not the usual. He was used to flashy women who thought in terms of dollars and cents, expensive clothes, and weekends "away." They were predictable and disposable. Once he grew tired of one, there was always another waiting to hop into the sack. If only he'd known just how different Wendy was. Not only was Mrs. Jacobs confused about herself—and in desperate need of psychological help for myriad reasons, her gambling not being the least of these—but also she happened to be married to the prick who was trying to get him fired. What a circus!

Al found a fresh pack of cigarettes and lit one. He was smoking too much. But who wouldn't with his life in such chaos? When the phone finally rang fifteen minutes later, Al took his time before answering it.

"Yeah?" he answered gruffly.

"It's Wendy." Her voice was soft, but unafraid.

"What can I do for you, Mrs. Jacobs?" He found a comfortable place to sit, sensing the conversation might drag on for a while.

"Don't sound like that, Al. Please."

"And just how would you like me to sound? Maybe I should be happy you've finally decided to let me know where you are?"

"You've known since you called Mel last night." There

was an icy edge to her voice. "Why bother to play games with me?"

"I just wanted to hear you admit you'd gone crawling back to your husband, that's all." He paused and waited for a retort. Silence was her only reply. "If you've called to explain——"

"There's nothing to explain," she cut him off. "I'm here, at home . . . and I'm going to stay."

"You're not coming back?" Al was stunned. He'd expected tears, demands for forgiveness. Wendy's coldness left no room for argument. "Just like that, you walk out?"

"You, of all people, know my decision isn't that simple. Look, I'd like to talk to you. Can we get together?"

"Get together?" he fumed. "And what the hell were we supposed to do this afternoon?" He stood up and began pacing. "We're supposed to go to the Emmys together."

"I'm going with Mel." She barely whispered. There was a long pause. "Look, I can't explain on the phone."

"Shove your explanations, Wendy. Let's face it: You don't know what the fuck you want out of life. First it's Mel, then it's me, now you're back with him again. You know, I'm beginning to think he was right; there *is* something wrong with you. You just can't treat people the way you do, jumping in and out of bed with every man who's willing to take you under his wing. One day you re going to have to face life and grow up." He nervously lit another cigarette. Christ, he was really letting it all hang out. But what the hell? He was pissed off . . . and Wendy had already made up her mind.

"Until a few days ago I would have been the first to agree with you, but no more."

"So Mel has shown you the way, is that it? He's finally going to make an honest woman of you."

"Look, I'm sorry about this, Al. If there were some other route. I'd take it."

"Don't hand me your noble shit. You've always been out for yourself—just like everyone in this fucking town. Don't try to back down now that you're flying your true colors." How the hell could he, good old smart Al Peterson, the man who knew women, have fallen for her line?

"I'm sorry I've hurt you, but . . ."

"Hurt me?" He laughed. "You haven't come within a mile." He rested his head against the wall wishing it were true. "Just do me one favor; call before you come to collect your clothes. I want to be gone while you pack. You've got your key. Let youself in and leave the key on the kitchen table on your way out. I'm sure you know the routine . . . you've had enough practice at it!'' He slammed down the phone before she had a chance to answer.

''Shit! Goddamned shit!'' He banged his fist into his other hand. ''Boy, do I get the winners . . . Rita Martin and Wendy Jacobs.''

He stalked into the bedroom and was immediately confronted with her camera and the stacks of contact sheets she'd been working on. For a second he saw her by the window as the sunlight danced off her golden hair, her cheeks flushed with the excitement of working again. ''*I* did that for you, Wendy! And how do you pay me back?'' he yelled into the empty room.

He picked up some black-and-white glossies and was faced with his own likeness. ''Just look at you! First-class sucker of the year. Mrs. Jacobs will take some of me with her because I can't stop it, but she's *not* going to take these.'' Within minutes the photos were reduced to a wastebasket full of shredded paper. ''Fuck you. Wendy Jacobs.'' His voice caught in his throat. ''Fuck you.''

Ten minutes later Al lay on the bed, his hands behind his head, his eyes closed. The apartment felt empty. Really empty. It wasn't like Wendy was out shopping or out having her hair done. It wasn't like she'd be coming home with some foolish, lovable comments about the strange people she'd seen in the streets, or the shocking prices of fruit at the Korean greengrocers, or how lousy the weather was. It wasn't just like that at all. Wendy was gone and he knew what to expect of the next weeks.

The provocative, residual smells of her perfume and cosmetics scattered in his top bureau drawer would eventually vanish. There'd be no more long waits to get into the steamy bathroom. No more cooking smells and the sounds of pots and pans banging when he returned from jogging late in the afternoon. There'd be no more petty quarrels about which TV program to watch or whose turn it was to drag the laundry to the Chinese place around the corner. And like a cheap laugh from the lowliest sitcom, there'd be no raised voices about who forgot to replace the toothpaste cap. There would only be silence.

Al's life would be peaceful once again, totally defined by his own desires and choices.

And it would hurt.

He dragged himself from the bed and wandered into the kitchen, not quite sure why he was there. Grinding a good Italian roast for espresso took his mind off the dull pain in his head. The coffee machine sputtered and groaned, then hissed to a halt. "Jesus Christ," he complained as he slapped the lumbering gold giant, "even you're against me today."

Finally he sat down at the table to clear his mind. He had to have a plan. Living without priorities was dangerous. It left too much time to think . . . to remember. What did he have to do today? Right now? Wendy had stood him up for the Emmy show and he needed a date. But whom? He immediately deleted Rita from the list. Sure, he'd done her a good turn last night, but she was poison. He hadn't seen Angela Brite in a while. She'd be available. No, he wasn't quite ready to admit he was that defeated.

He had an idea. It was a long shot, but . . . He dialed the phone, then waited anxiously. "Nan, it's Al. How're you doing?"

"Rushed, Al. I'm already late. What can I do for you?" She still had to get changed before the ceremony. With luck she'd still be able to catch the tail end of the cocktail party.

"Look, this is crazy as hell of me at this hour . . . but do you have a date for this afternoon?"

"I was planning to go alone," she lied without missing a beat. She'd planned to go with Don Sheridan, her safe, and obedient, escort.

"Then I'd deem it a great honor to escort you to the Emmy Award show."

"It's a deal, Mr. Peterson. In fact, I'd love it." She only momentarily wondered where the hell Wendy Jacobs was.

"Meet you at your place about twelve-thirty?"

"Meet me at the Waldorf at quarter to one," she quickly corrected. "I've still got a few errands to run." Emily had moved in with Nan a month before. Today she was home sick with a cold. It would be easier to keep Peterson away than to try and hide the reality of her ménage.

"See you then." He hung up just as the espresso machine chugged, grunted, and began oozing a trickle of coffee into a cup. "So, I get my coffee after all. Well, maybe this day won't be a total loss."

* * *

By twelve-forty-five the Waldorf ballroom was packed with people representing all facets of television. Script girls talked with game show hosts, actors gossiped with videotape engineers, producers rubbed elbows with the network management they were never able to get on the phone, PR people gushed, guests-by-marriage looked lost, and the bartenders and waitresses frantically tried to keep pace with this hard-drinking, fast-talking crowd. The daytime Emmy show was the New York television crowd's most glamorous celebration. It was one of the rare times the East Coast competed with the West Coast on a national level. And for this reason the room buzzed with excitement.

The ballroom itself had undergone a miraculous transformation. The stage had been converted from an ordinary proscenium into a glittering tinsel shrine to that greatest of modern deities—Television. The back wall vanished behind an enormous screen on which clips from nominated shows were to be projected. A lucite podium for the presenters and this year's MC—Peter Marshall, durable and congenial host of *Hollywood Squares*—stood stageright, and a low, golden staircase for arriving daytime stars jutted off into the wings, stage-left.

Numbered dining tables filled the main space of the ballroom floor and, on either side, temporary bars dispensed relief to the thirsty throng until one o'clock when lunch was to be served. Clearing the space by the two-thirty air time was impossible, so ITC, in the style of pretelevised ceremonies, billed this year's Emmy Awards as an informal occasion. It was Weatherhead's belief that seeing celebrities sitting over dishes and coffee cups would create the illusion of informality, while in reality there would be nothing informal about this production.

Nan Booth, dazzling in a taupe and vermilion frock by Kenzo, concluded a cozy chat with Dinah Shore, then scooted toward the nearest bar and a gloomy Joe Ericson. She'd dumped Peterson minutes earlier to get on with company business.

"Joe, darling," she proffered a kiss mid-gush. "Well, here we are at last. Excited?"

"Like a turkey the day before Thanksgiving," he replied sarcastically.

What an appropriate comparison, Nan thought to herself.

"With all your good news, I was sure you'd be spinning around here like a top! You are *so* unpredictable." She sounded like vintage Bette Davis, and loved every second of it.

"It's only habit," he smirked. "I taped my last show this morning. Tonight I head for the Coast."

Now that Rita was through, Ericson's sacrifice was gratuitous, but it did lend a nice feeling of credibility to Mrs. Elliott's dismissal. Nan feigned regret. "Are you sure you're making the right move?"

"Right move, wrong move, I've hung around New York too long. Don't feel bad, Nan. ITC's done me a favor. Getting caught up in a soap can be death for an actor—if he has any real ambitions. And I, for one, have real ambitions." He didn't have to confide in her, but she'd been so damn nice all along. It wasn't her fault the network had kept her hands tied. "Now don't get me wrong. I wouldn't trade my two years with *Time Nor Tide* for anything. I'm fairly well known now, and I think I've got a fair shot at lining up something in nighttime."

Nan took him by the hand. "I'll be honest with you, Joe. The main reason I didn't want to lose you is I think you're one hell of a fine actor. I'm being selfish—on the network's behalf."

"Coming from you, Nan, I consider that a great compliment." Ericson actually blushed. "You understand, there's nothing personal in my wanting out. In a way I'm thankful Rita Martin is such an obstinate bitch. If she weren't, I'd probably be doing the show for the rest of my life."

And without her you'll be doing toothpaste commercials in six months—if you're lucky, Nan thought maliciously. "Rita's not such a bad sort, Joe. She's mellowing with age."

"That's no longer my concern," he snorted. "There's only one thing I care about as I wave good-bye to daytime."

"And what's that?"

"One of those." Ericson pointed to the back of the stage where a shelf of Emmy Awards stood watch over the festivities.

"And no one deserves one more than you," Nan agreed. "You've done more to help *TNT* than almost anyone." And more to help *me* than you'll ever know, she thought.

"I just hope the awards committee sees it that way, too." He looked over Nan's shoulder and smiled. "There's someone I have to talk to; produces mini-series on the Coast. Take care, Nan, and thanks for everything." He kissed her on the cheek and pushed off through the crowd.

"Look me up when you're back in New York," she shouted after him, sure that in no time she'd be in L.A., too.

For a fleeting moment Nan felt a tug of nostalgia as she surveyed the crowd. She recognized most of these people on sight, she'd talked to many of them over the years, and even considered a few to be friends. Now that the move west seemed imminent, a vague sadness overcame her. It had been a long, hard struggle to be in the running for a nighttime position, and New York was very much part of that fight. She felt a little traitorous, being so anxious to leave; but her time in New York was up. She had to move on.

Nan worked the crowd, nodding to this one, kissing the cheek of that one, stopping for a laugh with her old friend Charles Nelson Reilly. She felt exuberant today, triumphant, in fact. As of a week from Monday—in just ten days—Rita Martin would be informed she was finished at ITC. And the network fully believed her removal would correct *TNT*'s troubles. Jason Weatherhead had already lauded Nan as the woman who'd found *Time Nor Tide*'s rotten spot and who had worked so tirelessly to cut it out. She'd heard enough network scuttlebutt over the past week to know Jason and his cronies were positively salivating at the thought of having finally snatched control of *TNT* from Rita's hands.

Of course, someone who commanded as much public attention and respect as Rita Martin quite often was untouchable. Any overt move against such an industry celebrity surely would cast a shadow on the network's business ethics. And the last thing Weatherhead wanted was a reputation as an ingrate. But thanks to Nan's diligence—and the constant stream of memos and reports—a case had been made against Mrs. Elliott. ITC had proof that dismissing their offending compatriot was their only recourse—facts didn't lie.

In the future, private talks with executives from other networks, Weatherhead, Goodspeed, the others on the fortieth floor, and Nan would express their profound regret over losing an oldtimer like Rita Martin. They would gladly cite the myriad things she'd done for ITC through *Time Nor Tide*, then they would sadly admit she'd finally lost her golden touch; she no longer knew what her audience wanted, she'd been unhinged by her husband's tragic death—as the falling ratings clearly showed.

In exchange for her diligence, Goodspeed owed Nan one. And he was the kind who always paid his debts. Her desire to segue into nighttime would come as no great shock. What the hell, it was no skin off his nose if she wanted out. He'd probably be glad to be rid of her.

Feeling absolutely ecstatic and confident, Nan cruised the room talking endlessly with everyone. She paid particular attention to a couple of newsmen by teasing them with broad hints about the upcoming changes. When they pressed her for details, however, she played coy.

"Now, I can't say any more, boys," she baited them further.

"But you haven't said *anything*," the stringer for the *Hollywood Reporter* complained.

"Well, all right. Let's just say there will be some *major* changes in ITC's daytime structure." She had to be somewhat discreet.

"Are you talking about ITC's soaps? Like *Time Nor Tide*, maybe?" the man from *Variety* asked. "Word has it around town that Rita Martin's about to get the ax."

Nan's heart leaped into her throat. It was done! The newspapers had it and were running with the story. Nan allowed herself to feel the sweet driving exhilaration of success.

"Nan? What's the scoop?" the *Hollywood* reporter interrupted.

She winked and blew them both a kiss. "Sorry, boys, you'll have to read about it in the newspapers."

Nan was about to find Peterson and their table when she spied Walter Kennelly and his wife having a drink near the ballroom entrance. Kennelly was ITC's nighttime vice-president in Hollywood. In fact, he had the job she wanted. The one she'd get eventually. Step by step.

"Walt, Lydia, you both look great!" Nan swooped down on the unexpecting couple, arms outstretched.

Walt Kennelly was just under five six in height and girth, and he perpetually smelled of aged cigar smoke. He sported a dark tan year round. Lydia Kennelly, at five eleven, towered over her husband. Her imposing, skeletal frame was as close to anorexia nervosa as Nan ever wanted to see. Her stringy gray hair was pulled unmercifully back from her bony face forcing her eyes, like a bullfrog's, to protrude. She was as pale as bread dough.

"Walt, you devil, you didn't tell me you were coming to New York," Nan cajoled. She slid her arm around his waist.

Kennelly looked stunned, then perplexed. "It was a sudden decision, Nan. I didn't know myself until last night."

Nan tightened her grip on his waist. "How long are you gracing New York with your presence?"

"I'm not sure." He looked nervously from Nan to Lydia, who had fixed Nan with a cold, icy stare. "Nan is our wonder woman. She's almost single-handedly reorganizing daytime out here." He sounded patronizing as if New York were just east of Calcutta.

"What a nice thing to say, Walter," Nan purred. He'd probably already heard about Rita. "But you're overstating the case a little, aren't you? I just helped with a little housecleaning. Daytime will get along just fine without me one of these days." A gentle hint of her desire to escape New York seemed in order.

"Get along without you?" Kennelly looked bewildered.

Nan said nothing.

"Oh, I see, you're joking." He laughed nervously.

Nan didn't join in the merriment. "I *wasn't* joking."

He absorbed the information somberly, then shrugged. "I don't figure it. Has one of the other networks made you a better offer?"

"What *are* you talking about?" She was slowly beginning to see that she and this jackass were talking at cross-purposes. "Why would I want to leave ITC?"

Kennelly stared thoughtfully off into the crowd, trying to fit Weatherhead's decision this morning together with Nan's present reaction. Jesus, it just didn't make sense, unless . . .

"You don't know, do you?" he gasped.

Nan's smile froze on her face. "Don't know *what*?"

He slapped himself on the forehead and quickly looked for an exit. "I was sure Jason had gotten to you."

"Just what the hell is going on?" Suddenly Nan was panicked. Her throat was so tense she was barely able to get the words out.

"Perhaps I should leave you two alone," Lydia Kennelly interjected.

"Stay where you are," Walter commanded. Then he broke into a big smile and shook his head. "Hell, what's the difference if I tell you or you hear it from Weatherhead himself? Christ, if you were going to be fired or something, I'd go straight back to the hotel and cut my wrists for having given it away, but this . . .

Nan shifted her weight from one foot to the other. Mentally she counted to three, then she closed her eyes. When they opened again she was back in control. "Then it's good news?" she asked warily.

"A little of both." Kennelly's eyes darted to his wife's, then back again. He cleared his throat, but when he spoke his voice sounded scratchy. "Jim Goodspeed had a heart attack last night."

"Jesus," Nan gasped, feeling suddenly light-headed.

Kennelly quickly took her by the arm. "Now, now, don't take this too hard. I know what good friends you are."

"A heart attack. It hardly seems possible," Nan mused as she tried to regain her composure. "Jim Goodspeed has always been one of the healthiest men I know. With all that jogging and meditation and health food . . ."

"Looks like he might have been better off with a cigarette and a very dry martini," Kennelly said, hoping to dispel the oppressiveness of the conversation.

But Nan was in no mood for gallows humor. Goodspeed's illness was far too serious to joke about. Her California plans allowed for no contingencies. "Is he okay? I mean, he's not . . ." She couldn't say it.

"He's just out of commission for a while, that's all."

"And *that's* why you're here in New York." No one had notified her of Goodspeed's illness. Why not?

"Jason got me and Lydia out of bed last night. There was a meeting of the board this morning at ten." He sighed. "With Jim out of the picture . . ."

"What do you mean 'out of the picture'?" Nan countered. "You just said he was only out of commission for a while."

"Jim had a real close call, Nan. Looks like all this Rita Martin crap finally got to him. His doctor's been after him for months to retire."

"Retire?" The word stuck in Nan's throat. "He'd never do that." He wouldn't. He *couldn't*.

"But he did," Kennelly contradicted her cheerfully. "Last night from his hospital room."

"Why wasn't I told all this? It's not like Jason to overlook . . ."

Kennelly raised his hand to silence Nan. "You couldn't be told until the time was right, until we'd come to a final decision. Hell, Nan, you were the *subject* of the meeting."

He touched her arm for reassurance. "I'm here in New York because of you, not Jim."

Without another word, the entire scenario unfolded before Nan. Goodspeed's heart attack. Weatherhead putting in frantic calls to the other members of the ITC board. Quick decisions. A hastily held vote. And the outcome was unanimous. There could never be a question in anyone's mind who should succeed Jim Goodspeed. There was only one person who had brought Rita Martin to her knees.

"Congratulations, Nan," Kennelly planted a wet kiss on her cheek, "you've been made president of daytime television for the ITC network. It looks like New York just can't live without you."

Al Peterson drifted around the ballroom feeling like a wallflower. He'd started in high gear by talking to Patty Fellows. She was in top form and played up her exuberant personality for all it was worth. But once she meandered off, it was downhill all the way. Seven months with *TNT* and he was still a virtual stranger. But that's the writer's lot—holed up alone putting words in actors' mouths and never getting the proper recognition, he thought philosophically. When I take command, things will change for the writers—as well as for everyone else. No way would Al Peterson make the same mistakes Rita Martin had.

A tap on the shoulder brought Peterson back to reality. He turned and for a moment wasn't convinced the athletic figure before him was really Tom Wesley. His skin glowed with a nut brown tan his hair was bleached nearly white from the sun, he'd put on weight and actually looked robustly healthy. And more than that. Tom looked happy.

"Jesus Christ, you look great," Al exclaimed, pumping his hand up and down.

"And I feel great," Tom agreed happily. "You know Bob, don't you?" He introduced his lover.

"Sure." Al shook hands with Bob Craig then stared in wonder at Tom. "We all thought you'd disappeared into the sunset. So, what's happening with you?"

"Nothing. Absolutely nothing." Tom beamed. "We've spent long, glorious days in the sun by the pool, taken up golf and loved every minute of it and . . . well, coming back to New York, I wonder how I ever managed to live here for so long."

Al grimaced. "Uh oh. Sounds like the old 'sunny California' routine to me."

"Don't worry," Tom laughed, "I won't bore you with stories about how wonderful it is out there . . . even though it is." He grew serious. "How are *you* doing?"

"Where to begin?" Al stalled. Tom had only been out of touch since January, yet in that short time Al's whole world had turned upside down. There was just no use even trying to relate that to Tom. "I'm doing okay . . . never better, as a matter of fact."

"I always suspected *you'd* hang on." Tom winked. "How about Rita . . . and Mel?"

"They don't know you're here?"

"It's my little surprise. I've got a sixth sense about today. If *TNT* wins I want to be here in person. I put the best years of my life into that soap."

Al playfully squeezed Tom's shoulder. "Looks to me like the best years of your life have just begun."

"Touché," Bob agreed wholeheartedly. Since abandoning New York Tom certainly knew he'd changed, but only Bob Craig had witnessed the totality of that metamorphosis. Not only had Tom stopped drinking, but he'd become—not a new person, but an old person—the old Tom with whom Bob had fallen in love ten years before, in the days before either of them had ever heard the name Rita Martin.

"Is *that* Mel Jacobs?" Tom gasped, seeing the Jacobses enter the ballroom.

Al whirled around. Mel and Wendy were just walking in, Mel resting his hand lightly on Wendy's arm for support. She looked beautiful.

"Jesus, what's happened to him?" Tom barely recognized the shrunken figure whose smile was as weak as Wendy's was strong. "He looks like death."

"It's a bad ulcer. He's going into the hospital for an operation." Al couldn't take his eyes off Wendy. The sight of her made him feel angry and lonely at the same time.

"Mel was always the last person I ever thought would get an ulcer. With his temper I thought he'd go to his grave shouting. But now . . ."

Mel spotted Tom and the others and guided Wendy toward them, despite Peterson. "Tom, you son of a bitch!" he exclaimed. "Is that really you?" He looked Tom up and down with undisguised amazement and ignored Al completely.

"None other than." Tom tried not to stare at Mel's obvious physical deteriorations.

"Seeing you has just made my day." Wendy kissed Tom lightly on the cheek. "You look reborn." She kept her eyes focused straight ahead, mindful that Peterson followed her every move. "I guess being a free man agrees with you."

"I'm still not quite used to it." Tom basked easily in the glow of this respect and admiration. It was what he'd always wanted from Mel and the others at *TNT*, and now that he'd broken away from that charmed circle, he finally had it. "I miss everyone and the show, of course, but I watch every day." He suddenly felt as it he might burst into tears at any minute.

"You *are* a masochist." Mel laughed to break the tension. "I always knew it."

"I put too much of myself into *TNT* to give up on it now."

"We all did," Mel agreed. "I wonder if it was worth it?" The pain in his stomach flared and Mel gripped Wendy's hand. Let's find our table, honey. Tom, it was good seeing you . . . you too, Bob. If you're in town for a while, give us a call." They struggled off, Mel obviously needing Wendy's assistance.

Tom turned to Al. "I wouldn't have believed it if I hadn't seen it with my own eyes . . . Mel Jacobs acting like a human being! Christ, what other news is there?"

"I'll let you discover all the dirt for yourself. This crowd is particularly good at giving away secrets," Peterson replied sarcastically. Being snubbed by the Jacobses had made him feel like a fool. "I assume we'll be at the same table, so I'll see you two there." He edged away toward Nan who stood alone at the bar.

As his humiliation at the hands of Mel and Wendy began to gnaw at him, Peterson quickened his pace toward Nan. He hoped that once embroiled in a conversation with his coconspirator he'd forget Wendy Jacobs completely. The bitch! She and Mel had *both* cut him dead. They obviously hadn't heard he was now top banana. Well, he wasn't going to let them ruin his day. He'd worked too damn hard to get this far and—Wendy Jacobs or no Wendy Jacobs—he was going to make sure he got the proper respect from the right people.

"A penny for your thoughts," he whispered in Nan's ear.

Nan leaped back and turned on him, her hand poised to

strike. "Don't *ever* do that again, Peterson, or I'll have your ass," she bellowed with rage.

"Cool off, Nan! You're not talking to Don Sheridan now."

"Fuck off, Peterson. Just get out of my fucking life," she growled, then stalked off into the crowd.

Jesus! Nan Booth shows her true colors, Tom Wesley returns to the scene of the crime, Wendy snubs me. What next?

"Are there any surprises left?" he asked the air, as he got himself a drink and surveyed the crowd.

"My God, that can't be Jeannie Elliott!" Patty Fellows squealed with delight.

"Without a doubt," Rita said proudly. "Jeannie, do you remember Miss Fellows?" Jeannie was holding Rita's hand and Mrs. Flannagan's skirt—for insurance.

Jeannie stared at her with a wide smile, then shook her head. "No."

"Well, I remember you, darling." Patty bent over and gave her a kiss on the cheek. "Rita, she's the most beautiful girl I've ever seen. Takes after her mother."

"After her father," Rita corrected. She leaned down and cleaned a corner of Jeannie's mouth. "Excited about the awards. Patty?"

"Last time I was this keyed up, I wet my pants," she confessed lustily.

"Let's hope that's not a precedent," Rita quipped with a sly smile. "Have I missed anything yet?" She'd planned to avoid the cocktail party entirely, but the taxi miraculously hadn't become snarled in traffic and they'd actually arrived early.

"Aside from acres of fresh shrimp and some pedestrian caviar, nothing yet. It's the same tired people saying the same tired things. If only there were some *real* excitement at these drab affairs."

Following Rita's instructions, Mrs. Flannagan began to hustle Jeannie off toward the table. "There will be plenty of excitement," Rita promised mysteriously. "Just keep your eyes on the podium."

18

At 2:30 P.M., Eastern Standard Time, the ITC Emmy Award ceremony for daytime television began.

Everyone in the Waldorf-Astoria ballroom grew silent in preparation for broadcast. As the array of klieg lights crackled to life and flooded the stage, a bolt of anticipation shot through the audience. In the era of film and videotape, a live television broadcast like this was the rarest—and most exciting—use of the medium. There was a magic quality in knowing that the performance on stage was to be seen simultaneously by millions of viewers across the country. The second the lights went up an avalanche of expectation was unleashed. Those present straightened in their seats, adjusting their clothes, pushing back their hair—they just *might* be caught on-camera during an audience pan. Particularly self-conscious and on their best behavior was the nervous clique of nominees clustered together down front for easy access to the stage.

And more excited but less self-conscious than anyone else in the ballroom, was Rita Martin. In less than ninety minutes her name would be called. She'd go to the stage to accept her award. And then she'd let them have it with both barrels! Emmy or no Emmy, she wasn't going to let ITC have the last word.

The color test patterns on the strategically placed monitors disappeared and the screens filled with soaring aerial shots of

New York City. The Emmy theme song—played by a live orchestra—swelled up in the background and the mellifluous voice of ITC's sexiest announcer proclaimed the ceremonies open. Down front, a floor manager, poised to cue Peter Marshall, held up one hand, fingers spread wide. At a signal from the control booth, he began to count off the seconds to air time—five . . . four . . . three . . . two . . . one. He pointed sharply at Marshall, the enthusiastic audience applause prompted by the flashing "Applause" sign subsided, and the show began.

"Thank you, ladies and gentlemen. It's a great honor for me to be this year's host of the daytime Emmy Awards." He smiled warmly. "You know I've spent so much time working on the *Hollywood Squares* I'd forgotten *real* people don't flash on and off like light bulbs."

The audience laughed politely, and Marshall's cue cards were changed.

"Seriously, being here is a very special treat for me. Daytime television is the most exciting field in which I've worked. Many people consider daytime a poor cousin to the glamorous prime-time shows, but take it from me . . . some of the most creative talent in television today is found in daytime."

There was scattered applause.

"The people here with me today are the cream of the crop—actors, writers, directors, producers, set designers—who have risen to the top of their professions. Today it is television's turn to thank them personally by awarding the daytime Emmys for outstanding achievement."

The *Applause* sign cued the audience to respond.

"Before we begin, we have a special treat for you. Here's a dance fantasy inspired by some of the most familiar theme songs of your favorite daytime serials." Marshall turned to his left, the director cued the camera aimed stage-left, and a troupe of dancers jetéed out from the wings.

Five minutes later Marshall returned to the podium. "I haven't heard such sad music since my agent called to say he wanted more money."

Everyone laughed.

"In just a minute we'll be back for the first award—Best Supporting Actor in a Daytime Drama Series."

A taped commercial cut in and as the lights dimmed, the ballroom's high energy level dissipated. People fidgeted in their seats, whispered to one another, took sips of cold coffee, and waited as the commercials rolled. After what seemed an eternity, the lights went back up, and the show began once again.

While Marshall himself read the name of each nominated actor in the supporting category, the giant screen displayed thirty-second clips of the actors' acting expertise. Both Joe Ericson and Rick Cologna were nominated. Rita smiled to herself as their names were read and their faces flashed before her one last time.

"They chose me to present *this* award, because the academy wants all those handsome guys to be in good company," Marshall ad-libbed.

The *Applause* sign didn't catch the quip, but the audience clapped anyway.

After a moment's tussle, he opened the envelope and read the name. "The winner is Rick Cologna—Frank Cameron on *Time Nor Tide*."

The audience burst into spontaneous applause. Rick Cologna, seated far from Rita, leaped to his feet and took the stairs to the stage two at a time. Rita felt curiously detached about him. Her fury was long since spent, and she found herself actually pleased he'd won. If nothing else it was good publicity for *TNT*. Cologna *was* a good actor, and he *had* brought the Cameron character to life. Watching him now, it hardly seemed possible they had once shared her bed. But now so much of what led to this day hardly seemed possible.

Cologna cleared his throat and the applause died. "As most of you know, I was murdered on Valentine's Day . . ."

The audience laughed heartily.

". . . so I'm no longer with *Time Nor Tide*. But I want to say that working on *TNT* was the greatest experience of my life. I want to thank my fellow actors, our director, producer, and the fine crew. And were it not for Rita Martin and her staff of writers. I wouldn't be up here right now." He held the Emmy at arm's length high above him. "I can't believe I won! Thank you. Thank you all." Cologna left the stage to a burst of applause.

"That was nice of him," Mel whispered in Rita's ear.

"He deserved it." She smiled.

"Let's hope the academy feels as benevolent toward the rest of us."

The show dragged on through endless awards, production numbers, and commercials. Finally it was the writers' turn.

"Everyone seems to forget that without words actors have nothing to say," Marshall began. "Writers are a special breed, giving voice to other people, making them happy or sad, good or evil. It takes real talent to write good dialogue day after day, week after week. The men and women—the writers—we are about to salute deserve the praise and admiration of their peers."

The applause was heartfelt.

"And now to present the award for Outstanding Writing for a Daytime Drama Series are Susan Lucci, the beautifully evil Erica Kane on *All My Children,* and Nan Booth, vice-president of daytime programming for the ITC network."

Rita quivered with excitement as Nan, tight-lipped but smiling, descended the golden stairs with the sultry Susan Lucci.

"I've never been so close to a television executive before, Nan," Susan read her cue card.

"Don't worry, Susan . . . we don't bite," Nan replied with a big, insincere smile.

"Then all those rumors I've heard are untrue." Susan's hand went to her throat, and she gasped with relief. "Thank goodness."

The audience laughed appreciatively.

Nan's smile froze on her face. "The nominees for Outstanding Writing for a Daytime Drama Series are . . ." As she read each name a representative vignette from the show was televised. *Time Nor Tide* offered Frank Cameron in the hospital cafeteria for the first time confronting Rebecca Danforth about her sordid past.

Rita actually gripped the edge of her chair. She'd been through this agony five times before and it never got any easier. Today she prayed for the Emmy to tie up the loose ends of her life. She'd soon be gone from *TNT*, and the award was the perfect bon voyage present!

Susan Lucci handed the envelope with the winning name to Nan who tore it open slowly and with great deliberation. "The winner is *Time Nor Tide*." She crumpled the envelope in her fist.

Rita sat motionless, not sure she'd heard correctly. For five years she'd heard *TNT* win, in her head. But in reality it had always been someone else. Now it *was TNT*, and she didn't know what to do.

"Rita, Rita, that's us," Mel nudged her. "For Christ's sake we won the damn thing," he shouted as he pushed his chair back.

Rita stared around her. Every face had turned toward her table. The audience applauded wildly, and suddenly Rita realized she had a lot of people on her side. They might not have appreciated her personal style, but they recognized a winner when they saw one. Rita tried to stand, but her legs buckled. She doubted if she could make it up the stairs without assistance. A strong hand came from nowhere to help her up; it was Al Peterson.

"It's all yours, Rita. They love you," he said gleefully.

"Mine?" she mouthed the word, still not entirely convinced she'd heard correctly.

Jeannie took Rita's hand. "That's you, Mommy," she said excitedly.

Rita broke away from Peterson for a moment. "That's *us*, darling. Now, you wait with Mrs. Flannagan. A little later I've got a surprise for you." She smiled and got up, saying under her breath, "But right now I've got an even bigger surprise for *them!*" she looked first at the ITC management's table, then up at Nan Booth onstage.

Mel took Rita's arm and Al, Tom, Patty, Evelyn, and Loretta followed in single file to the stage. Susan Lucci kissed Rita on both cheeks and mumbled something about how exciting it all was. Nan shook Rita's hand, then stepped back as far away from her as she could without drawing attention to herself. Rita looked out over the audience. They had risen to their feet. Her eyes filled with tears—her peers weren't cheering the Emmy, they were cheering her!

When Rita finally leaned into the microphone, the crowd returned to their seats. "I don't know what to say," she began. "I've thought about this moment for six years, ever since we aired our first episode of *Time Nor Tide*. Now that it's really happened, I'm speechless." She wiped a few stray tears from her eyes. "I would like to thank ITC for its faith in me—particularly Jim Goodspeed who believed in me through all the rough times."

There was a ripple of whispers from those who knew of his illness. Weatherhead had seen to it that the news was kept highly confidential, and many people unsuccessfully sought out his table as Rita spoke.

Rita continued. "And I would also like to thank the men and women you see with me—my writing team. Without them, this award would never have been possible." She stepped back and motioned the others forward to say something, but they were all too stunned to react. After a few seconds the *Time Nor Tide* theme swelled, and Nan and Susan herded the entourage backstage as the next presenters were announced.

"We made it, Rita. We made it!" Patty screamed, embracing her through a waterfall of tears.

"Guess I'll have somewhere to hang my hat from now on," Mel joked obviously moved by his award. "Jesus, I never thought it would happen."

Rita silenced them. "I meant what I said out there; every word of it. Without you—and our newest member, Al Peterson—we wouldn't have had a shot at the award. I only wish Ellie Davis were here." Ellie deserved to be, she'd worked on most of the previous year's scripts.

"Don't worry about Ellie! She's making a fortune doing sitcoms in Hollywood," Patty chirped. "I talk with her a couple of times a month. She always wanted me to thank you for firing her . . . but I thought it was tacky," Patty confided apologetically.

Rita laughed uproariously. "That's the second best news I've heard all day. I'll make sure she gets the award . . . I'll phone her myself."

The stage manager broke up their conference. "Please return to your seats during the next commercial. Mrs. Elliott, you stay back here."

"Why?" Rita managed to sound surprised.

"I was only told to pass the message along. Now, if the rest of you will follow me . . ." He started away.

The others looked quizzically at Rita, then filed back out to the ballroom.

In a few minutes before her special award was to be presented, Rita calmed down enough to go over her prepared speech. Thank God for Al Peterson's guilty conscience, she thought. She held the Emmy close and ran her hands along the smooth, cool contours of the statuette. So this is what it feels like to be an award winner. Not all that much different than it did five minutes ago, she mused.

If Ben were alive he would have rushed backstage, scooped

her into his arms, and drowned her with compliments and love. "But you *do* know, don't you, Ben?" Rita whispered. "This is as much yours as it is mine." She would have begun crying had not the stage manager taken her by the arm and led her back to the wings.

"When they call your name just walk out," he instructed. "And let me have that." He tried to take the statuette from her.

"Not on your life. I've worked too hard for this. Where I go, it goes.

He shook his head at her obstinacy, then vanished into a crowd of technicians.

Peter Marshall's voice boomed from the stage. "And now we have a special award. It is for dedication to excellence in the field of daytime drama. The recipient of this award has rigidly upheld the high standards of achievement so important to television, she has brought a new meaning to the word *professionalism.* She is an example of the best television can produce. Our recipient is talented, noble, self-sacrificing, generous, and has worked tirelessly to improve our medium when others said it was a hopeless task. Almost single-handedly she has created a reputation for excellence that others today can only imitate. She is a true original. The National Academy of Television Arts and Sciences is proud to present this special Emmy Award for excellence to Rita Martin."

This time Rita was not caught off-guard. She waited . . . five . . . eight . . . ten seconds before returning slowly center-stage. She held her first Emmy tightly in her hand. Here was the Rita Martin the audience expected—the dramatist, the actress, the woman who controlled every situation and demanded nothing less than perfection. Rita held her head high, kept her back straight, and walked with long, deliberate steps, smiling just enough to indicate she was pleased.

This was Rita Martin's swan song, and she was going to milk it for everything it was worth.

When Marshall handed her the second Emmy, she cradled them both in her arms like two babies. The crowd, once again on its feet, screamed with delight when Rita finally burst out laughing.

She stepped to the microphone. "I feel like the mother of twins!" She looked lovingly at her "children."

The crowd roared its approval.

Now Rita grew serious. "I had no idea this award was to be presented to me today, so I am totally unprepared . . . and completely happy." She paused. "Eight years ago out of a personal tragedy, *Time Nor Tide* was born. I had dreamed of creating a daytime drama that would be extraordinary because it was ordinary, because it presented *real* people in *real* situations. It's a difficult task to present reality as entertainment, for television demands the spectacular and the unusual. Simply put, I wanted to show that everyday life can be just as rewarding as the fanciful movies and comedies and dramas that are telecast at night. The viewers of daytime serials—soap operas—are special people. Each day they tune in to see how other people deal with their everyday problems. I knew our viewers consider these people their friends. They turn to them to draw inspiration for their own lives. I have never—will never—look down upon the soap opera viewers, because they are the real, solid people of this country."

The audience wildly concurred.

"When *Time Nor Tide* became such a success, I never thought I would leave it. During these years the characters were my only family. How could I possibly think of deserting them? But I have come to see that my television family is grown up now. They have lives of their own and no longer need a mother to watch over them." Rita pulled herself even taller. "I have another family now—my daughter Jeannie—who is growing so fast I can hardly keep track of her. Unlike my friends in Laurelton, U.S.A., Jeannie Elliott *does* need a mother now, and her welfare has become the most important thing in my life."

The audience began whispering and shifting uneasily, sensing a major announcement. Rita Martin had never been anything but a straightforward businesswoman and the inclusion of details of her private life was something very new and obviously not done without reason.

"Jesus Christ what the hell's going on?" Mel inadvertently asked Al Peterson.

"Rita Martin is one hell of a woman, Mel." Al smiled from ear to ear. "I think she's going to prove that we've all underestimated her."

Rita leaned forward for dramatic emphasis. "It is, therefore, with great regret and sadness, that I tell you—my viewing family—that I am leaving *Time Nor Tide*."

The audience gasped.

"I have instructed ITC by letter that I will not be renewing my contract." Rita's voice caught in her throat. Goddammit, this was going to be harder than she thought. "I would like to thank everyone connected with *TNT* for years of loyalty and good work . . . and I hope each and every one of you will accept my love. Thank you."

She swept into the wings to a burst of bewildered "Bravas."

Mrs. Flannagan waited backstage with Jeannie. Rita handed the older woman her Emmys, then swept her daughter into her arms. "You *are* getting to be a big girl, honey."

"Why are you crying?" Jeannie asked, touching Rita's tears with her fingers.

"Because I'm *so* happy."

The three of them left quickly by a back exit, entered the waiting limousine, and were gone before anyone had time to realize what had happened.

EPILOGUE

Two weeks after the Emmy Awards ceremony, in a private room at Memorial Sloan-Kettering, Mel Jacobs died.

Wendy spent most of that time by his side, reading when he was asleep and talking to him when he woke. Toward the end, Mel's conversations tended to ramble and oftentimes grew incoherent as the heavy doses of medication worked their limited magic. During his lucid moments Wendy did her best to comfort Mel, but there was very little she could say. Even though they had a silent understanding of his true condition he still chose to keep the words forever unspoken. Therefore, in the way of people accustomed to pretending, they maintained the happy belief that very soon Mel would leave the hospital a well man. They spoke of picking up the pieces of their life together. They'd start over—no regrets, no recriminations.

But in their hearts the truth reverberated.

"You've been very good to me, Wendy. And all the time I never thanked you," Mel repeated over and over in his reed-thin voice.

"Don't talk about the past," she'd say. "Let's think about what we'll do when we spring you from this joint," she'd joke.

Then Mel would plan trips and vacations, new apartments and country homes. Or sometimes he just painted pictures of quiet evenings with Wendy in front of a roaring fire. He often confused the past with the future, describing as fantasy something they'd actually done; their honeymoon in Acapulco, most often.

"Have you ever been to the Princess Hotel, Wendy? It's an Aztec temple built right on the beach. There are trees and flowers in the lobby! Waterfalls in the swimming pool and miles of beaches and palm forests, and horseback riding right at the front door," he described breathlessly. "We'll go there one day . . . just the two of us. We'll just lie in the sun and make love."

"As soon as you get well," she promised, although they had been there five years before. The Princess was also her fondest memory of life with Mel Jacobs. It was before all the trouble and the misunderstandings began. They were deeply in love and it showed. For two weeks they had done nothing more than lie in the sun and make love. Wendy thought her life was complete then.

When the surgeon's knife cut through Mel's viscera into his abdomen, it was discovered that Mel's body was riddled with tumors. In the months since Dr. Monroe's warning, the cancer had found a firm footing in Mel's healthy tissue and spread through his entire system. What was left of the stomach hardly mattered. The surgeon took one look, shook his head, and had his assistant sew Mel back up.

The disease, as if driven by a mind and will of its own, struck back at this surgical intrusion. Some malignant spark of primordial vengeance prompted by the operation triggered off Mel's final decline and within days he hovered near death.

"It happens this way, Wendy. The operation seems to aggravate the condition," Dr. Monroe informed her sadly. "I told Mel months ago he should be quick about this operation."

"He took a chance and lost," she defended him. "But even a successful operation would only have prolonged this." She tilted her head back to indicate Mel asleep in the bed behind them. "What kind of life is that?"

"I wish doctors could be of more help." He turned his palms up in exasperation. "But . . . if there's anything I can do personally, any questions you might have . . ."

"Thank you, no."

During the last hours of her vigil, Wendy sat at Mel's side trying to remember the man she'd fallen in love with. Was it possible she'd lived in such fear of this poor man who had become so pitiable? No. That Mel Jacobs had already died. And now she was confronted with a man she'd never seen, let alone loved. It was a cruel joke to say good-bye to a stranger. But it would have been crueler still had they not reconciled.

In truth, Wendy and Mel had made peace with each other. They'd even recaptured for a few moments the spark of compatibility and love that had drawn them together. And that, in the end, was all that mattered.

There was no funeral service. The announcement in the *New York Times* requested donations to a cancer fund set up in Mel's name.

The day after Mel was buried Wendy sat at home, the phone off the hook, staring out across the lush green of Central Park. A cold, heavy rain pummeled the city, shaking everything in its path. It was exactly the kind of day on which she'd met Mel. The outside world was hazy and uninviting, a threatening apparition, yet it beckoned Wendy, daring her to leave the warm safety of her private realm. Exactly when was she going to start living again?

"Tea, Mrs. Jacobs?" Mrs. Swedeborg interrupted. She carried the tea tray in.

Wendy eyed her without recognition. "I guess it might be nice," she finally managed to answer.

"A good cup of tea never fails." Lolly prepared a steaming cup with honey and handed it to Wendy. "I wish there were something I could do to ease your sorrow." Her eyes misted over.

"That's very kind of you, but I'm just going to have to wait this out. There's really nothing much anyone can do."

"Well, if you want anything, just call. I'll be in the kitchen." She rubbed the palms of her hands nervously on her apron as she left.

Wendy didn't miss Mel, though she mourned their lost years. They had tried to make something good of their life together. They had given their marriage their best shot; that was more than many people could say. Now she was alone. She was free. While she had once seen gambling as a form of freedom, now she understood that *not* gambling was another, stronger, more positive form of that same independence. Taking care of herself was far more satisfying than her dependence ever was. And she understood that in time this self-reliance would allow her to enter a relationship with a man as an equal—neither more nor less than her partner—and that she could never get lost as she had with Mel.

In that spirit, she'd accepted a lunch date with Al Peterson for the next day. It was only after she hung up that Wendy realized she was terrified of getting reinvolved.

Peterson poured a glass of Moët for Wendy. "This is a celebration." He raised his glass to hers. "To me and to my new job." He smiled and kept a close watch on her. He wanted her back, so this luncheon had to be handled with kid gloves. Keeping a light touch was essential.

"I'm so thoughtless," Wendy apologized. "I never did congratulate you on taking over *Time Nor Tide*."

"Who would've thought just eight months ago when I first met Rita Martin all this would happen?" He shook his head. "You just never know, do you?"

Wendy smiled indulgently.

"Rita's already gone. I hear she's off on a vacation somewhere." It was time to grow serious. "I felt sorry for her in the end, losing her husband, then giving up her show. But Rita's a dynamo," Al quickly added in praise. "She came into the office the Monday after the Emmys carrying five cardboard boxes, and within two hours she'd stripped the place bare."

"Why prolong it?" Wendy's voice was listless. Behind-the-scenes at *Time Nor Tide* had never interested her as much as the on-air drama. She'd spent five years of her life ruled by *TNT* and now that Mel was gone, she'd lost interest in it entirely.

"Personally, I think Rita was embarrassed she'd been given the gate," he said. "She's a tough cookie—she didn't leave many friends, you know."

"To hear it from you," she said sourly. Peterson's gloating was beginning to irritate her.

"You've got it all wrong. I still have the greatest respect for her as a professional. Other than *that* . . . ?" he shrugged. "Anyway, now that Nan Booth has taken over daytime, the name Rita Martin is strictly *verboten*."

"So you've become a corporation man after all. I guess when the price is right, we all are willing to change our points of view."

Peterson's face darkened. "Hey, that's a little rough, isn't it? After all, I was never in this for the glory. If pretending Rita never existed is what Nan wants, that's what she gets. He drummed his fingers on the table. "Besides, we're revamping the show . . . and just about everything Rita ever did is being shelved."

"I'm glad Mel's not around to see it. *Time Nor Tide* was the only thing in his life he loved without reserve."

"A lot of people who can't relate personally throw themselves bodily into their work like Mel did."

"And they end up sad and disappointed and bitter . . . like Mel."

"At least you don't have to worry." Al slowly edged the conversation around to his advantage.

"How's that?"

"You've opened up to me," he said. "That means something."

"I *thought* I opened up to you; I didn't really." She smiled. "I've done a great deal of thinking since Mel went into the hospital—about him, and me . . . and us."

"And what conclusions have you drawn?" There was no point beating around the bush; he had to get back to the office soon. He hadn't taken a call from Nan in order to duck out early.

"I used to think I was responsible for Mel's happiness . . . and yours. I believed I was always failing, that I brought out the worst in people. That's how it seemed all my life, anyway. People died, went away, got angry, and I thought it was my fault. Some ego, huh?" She looked him directly in the eye as she finished, "Now know I'm not responsible for the way anyone feels. Except myself."

"So where does that stunning revelation leave us?" It was over, Al knew. He just wanted to make her say the words.

"I'm sorry, Al, but I can't jump right back into the same kind of relationship I've had all my life just because it's comfortable and easy. I have to find out who I really am, not who I am in terms of someone else. Understand?"

"Sure I understand. It's simple." He swigged down the dregs of the champagne and poured himself another glass. "As Wendy Jacobs approaches middle age, she strikes out on her own. How very admirable!" His bitterness was undisguised. "What's the first step on your road to maturity?"

"I'm selling the apartment and moving into the loft I rented." She ignored his rudeness; she'd expected him to be hurt. "Then I'll be going back to school to catch up on a few lost years."

"Turning over a new leaf, is that it? Well, well. I wish you the best in your new life . . . even though there's no room in it for me.'' He checked his watch. Nan would have his ass if he didn't call her soon.

"I'm sorry to hurt you, Al, but I don't want another marriage like the one I had. Does that make sense?''

"I'll miss you,'' he admitted glumly.

"We can still have lunch . . . or dinner . . . if you have the time.''

"And what's *that* supposed to mean?''

"Whether you know it or not, you're already married . . . to ITC, to Nan Booth, to *Time Nor Tide*. You're head honcho, Al. And that means you're on call twenty-four hours a day. Admit it. You've worked too hard to get where you are to let anything, even me, interfere with your career—just like Rita. And the minute she let her guard down she was forced out.''

"You paint a pretty unattractive picture,'' he said coyly.

"And don't try to kid me,'' she laughed. "You love your work more than anything else. It's not exactly a fate worse than death to be running *Time Nor Tide*, you know.'' But almost, she thought to herself.

"It seems to mean losing you.'' He reached for her hand, and she withdrew it.

"You never had me.'' Now she checked her watch. "I'm late. I have a real estate agent coming over in twenty minutes to look at the apartment.'' She stood up.

He signaled the waiter, then finished his wine in one swallow.

Outside the restaurant Al kissed Wendy warmly, first on the cheek, then on the mouth. "So, this is the way it ends?''

She took his hands. "No, this is the way it begins.''

He laughed involuntarily. "Say, Mrs. Jacobs, with that line of dialogue, if you ever need a job, how about writing for *TNT*? I happen to know the head honcho very well.''

"I'll keep it in mind. And thanks.''

Wendy got into a taxi and sank back against the seat. Saying good-bye to Al was the hardest thing she'd ever done in her life. His words, his enticing looks, all conspired to draw her back. Al Peterson promised a life of security. And the price? Give in and become part of him. Live in his shadow. Forget the dreams of working again.

She fumbled her compact from her purse and stared in disbelief. God, she was a mess. After the real estate agent left, Russell Bates was coming for dinner—after all these years! He hadn't sounded the least bit surprised when she asked to see him about working again. It was as if they'd just spoken the day before and the five years in between had never been. Bates even promised to put up with her "artsy-fartsy" stuff, as he'd put it. He hadn't been angry, or condescending, or even disappointed. He'd just been happy that after an extended detour, Wendy was back on the right road.

Their conversation had ended with a simple, understanding, loving statement: "Thank God, you've finally come to your senses, Wendy," he said.

Al stormed tipsily into the *TNT* offices, headed for his office. Gloria Lake, the pretty blonde who had replaced Sandy Lief, handed him two phone messages from Nan Booth, both marked urgent. The bitch can wait, he thought. He threw his jacket on the couch and slumped down into the chair that once belonged to Rita Martin.

His desk overflowed with old and new work. Where to begin? Rita had left a taped memo that elucidated a few important matters, but the real mess wouldn't be untangled until *he* got down to work and began plotting July's shows. Thank God, the Penny Hewitt story was progressing nicely, but the satellite stories, the subplots involving minor characters, were still in limbo. Under the tight reins of Nan Booth, the show's image was drastically changing. Only yesterday Nan had decided *TNT* needed a whole raft of new, young characters to entice the younger, upscale viewers. As if he didn't have enough to do. If only his backup team weren't such jackasses . . . If only Nan would hurry up and find the right person to fill Al's old spot . . .

The phone jangled and he answered it brusquely. "What is it?"

"I left two messages. Why didn't you call?"

"Look, Nan, I just got in from lunch. I've only got so much time, you know."

"I'm not interested in your half-assed excuses, Peterson. If lunch interferes with your work, don't eat."

You lousy dyke bitch, he thought. "I'll order in from now on, how's that?"

"I don't care what you do as long as you increase productivity. I've got a dialogue writer lined up for you—good man with good experience. He'll be in to see you tomorrow at nine.

Al usually didn't get in until ten, but he said nothing. "What's the scoop on this guy? Has he done a script?"

"I read it yesterday. He'll work out. I want you to see him first, just in case."

"Thanks for thinking of me," he replied sarcastically. Since taking over daytime Nan treated him like a flunky. The two new assistant head writers had already signed contracts before he ever met them. "Anything else?"

"There's a meeting in my office tomorrow at ten to discuss *TNT*'s new look. Do a work-up tonight of any bright ideas you might have. Just remember—keep the young audience in mind. And for Christ's sake don't make all the young women student nurses." She hung up.

Maybe they should all be truck drivers, he thought viciously. Nan Booth had turned into an A-Number-One bitch. Al didn't know exactly what was bugging her about being head of daytime, but it was clear Nan hated her job and was determined to make everyone else feel the same way.

Al dialed Monty Welch's number. Monty had been negotiating Al's contract with ITC for over a week now; so far they were at an impasse.

"What's the news?"

Welch exhaled loudly into the phone. "Not good, Al. The network definitely won't go beyond a twenty-six-week initial contract."

"For Christ's sake I wanted a solid two-year deal. Twenty-six weeks is shit. That gives me just enough time to get this fucking show out of the hole before getting the old heave-ho."

"It's the best *I* can do. All *you* can do is take it or leave it."

"Have you talked to Nan Booth? She and I were pretty thick a couple of months ago."

"Who do you think I've been dealing with? Booth's a tough broad. She said, and I quote: 'If Peterson isn't happy with what ITC is offering, we'll find someone who is.' End quote. Get the message?"

"Take it, Monty," Peterson agreed reluctantly. "And keep your fingers crossed they'll renegotiate in six months."

"That's up to you, my friend. You'd better shine. Sorry I couldn't do better by you."

"It's not your fault. Thanks."

Al put in a second call. "Angela? . . . Yeah, it's Al. Look. I've got to cancel tonight. I'm up to my ass in work.

Let's make it over the weekend, okay? . . . Great, I'll call you then."

Angela Brite. Still beautiful. Still sexy. Still available. Three sterling qualities in Peterson's women. He was disgusted with everything. He was under the network's thumb so hard he could barely breathe, and with a pissy twenty-six-week contract, his job was on the line every minute of every day.

Well, he'd show Nan and the bastards upstairs who was working and who wasn't. It was probably just as well Wendy was off "finding herself" like some sixties hippie; there wasn't time to get involved anyway. If Nan wanted to play rough, Al could play rough. He wasn't going to take shit from anyone.

He jabbed at the intercom. "Dave, come in here."

Dave Hailey, Al's senior assistant, appeared at the door. Hailey was twenty-eight, intelligent, highly skilled, and a smart-ass. Peterson had taken an instant dislike to the punk as soon as Nan introduced them—and the feeling was mutual.

"What's up, boss?" Hailey perched on the edge of the desk.

"Have you finished that projection about Martha Reynolds's niece . . . the student nurse?"

Hailey hemmed and hawed. "I just haven't gotten around to doing it yet. Sorry, Al."

Pissed off though he was, Peterson let it go. "Scrap it. Work up something new that doesn't involve nursing. Try teaching . . . something."

"You got it." Hailey punctuated his insolence with a wink.

"And I want it before you leave the office today, understand?"

Hailey mumbled something under his breath and walked out. Arrogant son of a bitch, Peterson thought. He's going to be big trouble before long . . .

It was somewhere around midnight before Al got home and threw his briefcase on the kitchen table. He made a pot of strong coffee and rubbed his eyes. It looked like it would be an all-nighter; probably one of many. The coffee was good—hot and rich. It jolted his tired brain awake. He retrieved the endless sheaves of paper and notes from the briefcase and started making comments in the margins. What had Wendy said? That he was married to *TNT*, on call twenty-four hours a day? It was true. And it was also true, as she had said, he would let nothing stand in his way.

"Kathleen, will you please call the cleaners and ask them just where the hell my goddamned suit is?" Rita shouted from the bedroom. It was ten o'clock in the morning.

Mrs. Flannagan sauntered in from the living room carrying the plastic-wrapped suit aloft like the Olympic torch. "Is this what you're bellowing about, Mrs. Elliott?"

"What would I ever do without you, Kathleen?" Rita tore the plastic covering from the suit. She looked askance at it. "How do you think this will do in Hawaii? Personally, I think it might be a bit *de trop*." She reexamined the somber, dark gray suit.

"Well, I don't know what 'deetro' means, but if you ask me. I think you'll be hot as Hades out there wearing that. Besides, it looks more fit for a funeral than one of them fancy Hawaiian 'loulous.' "

"That's *luaus*," Rita corrected with a smile. "I guess you're right. Chalk up one suit." She threw the Chanel carelessly on the bed.

Mrs. Flannagan rescued it immediately. "Now it's not as if you're never coming back, Mrs. Elliott. Let's not burn *all* our bridges behind us." She tucked the suit away in Rita's bulging closet.

"Why not? After all, I was the one who built the goddamned bridges in the first place."

"Leave that worry up to the others. You're a free woman now."

"Free for three weeks, that's all. I've got a speaking engagement at Princeton coming up and a book to write, and Carson wants me back again." She happily rattled off her new itinerary.

Mrs. Flannagan shook her head. "Well, for the time being just pretend none of that exists. Go on, go out to Hawaii and have a good time with Jeannie; you both deserve it."

"Is she all packed?"

"She did it all herself," Mrs. Flannagan beamed. "Of course I had to go in and redo the whole thing . . . but she tried."

"She's trying more and more, don't you think?"

"Since she got her mother back, the little colleen has come

to life again. I was worried there for a while, I'll tell you . . . when Mr. Ben died. I had horrible images of her being sent off to school . . ."

"I'd never have done that," Rita quickly said, editing out the memory of those first weeks after Ben's death when she'd thought of doing *exactly* that. "Jeannie belongs with me, no one else."

"And thank God for it." Jeannie called from the other room, and Mrs. Flannagan responded. "Heaven forbid, she's probably undone everything I accomplished in there."

"Go look after her. I'll finish packing and call a limo."

Since the Emmys Rita had been doing everything a little too fast. That Monday she'd cleared out her office, dictated two hours of notes for Al Peterson concerning the intricacies of steering *TNT* on a straight course, signed a formal letter of resignation, and distributed gifts to everyone in the office—solid gold *TNT* pins for the women, *TNT* tie tacks for the men. And because she'd already booked her flight to Hawaii, she turned down ITC's offer of a testimonial dinner, truthfully saying the Emmy Award had been enough.

For the first time in her life, Rita Martin was satisfied.

After leaving her cherished office at ITC high above Manhattan, Rita found herself unwilling to deal with life as she formerly had. It finally occurred to her that *Time Nor Tide* might have been the cause of her daily anxiety, not the remedy. And, for the first time since sitting down to create Laurelton, U.S.A., and all its denizens, Rita stopped seeking more, and she started enumerating what she already had.

Late one night, a week after the Emmy show, she had sat quietly in her living room sipping a white wine. She stared out across the terrace to the glittering lights of the city and remembered. There was nothing New York had to offer that she hadn't sampled at least once—theater, restaurants, nightclubs, the glamour, success, prestige—everything. She had triumphed. She had conquered this city and used it as a road to fame. Yet it hadn't satisfied her. Her penthouse symbolized her restless search for something more. It was a closed world, bought and paid for with endless hours of grim determination and sacrifice. But in the end, what was it? Six tastefully decorated rooms with a nice view of the skyline. Night after night, year after year, Rita had come home, tired from the endless struggle, craving some peace of mind, to find six tastefully decorated rooms with a nice view of the skyline. All empty. When she closed that front door behind her, Rita Martin was alone, and it seemed nothing could remedy that loneliness.

Now she faced the prospect of countless days to be lived just like everyone else. Her pedestal had collapsed. But she was no longer alone.

Jeannie came scampering into the bedroom wearing a new blue dress. She was flushed with excitement. "Are we really going to Hawaii?" she asked exuberantly for the hundredth time.

"Yes, honey, we're going to Hawaii. We'll swim and play and do lots of nice things." In the early years, she and Ben had often talked about Hawaii, but there just never seemed enough time. Now, with Jeannie, Rita was taking that long-postponed trip.

She thought of Ben a great deal these days, wishing he were alive to see the changes in her. He never would have boasted he'd been right about Rita all along; he simply would have been over-joyed to see her finally relax . . . and begin to live. He would have been especially pleased that Jeannie had become the light of Rita's life. Who knew? Maybe in the end Jeannie Elliott might just teach her mother a thing or two about life.

The doorman buzzed, and a second later Mrs. Flannagan came bustling into the room. "The limousine's here, Mrs. Elliott. Do you have everything?"

Rita snapped her suitcase shut and quickly surveyed the shambles of the bedroom. "I think that's everything. If not, we'll just have to buy it there." She picked up the case and hurried into the living room, glancing for a second at the Emmy Awards standing proudly on the mantelpiece.

"You know, Kathleen, I think I'm going to sell this place when we get back. It's such a shame that big house in Connecticut is going to waste. New York can get along fine without me, after all these years.

Mrs. Flannagan silently thanked Saint Jude for answering her prayers.

Two days later Rita sat quietly on the terrace of her suite at the Royal Hawaiian Hotel staring down at the vast, pristine expanse of Waikiki Beach. Hawaii was truly the most beautiful place she'd ever seen. She and Jeannie had only begun to explore, but Rita was ready to admit she'd found paradise.

She slipped quietly into the bedroom and checked on Jeannie. She was still asleep, legs tangled in the covers, arms akimbo. After kissing her lightly on the head, Rita returned to the living room, restless as she always was until her daughter woke up. How ironic that for years she couldn't wait to get away from Jeannie, and now her day didn't officially begin until she'd kissed the child good-morning.

She finished her coffee, reread the newspaper, and wrote a few postcards—to Mrs. Flannagan, to Tom Wesley whom she planned to visit in Palm Springs on her way back east, and finally to Helen and Dave Moore. Rita and Helen were becoming friends again, and it was important Helen know she was in her thoughts.

Finished with her "tasks," Rita turned on the television out of desperation, half-expecting to find cheerful Hawaiians cavorting about in local programming. She was shocked to see the last ten minutes of *Time Nor Tide*. She looked at the clock: Nine-fifty. Apparently ITC's Honolulu affiliate, KWFD, had a mind of its own. It was their prerogative, but scheduling *TNT* at nine o'clock in the morning was hardly Rita's idea of prime daytime! Automatically she wondered how the ratings did at such an ungodly hour of the day. Then she laughed at herself. Fortunately, ratings were no longer her concern.

When Rebecca Danforth appeared on screen wearing a demure black dress and her signature strand of pearls, Rita quickly pegged this show as one that aired just after Rebecca's trial and acquittal. She was now a free woman. A secondary character—a nurse Frank Cameron had gotten hooked on drugs—had been convicted of the murder. Rebecca, true to her noble calling, tried to protect the nurse because she was young and had her whole life ahead of her, while Rebecca was getting on in years. Not once during the grueling trial had Rebecca divulged the murderer's name. And had not Sally Beauchamps, the actual killer, confessed during a very dramatic moment, Rebecca surely would have gone to prison without betraying her secret.

Rita settled back on the bed to watch. This was her own script—the last one she'd ever write for *Time Nor Tide*. She had completed work on it the night after the Emmy Awards ceremony. Rebecca's living room came into view.

* * *

Rebecca offered Bob Garrick a cup of coffee. "Cream and sugar, isn't it?"

He nodded, staring at her with unabashed admiration and wonder. "You know, you were playing a very dangerous game, Rebecca."

"I've taken greater chances in my life."

"This was toying with your freedom. If you'd been convicted you would have faced ten, maybe fifteen years in prison."

Rebecca smiled. "I must be getting old, Bob, because that just doesn't sound like such a long time to me."

"Life is different in prison. Out here you're used to having things your own way. It's not like that inside." He accepted the coffee and took a sip.

"Maybe it would have been good for me to let someone else take over the reins of my life. I've made a lot of mistakes, Bob. A lot of mistakes I can no longer correct. This was one time I could do something absolutely unselfsh." She sipped her coffee thoughtfully.

"You're one of a kind, Rebecca. I admire you."

"And you're a flatterer, Bob Garrick." She sighed. "I wish everyone felt about me like you do."

"Those who don't just don't understand you, that's all. They see you as domineering, demanding . . . a perfectionist."

"And you don't think I am?" she asked with raised eyebrows.

"I think you are that way when it suits your purposes. Personally, I think it's all an act."

Rebecca laughed a deep, throaty laugh. "And just exactly what am I covering up this time?"

"Under your tough exterior is a real, warm, loving woman who's just been a little misguided, that's all. You want to protect yourself from hurt and in doing so you invite others to hurt you. It's a trap."

Rebecca smiled warmly. "Maybe this time I've proved to some people that I'm human after all."

"You have to me, Rebecca." He took her hand and held it tightly.

Tears came to Rebecca Danforth's eyes. "I never knew before how important people are to me . . . and now most of the ones I care about are gone. But I like to think they understood me all along. Maybe they even know I'm still struggling, still trying to do the best I can with what I've been given, and that I've tried to make restitution to those I've wronged.''

''You're a remarkable woman,'' he said softly.

''Only because I've had the sense to see that it's not too late to start enjoying life. I do have some regrets, Bob, but I intend never to have another regret as long as I live.''

The camera moved in on Rebecca's radiant face and the picture faded to black.